CHECK TO YOUR KING

NEW ZEALAND CLASSICS

CHECK TO YOUR KING
ROBIN HYDE

Golden Press
Auckland, Christchurch, Sydney

First published 1936
This edition published 1975
by Golden Press Pty Ltd
16 Copsey Place
Avondale, Auckland
and
35 Osborne Street
Christchurch
Printed in Hong Kong
ISBN   0   85558   4483

To

THE PEOPLE OF A HOUSE
92 NORTHLAND ROAD, WELLINGTON
(not forgetting MULLIGATAWNY DAN)
and to three friends
GWEN MITCALFE, ROSALIE and GLORIA RAWLINSON

HIS TREES

And when there is no word more that I can say,
   No last defence for my frail, lost cities of thought,
Still the trees I have planted here will be wind-blown and gay
   And a surer way to the loveliness blind eyes sought.

When hope as body of mine shall be fallen in dust
   Still the full blue cups of a jacaranda tree
Were a flagon of beauty the tired heart might trust,
   There might be some content in the rosemary.

And the tiny leaves of a maple shall glisten wet,
   Or a young laburnum free long tresses of gold,
For the vanquished man shall leave his impress yet
   On that beloved country he could not hold.

                                      ROBIN HYDE.

"Suffer me that I may speak; and after that I have spoken, mock on."
—*The Book of Job.*

AUTHOR'S NOTE

The author has used a novelist's licence in constructing this book. Owing to the fragmentary nature of the de Thierry papers, it would have been impossible to present a biography which did not leak a little at the seams unless access to closer family records in France, England, among the Maoris, or even in the moon, had been suddenly made available. But nothing has been deliberately invented or misstated, and where the facts have seemed doubtful, or Charles inclined to draw the long bow, the author has done all she could to draw the attention of the reader to this without crudely calling the Sovereign Chief a liar.

Historical sources, the painstaking work of New Zealand and other historians, have been consulted, and are gratefully acknowledged. But the main source of information was written by Charles himself, and is preserved today in the Sir George Grey Collection of the Auckland Library, though probably it has not been read by a dozen living people. It is a manuscript entitled *An Historical Account of an Attempt to Colonize New Zealand*. I think Charles wanted this published, both in order to pay his debts and to induce the French to do something about his land claims. It is full of little admonitions: "To the printers"—"To the publishers—insert here." But the vanishing publishers were quite right. Even in Victoria's day it would have been asking too much that humanity should swim or sink in those seas of ink.

All quotations from this manuscript are given verbatim, as are all letters or extracts from letters throughout the book. The French pamphlet referred to and quoted from in the second chapter is also preserved in the Sir George Grey Collection.

Acknowledgment of kindly assistance is due to Mrs. Emily Morrison, a great-grand-daughter of the Baron de Thierry ; Mr. John Barr, librarian of the Auckland Public

Library, and Miss Maguire, his assistant; Dr. G. M. Tothill, who read the book in manuscript; the Rev. Father P. McKeefry, Keeper of the Roman Catholic archives in Auckland; the Rev. A. B. Chappell; and to Mrs. Rosalie Rawlinson and her daughter Gloria, who have such an encouraging weakness for the Baron as a character.

Since the events of this tale belong to old years, the author hopes she will not be accused of high treason if she adds:

God Save King Charles

CONTENTS

Part One
PAINFUL EVOLUTION OF A MONARCH

CHAPTER		PAGE
I.	CROWNS AND THRONES—WHAT ABOUT THOSE?	15
II.	DOCUMENT IN EXILE	19
III.	CONVERSATION PIECE	34
IV.	NOBODY IS BORED IN CAMBRIDGE	42
V.	SHIPS PUTTING FORTH	56
VI.	A CROWN FOR ULYSSES	69
VII.	A PEAK IN DARIEN	80

Part Two
ARMY WITH BANNERS

VIII.	NUKAHIVA	91
IX.	THE SUNSET GUN	97
X.	DUEL WITH QUILL PENS	109
XI.	CONTEMPLATION AND LOQUATS	119
XII.	GOD OMITS TO SAVE THE KING	130
XIII.	FIAT JUSTITIA	145
XIV.	TWO AND A HALF FRENCHMEN	160
XV.	THERE WAS A GLORY	174

Part Three
SOUND THE RETREAT

XVI.	THE KING GOES BACK TO NATURE	189
XVII.	SISTER ANNE, SISTER ANNE...	203
XVIII.	THE ROSY SOFA	212

CHAPTER		PAGE
XIX.	THE SMITHY IN THE WOODS	226
XX.	THE KING DECLINES AN OFFER	234
XXI.	KORORAREKA	249
XXII.	WIND OF THE SEA	260
XXIII.	PARDONNE	270
	EPILOGUE	283
	APPENDIX ONE: THE DEED OF PURCHASE	285
	APPENDIX TWO	286

Part One

PAINFUL EVOLUTION OF A MONARCH

CHAPTER ONE

CROWNS AND THRONES—WHAT ABOUT THOSE?

LEAVING the dictionary behind us, what constitutes a kingdom? Primarily, I suppose, a patch of ground, anything from a few acres to a few thousand miles in extent. We put a lot into this ground—our ashes and our dreams—and we take a lot out of it. The ashes don't count for very much, though one should waste nothing. But the dreams are another matter. Plant them for a few centuries—by that time your soil's malleable, practically every clod has achieved personal contact with humanity—and up come cathedrals, great red fighting-cocks of omnibuses, Tate galleries, social codes, treatises on virtue and value, sets of objections to the social codes, longer than the codes were to begin with.

All this takes time and space. But somebody has to start. And it's such a patient old planet.

A patch of ground, then, no more; and a little piece of silk or cotton, painted in gaudy colours. That's your flag, establishing sovereignty, or, at the least, independence. Wars have been fought over no more, no less.

Your kingdom; what about your king?

Of the hereditary monarchs I say nothing. But suppose, for the sake of argument, that there were certain mental or spiritual qualities, not necessarily hereditary, which marked off the chosen king? Suppose, in this modern age, that a man, lying up to his neck in the smooth, silken water of his hot bath, were suddenly to recognize these first signs . . . to find that the ground on which he must henceforth walk, the very bath-mat on which he must stand to dry himself, were no longer just ground and mat, but the root-woven soil of the waiting kingdom?

Suppose, as he walked down the steep stretches of bitumen, that the preoccupied pink faces passing him by were no longer merely faces, but his people. His mind filled, tossed and disordered with phrases like streaming banners: "I must do this for them . . . I must take care that they step clear of that . . . I must point out to them . . ." What's to be done about it ?

Take up golf, my dear chap, take up golf. Something stable in the swing of that innocent little niblick.

But if the golf didn't work ; if the tattered banners blew wilder and more prodigious than ever ; if the soil cried out with a deep voice, and the faces passing by seemed to slide into the one appeal ? What about it then ?

Give yourself up, of course. Surrender to the white Mona Lisa smile of the hospital ward, and the doctors who have heard it all before. Humanity is no longer in the vein.

I cannot too strongly emphasize the fact that the call to be a king differs in essence from the call to be a dictator. A dictator has a shouting part, and it matters nothing what he shouts. Leather lungs, bull neck, that's the lot. But a king's is a speaking part. It means a saying of quiet things which hang together and make sense. One might almost say that the urge to make sense is behind the self-appointment of most of our best kings.

Humanity is no longer in the vein.

A hundred years, however, they did it, and with *élan*. There was the Stanhope woman, riding like mad on a white horse across Syria. There was Byron, setting out for Greece—only a liberator, but didn't the little man hope the Greeks would notice how chastely becoming is golden crown to liberator's brow ? There was the classic example of Napoleon. Black men were trying on crowns, east and west. As a revived style in millinery, the crown was enjoying a vogue.

Our Charles, you might say he was born stuffed with all this monarchical business. That father of his, the Sieur de Thierry—or Baron de Thierry de Laville, if you're going to give him as much titular grandeur as he wanted—running about Paris intriguing in keyholes against the revolutionists, happy as a mason-wasp ; emigrating to England just in time to save his skin, then sentimentalizing for ever about the dear departed Louis XVI, the Austrian, the aristocrats. God forgive us for mentioning it, but that bunch, the whole of them, looked better with their heads off. The boy, however—little Charles de Thierry, London-born son of his noble *émigré* papa—grew up seeing everything royal or aristocratic as both beautiful and fine. He didn't have to live in it, that garden of the dead.

There may be some debate as to whether this little Charles —later Baron de Thierry—is entitled to be recognized and written about as a bona-fide king. King of Nukahiva, Sovereign Chief of New Zealand—those were the damages he claimed against history. His Nukahivan monarchy was never recognized by the Powers, and as to the Sovereign Chieftaincy in New Zealand, there was a dog-fight about that. But he hoisted an independent flag on Nukahiva, a flag that had bagged the royal salute three times—once on the Atlantic, once leaving Pointe-à-Pitre, once from the old pirate-haunted city of Panama. He declares, and no Nukahivan evidence has been produced to contradict him, that the Nukahivan Islanders readily accepted him as their King, and anointed him with the sacred oils. He certainly issued documents signed, "We, Charles, King of Nukahiva." Copies of them remain in existence. After that, I can see nothing against him as a king. Besides, he enjoyed it so much. . . .

Here is warning. Faces, milestones . . . if you don't like them, stand clear. Salomon, Vigneti, Bertholini, Morel, Feraud, Captain D'Orsay of the *Momus*, the little people of this book . . . what do I know about them ? I know that Salomon was a fat brown man, and Vigneti a thin, solemn one, always seasick. Faces . . . queer, blurred old portraits, in a gallery which nobody visits; a gallery where the lonely footstep echoes terribly, and which is now growing very dark. Charles says they were a pack of scoundrels, who either robbed him, owed him money, or refused to lend it to him in his extremity : a much meaner offence, since, if you need money yourself, it's natural to take it from somebody who appears better fixed ; but if you are in funds, there can be no excuse for refusing to replenish your fellow creatures.

Then again, if Charles had only kept in one place . . . a great city, even a great desert. But he was the fauna of everywhere. One finds him flourishing in pestilential swamps of Panama, persisting on a New Zealand mountain-top, surviving somehow in Cambridge itself. This keeps a biographer moving. Perhaps one could do a graph of him, and plant it at the end of the book. But it would certainly be inaccurate. So was Charles.

It would be possible, it would even be probable, to treat him as though he and his kingdom were funny, nothing more.

Be at peace, awful spectre of our Charles. Apart from the fact that this would be bad art, I do not think it would even be true. For, look you, there is such a thing as being funny in the passive, more than in the active. People who never in their long lives have taken any misdirected step can be funnier, in a dim way, than any naked maniac who ever stood on his head and waved his legs in the air.

Suppose there were seated somewhere a personal and cruelly inquisitive god, who made leopards and butterflies because he liked their suggestions of action, a god understanding all the possibilities open to the creatures of this world? Can you see this god leaning down from his throne, a dry cackle beginning to form in his throat? "What's this you're telling me . . . you've got a man there who never wanted to fly? Comic sort of a fellow . . . What? Another man who has never been in love? Get along with you, you're trying to fool me. . . . What's that? Oh, that's too rich altogether. Get out of my way, I want to have a look at him. Isfrael, Isfrael, come here. Ha-ha-ha . . . !" (The skies begin to crackle with straw-coloured lightning, with the violent, dangerous laughter of God.) "Don't block the gangway, you old scoundrel. I want to see. Ha-ha-ha . . . ! There's a man down there who says he's never made a fool of himself."

CHAPTER TWO

DOCUMENT IN EXILE

To begin the history of a life with the words "I don't know" seems, perhaps, odd.

On second thoughts it is insufferable. One must then resort to strategy. This is best done by the immediate imagining of a stage, on which the puppets can do a little explaining for themselves.

Ring up the curtain. . . .

To the fore of the stage a staring notice-board bears the legend, "LONDON, A.D. 1804." The darkness is no kindly twilight, but pea-soup fog. Softly, from chimney-pots, high iron fences, and tall, discouraging buildings in Berwick Street, drift the deciduous yellow leaves of this vapour, piling up in a great sad dream valley, as though centuries of autumns lay perished there. Between the street's façades of veiled grotesquerie slouches a boy of eight years old. Look at him quickly, we have only a minute : yes, perhaps some resemblance to a scared rabbit, with his enormous and terrified hazel eyes, the wisp of chestnut hair pulled over his high forehead. . . . Our Charles, none other.

No. 35 Berwick Street. For a moment he gazes about with a trapped expression, like one of the shy and youthful damned constrained against his will to make the devil peevish by hammering on the gates of hell. The door slams open; he is beckoned into the most undignified hole in London, to wit, the Sponging-House, politely transcribed for posterity as the Debtors' Prison.

. . . .

One's horizon is always being enlarged. Here is Papa in prison. But does one inevitably want this enlargement? Sometimes little horizons seem the safest . . . the tent bounded by the four bandy legs of the sitting-room table, the worn hearth-rug, overcast with the golden ghosts of flames. The horizon is larger if one opens the door and ventures into the corridors, but then there are the old ladies with terrible teeth and knobs of hair, old ladies with bony fingers. They are Papa's *pensionnaires*. If they pay their rent, they are invariably on the point of leaving the house. If they don't pay, they stay for ever ; and *Maman*, though her bosom heaves indignantly when she is alone with Charles, is afraid of them face to face.

Looking through the window of one's attic bedroom, one sees another horizon. But it is cold, with little bits of soot, like fly-specks on an old painting. The street, centuries ago, made a weary joke and had itself christened New Road. It was never new, however ; not as warm new-laid eggs are new, or even with the red but fascinating newness of new babies, of whom Charles knows something, since God sends him small brothers in an apparently unending stream ; and how they are to be supported *Maman* never knows ; Papa only when he is in his sanguine mood, which results in such unexampled trouble.

The large red horses, plodding down New Road, lift up their tails and supply the middle of the street with piles of steaming straw-coloured manure. One feels it is somehow indelicate of them, a situation demanding that one should look away. But the sparrows, friendly on the sills of the attic windows, take it in a jolly spirit. Sparrows are the soul of London.

Other things happen in New Road: things like the faded passion in the smell of violets, as a flower-seller trundles his barrow past ; tragic, humped, unshaven things, dragging their aimless limbs by, shrouded in rags ; waif things, as when the little girls appear at five in the morning to whiten the doorsteps of the wealthier houses, a ha'penny the doorstep. The lamps are still guttering dimly then, and along run the little girls, so small, with such white faces and such great eyes, that they are like a sad breed of fairies. (Forests grew here once, even in London. The forests were hacked down ; the fairies had to make the best of it, like us, the *émigrés*.)

There was horizon-widening of a different sort when

Papa lifted the lid of the piano and played. Strong, steady, sweeping notes, like the battle of a swimmer against mighty waves. Despite all the talk, the enthusiastic gatherings of minor Royalists who still drifted in when Papa had any money to spend, Charles felt most certain that his father was a Somebody when he played the piano.

And now Papa is in prison. Not a bad prison of its kind—the enemies and detractors of the Baron de Thierry would say it was too good for the old fraud. No toads nor rats. Scourge and torture kept well in the background. Fleas, perhaps. A tiny room, bare of everything but bench and deal table on which are cheap paper, ink-horn, quills, and two mean tallow candles. Already Charles knows his papa well enough to suspect that, once give him writing-materials, little else is necessary.

Naturally, it's a much more outrageous thing to arrest a baron and clap him in gaol than if he were a common man, and, from the way *Maman* talks, the least Monseigneur the Comte d'Artois will do when he hears of it is to have the whole rascally English nation whipped at the cart-tail. On the other hand, in a frightening way, it does give more life to those old tales of which Papa is so full: the tale of the king whose head was cut off, of the queen who played at shepherdess, and the dauphin shut in the temple. At thought of the lost prince, favourite dream-playmate, tears of mingled pity and excitement for all prisoners rush to little Charles de Thierry's eyes. "Papa, Papa," he stammers. The old Baron, seeing his son *emotioné*, would not dream of losing the moment. Instantly he makes a speech. . . .

The old fraud, his enemies would say, and do say. There are bills everywhere. Ah, such bills! Butcher, baker, candlestick-maker—one can only suppose that he has hypnotized the lot of them. His reply to any charge is magnificence itself. "What would you have? One is not born to it. I am not a lodging-house keeper, I am a Baron."

God knows, indeed, whatever inspired the old gentleman to begin with his lodging-house; one of those extraordinary and perverted visions which keep popping in and out of his brain—and while they last, mind you, they glow like roasting chestnuts. Maybe he saw the lodging-house as a *rencontre* for Royalist intrigue. He would love that; he flourishes on intrigue like a bed of nettles. Or else, in his view, his title and romantic circumstances were sufficient to guarantee *pensionnaires* of the gentler sort. But the actuality . . . ! If the Baroness de Thierry is terrified of her guests, not less so, in his way, is her husband. "Figure to yourself," he cries. "They ask, the English, for boiled mutton in the middle of the day. *C'est incroyable!*" And then, if he puts his nose out of his bedroom to venture along to the lavatory, he is sure to hear another door slam, and to catch a glimpse of a nightcapped head, suspicious as a snail's, retreating into safety. "The virgins," he says, helplessly; "they consider, it seems, that I wish to seduce them. Nevertheless, they wear flannel night-gowns. The English are not *practical.*" His hands wave again; he mutters, "Figure to yourself."

The little Baroness looks almost shrewish. Figures are the bane of her life. God keeps sending the little ones. First Caroline, when they had barely fled from France, and were tarrying awhile in the Netherlands. That was well enough—the child was born at the Orange palace of Lackeu. She mightn't have been, it is true, but she came prematurely; and the good young Prince and Princess of Orange could not bring themselves to request the Baroness de Thierry to move, when she had actually, and with such determination, started her labour.

Then Charles, in London. After him, in succession, Francis, Louis, Frederick, little Cecil. At the thought of Cecil, her tired hands go to her eyes. The house in New Road killed Cecil. There was typhoid in the place; the *pensionnaires* decamped, mostly without paying their rent; and the end of it was an infant corpse under a sheet soaked in disinfectant. Children of exile . . . it is easy to understand that they might be better accommodated in heaven.

Do we see, then, in cellar cool at Berwick Street, an old knight disarmed? Look again at the ink-horn. Among many uncertainties one unfailing de Thierry trait stands out plainer than Cleopatra's Needle. No de Thierry, given the use of writing-materials, may be considered forlorn. They adored writing pamphlets.

The great pen flourishes, swoops like an eagle on the defenceless paper.

To His Royal Highness,
Monsieur,
Brother of Louis XVIII,
King of France.

Monsieur,
In this life arise painful circumstances which call for the sort of explanation honour now compels me to bring beneath the eye of your Royal Highness. Only to yourself and to my King need I render account for my conduct, which has ever been to uphold throne and Church. My devotion lies with the illustrious family of the Bourbons. That deep love, graven on my heart as on the hearts of all my family, has been the cause of unjust and slanderous reports which secret enemies have had the wickedness to put forth about me. Always, they cry, I thrust myself to the fore. Far be it from me to deny this truth, but it should be looked at in daylight, not in the colour given by jealousy. A score of times I have come near losing my life. Why are they not in like case? I have never thrust myself forward here, in the nest of the French Republic's envoys. Always in my works and speech I have made plain what now I write, that my device has most constantly been, "God and my King."
It would be tedious here to establish my own descent and that of my wife. I will take only the liberty of recalling to your Royal Highness that it was one of my forefathers who replaced the Seneschal de Molac, and, at the famous Battle of Pavie (February 24th, 1525), saved the life of a French king by laying down his own life. The King did not then reproach him with thrusting himself to the fore. *Those incapable of a like devotion would heap on him ridicule, such as they have heaped on me for more than forty years; a ridicule which does not blush to accompany its sneers with the vilest calumnies, even against Madame de Thierry; not against her virtue—that, not the boldest dare dispute—but concerning her birth. Yet your Highness knows that Madame her mother was daughter to the Marquis de Monbion, officer of the Gendarmes of the Garde. She married M. de Laville, inspector of wide districts, and a man whose probity is vouched for on all reports. The Queen had the goodness to award Mademoiselle de Laville a pension of 1200 livres for her education, and a few years later gave to her brother the*

consulate of *Drontheim*, in Norway. It was with their Majesties' consent that I obtained Mademoiselle de Laville's hand, and after our marriage we were presented together to our King and Queen, who said to us, "Be happy." I thanked her gracious Majesty for that pension of which I have spoken. "I do not withdraw my favours except from those who no longer deserve them," she answered. "The King and myself will do everything possible for your happiness."

Little Charles, bored with the muttered words of what is a very old tale to him, lets his mind wander back to his mother, that former Mademoiselle de Laville of whom Papa writes.

"Charles, Charles, you're to attend at once on your father. Your father is writing an appeal to Monsieur. Your father says you must take the papers to the printer's. . . ." And that final "Charles!" wailing after him just when he's on the door-mat. The little *Maman* opens her arms with a dramatic gesture, revealing her bosom: needing a safety-pin, but still rounded and white—an odd thing, considering the number of little ones God sends. He rests his face there a moment, her mouth touches his cheek. Many things go into that kiss: affection, worry, fear, the vaguely improper humour of the stranded and desperate, remorse that life isn't spoiling little Charles, as our eldest sons ought to be spoiled.

"They won't cut off my head at the prison?"

"Silly cabbage. . . . Here in England, they haven't even a guillotine."

She forbears to mention how readily, with their own rough dexterity, they will hang, draw, and quarter you on the briefest acquaintance.

Prison without guillotine and executioner seems out of all tradition to Charles. Rubbing his eyes, he tries to make out the signs marking off this tiny room as a real cell, and suddenly has it. The candles, stinking tallow, where the de Thierrys, in their worst days even, had wax. There were wax candles, their flames budding like little miraculous snow-roses, at that unlucky memorial service which had really precipitated all this trouble. . . .

The old man, staring through the wall at the face of a

young queen who had been gracious, sees other pictures. Pictures and memories; nothing else left until the end.

The fiddles in the darkness strike up their deuced melancholy wailing, very softly. "O Richard. . . . *O mon roi.* . . ."

It is too late, my sentimental Blondels. King Richard is very dead; no deader, however, than your King Louis XVI will be when this Paris mob has done with him.

Paris, beginning the final decade of the eighteenth century. The avalanche grows ready to fall. Among the Bourbonists, a little less important than he thinks himself, but not to be surpassed in brutal energy, is the young Baron de Thierry, recently married to a Mademoiselle de Laville. At his house some of the deputies have formed a habit of dropping in. He sets himself to weed out the destructivists from those still Royalist at heart, pumping them for all he is worth. He wheedles his way into the dens of the rising bureaucracy. ("Always," cry his peevish critics, "de Thierry thrusts himself to the fore.")

Comes the opportunity for a more spectacular part. At the moment when the *Gardes Françoises* abandon their king, the little Baron claps wings to heels and runs to the houses of Versailles' loyal gentlemen. "It is necessary to guard our King!" he cries. "Drawn swords in hand, if we can't get muskets!"

The gate-sentries supply a score or two of rifles, and within a day, under leadership of the Commandant, M. de Poix, the Gentlemen's Guard of Versailles has been formed. "In which," he writes, with conscious virtue, "I wished merely the rank and title of Captain."

One drama leads to another. Here we have the Baron de Thierry beguiling the populace into stripping themselves of jewels and gold watches for something he refers to vaguely, though passionately, as "the cause of the people"; here rescuing the Comte d'Artois. His Majesty, with the Comte de Provence and the Comte d'Artois (the "*Altesse Royale*" of the Baron's passionate appeal from his sponging-house), leave the assembly, to proceed to a château. Preceded by the deputies, Baron de Thierry also makes his departure. At the palace gates he espies a group of brigands, armed with stones and brickbats, and crying with one accord, "It is necessary that we kill the Comte d'Artois!" "Down with d'Artois!" and other slogans of the sort. On the whole, a none too original idea, since d'Artois, from birth to death, remained the implacable autocrat, wholly out of sympathy with the people.

Already the deputies, quitting the palace, were in the Avenue de Paris. De Thierry raced after them, recalled them, and, bidding them link arms, thus formed two rows, between which slowly advanced the royal party. At the high iron gates reserved for royalty, the mob thronged and eddied, and made remarks. The Baron skipped ahead of his King, crossed the rifles of two Swiss guards against the grille, and held them there until the party had passed.

("His Royal Highness, Monsieur, now rightful King of France, will not, I feel sure, have forgotten this. It was then that the King said to me, "Withdraw, my dear fellow, you will be killed." Far from reproaching me with *thrusting myself forward*, he had the goodness that evening to send M. de Saugest to my home for news of me.")

A discussion is arranged between the King and General la Fayette. Drawn swords in hand, the Royalist "gentlemen of goodwill" march afoot as bodyguard to the King's carriage, two chevaliers of St. Louis clinging to the great gilded doors as the state coach trundles through Paris. Parisians and monarch meet. . . .

("It was at this moment that M. Bailly, offering the King the keys of Paris, spoke those all too significant words, the most cunning and ominous expression of Jacobinism. 'Henri IV conquered his people,' he said. 'Today, the people conquer their King.'")

At five, Louis takes to the road again. The Paris guard link up with that of Versailles around the gilded coach. His Majesty begs to thank his gentlemen for their services. "It grows late, my family will be anxious," he adds, his eyes darkening. "Already I have sent three couriers to the Queen." "Try to march faster, His Majesty is hungry," whispers the Duc de Vilquier to the sworded and sweating bodyguard. But, though an attempt is made to break into a trot, the Parisians swarm around the coach, forcing it to proceed at snail's pace. At Sèvres they fall in with more of His Majesty's loyal guards.

The palace is reached at last, and how strangely mockery mingles with the moment's enthusiasm, as the Parisians roar, "Long live the King!"

Bread and flour are now of unexampled scarcity. Behold the Baron de Thierry perched on the seat of a lumbering blue waggon, whipping up his horse for Versailles, with a load of the precious wheat. Versailles is to be provisioned at any cost; King Louis has given *carte blanche* to his gentlemen (who never again see the colour of their money). The Parisians steal the Versailles conveyances, but de Thierry triumphantly brings three cartloads of grain to the palace doors. In the city, where the famished pillage every baker's shop, a determined effort is made to hang one baker, the Sieur Fontain, of rue Notre Dame, for his indiscretion in selling rolls to the Court. The Baron de Thierry contrives the escape of this worthy, then distributes several bushels of grain among the prowlers outside the palace gates, and offers money to those who look hungriest. "They listened to reason," he writes, with a lack of logic which is superb in its way.

His Paris days are numbered. The little Gentlemen's Guard still turns up its nose at the tricolour, disporting itself in uniforms with cream and blue cockades, and bright buttons graven with the words, "*Pro Patria et Rege*". But on November 29th, 1790, the *procès* instituted by the Duc d'Orleans begins, its avowed object to discover conspirators against the national welfare. Four Royalists are at once proscribed—Boucher d'Argis, Duvalnampti, Delasser, and de Thierry, who is at the moment busying himself with a secret society of King's friends, under the encouraging title, "The House of Fraternity". That house is never builded. The first de Thierry to lose his head over Lady Guillotine does so in 1792. Before the Revolution is over, fourteen more of the family go the same way. The widowed Madame de Laville, daughter of the Marquis de Monbion, who came to Paris to see her daughter married on Marie Antoinette's bounty, met a different end. She took refuge in a Paris church; fifteen pikes pinned the terrified old woman to the altar.

The Baron and Baroness de Thierry were safe in Grave when the news of Louis XVI's execution came through. Ah, what a tragedy! Weeping copiously, the organizer of the little Gentlemen's Guard arranged the first memorial service held abroad in honour of the martyr. The Hollanders joined in with the *émigrés*.

It was an unlucky step, that memorial service, as the Baroness de Thierry would freely have told you. The tiger has tasted blood.

The family was in luckier case than most. The Princess of Orange befriended them ; the Baroness, as has been narrated, was accouched on the royal premises. When they departed for England, the baby Caroline carried around her little neck a huge gold medallion, in which was twisted a lock of the Princess's hair. Letters from the Orange household saved them from the pestering of the Aliens Office in London.

In England the father of the family was restless as a spectre on a lost battlefield—always underfoot, writing pamphlets on the Revolution, dedicating them to those Bourbons who yet survived. In London the eldest son was born, and at once assaulted with the names of Charles Philip Hippolytus. But they made something of that christening. The Comte d'Artois, by that time head of the Royalists in London, stood godfather.

Charles may have been London-born, but he was reared in a tiny travelling circus of a France. From London to Bath, from Bath to Weymouth—where he was taken for Jacobin and spy—prowled de Thierry *père*, succeeding in plunging the whole family into disfavour with English and *émigrés* alike. Shady rumours started to get about. He harassed authority for permission to revisit France, where an aunt of his wife's had left an estate which would shower gold upon him . . . if he could once get at it. In 1802, d'Artois gave the required permissionn. To France, camouflaged as an Englishman, went the adventurer, rejoicing. In Dover, his family waited with what patience they could muster for news of his execution.

Once in France, he seems to have made little effort with his English masquerade. His snuff-box flourished a miniature of the excellent King Henri IV. Providence seems at times to have kept a soft spot for the erratic de Thierry. He moved among his own kind, ghosts, men who remembered dead glories, dead faces. After six months he won back to England with unscratched complacency, and reported to a pardonably surprised Comte d'Artois that France was still Royalist at heart.

Naturally, most of the *émigrés* took him for a spy. The de Thierrys, father and son, did so many things obviously insane in the eyes of a reasonable person that reasonable persons, discovering them quite normal in conversation and habits, at once put them down for deep scoundrels. But honesty was always one of the few real de Thierry addictions.

That visit was the beginning of the end. People dropped him. He started the lodging-house ; the *pensionnaires* wished boiled mutton at midday ; the virgins regarded him as though they expected him to seduce them, and yet they wore flannel night-gowns. The little Baroness, it is true, would not have minded if he had seduced the English virgins, who might then have been pleasanter to her. How many times must she have taken to her kitchen, her bosom heaving, the tears welling piteously over her still pretty little face ?

But lodging-house keeper was no role for the Baron de Thierry. To have, on the contrary, a real speaking part . . . He had it. Another memorial service, celebrating the anniversary of the martyred dead, Louis and his Antoinette.

Thomas calls himself an *entrepreneur*, but the fact is, he's a villain and a robber. One commits oneself to his hands. What happens ? First, a series of postponements. We will have the memorial service here, we will have it there. . . . One might run one's legs off following him. Then comes the horrible news that the French Protestants will not attend the service unless the Catholics are excluded ; while the Catholics are waiting for an assurance that no Protestants will be admitted. It takes a de Thierry to handle a thing like this. . . .

Three hundred *émigrés* waited outside St. Patrick's one day in pouring rain. At last the Baron de Thierry, resplendent in his old uniform, appeared under an umbrella with key and clergyman, and triumphantly entered the church. It was all very damp, but tall white candles fluttered little flags of flame over kneeling men and women ; the names of the dead were spoken in devoted voices . . . prayers of ghosts for ghosts.

On leaving the church, however, the Baron de Thierry was at once arrested. A carpet-weaver charged him with debt. A wine-merchant, a good fellow, promptly bailed him out. But then the iniquitous Thomas spread rumours concerning the subscriptions collected for the memorial Mass, of which fund the Baron was treasurer. (This was not past understanding. Since early morning, Thomas had been besieged by both Protestants and Catholics, unanimous at least in wanting their money back.) Rumour coursed; the amount swelled to a fortune, on which the Baron, leaving his bankrupt lodging-house together with his wife and large family, was to turn Jacobin and flee at once to France.

The fact that the Baron was in bed, and his wife sitting beside him wringing her little hands and weeping piteously, did not alter the case. He was arrested, forced to appear at the King's Bench, then confined at the Berwick Street debtors' prison. He protested he could give a full account of the 76 livres collected. His enemies murmured that it was rather a little matter of 1500 livres. *"Ah, quelle différence...! Ah, quel sort!"* cries the accused, driving his pen into the ink-horn, and launching out into yet another paragraph of his appeal to the Comte d'Artois.

(In this year of 1936, the full text of the appeal, in the pamphlet form in which it emerged from the printing-presses, still survives with the papers of the de Thierry family. And on it, in faded ink, an old man who was once the little boy of New Road and Berwick Street has traced these words: "Very important for the family. Written by my father.")

Think what a ghostly thing is a spinet. It is a sort of near-missing link in music, a chain of flowers between past and present. It still stands, spectral, in a few music-rooms; light hands touch it from time to time. But its silver cord is almost severed.

There is no portrait of that Mademoiselle de Laville who, by marrying the Baron de Thierry, became the mother of Our Charles. Her Christian name is nowhere mentioned; neither are the date and circumstances of her death in exile recorded. But there is a casual mention that she played the spinet.

A pair of white hands on a spinet. Nothing more.

We are now faced with a problem. Was the old gentleman who so forcefully recalled his services in this appeal to d'Artois really the victim of injustice? Was he punished too hard for peccadilloes, while fine services were forgotten ? Or was he, on the other hand, a lunatic ?

If we take the circumstances recorded in that appeal as gospel, we have a personage—a man of valour, however he may smack of Ancient Pistol, and, never let us forget it, an authentic baron.

Yet, for a man of the attainments to which the elder Baron de Thierry laid claim, one might have expected some break in history's conspiracy of silence.

There are some who have been definitely unkind. There is a Maurice Besson ; he alleged, in an article written for the *Bulletin de la Société des Études Océaniennes* (June 1933), that our Baron, arriving in London with the titles de Ville d'Avray glowing like a comet's tail behind him, was no nobleman at all, but the nephew of King Louis XVI's faithful valet ; and that he justified his claim to the "de Ville d'Avray" by possession of a wretched little shanty at that spot.

It is true that elsewhere, when he plunges into detail concerning New Zealand, M. Besson is a mine of misinformation. It is also true that, by some confusion of generations, he attributes to Our Charles (blithely unborn at the time of the revolution) all his father's adventures as well as his own, which would have made him a centenarian long before he had time to become King of Nukahiva, Sovereign Chief of New Zealand.

On the other hand, some explanation for the elder baron's fall from being the right hand of the Bourbons (as he says) to becoming the debtor of the wine-merchant and Thomas the *entrepreneur* does seem called for.

One can imagine it. London, following upon the incipience of the Revolution.

"The Baron de Thierry . . . his estate, where would that be ?"

"It escapes me also. But, my dear fellow, if a man tells me he is a French baron, naturally I take it that he is a French baron. What else ? French barons are about as popular as the plague in Paris, and two a penny in London. If he weren't a baron, would the chap say he was a baron ? Come, now. There's everything against the supposition."

"Yes, but it's different here in England. The English, you know, they're such snobs. They don't like anybody without money to virtual desperation, but, if it comes to the point, how much better, they reason, a baron than a butcher. And, suppose this old de Thierry is really the nephew of a valet, as I've heard it whispered . . . can't you imagine the expostulations ? There is, I assure you, a perfect system, a sort of round game. 'Have you the butler of my grand-aunt ?' 'No, but I have the housemaid of your great-uncle, the one with the long nose. My cousin Derek's gardener's wife has the child of the cook, who is also the child of my cousin Derek, but, oh no, we never mention it.' A place for everyone, you understand, and everyone in his proper place. Well, this de Thierry, he dramatizes. Can one dramatize to effect while pressing trousers ? If he assumes a title, it is to do what his circumstances call for."

Some evidence, however, may be mustered in support of M. le Baron's authenticity. There are attested copies of certificates and papers : a passport, signed by M. M. Necker and M. le Comte de St. Priest, August 18th, 1789, issued to 'Sieur de Thierry, Capitaine de la 18ième Compagnie de la Garde Bourgeois de Versailles" ; a certificate from M. le Marquis de Quenille, April 20th, 1792, stating that "the Sieur de Thierry is in every way worthy of the regard of the Princes", and that, arriving that year in Coblentz, he was presented to the Electoral Prince and Princess. The most interesting document is a copy of a certificate given in London, May 30th, 1797, and signed by the Comte de Vaudreuil, *Grand Fauconnier de France, Chevalier des Ordres du Roi et Maréchal de Camp et des Armées* :

I certify that I have seen and examined all the titles that M. the Baron de Thierry de Laville cites, and that they are in correct order and prove in plainest manner his zeal, faithfulness, and strong attachment to the King and the Royal Family, also the services he has rendered and attempted to render on their behalf : in belief of which, I sign the present certificate.

There was a time, you know, when history was peppered with virgin births. Madame the Queen was the happy mother, you were told ; Apollo, Jupiter, Bacchus, old dogs of that sort, were the proud papas. Did one inquire too closely ? It made the world more picturesque, and added a glamour to being cuckolded. After the French Revolution, London was doubtless the same sort of hunting-field.

Long afterwards, in New Zealand, Charles, full-blown Baron de Thierry, told legends enough of his youth, but more often of the early, poverty-stricken days than of the later ones, when some benign influence—either that of the Comte d'Artois or of a wealthy unknown—had redeemed the de Thierrys from pawn and set them down in gentle and financial circumstances in Somerset. That lodging-house! It killed off little Cecil, it frightened away the *pensionnaires*—for those who would bear with the typhoid and the flat pink bugs behind the wallpaper took exception to the old Baron. Only one conclusion is possible. Authentic or not—Great Auk's egg, or simple cuckoo—the Baron was no lodging-house keeper.

Perhaps it is appropriate that his son first appears out of the fog at the sponging-house door, a queer little figure, saddled with a devotion to this papa who, even after borrowing from the wine-merchant, never had enough to pay both the carpet-weaver and Thomas the *entrepreneur*. Perhaps it is fitting that the little Baroness should stand, her bosom heaving with indignation, her tears falling roundly into the saucepans. For their son, Charles de Thierry, lies now in a grave as obscure as any day of his childhood.

Somerset's sweet apple-orchards are a pleasant enough background for later youth. It is astonishing how much better things move when one has money. It restores one's faith in the aristocratic way of life.

Where that faith led Our Charles can now be followed by clearer trails. Once the many doubts and fears concerning his fledgling years have been dragged into daylight, the rest, by comparison, seems very nearly lucid.

CHAPTER THREE

CONVERSATION PIECE

The white-starred négligé of the jasmine sprawling over the dank little summer-house was cautiously parted by an arrow's point. A peculiarly complacent-looking cat, very spruce in black doublet and spotless white hose, sat sunning itself on the brick wall against which an elderly apricot had brought forth golden abundance. The arrow whizzed, pinking a splendid apricot, clean missing the cat, which, heedless of this boon, called upon its gods and launched itself into space.

The hunter, crestfallen, came in sight, his shoes gloomily scuffing the pebbles of the garden path, in whose borders old-maidenly flowers, pink thrift, scarlet pincushions, and dim, dreamy lavender bushes, nodded their heads tremulously. The boy stared at the spot vacated by the cat, as if his miss were a far more living reproach to him than anything these prim spinster flowers could imply. His bow, trailed behind him, was at least twice as long as himself.

"Charlie, Charlie," drawled a voice as lazy as the windless pause of the trees, "did I give ye that bow to keep your eye trained proper at the targets, or were't to go shooting cats and vermin?"

" 'Twas no vermin," answered the boy, with a flat disregard of the laws of evidence which seemed to amuse the tall, limping, club-haired old gentleman, whose eyes were no less twinkling blue than his periwinkle satin coat. " 'Twas a heathen cannibal."

Green turf, smooth as though abigail had pressed it with flat-irons, invited them. The gentleman squatted down beside Nimrod, who, after a moment, forgot his wounded dignity, and flung himself full-length at his tail companion's side.

"If it were a cannibal," said the elder, seriously, "you'd have more sense, Charlie, on coming to my age, or even years enough for a saucy little Jack midshipmite, than to go fighting the wind with a great cumbersome weapon like that. What use would your bow be across a dirty little grey creek with the trees twisting all around, like as old Mother Cranston down the way had put the twitching palsy on 'em, and a stink of musk coming out of the swamp, where ye'd see a big, ugly snout hitching itself under the nose of your canoe ? If it came to fight, there'd be neither sight nor sound of the enemy, but you'd see the man in front put up his hand to brush a gnat from his cheek ; and 'twouldn't be no gnat at all, but a little bit of a sticky dart, come from one of the savage blow-pipes. A moment later, ye'd see that man pitch forward, Charlie . . ."

"Poisoned ?"

"Poisoned," nodded the lame gentleman, sombre satisfaction in every crinkle of his mahogany face.

"Captain Pete, next time you're at sea, couldn't you bring me back the littlest scrap of that poison ? I wouldn't use it, not even on the cat. Just to keep it, Captain Pete. Who knows the savages won't be coming to England one day in their canoes ?"

"I'll be going no more to sea, Charlie. They don't want lame old sea-dogs for a man's work, you know. Besides, there's no Captain Cook for me to sail with now, as in my boyhood. There was a man, Charlie. The southern seas will never see a better. And he was too fine an Englishman to go poisoning savages, as I fear many will do in times to come. Where he found them to be men, ay, and gentlemen, he could treat 'em as such. Maybe the ideas he put into me in boyhood have stuck with me yet. But if you want a gentleman's weapon for fighting the savages, Charlie, don't go using long-bows, nor yet poisoned darts.

"Put that club of greenstone I brought you from New Zealand against your cheek, and ask it to sing you its battle-song, as the natives swear it will. If it would do that, you'd hear a long story and a fine one, Charlie. Generation to generation, those clubs are handed down among the Maoris, the tallest and bravest race of fighters the world can show a sailor. They're poets, too, in the savage fashion. That stone your club's made from, they call it 'robe of the sky'. Do christen their clubs like babies, and give 'em titles of honour after a battle, as the old kings would knight a man." He shaded his eyes, watching a tiny fountain bubble in a white jet of laughter between the hands of a leaden naiad.

"Before Cook was slain, Charlie, I used to dream that a man might do better than go to those southern seas to fight with the people. It's a fair world, and deserved more than greed and bloodshed, if so be it we can't let it alone. And the people . . ."

"They're good people, Captain Pete ?"

"Last time I sailed with Cook, and not much older than you are today, I lay sick ashore on the north island of that New Zealand. Friendly enough, the people were. Do live in huts like bee-skeps, and wear great cloaks made of feathers, or the leaves of a strong plant, dyed black, vermeil, and white. They've ovens with red-hot stones in them, under the earth, and water-springs that come singing like the steam from a kettle out of the ground itself, though that you won't believe. I've seen trees burning fiery red with flowers there, and in the morning, the most beguiling sweet bird with surplice of white on his breast, like Robin Hood's parson, wakes the heart up with his song. Cook, the scoundrel, had some caught and baked in a pie. Marvellous sweet eating he said they were, but I couldn't bring my stomach to it, after that morning song. Sweeter on the bough, say I. A lovely place, Charlie."

"I'll go, Captain Pete, and I'll wear a cloak of feathers and carry my green club and be their king, as our Louis was in France till they cut his head off. I'll be a good king."

"Maybe, Charlie. Heigho, it's the sunshine and old age make me prosy, dreaming of the green isles where I can voyage no more. And fine I'll be scolded by Mistress Caroline, who sent me out with news of a bowl of strawberries that seems to be waiting about in the larder for you. . . ."

A moment, just one, before scrambling to his feet. Sometimes, when you're unspeakably happy, or the reverse, the touch of some insignificant thing will fix the memory for ever. In the New Road, on the last night before Papa forsook his lodging-house, a hand outspread, cautiously, like some queer white creeper on the stone wall, seemed to take and hold everything that was London. The misery, the running children, the old, slow lichens, trying to be golden-green, succeeding only in being sooty. Men speaking in voices as despairingly brutish as those of Circe's enchanted tigers and swine. The red horses. The sparrows, soul of London, hopping cheerfully over the manure. A solemn moon, quite beautiful, like a princess astray in New Road.

Now, under one's fingers, the sunburnt feel of smooth turf. We are rich, quite safe, or, one knows instinctively, we would not possess such smooth turf. . . . .Take and hold the moment while you can, outspread fingers of little Charles de Thierry.

. . . . . .

Four steps, whistle your tune over again. (Somerset is the lovely cool green, Hesperidean colour of dusk tangling in the apple-trees.) In between whistling, rehearse what must be said, as befits a man of affairs.

He is, in fact, almost a great man now. Twenty, the head of his house, the Baron de Thierry ; and successfully through no less a mill than the Congress of Vienna, which from 1814 until this year of 1816 has drawn half Europe to their city on the sentimental blue Danube.

The Corsican's done for, the scare of the Hundred Days was no more than a sky-rocket, flaring and falling against that horizon where the Bourbon monarchy's star has risen again over France. Be grateful, France ! Napoleon is strait-jacketed on St. Helena. The English will keep him tight there ; don't disturb yourself. They have no manners, no sense of *mélange*, but in their rough way they are efficient. Louis XVIII occupies the throne of France . . . and how fully ! The old man didn't get slim in exile. The *émigrés* are not forgotten. In the pocket of Baron Charles de Thierry, personal secretary to the Marquis of Marialva at the Congress of Vienna, now crackles a bit of parchment—no less than the letter which appoints him attaché to the French Legation at London, and assures him of Monsieur's "very perfect consideration".

Click the gate. Underfoot are the same round white pebbles that Captain Pete and a ghostly little Charles used for playing knuckle-bones, years ago. The house, with its benevolent, shaggy eaves, hives a multitude to welcome him. Not alone Caroline, Francis, Frederick, Louis. . . . But there is the ghost of his mother, her hands white on her spinet. The rinds of cucumber and lemon that she used, poor *Maman*, to scrub off the feel of the cooking-pots! And the memory of his father, who used to sit in the sunshine, solemnly nodding assurance that again a king would sit on the French throne, and the lost diamond of *émigré* valour glitter from the dust. There was a time, mind you, when the scoundrels said we were only French paste.

Moreover, every moment when Charles put doubt from his mind, and assured various stars and apple-trees that the way to Fame was open, will now have crowded into the house to welcome him. You will perceive that while French royalty and the *émigrés* lay tumbled in limbo, this house, its occupants and its hours, did not live at all. They were suspended in a dream; and at times, as into the mind of the dreamer glides the shadow of a haunting fear, so they were pestered by the idea, "Will we ever be able to wake up?" Now, all over the houses, the little clocks of Victory are striking, slow, solemn, and clear. They are very ornate clocks, some enamelled with painted shepherdesses, others adorned with the gilt figures of Noble Qualities. You would not, I am sure, permit them in your drawing-room today. . . . Our Charles, however, has come home to set them ticking. "There is a king again; and, I can assure you, I am quite a success for one so young."

The Abbot Vaggioli, author of *La Storia della Nuova Zelandia*, comes to light with a reference to the Baron de Thierry of this date, mentioning him as attached to the Portuguese delegation at the conference of Vienna, "where his musical talent attracted much notice". I like better a passage underlined in a newspaper description of a Court masquerade in Vienna, which the Baron himself evidently retained among his treasures for sixty years.

"At the masquerade, the Baron de Thierry played a harp solo, and an Imperial lady fell in love with him." Who was she, the unknown whose eye brightened as the little *émigré* wandered through his golden forest of harp-strings? One thing is certain: if she were really an Imperial lady, Charles would have been beside himself with delight at her attentions, even though she had a face like a gardening-trowel.

There was a picturesque world for a young man to choose from, since Metternich, the great chancellor of Austria, had brought to Vienna half the damsels and courtiers of a continent, possibly so that the clack of their tongues would either lull or deafen the foreign diplomats. From Paris came those hussies whose petticoats were cut like mares' tails ; whose shoulders, what with puffs, ruffs, and frills, stood up higher than their ears. One is puzzled. How was so much of immorality possible, against the voluminous shapes of the prevailing fashions ? Ladies, you remind me, do not invariably retain their petticoats. Naked they came into the world, naked they . . . But it must still have taken such a time to disrobe. Yet their charm laughed over the taffeta barricades. Tiny spring-song bracelets, white lilac and rosebuds, caught their sleeves again and again to their arms. There were soft bare shoulders ; the hair of the older dames was delicately rimed with powder, as in the days before France put her eggs into the revolutionary basket. . . .

Yet with all the world sending embassies to Vienna, secretaries must have been as plentiful as blackberries.

"Who is the young man in green broadcloth, the one with the air of an infant Byron, and a slightly long nose ?"

"That is the Baron de Thierry, a son of *émigrés*."

"Psst ! . . . Vienna is full of *émigrés*, half of them sons of the Bourbons, bastard and otherwise, and all borrowing."

"He is personal secretary to the Marquis of Marialva, of the Portuguese delegation."

"A secretary . . . we waste our time."

"Yes, but he has an uncommon musical talent. He plays the harp, the grand piano, the penny whistle also, for anything I can tell you to the contrary."

"A musician . . . something for our women to listen to . . . now that's a profession of discretion. We shall ask the young man to dinner."

Harp solos. A little tempest of hand-claps in the porcelain teacup and Our Charles harping and blushing furiously. Marialva, it would seem, comports himself pleasantly with his secretary ; for, years later, Charles, trying to refute one of the many libels bruited about among the unimpressionable English, refers haughtily to "the Marquis of Marialva, to whom I was as a son".

As attaché to a legation, one acquires a passport here and there. From twenty gloriously stamped and sealed documents, still preserved, emerges a Charles de Thierry with a long nose, a nose rather thick at the end, a sideways-inclined nose. One official gives him grey eyes, another insists on brown, a third offers orbs of viridian green ; summed up, it comes to hazel. They describe him as sun-tanned, pale, and of swart complexion. (Perhaps he had been seasick after one Channel crossing, scorched during another.) Of two things alone they cannot rob him. He remains a slender young man of middle height, and with chestnut side-whiskers. An Imperial lady fell in love with this. . . .

Suppose, now it's all over ; that some affable Djinn, astray from the Arabian Nights, were to stand whispering in his ear, as he walks up the pebbled drive of the house in Somerset ?

"Well, my little Baron, let's have it. You have seen the lot of them ; a poor crowd compared with the old hands, but the best we can get, now that history no longer does itself in style. For yourself, my boy, what shall it be ? An emperor, perhaps ?"

"Emphatically not an emperor. To be an emperor is both too much and too little. There is something of unreality in the office. One would suspect always the presence of the little toy nightingale, the dolorous bird, flying about the palace and singing, 'We are all alone, Emperor, you and I and Death.' There was a brace of emperors at this congress. But look at them . . . Alexander of Russia, weak, melancholy, swayed always by his desire to sway other people. And the Emperor of Austria, what was he, poor devil, but an opportunity for this Metternich to show how sharp he was ? Both of them had no companion but the nightingale."

"A duke, then, all done up in strawberry-leaves ? Come, don't be modest !"

"Mmm. The devil of it is, these dukes, these lords, these earls . . . they're all so busy running after the king."

"What is it, then, that you would ask ?"

"I would like to be a great leader of men."

"I am surprised, my little one, that you shouldn't have selected a profession with more cachet. But no matter : it would please you, then, to be a demagogue ?"

"Monsieur, you wish to insult me. I am a baron, the son of noble parents, godson to Monsieur the Comte d'Artois, who is brother of King Louis XVIII. You would compare me to a politician. I would lead the people, as it has always been the duty and privilege of the noble to lead the people."

"Then, since you won't be a politician or a duke, you insist on being the man apart? That is to say, the king?"

"There are possibilities in such a position. I often wonder they don't see it."

"Kings are a lousy lot."

"Perhaps. But I would do things differently. I would civilize my subjects."

"You will, in this kingdom, personally wipe all unseemly noses, chastise all unrepentant behinds, and reward the virtuous? *Aussitôt dit que fait*, my little one. Long live King Charles!"

The Djinn disappears. All the bells of Vienna echo softly in the air, drowning the dull rasping of Ethics, Moralizing, and Philosophy. Charles, putting aside the question of a kingdom, stands on the thresholds of a diplomatic career and a kindly old house in Somerset. He is already attaché to the French Legation at London; Monsieur assures him of Monsieur's consideration *toute parfaite*. . . . Things could be worse.

CHAPTER FOUR

NOBODY IS BORED IN CAMBRIDGE

NOBODY is bored in Cambridge ; it is the thing, in the execrable idiom of the inhabitants, that is not done. One becomes, perhaps, a little set in one's ways. It is said that the first five hundred years are the worst. Everything is under magnificent discipline. The lean, narrow face of Erasmus looks down, as Holbein the Younger caught it ; Elizabeth Woodville's painted face has quiet eyes. The bluebells, their stems brave as ships' masts, thrust up azure through the pale tidal wash of grass among the flowers of the Cloistered Court. They look fragmentary, part of an old Roman mosaic telling the story of Flora's passing through this earth. But when you inspect them more closely, you see that they are regimented most carefully. In long garden-plots, the roses, white Yorks and crimson Lancastrians, come later to march side by side. It is forbidden that they argue. Everyone contributes—contributes what little of an air he may have. We are all poured into this mighty vessel of the past.

"But suppose that is just the trouble ? Suppose one wishes to be not merely a shadow, disciplined by the hoariness of the sun-dial on which one is cast, but one's own vigorous self ?"

"Come, then, my brave young man. Apart from a pair of chestnut side-whiskers, a pair of not inelegant pantaloons, what is this self ?"

"I am a baron, son of *émigré* parents. Charles Philip Hippolytus, Baron de Thierry, now, in this year of 1820, attained to twenty-six years."

"The Charles Philip Hippolytus doesn't make things any better. As for the title, it may be ornamental, but your continental nobility were always so profuse. What are you, in yourself ?"

"At eighteen I was attaché to the French Legation at London . . ."

"There is a career in diplomacy, for the duller sort of scoundrel."

"But I gave that up."

"You did well. What then?"

"I was attracted to the military career. Owing to the favour of the Duke of York, I received a commission in His Majesty's 23rd Light Dragoons."

"Not so bad. To sit a cavalry charger on a frosty morning is an invigorating thing."

"However, I resigned my commission. I found that I liked horses, but could not endure the monotony of my brother officers."

"What hat did you try on next?"

"I am an author. I wrote a novel called *Isabel*. My heroine was a paragon of the virtues, a hecatomb of the tragedies. A London firm made arrangements for publication. It was not, however, a popular success. Frequently the publishers send me accounts . . . a matter of £50. I decided, therefore, to regiment my abilities under the discipline of university life, and entered Oxford as a gentleman commoner."

"A noble university."

"But shortly afterwards, I married my wife Emily, who is daughter to the Archdeacon Thomas Rudge, of Gloucester, a divine of eminence in the Church of England. A solid papa-in-law, I can assure you of that. Always we enjoy roast beef on Sundays. Always he scatters snuff on the carpets. It was his idea that I should come to Cambridge and apply myself to the study of theology and law. 'Charles,' he declared, 'Nature herself has made a talker of you. There are offices where eloquence is not misplaced . . . the pulpit, or even the bar. You will be better applied in these directions than in galloping about Oxford, with some Quixote maggot for ever in your brain. It is due to my daughter Emily that you should settle down.' (This I recognized, for, at the time, Madame the Baroness was already expecting.) So I entered Cambridge as a fellow commoner. But . . ."

"It can't be that you are tired of it already? Nobody is bored in Cambridge."

"I appreciate that. The trouble is, I'm only twenty-six; Cambridge is so many centuries. It doesn't leave one much scope for initiative. And my wife is once again expecting. . . ."

Love, in itself, is a university of tradition. Before ever Charles was settled in life as the husband of fair-haired little Emily Rudge, daughter of the snuff-taking Archdeacon, there was also Eliza.

A leaf whirls for an instant on its bough, then, with a dry and tiny sound, like an infinitesimal fairy sigh, it is fallen to grass. That was Eliza. It was a funny little name, which should have belonged to a very old-fashioned flower, loved by all the bees. But then, Eliza was a funny little girl. It is hard to extract from Charles's records any account of her other than purely sentimental reference. "My lost love, Eliza. . . ." And then, years later, when his baby daughter at last arrived, there was that business about the poppet's christening.

When she slipped away from him—after a quarrel in which he had been stigmatized, with justice, as a stupid, conceited boy, who did nothing but ride horses and tell fairy-tales—it was as if she had gone into another room, a strange room; but not out of the dear, warm house of memory and life. He had been hurt and angry after he said good-bye. He could just remember her black-and-cerise shoes, showing under a looped petticoat of three enormous flounces, her hands curled up like squirrels in the prodigious fur muff, as she ran up the stairs of her house in London. A door had flashed open for a moment, a beam of light slanted out, dusty gold, over her cheek and bonnet, both a little wet from the sprinkling of summer's rain. Then she was gone. And it was no use waiting, he learned that.

He had paid court like a schoolboy. And she, white now, no longer the gay Columbine, had fled away from such clumsy loving, away from any human love at all.

Thrust them out of sight, the useless thoughts; drown them in the brittle white sunshine of Cambridge mornings. At twenty-six it becomes a duty to have established one's self in life, to have a professional and an assured future, disciplined like the bluebells. One must be a rational part of the mosaic. If one is bored, the evidence must be controlled. . . .

A piece of orange-peel on a pavement may alter the physical

circumstances of a man's life. But to take a mind and its armada of dream, to set the sails moving into the blue . . . that seems more difficult. In Charles de Thierry's case, the wind of destiny blew, the gates of the ocean were unlocked, when, at the far end of the world, an English missionary named Thomas Kendall seduced two cannibal chieftains into an itching desire to look on the face of His Majesty, King George IV of England. A cat, thought Mr. Kendall, may look at a king ; why mayn't a cannibal ? Besides, he wanted the trip himself. Things were getting hot for him in New Zealand, it was convenient to run before the storm.

In the younger of his two charges, Shunghie, paramount chieftain of the warlike and energetic Ngapuhi tribes, whose might went for law in the northern parts of New Zealand, the Rev. Thomas Kendall beheld an intelligence, a shrewd power of reason. The more Shunghie learned from his English visit, the more he consolidated his powers in that wild and feud-tangled North Island, the better Mr. Kendall would like it. Mr. Kendall had plans. . . .

The second chieftain, Waikato, was a man of dignity and reputation, physically a tattooed and mahogany-brown giant, who could no more fail of making an impression in England than a double-headed giraffe. He was, moreover, a leading agriculturist in a nation which possessed considerable primitive skill in this art. Agriculture, everyone knew, was particularly close to the heart of His Britannic Majesty. There was little chance that Waikato should not prove a great attraction.

Our forefathers were, above all things, unselfconscious. On the modern stage, Mr. Kendall, with his dives into intrigue, his passionate declarations of independence, his affairs of the heart—mostly, one regrets, with pretty little Maori maidens —and his orgies of repentance, in which he would do everything but thump his head on the floor, would be received as rather exaggerated. But in 1820 his confidence was invaded by no foreknowledge of times when professional sinners and penitents would not be encouraged to take themselves so seriously. So, the perfect bear-leader for his chiefs, Mr. Kendall strides on to the Cambridge stage. He has at least one unexceptionable pretext for bringing Shunghie and Waikato to London, though he has dispensed with the formality of getting the Church

Missionary Society's permission for this step. There is no Maori grammar or vocabulary in existence, and Professor Lee, of Cambridge, is anxious to compile one ;* Shunghie and Waikato are willing to supply requisite material. The three of them will be the guests of Cambridge, received with interest, honour, and curiosity. Nobody is bored in Cambridge, but cannibal chieftains are a novelty, especially when so good-looking.

Behold, then, a thick-set gentleman in early middle age—dark hair, a proud brown eye, complexion pleasantly tanned by years of open-air life. (Thomas Kendall was one of the first missionaries to settle in New Zealand.) He looked like anything in the world rather than a churchman . . . something of the explorer, something of the dreamer. Missionizing, in New Zealand, was a man's job in those days. It was essential that the missionary should be craftsman, tutor, labourer, mechanic, diplomat, nurse, general. All of these things Mr. Kendall was, to a degree a little too outstanding for his general popularity. Already he had incurred the distrust of old Samuel Marsden, father of the New Zealand Mission—though Mr. Marsden was now stationed in New South Wales, and only occasionally swooped down on the New Zealand fold. Smaller fry among the whites envied Mr. Kendall, feared his influence with the powerful chief Shunghie, and pretended to be scandalized at his behaviour. Contradicting the roughness of his personality—a manner deliberately assumed—was the slow, musical voice. The only educated man, and the most rebellious one among the first batch of missionaries sent to New Zealand by Samuel Marsden, Kendall could talk like a book.

Shunghie—the historians of the day spelt his name according to the soft phonetic pronunciation, but the modern spelling is Hongi-Hika—was lord absolute of the dreaded Ngapuhi tribe, King of the carved *pa* whose palisades were the grimmest threat in the North Island. He was already a veteran in warfare, and in the custom of cannibalism. During that war, in which he engaged soon after his return from England, three hundred prisoners of Shunghie's were killed and eaten. Waikato, the agriculturist, won the heart of King George, as expected, and was presented by His Majesty with a magnificent fowling-piece

---

*Tui and Titoria, two of Marsden's pupils, started on this work with Professor Lee in 1817.

bearing the royal name and message of goodwill on a plate of gold.

In Sydney, where Thomas Kendall and his charges arrived in March 1820, aboard the sturdy little coastal barque *Captain Monro*, Shunghie and Waikato explained their intentions freely to the editor of the *Sydney Gazette*. These were, to see His Majesty the King of England ; also to observe the number of his people, their different occupations, and the manufactures and produce of the country. On arrival, they were introduced by Mr. Kendall to the Honourable Committee of the Church Missionary Society, and, after a few days, journeyed on to Cambridge,

where they were entertained in the most obliging manner by Professor Lee, and were introduced by him to the Vice-Chancellor, Rev. Dr. Clarke, the Rev. Mr. Mandell, the Rev. Mr. Gee, Professor Farish, Mr. Farish, Surgeon, the Baron de Thierry, and many other distinguished officers and members of that university. They had the opportunity of taking a survey of the county in time of harvest, and were entertained by many, including William Mortlock, Esquire, and Lady Jane Pym.*

For better, for worse, the deed is done. Our Charles, through the instrumentality of the Rev. Mr. Thomas Kendall, has become acquainted with the people of Captain Pete's unforgotten stories. Here he is, his abandoned professions trailing like beggars at his heels, suddenly in his element as companion, part-time host, and eager listener to a couple of authentic and ornamental chieftains, accompanied by a suspiciously eloquent interpreter. The period of Mr. Kendall's stay in Cambridge was one of the happiest times in Charles de Thierry's life.

Mr. Kendall has his plans, and it is not impossible to fit one so young and ardent as Charles into the exact centre of those plans, particularly as, just then, Charles was in possession of a loose thousand or two. (Don't ask me whether he had borrowed it from his father-in-law, the Archdeacon. It was there, though not for long.)

If Charles, at Cambridge, was already becoming filled with the idea that the Church was not suited to him, something

---

*The *Sydney Gazette* of June 2nd, 1821.

of the kind may also have crossed the mind of the Rev. Thomas Kendall before ever he left the Antipodes on this trip. Thomas Kendall had talents, but was the Church Missionary Society the place for them? He began to doubt this, and while in England never mentioned to the Society that he had whisked Shunghie and Waikato away without so much as a by-your-leave to his fuming superiors. Scarcely had he returned to New Zealand after this English visit when the ominous rumblings formerly heard from the Society became a perfect little Vesuvius. There was a scandal. Mr. Samuel Marsden was willing to pray for Mr. Kendall, but not at all willing that Mr. Kendall should remain in his New Zealand office. The chieftain, Shunghie, continued to extend his patronage and liking to the discredited missionary, and might have protected him indefinitely, but Mr. Kendall, in one of those wild fits of penitence and despondency to which he was subject, threw in his hand, retired, as Samuel Marsden commanded, to New South Wales, and later perished miserably enough by drowning off that unattractive coast, which is, to make the matter worse, everywhere infested by sharks.

During his Cambridge holiday, however, Thomas Kendall had no intention of going into a fit of penitence, much less of being drowned. His idea was to consolidate his own doubtful position by inducing a few gentlemen to buy from Shunghie and Waikato, or their relatives, some of the enormous land-tracts available in that wild and lawless country, the No Man's Land of the southern world. There may be complications, perhaps, with the Church Missionary Society. But if there is at hand a colony of white men, a colony wanting the services of an educated man with a thorough understanding of the natives, a strong influence with Shunghie, the most powerful chieftain of all ... It was not a bad idea.

From the first, at all events, Mr. Kendall talked New Zealand colony into the head of the most willing audience that a shrewd business man, interesting himself in land deals under cover of much talk about the welfare of the natives, could have wished to meet. As for Shunghie and Waikato, there is reason to think they had a very friendly mind to the young Baron de Thierry. The Maori, for a while, stood hesitating on the brink of white civilization. The *pakeha* in New Zealand had an almost supernatural prestige, when he had sense enough to go in peace among the natives. Even the most miserable and squalid of escaped convicts from Van Diemen's Land and Botany Bay were sheltered, adopted, and enriched. One writer has described the white new-comer to Maoriland of that day as "a tame god". White men's law, white men's institutions . . . these were eagerly and hopefully watched.

"During the two months of Mr. Kendall's stay in Cambridge, I saw much of them, meeting with the chieftains almost daily. Mr. Kendall's representations were such as would have excited less sanguine persons than myself. I gave my deepest attention and consideration to all that Shunghie and Waikato wanted me to do for them. . . ."

Hours of listening to Mr. Kendall, while Professor Lee gathers crumbs of information for that *Grammar and Vocabulary of the Language of New Zealand*, published late in 1820 by the Church Missionary Society. There is talk of the whalers, standing in from far parts of the world ; of outrages among the natives, cannibal vengeance, reprisal charring the flax-thatched villages out of existence. From Sydney the Church Missionary Society reaches forth, but its outpost in the northern part of the country remains a lonely venture. The rest belongs to nobody.

"We live, my dear Baron, because the Maoris also worship not idols, but a spirit . . . something invisible. They build carved houses for temples, very elaborate. From the grim faces and squinting shell-eyes patterned on these, you'd take them to be idolatrous enough, but not the most intricate shrine means anything to the Maori until it has been consecrated by their *tohunga*, or priest. Then, no money will purchase such a shrine. Among the whites there are good and bad. Some love the native just as the slave-owner loves his slaves—not that the Maori will ever work as a serf, but the provisions resulting from his labour come in useful when they can be bought for next to nothing. Other whites pare off free land for themselves and their families. . . ."

Charles learned of the continual escape to New Zealand of convicts from the penal settlements, safe from justice in these wild islands, where neither British law nor that of any other civilized country had sway. Around the missionary outposts grew up the defiant stores and settlements of the white traders, some of them white men gone Maori. Not a few took advantage of their prestige as whites to drag the native women down to vice and disease. Men had nothing to lose but their lives, and the lives of many were forfeit already, or branded by the chains and brutality of their prisons. There was no law other than the infamous club-law system, which allowed a few powerful whites to dominate all.

Yet behind this little rum-swilling, dangerous world stretched the green place of old dreams. Great *kauri* trees, tallest of the pine family, soared up, ready-made ships' masts. Under the bloodshed and the cannibalism was a simplicity of lovely legend, of natural poetry and music.

"Crushed between the upper and the nether millstones, poor souls. Behind them is the blackness of their own cannibal customs; in front, if we were honest enough to admit it, a white civilization which without law must remain a mere cesspool of the vices. The Church does what it can, but what is the Church without law? What control has the Church over the riff-raff of our own race and the other whites when no law exists? White colonists could soon establish law. Why do reputable Englishmen shrink from such an adventure, and such a humane interest? Surely England had more spirit a few years ago?"

Charles discovered that land which would cost a fortune in the Old World went cheaply in the new.

"Trade, my dear Baron, and *such* trade. Gimcrack, bright cloth, a sniff of gunpowder, an antiquated musket. There's nothing they won't do for muskets. A warlike race, the New Zealanders. What will be the end? Will they exterminate one another, tribe against tribe, or will the white man swallow them all and name his crime civilization?"

"Do live in huts like bee-skeps, and wear great cloaks of feathers," thought Charles, wishing he could see Shunghie and Waikato as Captain Pete had described the race. A loathing of their European clothing came over him. Was it indeed true that these bronze bodies, and thousands like them, must be vitiated and spoiled by the contact of a degraded civilization? Was there to be no equal footing of speech and thought?

"Teach English, all English, and nothing but English,"

runs an outburst in his monumental record. "One universal language for the races of the South Seas, raising them to a level where they can properly meet civilization." And long after the last shred of his English affinities has been torn away, and he is the hated "French aggressor" of English settlers' nightmares, he continues to urge that the native dragged into a civilized world should be given the language of civilization.

The friendship between the queer quartette, white and brown, continues. Before Mr. Kendall has shepherded his flock to London, where the King is pleased to grant them an audience, the rough outline of a New Zealand colony, a little Utopia to be peopled with strictly respectable Englishmen and Maoris, settled, if possible, under British protection, and at all events a model of British institutions and justice, has been designed.

"Mr. Kendall took with him to New Zealand a well-drawn-up deed, with blanks, promising to purchase all that part of New Zealand from the narrow neck of land in the North Island upwards. To this end, I entrusted to him considerable property, and gave many presents both to Shunghie and Waikato and to Mrs. Kendall, who was in New Zealand. My last gifts to Shunghie and Waikato were a gun for each, engraved with their names and my own on silver plates. And with a copious flow of tears, which the New Zealanders can so readily command, and which Mr. Kendall also managed to shed, and with mutual expressions of due regard, we parted."

They have seen many things, the old Cambridge towers: Milton mooning under his mulberry-tree, kings and queens with their prodigious trains, poets casting their eyes to heaven or their fists at their persecutors. But Our Charles, Mr. Thomas Kendall, and the two enormous bronze chieftains, all in tears, such large tears . . . that, also, must have been worth a spire's craning its neck a little.

Not immediately did Mr. Kendall leave for New Zealand. John Mortlock, Esquire, created a sensation by presenting the two handsome savages to the House of Lords. They had private interviews with half the peerage, and more public intercourse with the lions in the old Strand menagerie, which probably pleased them a great deal better. Their visit reached its climax when Mr. Mortlock had the honour of presenting them to His Majesty,

who treated them with the greatest condescension and affability, conducted them to his armoury, gave them several valuable presents, and allowed them the honour of kissing his hand. They also visited the Tower of London and the Museum, and sailed for home on December 10th, in the best of health and spirits.*

On his visit to the royal armoury, Shunghie was invited by His Majesty to choose some token of the kingly regard. He settled on a suit of armour. In Sydney, the warrior chief declared that lesson which his English visit had taught him: "One people, one king." He sold all the gifts he had received in England, with the sole exception of this suit of armour, receiving muskets in exchange. Returning to his native land, he immediately put his new creed into practice, slaughtering vast numbers of enemies, and eating a very handsome collection of them. In his every battle shone the armour given him by the English George. On the day when he left it off, fortune deserted him, and he fell mortally wounded . . . an end to a reign of blood and terror not easily surpassed in minor history. Incidentally, Shunghie's ardour, as well as the remonstrances of Samuel Marsden, may have had something to do with Thomas Kendall's acute fits of penitence. It takes self-possession to ride a cannibal whirlwind.

"It is Mr. Kendall's intention to re-establish a school among the natives, having been given supplies for that purpose by the Church Missionary Society, and by several private ladies and gentlemen," hopefully states the *Sydney Gazette*, having interviewed Mr. Kendall on his homeward journey. Unfortunately, Mr. Kendall's good intentions fell by the wayside. He lasted just long enough in New Zealand to drag Charles de Thierry, among other people, into the whirlpool.

A curious two years must have been spent by Emily de Thierry. She had married a lovelorn youth, was a mother almost in girlhood, and before they left Cambridge was manufacturing lordly white long-clothes for another defenceless male, Richard de Thierry, born two years after little Charles

---

*The *Sydney Gazette*.

Frederick. She was linked now with Quixote, firmly seated on his hobby-horse. He took her to Paris, introduced her to Court circles. She curtsied, as became a modest lady. He set her in a canoe and dragged her, with a baby in her lap and other infants frisking at her side, up the fever-ridden river Chagres, over the Isthmus of Panama, where everyone warned them that they must certainly fall victims to the yellow pest, and thus perish ingloriously, with none but glum Indians and tobacco-chewing peons to put up a show of lament for them —which they would not do, if paid in advance for their services. She remained in excellent health, nursed her baby, and pulled through the Panama fever an extremely unpleasant, quite useless smuggler from the Demarara coast, whom her lord had gathered into their party.

I think Emily de Thierry loved her husband with a most gentle and tolerant love. There is a curious pathos in one relic preserved in a New Zealand home—a bunch of flowers, pressed for so long between the pages of an old book that they have quite lost their colour. Nobody would dare to handle their dry and brittle fragility, but it is obvious that they were violets. Round their stalks was twisted a scrap of paper on which a woman's hand had written:

Gathered at Bunthorpe Hill, March 1826. Good-bye, England.

Early in 1823 came the letter which Charles had long expected. It was dated from the Bay of Islands, New Zealand, December 2nd, 1822.

My Dear Baron,
Owing to the wars of the natives and various other disturbances, I have not been able to procure you any land before this. I have, however, at length done as well as I could for you. The chiefs mentioned in the deed are friends to Shunghie and Waikato. The heads of the river are in latitudes 35-32 on the west coast of New Zealand, opposite to us. I have walked through part of the woods, which are very extensive, but the boundaries cannot be better described than by giving the names of the districts or townships. I cannot recommend you to send your brother,

because I should not think it prudent for any person or small number of persons to settle themselves now under a heathen government. I shall, however, be happy to serve your brother if you determine on making the attempt. I hope the Baroness is in good health. Be pleased to favour me with a line when you receive this.

And am, dear Sir,
Your faithful servant,
Thomas Kendall.

The letter lay folded in a package of gifts which made Charles's eyes glisten; for they were from Shunghie and Waikato. Shunghie's gift was a princely one, his greenstone war mere, a weapon with a notorious history of bloodshed behind it.

But the thing he could not weary of reading, the thing he fingered as though its sheets were jade, beautiful to touch, was the deed enclosed with Mr. Kendall's letter.

In 1823, Baron Charles de Thierry, noted in this deed as "of Queen's College, Cambridge, and Bathampton, Somerset", became, by purchase from the chiefs Nene, Mudi Wai, and Patuone, absolute owner of about 40,000 acres in the North Island of New Zealand, land lying on the western banks of the Hokianga River—quaintly spelled in the deed as "Yokianga" —deep-wooded with *kauri*, and threaded with streams whose fishing-rights were carefully preserved for its new lord.

The deed was signed aboard the ship *Providence*, with Thomas Kendall, James Herd, master of the *Providence*, and William Edward Green, first officer, as witnesses. Nene, Mudi Wai, and Patuone made their mark, as was customary in all land transactions with the Maoris.

In all, the property entrusted by Charles to Mr. Kendall— chosen, he says, according to lists made out by the missionary and the two chieftains of the trade best likely to warm the cockles of native hearts—was worth a little over £1000. That was Charles's account, and, as the modern heathen say, he stuck to it, with few divagations. The Abbot Vaggioli, for instance, says Mr. Kendall was a terrible robber, he deprived Charles of *many* thousands of pounds. However, by that time a certain amount of incoherence was justifiable. And, in his half-finished memoirs and other documents, the figure £1000 crops up so persistently that one feels there's something in it.

In the deed, the price mentioned as paid to the chiefs for their 40,000 acres was thirty-six axes.

From a benefactor of the natives, does that look well?

Over and over again, Charles says, he asked himself about this point. But what could he do? Here he was, the deed in his pocket. Mr. Kendall, Nene, Mudi Wai, and Patuone were all of them thousands of miles away. Mr. Kendall must have done something with the rest of the £1000. Maybe he gave it in palm-oil among important chiefs. As for the deed, there's nothing wrong with that. Look at it back, front, or sideways, it's a lovely deed. It preserves even the fishing-rights. Fishing-rights and rights of man. . . . "I'll be careful of those," Charles assures his fire.

Utopia, Utopia, you are no longer between the pages of an old book, a thing that one takes gently down from the library shelf and as gently puts back again. You are between two arms of land, widening to embrace a blue sea. You are the rounded bosom of a hill in an unknown land. Faces, brown-eyed as rabbits, peer out from the undergrowth.

He sees it, sitting there watching the little phoenix-wings of flame mount and tumble in the gullet of a vast sooty chimney. It is intriguing, this occupation. And, does it not prove what we have said? It is dangerous, it is tempting Providence, to be bored in Cambridge.

CHAPTER FIVE

SHIPS PUTTING FORTH

THE notice-board, lugged forth from years of oblivion, leans drunkenly over the stage. (We couldn't contrive without it.) "Budge Row," runs the legend, "London, A.D. 1825."

Almost empty, the vast theatre. Motes of dust take on a rainbow life in long, solemn beams of light. One has the idea that they are more alive than dust-motes have reason to be. Perhaps each is the spirit of some old playgoer, not to be whisked out by any attendant's broom. In the wings are men with unshaven chins and unimpressionable faces. Those are the scene-shifters, but some folk call them The Years. Hear them whispering. . . .

. . . . .

"You're a dead man, Charles."

"Not quite, Francis, but it's damnably hot. I wouldn't mind that, either, except for the flies and the Poles. They're both difficult to get rid of. On the whole, I'd rather have the flies. They aren't so plaguy ambitious. Look at these."

On the desk of the close little office hung a tremendous banner of crimson and silver. There were samples of scarlet cloth, numerous twinkling buttons. A lance stood proudly in one corner of the room.

Francis de Thierry began to laugh.

"For pity and piety's sake, Charles, what's all this? Are you fathering a mere colony, or starting a crusade? Have you turned Chartist, and mean to introduce some colour into their processions?"

"No laughing matter, Frank. It's the Poles. A deputation of them waited on me today, with Budge Row staring from every window as though the world were coming to an end, and I the angel Gabriel, getting ready to hoot on the trump of doom. The desire of my Polish pests is that I should form a regiment of Lancers to accompany my settlers to New Zealand. Wouldn't take 'no' for an answer. 'You will find the uniforms very becoming, *mon general*,' says a swarthy fellow, all gimlet eye and onion breath. So away they go, leaving me to think it over. How the devil am I going to get rid of that confounded lance ? Then here's a letter representative of a considerable number of French foot-soldiers, who are very willing to act as my infantry. In God's name, Frank, doesn't Europe think of anything at all beyond slitting throats ?"

"Or stretching necks, dear lad. But this time there's no shortage of emigrants."

"Shortage ? There's clergymen in dozens open to clerical appointments. There's lawyers who tender me their services as magistrates, physicians and surgeons innumerable, authors who'll write books for me, and odes even . . . at a price . . . penny-a-liners anxious to sell their eloquence. Actors aren't few, barbers and fitters enough to found a colony on their own, and then we've the gentlemen, bless them, who for the most part insist on telling me more about their private affairs than I have any wish to know. There are so many schoolmasters offering that, if I take the lot, I can teach every native in New Zealand English at one fell swoop . . . best thing that could happen to them. The most interesting of today's bag was a young American surgeon, offered me a neat little invention for use when Sawbones wants to make the vile body viler. The spring lancet, he calls it. Why, by the time the day's out, my brain goes round when I try to sort sense into the mass of information and lies I've received."

"So in rolls Captain Billy Stewart, hitches up those great elephantine britches of his, and says, 'Baron Charles, me lad, away with you to the 'Saracen's Head'," or some other hovel of all the vices. I don't like your tarry friend, Charles."

"Oh, he's a good fellow, and knows the country. But tonight I'm too weary for Captain Billy. I'm for home, if you call three rooms in a London hotel a home, though the children are happy enough there, stuffing the pigeons from the window-sills. Don't forget New Zealand in your prayers, Frank."

Much water has flowed under London Bridge since Thomas

Kendall and two handsome chieftains waved a fond farewell. Barons, naturally, do not pipe their eye. Otherwise one might declare that a proportion of this water was tears, to which Our Charles had contributed most handsomely. . . .

If a man wasn't in earnest, would he have the sheer audacity to stick flippant beauty-patches all over the face of London? You know the sort of face London has: beautiful, in a relentless, grimy way, especially when the tree-tresses are all in young leaf again, but not by any means a hail-fellow-well-met face. All through these stifling months, Londoners have discovered the stone face of their city plastered with huge coloured bills. The handsomest bear portraits of savages with large bare legs and blue tattooing over their beaky noses. All refer in enthusiastic terms to the merits of this New Zealand. A Baron de Thierry, it would seem, is running an expedition there this year . . . promises to make a fortune for the lot of us. Where the deuce, then, is New Zealand? Stuck on the tail end of the world; people walking about like flies on a ceiling. Nothing to be seen but convicts and cannibals. That's the gag at the back of those Australian penal colonies, you know. The cannibals were expected to eat the convicts, but our lads turned out too tough for 'em. Oh, there must be more to it than that. Come along to this office in Budge Row, as the posters advise us. . . . The Baron will tell us what's in the idea.

An Appeal to the People of England, in the Matter of a New Zealand Settlement. That's the title of the brochure published early in '25, under the sign and seal of Charles. New Zealand, it is evident, possesses everything desirable: metals, tangled in the fibrous hair of old earth; *kauri* spars, for which sea-captains will come begging you on their marrow-bones; then there's a strong plant, *Phormium Tenax,* which is to corner the world's rope market. And the land will grow anything. Cannibals? Pish to that! . . . The Baron has been on intimate terms with the chieftains; he corresponds with them still, and swears they'll live with his settlers like brothers. Framed on his office wall there's the deed which proves him owner of 40,000 New Zealand acres. He got the land for thirty-six axes . . . seems a shrewd fellow.

The expert on the natives and their passion for axes

is, however, not Charles de Thierry, but Captain Billy Stewart.

It would be convenient, if one had a map, to glance at an island of the three red dots that make up New Zealand. Not the scraggy topmost one, like a fish—though that's where Charles and his settlers are bound. Not the middle island, shaped rather like a sheep-skin. That little one at the tail end, south of nowhere. It grows beautiful oysters, and the whalers used it a lot for boiling out blubber in their great tripod-legged iron pots. However, that's not the point. The name of this islet is Stewart Island, named after Captain Billy Stewart. He may be a bit of a rough-neck, but he's also a Jacobite. You have observed the name? He says he's one of *those* Stewarts, the ones whose posteriors have a right to the English throne, who got their heads chopped off or were chased up oak-trees, and who, despite hard times, always maintained a sufficiency of glamour and mistresses. That gives Captain Billy a little in common with Charles. How we kings love one another!

Of course, there's the usual little something of irregularity. Captain Stewart was a deserter from the King's navy, then prize-master on a privateer, and didn't put his nose inside an English port until an amnesty was declared, some few years ago. But bygones are bygones, and, besides, Captain Billy is reassuring about Thomas Kendall's thirty-six axes.

"Payment, lad? What payment d'ye think your mouse-livered little friends the missionaries made to the Maoris for the thousands of acres they've whittled off in their settlements . . . ay, and dug themselves in so pretty it 'ud take Shunghie on the warpath to get 'em out again, even if a squeal out of 'em wouldn't bring the warships over from Sydney? I tell you, the missionary, for the most part, makes it a matter of condescension to risk his bacon among the heathen. Spreading the word o' God among the Maoris . . . maybe, maybe, but they spread it at a price, my boy. The native Bibles and prayer-books that get round among the Maoris don't drop from heaven, not by no manner of means. They're paid for in kits of sweet potatoes and hogs, which have come on wonderful in New Zealand since Captain Cook had the brains to turn 'em loose there. This Kendall, I'm not saying he's more or less of a scoundrel than others. But you can't quarrel with his thirty-six axes as payment for New Zealand land. The Maori will give more than a few acres for a matter of axes."

One wishes to do things in orderly manner. Olympus, of course, is the British Colonial Office, Jove the supremely indifferent Earl Bathurst. Those old geese up yonder won't lay anything beyond an occasional china egg. There's an Under-Secretary named Horton, who does my lord's "Answers to Correspondents". It hurts him to talk, though. Of course, the Duke of Wellington's behind the Colonial Office policy. He sticks that surpassing beak of his in the air and says England has too many colonies already.

"The Baron de Thierry has the honour to present his compliments to the Right Honourable Earl Bathurst. . . ."

Over and over again, processions of compliments. The Right Honourable Earl never turns a hair.

Would the Colonial Office in any way assist a new settlement accepting the Baron de Thierry's title deeds of land as guarantee, with immediate repayment promised in "cowrie spars"?

The Colonial Office would not.

Would any protection be offered British settlers making their homes in New Zealand?

New Zealand not being a possession of England, settlers there must shift for themselves.

The correspondence develops into a one-sided duel. The Baron de Thierry, hearing this stricture or that passed in the House of Commons concerning his beloved colonizing project, sits down and tosses off another letter to the Earl. He begs to assure all that he will certainly not, as has been suggested, permit his settlement to be the happy hunting-ground of escaped convicts; he will rather return such persons at once to their proper habitation. He volunteers to supply the Colonial Office with any information it may require concerning New Zealand.

The Colonial Office remains mute.

In spite of indifference and jests, in spite of the want of adequate finance—much more serious—the first expedition in 1823 had begun to take shape fairly well. The *Princess Royal*, a barque of 360 tons, was fitted out—the first ship ever chartered to colonize New Zealand. Settlers were welded together. Then the Press broke out in a rash of warnings. There were shouts in the House of Commons of a second Poyais expedition. Cannibalism enjoyed a vogue in the Grub Street limelight. Before Charles's eyes, his expedition melted away, all but a few gentlemen of quality joining in the *sauve qui peut*. He thanked his gentlemen of quality . . . but, alas, one can't spread a single teaspoonful of jam, even the best strawberry, over 40,000 lawless acres.

Yet there were men in England whom nobody wanted. No journal would have uttered a protest if every cannibal in the South Seas had made arrangements for dining on them. The parishes offered the *Princess Royal* expedition their paupers, with £5 a head thrown in.

There were men here who had grown up, from sickly childhood to pallid and dejected youth, in the shadow of the workhouse. For the poor, England of that day was a bitter place. Danger was rising on the wind, Chartist murmurings were heard, and the hand of Authority, of the old and hard-headed, grew tighter on the reins. These men would crush rebellion by trampling it into the dust.

One does not forget. One fails, is helpless, but one does not forget. Forty years later one's hands, though no longer so confident and strong, take pen and paper, and write.

"They were men weighed down by poverty and destitution, and I would willingly have befriended them. They were suffering, and it would have been my most earnest wish to relieve them. They were without homes, and to settle them in a new country where they might be comforted and made happy was a bright dream. . . . And I could not realize it. There were men among them who begged me with tears in their eyes for their chance in that new world. Had the Government aided them, ever so little, we might have contrived what they asked. But the poor-laws of England do not fall on the Government, and if the poor starve and suffer, there is money enough still to be squandered by the wealthy man. . . . Think: a few of those millions thrown away on warlike armaments, a few of the thousands of men whose blood fertilizes the fields of an enemy—with no more than that we could carry civilization to the very ends of the earth."

There were, of course, other possible supporters than England. The Dutch discovered New Zealand ; there's a whole sea named after their navigator, Abel Tasman. But Baron Tagel, Holland's Ambassador in London, blandly disclaims all interest in the country when Charles pops in to talk the matter over.

France, then, perhaps ? After all, the de Thierrys are Frenchmen at root. . . . And Paris, for *émigré* barons, was a happy place just then. The former Comte d'Artois, godfather to Charles, was by this time King Charles X.

You remember Caroline, the first little de Thierry, the clever one who got herself born at the Orange palace ? She is now Madame Caroline de Cordoza, a personage of credit at Court. It all helps. Madame the Baroness de Thierry accompanies her energetic husband. Hers is a singular life. Now her lord is exclaiming over the duplicity of the French enthusiast who received the colonizing project so kindly, and then departed hastily for America with the large fund raised for the expedition. . . . Now he is receiving from M. le Duc d'Aumont an invitation to the games at the Tuileries. . . . Now he is in despair again, because the French, the moment you say "colony" to them, fly into raptures about Brazil, and can be tempted by nothing but the smell of coffee-beans. "*C'en est trop !*" wails Charles.

The little Baroness might also, for her part, feel she has had rather too much of a good thing. She is again expecting—this is the third time—and really, when one has no settled home, when one does not know whether the next *pied-à-terre* will be a palace or the attic of a detestable London lodging-house, three pregnancies are, if not too much, at least sufficient. The first boy was Charles Frederick ; the second, born at Cambridge, Richard. The third, if it's a boy—and she knows from the way the little creature disposes itself that it will be a boy, though Charles, when not harping on New Zealand, is demanding of her a daughter—will be called George. One born in London, one in Cambridge, one in Paris. As for the others, God knows where they will take it into their heads to arrive. One marries an innocent, who agrees to study law and theology. One finds oneself attached to a species of Ulysses, expected to have babies all over the world, girls preferred. . . .

George, however, is a boy all right, and the French, enraptured with their coffee-beans, won't look at the project of a New Zealand colony, though out of the wreck Charles does save certain vague but extensive promises from influential sources of French support for his colony, *when* it is settled and in good working order. They return disconsolate to London, and Charles gets up early to go out sticking bills. It does not seem dignified, but it works. Over four hundred people call daily at the office in Budge Row.

At the Tuileries the Baroness de Thierry was presented to the Dauphine, who, hearing with interest of the young couple's romantic past and future, presented Emily with a token of her regard. This token now holds up gilt candlesticks in one of the three London rooms where, as Charles has said, the children make far too much fuss of the pigeons.

Look well at the tiny Sèvres figure. She is, in a way, the genius of the story. Though exquisite, she has that abstracted porcelain look which might make her face quite insipid, if one didn't wonder, "Does she ever think at all? What goes on behind those painted blue eyes? Do the little china breasts over her robe never heave with womanly emotion?" She has already seen so much, this figurine, whose gilt candlesticks support the clear tapers of which Charles, at his most impoverished moments, must never be denied. This little shepherdess of the Dauphine's was standing on a writing-desk in that apartment of the Tuileries from which King Louis XVI was dragged away to imprisonment and death. Irreparable day! Unimpressionable shepherdess! To have seen a king ruined, yet to maintain a china smile, a china elegance! The figurine always travelled with the de Thierry circus. In New York—what won't the Yankees do?—a trusting thug stole the candlesticks under the belief that they were gold, so they had to be replaced with others less fine. But in New Zealand the shepherdess lighted strange scenes.

The summer wears out, hot and torpid over Budge Row. There's an unexpected crack of thunder when Captain Billy Stewart, tired of gentility, not only deserts the expedition, but associates himself with a rival one, bound, as is the de Thierry armada, for the Hokianga district in the far north.

But this desertion comes too late in the day to do much damage. though it's a disillusion to find that kings don't love one another so much after all.

The ships are the things to consider now, beautiful, living, and mettlesome ships. The *Swiftsure*, a brig with sixteen nine-pounder guns ; the *Calista*, a vessel of three hundred and fifty tons ; and the *Woodbridge*, of five hundred tons, all chartered by Charles and his brother Francis, who has been like the right hand of this expedition. They are getting ready for sea towards early autumn, 1825.

There was a curious tale that the rats had formally declared the *Swiftsure* a ship of ill omen, trooping ashore in a hustling grey tide at Portsmouth. But the majority of Charles's recruits were either strapping fellows from the country or cheerful little Cockneys, unmoved by deep-sea superstitions. The sailing-ship was then in the heyday of its pride and glory, and the vessels chartered for the expedition were almost new ; clean-cut, shapely, with the towering splendour of canvas like a shining cloud above them, as they swam in state up London's river.

A day of blazing heat, of gnat-like worries and details. And then came Francis de Thierry, running, white-lipped, into the office.

The trouble on the *Swiftsure* had been so little . . . a cabin panel damaged by the fall of a piece of furniture. The ship's carpenter, putting this in order, came on a plank of rotten wood. He was ordered to remove it.

Under the rotten plank a broken futtock was revealed. The carpenter sucked in his breath, worked on. Another broken futtock, and another. . . .

In one morning they discovered twenty-two broken futtocks. Francis, who was in charge of the *Swiftsure* for the expedition, sought out the shipmasters from whom she had been chartered. Their captain, a weazened little Cockney, was discovered in a crimping-house.

The ship had been on the rocks at Trincomalee. The incident had never been logged. But for the trivial accident of the cabin repairs, it would not have been discovered save in the might of a storm on the high seas, which give up no dead nor their secrets.

The *Swiftsure* was condemned as unseaworthy.

"There's still the *Woodbridge* and the *Calista*. We've got to manage with two ships, I tell you. England won't forget this, not in twenty years. There'll never be another de Thierry expedition raised from this country if we fail now."

"Come down yourself, for God's sake, and see if you can shout sense into your emigrants. You're working against Billy Stewart now. How soon did he know of this? The moment one of his own paid men could duck from your crew on the *Swiftsure*, and pass him the word. Do you know what tale is going round? That to beat the other expedition at the post, you're putting out in death-ships, and you'll see the emigrants drowned before you'll let him win. Yes, and now that things are going against us, there's the cry of cannibals too. Another day of this and I tell you they'll stampede like a mob of sheep. I wouldn't put it past Stewart to have had a hand in selling you this pup. There's something queer in the way that Trincomalee business was kept dark, until now, when it can smash us."

"I'll come," said Charles mechanically. He reached for his silk hat; one looks best in one's silk hat. Yet he knew, as he closed the door of the office in Budge Row, that he had closed also a chapter of his life, and one which had promised well.

She looked proud and lovely as ever, the *Swiftsure*. Men had broken her with their drunkenness, their cringing lies. Otherwise, no doubt, she would have been proud to serve the expedition.

"Why do reputable men shrink from such an adventure and such a humane enterprise? Surely, my dear Baron, England had more spirit a few years ago."

"Yes, but , . . it's faith that has somehow gone out of the world, isn't it, Thomas Kendall? As though youth had left the loins of a man. . . ."

Men and women who were to have sailed within the week, sat on the docks, squatting on boxes and coils of rope, arguing, staring, shouting. Something a little blind and animal about them, a half-satisfaction in the sheer excitement of trouble. They're good enough, people you know, but not like the paupers, who, poor creatures, had such an extreme longing

E

to escape at any cost. These people are conservative ; it was a tremendous step that they should uproot themselves. The suspicion that somebody is trying to fool them is too much.

That they wouldn't hear him speak was not much more than he had expected. The crowd has a funny way of expressing its will. A sort of treble S sound, made with the tongue pressed hard on the front of the palate. Gigantic coils of serpents . . . then separate little cries bursting out. "The *Calista*, they said, was cranky. . . . The *Woodbridge*, the noble *Woodbridge*, with her lofty 'tweendecks, they said she was fit only for a prison-ship."

Some of the more talkative, inflamed by free liquor passed round by a curiously sympathetic little knot of sailormen, barred his way. "A death-ship . . . ! Taking us out to sea, to drown in your bloody death-ships !"

The *Calista*, encompassed in the evil spell of her sister ship's disaster, had been new painted in white and green. Her figurehead, the head, shoulders, and breasts of a woman in a robe blue as larkspurs, rose up high and undaunted. There were seagulls with coral claws and wings of white and grey, fluttering around sails that hung slack now, yet shone where the sunlight caught them.

Charles turned away.

Thirty years later, round the jutting yellow of a headland which flaunted great garish tree-banners of crimson blossom, the ship *Calista* stood into Auckland harbour, the chief anchorage then in the north part of New Zealand. The deeper and wilder blue of the New Zealand sea shone up under her keel, the figure of the proud blue-robed woman thrust forth before her. Watching her draw close, unnoticed by any person of importance in the little crowd which always greeted a ship from England, stood a rather shabby old man, in decorous but distinctly outmoded clothing.

On she came, sails full and gleaming in that clear sunlight. And in that old man's eyes was such a look as not even this world, with its losses, its disappointments, its cold cruelties, dares often to paint on a human face. She had kept her own nobility, had outlived the old slanders which set a London crowd snarling. So she moved easily and most graciously through the waters where he would have brought her on a gallant enterprise. It was thirty years too late that the death-ship *Calista* vindicated herself. Thirty years can do much to a man and to his hopes. Yet, watching the larkspur robe shine against the bluer sea, he was glad that among all perishable things so much of loveliness had lived on.

The rival expedition, under Captain Herd in the *Rosanna*, sailed late in this year and made land in the Hokianga river-mouth, not far from the Baron de Thierry's land-purchases. Its success, however, was quickly turned to mourning, or to low comedy, as one chooses to look at it. The emigrants had no title to land, though they bought two islands in the Hauraki gulf. The chieftains ranged themselves against the expedition, either in genuine annoyance or, much more likely, for the fun of the thing. On either bank of the river they lined up and did war-dances. Is this neighbourly? They jump about, they roll their eyes, they protrude their tongues, their navels, and their abdomens, waving formidable weapons and shouting all the time. With the exception of four men, the terrified emigrants refused to leave ship, and insisted on being taken direct to Hobart Town in Tasmania, where, comforting thought, the natives had already been exterminated. The four who stayed in New Zealand were (need I say it?) Scotsmen. They landed, unmolested by the Maoris, and remained there as peaceful and prosperous settlers for the rest of their lives.

In New York, late in 1828, Charles met with an officer from the *Rosanna*. It was in a hotel parlour. The officer was a good deal more than half-seas-over. Charles says he was sober himself.

"Your expedition, sir, was a failure . . . hic . . . failure," warmly declared the officer—by then attached to a heart-breaking old she-devil of a merchantman. "But ours, sir, ours . . . hic . . . was a burst."

Budge Row, at least, is done with. "Good-bye, England," says the Baroness de Thierry, formerly Emily Rudge.

Where now can one promote an expedition to further the brotherhood of man, white, brown, and café-au-lait? In heaven, perhaps, with rebel angels for settlers. Then there is the United States. "A gentleman who owed me a considerable amount of money had departed there," writes Charles. That seemed to settle their course.

Budge Row escapes the excitement of further Poles, banners, and lances. Brother shakes hands with brother. Charles won't have the parting as "Adieu". For years he keeps writing, "We shall meet in New Zealand yet."

"Adventurer . . . yes, as Walter Raleigh was an adventurer," writes Francis de Thierry, twenty years later, trying to give some account of his fantastic brother to a Paris journal, *L'Armoricain*. And to Charles, separated from him by the width of a world, he writes, "Don't, I beg of you, write to me in English, the tongue of our exile. Ah, that accursed New Zealand, it has cost you everything."

CHAPTER SIX

A CROWN FOR ULYSSES

A YOUNG lady is seated in a swing, beneath an elm in a Baltimore garden. She is attended by a youth of about ten years old, with large red ears, and that patience shown only by dumb animals, or by young men suddenly infatuated with little Titania. The young lady's eyes are shut, but between her lashes she can see a glory of shattered sunrays, crimson, orange, delicate green . . . the most exciting colours. Her head is thrown back in ecstasy, her brown legs dangle bare and shoeless. This is perhaps out of place in a princess, and provides an unseemly moment for her introduction to the public. Moreover, it may be argued that the Princess is callous, since her good papa is barely recovered from the cholera at present devastating the Southern States of America, whilst her good mamma and her brothers Frederick and George are still in the grip of the malady. Later, indeed—when Margaret Neilsen is brushing her hair at night, and pulls so hard that all the tangles, indignant, make it a tug-of-war—the Princess remembers her family misfortunes, and weeps so loudly that she has to be given strawberries and cream in a bowl decorated with three pigs.

But at the moment the swing swoops gorgeously downwards, and the Princess, kicking her legs in the air, shouts "Whoosh!" Can I help it? It is just so, with bare feet, and the airs tender and delicious about her brown face, that Isabel de Thierry's ghost may sometimes hunt up streets and down streets for the Baltimore garden.

It is nowadays fairly easy for an American lady to become a princess. She has only to drop the little slipper—not glass, but diamond of a reasonable carat—and from Europe Prince Charming will arrive on the run. But Isabel, five years old when her red-eared cavalier pushed the wooden swing, arranged things differently. She became, at ten, a princess in her own right, and without any business of matrimony, which may or may not turn out well. Her father, having by perhaps unconventional methods achieved the Kingship of Nukahiva and the Sovereign Chieftaincy of his little demesne in New Zealand, was insistent about only one thing. It is incorrect to say that he took a crown with him ; those who hold out for a throne and sceptre are, believe me, just liars, enamoured of the picturesque, like golfers and bigamists. But he did enjoin those who linked their destinies with the de Thierry expedition to call his daughter Princess Isabel.

It was a dignity she wore charmingly, no doubt . . . she with the black curls and the serious dark eyes. Yet in her case, as in that of her papa, the King, you might seek in vain for the grave of the only American-born princess who ever leaned from the side of a ship, and, as the vessel drew away from Panama, heard the guns of a city thunder out the royal salute.

· · · · ·

Exactly how Charles de Thierry fared during his eight American years is somewhat obscure. We have already mentioned the known facts, that in 1826 he departed thither from England, not merely sickened with disappointment, but very anxious to come into contact with "a gentleman who owed me a very large sum of money". Whether he ever grasped the coat-tails of this person is doubtful. The de Thierrys had their ups and downs in the States. It is certain that they were often happy, often befriended. They made no settled home. There was no restraining Charles from new assaults upon his colonizing project. Up and down he travelled, lecturing here, scribbling another pamphlet there, leaving a trail of more or less unwanted information about New Zealand clear across America. He scatters his leaflets as a broom-pod scatters its little brown seeds to the winds ; and, though no American had the honour of accompanying him to New Zealand in the long run, for the first few years after he actually arrived at the Canaan of his descriptions he got shoals of letters from the States, all with Royalist superscriptions on their envelopes.

Among his papers is a draft of a novel, *The Emigrants : A Story of America*. Perhaps he meant it to be funny. In either case, it is. Our Charles was anything but a literary expert. But in later years, when his children were as much cut off from ordinary social recreations as so many young Crusoes and Fridays, he used to gather them round the fire and read aloud what he had written in the course of the day. *The Emigrants* has for its hero a benevolent old Dutchman, of a huge income. He changes all his T's into D's, and R's into W's, but, just the same, he's always popping up to advance the needy another hundred dollars or so. At this stage of the game, Charles must have felt the need of a fairy godfather.

"Ten years of adversity should certainly do something to mellow a man's feelings. What I lost on the one side, I seemed to gain on the other, and the Blind Goddess appeared intent on the equitable adjustment of her scales. I got rid of some of the vanities of the world. . . . However, I had not now at my command the amount of means which I had formerly possessed. Those means were not great, but I had other available resources, and the fund thus disposable might have done much, had I been otherwise treated."

He seems to have lost some money and gained a little philosophy. Then there was the better reason for happiness. She arrived on January 3rd, 1828. Charles tried very hard not to be quite so proud of her. But they were allies, conspirators, from the first. The boys were fair, firm-thinking, slow-spoken little fellows. Isabel, when first her puckered face, its mouth screwed up like a button rosebud, was uncovered, appeared dark and impish. She looked at him straightly for a moment, then she winked.

There was a hand curled in his own, and to resist going where it urged was quite beyond thinking. A baron is a baron, but still he can play at horses. Can one imagine Charles as sly ? However, he desperately wished to name his daughter after "my lost love, Eliza", and hadn't quite the pluck, for, as he frankly admits, his wife would have been jealous. Nothing could have been more reasonable on her part. Is one to go to the expense and trouble of producing a daughter as incessantly demanded by Charles, simply that another woman may get all the sentimental credit ? Charles, however, discovered in an old dictionary of names that Isabel is simply another version of Eliza. Isabel, the dark lady, came back from the christening-font.

Another Isabella, from the day of the baby's birth, steps into the de Thierry fold, to remain there as a permanent fixture. But instantly, that *la petite* might have no rival, Charles induced the new-comer to let them employ her second name, Margaret—Margaret Neilsen.

Here is the Faithful Nurse, the essential we have lacked all along. One wonders how ever we did without her until the Baroness de Thierry's fourth *accouchement*. Margaret Neilsen is ideal of her kind—Scotch, and a little body, with mouse-coloured hair screwed into a bun at the top of her skull and affixed with steel pins like daggers. At some time she has been married, and is either widowed or (can it be ?) divorced. But any allusion to this she puts aside with the grim sentence, "Don't talk to me about Neilsen," and nobody ever does. She says her prayers with regularity, is not above taking a hair-brush to the seats of the mighty if they need it, and yet spoils them to distraction. At the moment, having seen the Baron himself in and out of the cholera, she is torn between the ailing Baroness and the two sick boys, and the feeling that the others, especially Baby Will, can't possibly survive without her. She quarters them safely in a disinfectant-reeking Baltimore house, weeps and prays a great deal, but never burns the porridge. . . .

Baby Will ? Certainly. In long-clothes, and not six months old. He is, however, the last of the de Thierry series. "Not before it was time," sniffs Margaret Neilsen, not greatly impressed with nineteenth-century fecundity, which she considers plays into the hands of "the men". She likes, pampers, and admires men, but disapproves of them on principle.

A gentleman in reduced circumstances, and very seldom of fixed abode, falls sick with the cholera in 1833. Other members of his household follow suit, but all survive. Upon their recovery, seeing the pest still raging throughout the whole of the southern States, and having, besides, remained a long time without profit in the land of the free, the gentleman decides that he is tired of America. His failures in Europe are too bitter for him to consider returning there. Somehow he must get to New Zealand, where, as he never tires of telling anyone who will lend him even half an ear, he is a landed proprietor to the tune of 40,000 acres. An ark is at hand, in the shape of a little vessel bound for the West Indies. The gentleman steps aboard, accompanied by the following entourage: a wife, one ; sons, four, including the squalling bundle done up in wool and napkins ; a daughter, one—handle her like glass, she is to be a princess ; a faithful servant, one, with an incredible bit of straw millinery perched like a second Babel on her bun of brown hair.

This is at least rational. But the gentleman who goes to the West Indies comes out at the other end of his journey a king. A recognized government—not much of a government, certainly—turns a serious ear to his proposals, and, by acclamation, grants him a concession of enormous importance. And he has real money in his pocket.

It is unbelievable, but it happened.

In Jamaica, every one of the laughing negroes burned a candle at night before his pile of melons and delicious tropical fruits. It was like some dusky Feast of All Souls, the little flames fluttering unleashed in soft wind from a black-and-ivory sea. There were old houses, colour-washed yellow and pale blue, in Martinique, narrow alleys, trees touching hands across white squares, and everywhere the stiff, dry sabre-rattling of palms. Hundreds of French *émigré* families were scattered through the Indies, and with many of them Charles had ties of mutual acquaintance.

This does not explain how the de Thierrys, after their exodus from the States, continued to support existence on their reduced income. The indefatigable M. Maurice Besson claims to have discovered that the Baron de Thierry lent himself to the tuning of spinets whilst in the West Indies. At first I was inclined to sneer at this ; Charles had a touchy pride. Occasionally, when the tide has turned against him, he records haughtily, "I did as better men have done : I had recourse to the use of my talents." Is the tuning of spinets to be reckoned as a talent ? After all, why not ? To rid from their asthma and catarrh all those light, laughing, breezy little spinet voices, no doubt to demonstrate to amateurish owners how they should be played . . . possibly it was talented.

I once knew an old shoemaker who was talented. He was also, as it happens, a lunatic, and I met him one morning shambling up from the lunatic asylum. He was harmless, and permitted to prowl. He walked around me in a circle, grinning and pointing at my shoes. At first he could manage to say nothing at all, but finally the words came stumbling out :
"Blue shoes . . . You've got blue shoes on."

The magnificence of my blue shoes had evidently burst like a couple of blue moons into the darkened attic of his mind. In this one may perceive that complete intimacy with a subject which is in itself a very high order of talent, whether it relates to shoe-leather or spinets.

At all events, at Pointe-à-Pitre the Baron de Thierry gave a concert "de harpe". And the harp which had pleased Vienna, including an Imperial lady, cleared a profit of 400 francs for the musician.

It was at this same Pointe-à-Pitre—though one wouldn't expect a place which puts only 400 francs in the bag for the Arts to be much of a hunting-ground—that the climax of his career was reached ; that great affairs were mooted, and a crown offered Ulysses.

Through the West Indies they progressed on brief and charming journeys. At this time Charles must have been in funds again, for he chartered his own little schooner. From Martinique they went to Guadeloupe, thence to Dominica, where they put in to visit French friends who had been their hosts during their visit to Paris in 1824.

They bore a charmed life, these de Thierrys. Far out on the horizon, that day, showed an ugly white snout of foam, and Charles was warned by his skipper that if he wanted his cockleshell out of the tail of dirty weather, he must put off immediately. So there was kissing and compliment, and from shore bright scarves and kerchiefs were waved as the schooner stood out to sea. An hour later they were rolling sickly in long furrows. Their boat was out of the line of danger, but over Dominica the sky had turned dark green, with a curious coppery glare. The skipper, very nearly the same shade, and with his eyes popping out of his head, continued to cross himself and solicit the attentions of the Virgin. They had missed a hurricane by an hour. Meanwhile, like a great leaden fist from the clouds, down smashed the storm on Dominica. It kept a narrow, twirling path, but where it passed hundreds of the lighthouses lay in ruins, and not a ship at anchor in the harbour escaped. The de Thierrys' friends, like hundreds of others, lay dead under the ruins of their home. France and the West Indies went into mourning. Charles, a little white about the gills, felt that Providence must after all have a sneaking regard for him.

"I set out from Martinique without an idea that at Guadeloupe the conversations so often indulged with a dear good friend should have been productive of great developments. I was, as it were, the parent of a settled scheme, which appealed to others, who had at their disposal the means I no longer possessed, as sufficiently promising to justify the expenditure of their capital."

At Pointe-à-Pitre, July 23rd, 1834, the French brig-o'-war, the *Momus*, under Commandant d'Orsay, came from Bafre-Terre, its captain having the express purpose of visiting the Baron de Thierry and plunging with him into majestic plans. In the cabin of the *Momus* were first discussed the projects which raised the de Thierry New Zealand colony to undreamed-of glamour, and a risk of real importance.

A moment. Did I mention it? Charles, perhaps finding that he was not much of a success with the lower middle classes, developed in middle life a habit of ennobling the friends who did the decent thing by him. One finds his record full of barons and *comtes*; the grain of salt is recommended. This Captain d'Orsay of the *Momus* is the first of them. Invariably, so far as Charles is concerned, the gentleman appears as *Comte* d'Orsay, a touch which for a moment threw me into a wild confusion of ideas, making it seem possible that Byron's friend, the dandy of the age, was leading a double life on the Atlantic Ocean, hobnobbing with colonists and king-makers. It would have been pleasant, but it cannot stand the light of day. The real truth is inescapable. If a man showed a noble frankness in his dealings, Charles simply couldn't bear that the poor fellow should not be either a baron or a *comte*. He exercised what is, after all, an immemorial prerogative of kings, and filled his records with nobles quite unknown to history. An alternative appellation, used once, was "the excellent Captain d'Orsay". We had better lean to this if we must keep to facts.

According to himself, Charles began to dream of the Panama Canal's possibility years before, when in Paris. But at the time he said little, knowing nothing of the conditions and government prevailing over Panama. Evenings of long conversation with the rovers who knocked about the Indies shaped his project more plainly.

"It was no longer merely the colonization of New Zealand that was planned, but the founding of a new state, the cutting of the Isthmus of Darien, a new highway across the globe, for the benefit of all nations and the emancipation and civilization of the New Zealand aborigines."

This, of course, was not the first Panama Canal scheme. The Spanish had long dreamed of the enterprise, more than once had half-heartedly taken it in hand. But difficulties seemed insuperable. Political intrigue, corruption, lassitude, disease, were the joint governors of that area through which the canal must pierce, until on the Pacific coast it emerged to bring new wealth to the old Spanish city of Panama, the treasure-stronghold upon which for centuries pirates and filibusters had cast envious looks. The fortifications of the city had kept those crows off. Panama City remained Spanish in architecture, in listless resignation to a diminished destiny. Spanish most of all in its decay.

Less than fifty years before, the territories of Panama, isthmus and cities, had come under the sway of New Granada, and now looked to the Congress of Bogota for its legislature. It was a step towards progress, though Bogota also was festivals and fevers for the most part.

Meet, then, the men of affairs, crowding into d'Orsay's cabin: M. Auguste Salomon, a man, according to Charles, of remarkable business capacity and large capital. (The first is doubtful, the second a moral certainty. M. Salomon advanced Charles 12,000 francs.) Birds of brighter plumage, if less financial importance, arrive from the Governor's residence at Guadeloupe: M. Vigneti, formerly private secretary to his Excellency, and Major Edward Fergus, the Governor's long-legged aide-de-camp. Then there are Bertholini and Morel . . . both of them, not to mince matters, straight-out blackguards. Morel, in fact, turns out to be a notorious smuggler from the Demarara coast, at which Charles is indignant when he finds it out. But both are sitting in Salomon's pocket, and consequently are voted unanimously into the Syndicate.

Who can tell how brightly the phoenix displayed its new plumes ? The Governor's residence at Guadeloupe lost two of its ornaments. Major Fergus and Vigneti both decided to cast in their fortunes with that of the Baron de Thierry. "The Canal was to be cut from Navy Bay to the River Chagres, and from Cruzes on the Chagres to the Rio Grande on the Pacific Ocean." The Canal once opened—with the assent of the Congress of Bogota—a quick linking-up of distant places was planned, a packet service from England to Chagres, via the West Indies, from Panama, and thence to New Zealand. From New Zealand the service would be kept open with Sydney and the East Indies as ports of call, the packets passing through Torres Straits. Sailings were planned for at least once a month, cutting in half the time and space between Europe, America, and the Antipodes.

"How near all these plans were to success might be made plain were I to show to Your Excellency the official documents I received then from Paris. But the French have long been remarkable for being too late in these eventful affairs." (This extract is from a letter written by Charles de Thierry in 1840 to Captain Hobson, then Lieutenant-Governor of the new British colony, New Zealand.)

At the other end of this "new highway across the globe", no British colony, not even a French one, was to welcome the packet-ships. Here, on the mouth of the Hokianga, would flourish the tiny independent state ruled over by Charles ; the state with its own sovereignty, its unlimited brotherhood between white and brown men, its astounding productivity. (As a matter of fact, before ever he sailed for his state, Charles had accomplished detailed arrangements for selling its produce to reputable merchant houses in Pointe-à-Pitre, Panama, Paris, and London. And the full ground plans of Utopia were drawn to the very inch, as you will hear.)

The tiny state—that's more likely to appeal to the Congress of Bogota than to put them off. They're a bit afraid of the Big Stick.... England, France, America—once let them in, and we all know the merry time a poor republic will have persuading them to go out again. Utopia... the Sovereign Chieftaincy... is different. There are other reasons in favour of the declaration of Utopia's independence.

"Could a public loan be negotiated in London for the Baron de Thierry, or for M. Salomon? Certainly not," writes Charles, with truth. He goes on to say, "Either an Act of Parliament must incorporate a company, or it must treat with some foreign state.... Everyone but myself was of the opinion that I must take the title of King, but this I refused."

A meeting in Guadeloupe. M. Salomon, M. Vigneti, Major Fergus, Bertholini, Morel, one and all offer to take the Oath of Allegiance to the Baron de Thierry, future ruler of the little kingdom to be founded on his 40,000 acres. However much the project may have appealed to him, he had his doubts as to whether 40,000 acres was quite the same thing as the whole of New Zealand, and so rejected both Oath and Crown. It was settled that he should assume instead the title of Sovereign Chief of New Zealand, a title more likely to place him at one with the natives. It's a dignified title, perhaps a little misleading, but it should be understood that he only referred to his beloved 40,000 acres, and was not, as some say, trying to grab the whole country.

Offices were then settled among the others. Salomon was to remain at Pointe-à-Pitre, acting as treasurer, general agent, and deputy for negotiation of the loan necessary for the Panama Canal project. (The 12,000 francs advanced by Salomon was for the New Zealand end of the scheme.) Vigneti became "Secretary for the Foreign Department"; Major Fergus came as soldier and free lance, to take on what service he might find. The capacities of Bertholini and Morel were from the first doubtful. Only one thing seemed certain about them. They steadfastly refused to pay their own expenses.

It has been said that M. Salomon was the Baron de Thierry's dupe, the Panama Canal project a cover for a pick-pocket.

But, unfortunately for this theory, M. Salomon's own letter to Charles, written long after the little state had crumbled to ruins and the ghost of the crown been whisked away, remains to testify otherwise. Does the wronged man write to the thief, "We were both of us deceived by others. Do not think that I meant to abandon you" ?

Salomon, Vigneti, Fergus, Bertholini, Morel . . . dark faces, lost in the old gallery. Perhaps at times Charles would have drawn back from his grandiose schemes. In his old age, he knew that when he had turned away to star-gazing he had made mistakes. Yes, he had made serious mistakes. He was humiliated to think of them.

The year drew into summer heat and ripeness. Round their house poinsettias burst into vivid flame, the coral-trees pricked up goblin ears. They seemed to be living in the heart of a bonfire. Up from the sea at night swung the red lantern of the moon.

On December 1st, 1834, the brigantine *Momus* was by command of the Governor of Guadeloupe sent to transport the Baron de Thierry and his party to St. Thomas, where they would make preparations for their New Zealand expedition, arrange for the Panama Canal concession, and themselves cross by land the Isthmus of Darien.

It is odd, that. Emily, lying on the borderland of sleep, and thinking in a confused way of crowns, which have never seemed very serious to her, reflects how this one and that will speak of a great triumph, a romance, and say, "This was the crown of my life." Her husband has a crown, or the next thing to it, and this doesn't matter. It falls off and trundles away into the shadows, like a hoop. But what will be remembered always is the moon's edge, dipping into velvet water, the fragile scent of flowers in this garden. She feels that these might come back to her in the instant of death, and say, "We were the crown of your life." Not success, not the little triumphs. She would forget these ; they would go past like the fleet waves breaking under the moon.

CHAPTER SEVEN

A PEAK IN DARIEN

AT St. Thomas, where the *Momus* landed the party early in December '34 (popping off her guns in the royal salute as she stood out again to sea), they laid in stores of swords, epaulettes, gold lace, scarlet and sky-blue cloth, firearms, plumes white and flamingo-hued. Hundreds of gaily coloured cotton and flannel shirts for the natives were added to the baggage, and a huge supply of negro-head tobacco, the last somewhat against the wishes of Charles, who, as a strict non-smoker and non-chewer, regarded tobacco as a vice.

They intended to recruit no soldiery for the settlement's defence. The plan was a combined militia of settlers and friendly natives, mustered and drilled by Major Fergus, who was dying for a chance to sport his plumed helmet. The settlers, they decided, had better be raised in Sydney, where their provisioning and journey money would fall less heavily on the Royal Exchequer.

Charles says that at this stage most of the expenses came out of his private purse. What is this about a private purse? There are the other de Thierrys over in France, Caroline and Francis, keenly interested in the expedition. Now that the Atlantic sea-birds are startled out of their scant wits by the poppings of the royal salute, it may be that they clubbed together to help.

Major Fergus, for the honour of Britain, be it said, is the only one who hasn't an invincible objection to paying his way. Charles, however, develops a real affection for his Secretary for the Foreign Department, Vigneti, a pale, serious, scholarly young man. It may be that there is a little of the motherly spirit in the Sovereign Chief. Poor M. Vigneti, he becomes with ease so terribly seasick. All the way to St. Thomas, nothing but one port-hole after another. One tries him with green apples, with champagne, with ghostly consolation. "Don't look at the deck-rail, my dear fellow, that will make you worse. Keep your eyes fixed on mine." A terrible glare between them, Vigneti's eye glaucous as a frog's egg, the Baron's sinister with attempted mesmerism. It is useless. Vigneti rushes again to the side of the ship.

Bertholini and Morel already are showing themselves in their true colour. It is black, alas . . . black brows, black finger-nails; even, Charles begins to suspect, black designs. But the flood-tide pulls; there is no time for a rearrangement of the expedition.

Frederic, Baron Oxholm, was then Governor of St. Thomas, and made himself most amiable to the de Thierrys, manifesting a friendly interest in the Panama Canal project. One becomes familiar with his copper-plate handwriting:

M. le Baron,
 I have the honour to thank you for your letter. The great and general usefulness of the enterprise you have in hand without doubt deserves the interest and support of all. . . .

Many further civilities are stored away with those hoards of paper. However, it is fair to state that Baron Oxholm seems to have been a more impulsive man than the average Excellency of his day; indeed, Captain Fitzroy, of the ship *Beagle*, meeting later with the Baron de Thierry, was either libellous or frank enough to say that "St. Thomas was a nest of pirates, and its Governor no better than a protector of filibusters".

On December 12th, Charles chartered from Joseph Plise the schooner *Roarer*, paid for by four hundred milled Spanish dollars in gold, and with Captain Nickerson as skipper continued their journey without incident as far as Chagres. Here they spent three days preparing to cross the Isthmus of Darien.

Everywhere they were warned against fever. Panama City, their goal, had a special fever of its own, a recurrent malady. Once catch it, and one was always turning blue and chattering like an ape. Then there was the yellow pest. Both these plagues, and several others, hung miasmic over the Isthmus. There was, however, no turning back.

F

Margaret Neilsen, brushing out the hair of her Baroness, talked loudly about the probable wrath of God, but bundled into their hired canoes next morning. They made their way by river to Gorgona, one of the canoes, laden with gorgeous military paraphernalia, coming to grief in mid-stream.

At Gorgona they hired horses, with peons as carriers for their luggage. The rest of the journey was vague to Charles, who was seized by the Panama fever, and found it difficult to sit his horse. Morel tumbled down in delirium before the end, and finished in state, carried in a litter. Isabel rode with Major Fergus, who was immensely civil to the womenfolk, and made it a point of etiquette to call the dark-haired lady "Princess". He also presented her with a marmoset, a sad-faced, wise, and wizened atomy, promptly christened Alexander the Great. The Baroness rode placidly ahead, her habit of chestnut cloth restrained and decorous among all the irresistible, shrieking parrot-greens of the tropical verdure.

At sunset they topped the rise above Panama City and reined in their horses. The carriers dropped down, sprawling limbs pouring sweat. Negro-head tobacco was doled out, a fig to each man. Most of them chewed it steadily. They conversed but little, and in grunts. A mixture of Mexican and Indian blood, they did not appear a communicative or versatile race.

As Cortez had once seen it from his peak in Darien, that untrammelled ocean shone out, deepened and paled at last, far beyond man's sight. There was a ring of foam, hard-white as salt, on that honey-yellow which was Panama. Palms leaned out with lashing fronds. But the sea from its shallows deepened to a colour of harebells, and beyond that fringe the green tourmaline of shifting currents showed beneath it, as beneath a transparent robe. At last it was nothing but a vast bubble, a blue crystal of ocean hermetically sealed by sky, and all power of time and thought lay enclosed in this. A ship moved white-sailed across the nearer bay, but Charles knew it could never escape from the sealed bubble. A ship in a glass bottle. . . .

Panama was a dream in deep slumber, honeycomb-yellow save where the sun flared on windows of old stucco and brick houses, with cavernous pitted balconies and high-walled courtyards. It was no wonder that the waves emptied their strength quietly on that entranced shore. The wonder was that they should break at all.

They set their horses at a canter for the city. There was a crackle of fireworks here and there, and the isolated stroke of a bell was laid severely on the air. It was New Year's Eve.

"And I issued in the New Year with that broad expanse of the Pacific before me."

Everything here is done in the grand manner. Charles takes two houses, one for his family and Major Fergus, one for the rest. (I suspect the Sovereign Chief simply could not live with Bertholini and Morel, whom he denounces as "swaggering, insolent, and coarse", though the Baroness is humane enough to pull Morel through his sharp bout of fever.) However, there are outdoor resources. Charles hires twelve horses; Major Fergus constitutes himself instructor of the junior cavalry. Charles Frederick is rising seventeen now, as tall as his papa. The other boys, Richard and George, shoot up. Everyone except Baby Will, who remains placidly under his mosquito-netting, learns the excitement of morning rides, crisp yellow sand scattering in fine spray under the flying hooves.

An American consul as Panama god of affairs should be useful. Mr. J. B. Feraud is a friend and business associate of M. Salomon, and, in addition to his consular status, his general store is the most delightful place in Panama. The children use it when disporting themselves as pirates and treasure-seekers. The store looks rather like a big yellow doll's house, a stair curling through to the second storey, and an attic festooned with cobwebs. Here are chests which might contain treasure. (One discovers, on investigation, that they hold nothing but fragrant China tea.) Mr. Feraud, looking, with his wrinkled, leathery face and goatee beard, exactly like the newspaper portraits of Uncle Sam, makes himself very friendly to the treasure-seekers by day. By night he collects Papa, and lugs him off to the brown brick house on the hill. Here they plot and plan, evening being the time for business and politics in Panama.

A communication from Salomon indicated that for the

Canal scheme a preliminary loan of 100,000 francs must be floated; then, a step of equal importance, the assent of the Congress of Bogota to the actual cutting of the Canal must be obtained without delay.

Eventually a deputation of three was sent off to conciliate this Congress: Captain Labarrière, a well-known resident of the city, the Hon. Marianoa Arofsemena, and the Hon. José Albadia, Congress members who had become keenly interested in the Baron's undertakings. The full text of the Canal proposals was printed for distribution, and this document, bearing the signatures of the deputation, still survives. It appears as a pamphlet: *Documentos Importantes sobre la Apertura de un Canal Fluvia entre los Oceanos Atlantico y Pacifico, Por el Istmo de Panama : Los Publica, La Sociedad Amigos del Pais, Panama. Imprenta de José Angel Santos, Ano de* 1835.

To keep Salomon apprised of the expedition's progress and assist in raising the preliminary 100,000 francs, Vigneti is parcelled off to Guadeloupe, supplied by his Sovereign Chief with a thousand francs journey-money. The vessel, laden with grain, sprang a leak and put back to port. Less than a week after his exit there is a knock on the door. Outside stands a deplorable figure. It is Vigneti, who, by fatal chance, has lost the whole of the journey-money.

The motherliness which the Baron developed for his Secretary for Foreign Affairs now comes to the fore. Vigneti, warmed like a serpent at the hearth, tells how the passage from Carthagena became unbelievable. He himself was seasick. . . .

Charles pulls a long face. This, anyhow, is credible.

Pulling out his handkerchief as he stood at the deck-rail, doubled up in a paroxysm, M. Vigneti pulled out with it the whole thousand francs. Over the side they fluttered, a meal for the fishes.

Our Charles concludes the affair thus in his records: "When a man in whom I trust makes a statement to me, I am bound to accept his word."

Vigneti's expensive bout of seasickness is accepted. Once again he is furnished with funds, and starts afresh on his mission to Pointe-à-Pitre.

Did he look back, as he turned away? The Secretary for Foreign Affairs never saw the Sovereign Chief again. For years the man whom he had deserted refused to hear a word against him, insisting that he had certainly been shipwrecked. In his last days the Baron wrote of the vanishing Vigneti: "One on whose single-minded disinterestedness I would have staked my life."

From the first the bills were mutely handed over to Charles. "Doubloons lessened in bulk, and a something of doubt crossed my mind," he writes. But things got moving. . . .

How far Mr. Feraud, in conjunction with M. Salomon, went in promises to assist the New Zealand expedition can only be a matter of broken record. As far as the documents in the case go, everyone says frankly enough that everyone else was a thief and a shameless liar. Salomon, in later letters to Charles, accuses Feraud of grossly neglecting and betraying the interests of the colony. The most definite assurance seems to have been the charter of an armed ship, to sail from Panama as escort to the settlers. Whilst the cutting of the Panama Canal was being negotiated with the Congress of Bogota, attempts were certainly made to arrange the charter of the frigate *Columbia*. A further expectation, most bitterly disappointed, was that Vigneti should follow Charles to New Zealand, bringing fresh resources and settlers. From Tahiti, Charles wrote sadly to Sir Richard Bourke, Governor of New South Wales, of "the armed ship from Panama, which I still expect . . . though a deep and painful mystery hangs around its non-arrival."

The mystery, painful enough to Charles, was not so deep. Possibly there was enthusiasm enough in that fantastic company which at Pointe-à-Pitre decided to cut the Isthmus of Darien, furnish the globe with a new highway, found an Independent State, attend to the brotherhood of man. But the expedition suffered its morning after. The New Zealand end of the project, in which the Sovereign Chief's whole heart was wrapped up, seemed vague, dangerous, and expensive. The Panama Canal, on the other hand, looked like turning over a profit. But did they actually need a king? Mightn't the civilized world laugh?

However it went, nobody ever sends an armed frigate

chasing after the expedition. M. Vigneti evaporates, Bertholini and Morel are so communistic that the King fires them half-way across the Pacific—when they at once return to Panama, and spread the most damaging reports, swearing he is a crazy Robinson Crusoe, beached high and dry on a coast of dreams. Fergus is the only sticker of the lot.

"At the opening of the Panama Canal, the Chairman was good enough to say that the Baron de Thierry had originally held the concession for cutting the Canal, but had lost his opportunity through the dishonesty of others."

This is all for the future. Meanwhile, the expedition has a fine send-off from Panama.

Between J. A. Phipps, master of the *Active*, and Charles, Baron de Thierry, Sovereign Chief of New Zealand, was signed a charter for the voyage to Otaheiti (Tahiti) in May 1835. It was covenanted that the *Active* must be tight, staunch, and strong, carrying fifteen passengers if required. For the voyage to Otaheiti—then a mid-Pacific native kingdom, now a French protectorate—the said Baron de Thierry was to pay 1220 milled Spanish dollars in gold. He also had right of charter over the *Active* for a second voyage, when the vessel would pick up Vigneti and his recruits. The deal was made in Feraud's country house, a few miles from Panama, the American consul having proved very obliging in finding a good ship. The party's last breakfast in Panama was eaten at Mr. Feraud's house of brown bricks, gorgeous purple masses of bougainvillaea sprawling over its exterior.

A great send-off. . . . Everyone at the breakfast-table is dressed to kill ; the little Baroness in cerise and black. Her pelisse of cherry cloth, stitched with satin flowers, falls softly to touch the panniers that widen the skirts spreading from a figure not yet too matronly. There is a prim starched cravat, a bonnet with black plumes and fluting of silk beneath its brim. Hair is worn curled, a cliff of ringlets dominating the nape of the neck. Fifteen years of an Odyssey that has taken her half round the world, the remnant of her life to be spent heaven knows where, but unfailingly among carnage and cannibals, and she looks as demure as when he first saw her in the Archdeacon's study, straightening up stray pages of sermons and removing the traces of Papa's gillyflower snuff.

First the earthquake. It is as if an enormous cannon booms from the hills. The coffee-cups fling themselves into the laps of the company, the dishes slide off the table-cloth. Before there is time to cry out, the lower wall in front of the house is seen to split quite quietly, like a big brown fan unfolding. There is a cloud of brick-coloured dust. "Still . . . keep still . . . it's a 'quake"—from Mr. Feraud, whose face is sickly green. The world hesitates, steadies itself, though above the table the little crystal pennants dangling from the lamp-bracket continue to swing violently from side to side. The negro who served the coffee patters back, a peculiar colour but otherwise unimpaired. "Earthquake, saar." He picks up pieces of crockery, while the crystal pennants still swing to and fro.

At three in the afternoon the party, with Fergus, Bertholini, and Morel in the wake of the de Thierrys and their faithful Margaret Neilsen, went on board the *Active*. It was June 1st, 1835. Sunlight sparkled on the glorious harbour.

Before Feraud's store were mounted some of the old fortifications, pieces of ordnance, growing civilized since the days when they held off the shifty craft flying the Jolly Roger. As a mile of water brightened between the *Active* and Panama City, the guns spoke again and again. The deep vault of the afternoon echoed with their rumbling voices . . . twenty-one guns, booming the royal salute to the man who goes forth to found a kingdom.

"Look, Papa, look!" Isabel's voice, her hand pointing upward. In St. Thomas they had purchased three flags, a great silken banner of crimson and azure, and two smaller bunting pennants. Now, as he watched, the sails leaned into the slight wind, and his own colours took the breeze from the west and shone out between sea and sky.

For a moment he could not take his eyes from the sparkling of the water, painful as little needles between the eyelids. When he did look up, the tears were on his face. He couldn't have checked them if he would. But the bitterness of the wasted years, the sudden feeling of standing naked and ridiculous as a radish, quarrels with the trivial, friendship offered and quietly withdrawn—each had its second in memory now, and so slipped into the smother of foam, lost for ever in the wake of the ship.

"We sail under our own flag now, my darling. And this tiny track over the water ends in our own kingdom, where the world's fair and the sunshine builds us a gold castle in the woods. Watch the waves curtsy to their Princess. . . ."

The wind took up the black curls, fondling them as it did the crimson and azure—a light-hearted, unstable wind, fond of any novelty. The rest laughed and shouted. But the child in his arms stayed intent, her eyes never moving from the flag. He had a feeling that she was indeed a princess, a little spirit with her own sovereignty over the fleeting and intangible loveliness of this life. There were many invisible corridors in Charles de Thierry's mind. But no matter where he went, at the heart of the dream he was sure to find Isabel.

Part Two
ARMY WITH BANNERS

CHAPTER EIGHT

NUKAHIVA

SOMETHING more than ten thousand little fishes, dapper in burnished silver, and not one of them over a centimetre from top to tail, suddenly took it into their heads to proceed in a great hurry up the bay. Half-way across, they changed their collective mind and darted inshore, flirting through the water in elfin speckles of light. A shadow passed over them, black, cool, and velvety. Could organisms so tiny have known it? Much is denied the minor order of fishes. The ten thousand suspected nothing of the excitement for which even the Nukahivan palms seemed leaning seaward, craning their necks.

Like a black swan, the shadow of the *Active* swam up the bay. From her decks proceeded an extraordinary sound— the laughter of white children. Escorted by the fairy shoal, the ship moved safely to her anchorage in the loveliest harbour of the Marquesan group.

The master of the *Active* had his guns trained on the white shore, and begged permission of the Sovereign Chief to announce their approach with a salvo . . . mayn't it impress the natives? Charles refused. To shatter that calm would have been most unlucky, like breaking a looking-glass. Besides, this was *his* world. He had recognized it the moment the scent of the orange-groves penetrated his consciousness.

For weeks everybody aboard ship, crew and passengers alike, had gone short of water. The 1400 gallons with which the brig put out from Panama were plainly insufficient, but Panama was cursed with a tiny worm which riddled the wood of drinking-casks, making the stowage of large supplies impracticable. Two days they loitered at the dot-sized isle of Taboga, within fifteen miles of Panama City, taking on water and provisions. Here they jettisoned the armourer Charles had incautiously picked up in St. Thomas with the white and flamingo plumes and all the other opulence. It is all very fine for a king to possess an armourer, but this one bragged too openly that he meant to desert at Sydney and try his luck selling small arms to the bushrangers.

Strife did not precisely flee the *Active* when they dropped the armourer. Bertholini and Morel continued to be so rude. Unable to feed them to the sharks, unwilling to offend Salomon in the person of his lieutenants, Charles barred them from his cabin table. The rest, however, were good seafarers, and the children shared their water-ration so that Isabel's horse, Black Aladdin, too great a favourite to be left in Panama, travelled in comparative luxury.

The trades were too fresh for the *Active* to put in at James Island or the Albemarles, where she might have taken on water. So she beat towards the Marquesan group, and lay now at anchor before Nukahiva, one of the largest of this lonely peppering of islands.

It is hard, at times, to decide whether Charles's luck was incredibly bad or incredibly good. Look at this selection, for his first real glimpse of a native people, of Nukahiva. Anyone who wishes to idealize and etherealize the coloured races cannot possibly take a pot shot at the Pacific and come off with illusions undefeated. The Pacific, like other oceans, has its seamy side. There are whole archipelagos where few women past their early teens turn the scales at under twenty stone ; islands where the inhabitants stiffen fuzzy hair with scarlet clay, practise scandalous methods of midwifery, abortion, head-hunting, and braggadocio ; are rapacious, insolent, and dirty. The crimes of savagery have always a sort of innocent directness which may appeal to the mind nearly unhinged by its own complexity. But even Charles de Thierry could not very well have romanticized his reception, if they had showered coarse insults and spears upon him, and then proceeded to carve steaks from his thighs.

But Nukahiva ! . . . Merely because the trades were fresh, and the Panama worm interfered with the carriage of water-supplies, to have hit on Nukahiva.

The long-boat was scarcely lowered before they were greeted in person by the islanders, who, slipping into the water, were soon splashing around the boat like so many seals.

Dark heads bobbed up almost under the keel, brown hands clutched the gunwale. And there was laughter and a flashing of excellent teeth as some youth, showing off his aquatic powers, rolled in the water. So the past became for Charles a great painted book of many pages, and out of it splashed the merry people of his dream.

The Nukahivans were very fair for an island race, and went naked to the waist, or, in the case of the young fry, untroubled by any clothing at all. On the perfect breasts of the girls lay a red-and-white laughter of flowers. (It is curious. Charles was eminently shockable, sometimes almost a prig. But not among these Nukahivans.) The hair of man and woman was straight, black, and lustrous. They were peace-loving folk, a species of overgrown fairy, possessing the remnants of a tradition too old and severe for them, in those great stone platforms of debate to be found amid their orange-groves. Everywhere orange-groves. Green and gold moonlets of fruit, and that delicious breath of perfume. There again, you notice how the luck held? Almost anywhere else in the Pacific his nostrils would have been violently assaulted by rank copra.

In all this island there was not a single mark of cruelty or mistrust.

Thus, from a ship flying the de Thierry flag, landed in 1835 almost the first white men Nukahiva had ever seen; probably the first white women, Emily and her Margaret; indubitably, and of much more importance from the native idea, the first white children, the first horse, the first marmoset, the first long-faced, droop-tailed, and melancholy monkeys, the first scarlet-and-green macaw—sidling up and down Charles's arm, and swearing frightfully—the first green Mexican parrot.

All of which were well received. But the parrot was a sensation, and might have become Nukahiva's god had its owners wished to part with it. As for the monkeys, their trustful mugs and glum scolding were regarded most intently at first. Then the natives sensed the comedy of these sad little tailed men, and forthwith the tribe fell to laughing, as heartily as though laughter were their dinner.

White children, with their elegant pale skins, their remarkable eyes and hair, their clothing ... the Nukahivans could not be held away from them. But all they did was to take possession of the young de Thierrys, petting them, fondling them, carrying them pick-a-back through the orange-groves, where the morning and the birds were disturbed by great gusty shouts of laughter. And the *Active's* useless guns showed there, black against that bluest sky, and for once Charles had reason to thank his God that he had sense enough to believe in the impossible.

Thus the two worlds met, the world of the waiting isle, the world of the seeking ship. They conversed by means of interpreter, the *Active's* third officer, a half-caste and a bit of a dab at Polynesian languages, having full play. The informal welcome went into stages of ceremonial punctilio. An old fellow with white-plumed hair, girdled in a dignified snowy garment of tappa, stepped forward and delivered a harangue replete with poetic courtesies.

"With the full consent of the chieftains and people, I annexed Nukahiva for New Zealand," writes Charles. He goes on to relate how the blue-and-crimson flag was hoisted there; how the Nukahivans, generous and simple creatures, had no objection at all to his becoming their king; and how they consecrated him with the ceremony and sacred oil of chieftainship. He makes an effort to explain that the isle would have been a valuable depot for ships between Panama and New Zealand, an addition to the latter's possessions.

But why give reasons for falling in love? That is precisely what the Baron de Thierry did, stepping off the *Active* into a little Eden. In the best sense, its people were his people. The most consistent act of his life was getting himself accepted as King of Nukahiva.

Sun had soaked into the world, into golden-brown bodies moving around him, into vividness of leaf and wing, the amazing sapphire arches of sea and sky. The ideas of the past, old and dishevelled, were no more than tattered garments, to be thrown off in the clean sunlight. After the banquet, one wanders, one discusses most eloquently the island's future. There is to be a harbour-master, who will collect dues from all trading vessels. (Only, it is consoling to remember, a dollar per ship.) This money, after the harbour-master has reimbursed himself, is to be devoted solely for the benefit of the natives. Who says so? "We, Charles, King of Nukahiva."

In Nukahiva, also, it is not improper to fall asleep in the afternoon heat. Charles awoke in early twilight, a little bronze hand gently shaking his shoulder. And there was a face, looking down at him through the half-darkness of the palm-thatched hut, so merry, so intelligent, and so friendly that he would have given ten years of his life to be able to speak the stranger's tongue and say only the one word, "Brother".

Little curious face, looking intently at me through the fronds of shadow, and so picturesque that probably you are simply some old idea of mine, a waif taking on elusive life for just one moment : tell me, what is it, then, that I can do for you ?

I am different, I have a pinkish-white face, my watch-chain appeals to you, and the peculiarity of my clothes ? Because my ship is larger than your canoe, you would possibly take me to be your superior, and even wish to be like me ? Now, God forbid.

I am well enough in my way ; but I need considerable modifications. There is something, Brother, something that we both desire, I more painfully than you. For the wistfulness only comes into the shallow brown glass of your eyes when you see the bright trinkets I have about me. Otherwise, you are satisfied. But I . . . I am always conscious of my lack. There is something. . . . Brother, let us seek it together.

We have certain things in Europe : knowledge, an appreciation of the Arts, a distorted and much-abused regard for life and property, which we could possibly pull into the shape of decent law if we put our minds to it.

We have a God. But I must tell you that the road to Him is very painful. We did not, you see, explore behind Calvary.

You cannot imagine, Brother, how high the cathedral towers reach in Europe. And the higher they climb, poor suppliants, the farther they fall short of God. I am inclined to think that God is something very lowly. Perhaps He is the warm sand under the ball of your naked running foot.

Yet, on the whole, I think this is what I have to give you : aspiration, the words to express that vague, dumb longing which occasionally moves behind your eyes.

I am not insolent in what I offer. You have a far greater thing to give me. Its name is Innocence.

Somewhere between us, lost, lies a state. Let us seek it together. O, my Brother, both of us are without homes. You lack the knowledge of your residence in immortality. I, how lost and orphaned I am, without your knowledge of the simple needs and beauty of the flesh.

I could not, of course, talk to you so freely, if we were more than two dreams in a twilight. Nay, *I* cannot talk to you, my words stumble. But my heart speaks. Let me touch your hand. We know one another in understanding, my Brother.

(Over this island lay the shadow of a destiny which for horror finds no equal in the story of the Pacific. Where the *Active* lay anchored, the Peruvian slave-ship would slink in like a jackal, and her gifts to the Nukahivans would be murder, slavery, outrage, and death . . . death by the ravaging pests of smallpox and syphilis, death throttling in the stinking holds where she carried off hundreds. The English came; native labour was requisite. What was the best bribe? Not such foolish toys as made their eyes shine and their white teeth flash, when Charles de Thierry distributed gifts among them —but opium. Many years later, the author, Frederick O'Brien, visited Nukahiva, to find a handful of natives living in degradation and misery, where once a happy people had played with the first white children.)

Nukahiva. . . . Ah, the kings are doddering old fools nowadays; nobody listens to them. The dictator has the shouting part, the butcher presides over the shambles as to the manner born. But is it a wonder that your civilization has grown senile, that its loins are drained of virtue, when these unexpiated crimes lie on its conscience?

Captain Phipps touched Charles on the shoulder. The long-boat had travelled again and again between ship and shore, weighed down to the gunwale with fruit, water, and coconuts. A rim of moon showed over the water's edge, red as the island flamboyants.

Perhaps there is still some such place in the world, which, for a day at least, by the appeal of its sheer helpless loveliness, can hold at bay the human heart.

So passed out of Nukahiva's story one man who saw it naked and beautiful as Eve's body in Paradise; who remembered it thus to the last day of his life.

So passed out of Charles de Thierry's reach the innocent kingdom which accepted him.

CHAPTER NINE

THE SUNSET GUN

NUKAHIVA was an Eden. It seems rather a shame, on top of that, to confess that Tahiti, where there was any amount of sin and copra, was more typical of the Pacific. But the fact remains that Tahiti—variously spelled by old mariners as Otaheiti, Otaheite—was one of the few places on earth which became definitely more respectable after the French took it over.

At the time when the *Active* entered Papeete Harbour, Tahiti was still a native kingdom, under the autocratic rule of Queen Pomare. Great native rulers are not uncommon. One may find anything among them from a Napoleon to an unbridled altruist. Pomare, though large, was not great ; one therefore found in her, as in the ruck of little rulers, equal parts of superstition, vanity, and childishness. She had her virtues . . . generosity, friendliness, those inseparables of the native character. However, Tahiti had been too long the rendezvous of thousands of sailing-ships to be an uncomplicated kingdom, and its queen was not the best of riders for the veering wind of her day.

Wherever civilization has come into contact with a native principality under a weak ruler, one looks about for the white man who has dug himself in as power behind the throne. Sometimes he dispenses gin and muskets, sometimes his stock in trade is religion. If he is not juggling with the idea of a native army, he appears in the capacity of Ghostly Discomforter.

Pomare was an autocrat, but the gentleman who alternately bellowed and whispered in her ear was the Rev. Mr. Pritchard, a seasoned missionary of the Church of England. Mr. Pritchard was a man of forceful character, shrewd humour, energy, and enterprise. He was as respectable as is possible with a sectarian bigot, who, one must remember, is always being urged by his God towards acts of violence.

The landing at Papeete Bay was accomplished without

hitch where the de Thierrys were concerned, but it ended the voyagings of M. Bertholini and M. Morel. Charles had endured enough. Finding that no white man could land without the permission of Queen Pomare, he sat himself down in his cabin and scrawled a confidential letter, duly interpreted to Her Majesty by Mr. Pritchard. The end was that Bertholini and Morel were not permitted to land, and the last Charles saw of them, as the long-boat pulled off from the *Active*, included two furious faces and shaken fists, whilst on the breeze, already stiff with copra, proceeded language which made Margaret Neilsen stuff her fingers in her ears and shriek to her charges to do likewise.

Shark-toothed mountains rose up steep and purplish, framing the glitter of the harbour. There were many ships at anchor, British, French, and American colours bobbing bright in the wind. Among them, stately, streams the de Thierry crimson and azure, a totally new variety of flying-fish.

Charles's own ideas of what was *comme il faut* for royalty were perhaps a little ponderous. His first audience with Her Majesty of Tahiti relieved him of some illusions. From the beginning, Pomare shocked him. Those twelve ladies-in-waiting . . . Charles says they were no better than geisha girls of the Pacific, each of the hussies having her favourites among the sea captains, who brought them back presents, the costliness of which would have made many a Liverpool wife cry her eyes out. (Well, indeed, would one have wished the white races to add stinginess to all the rest?) He says, hotly, that one could not walk along the beach without seeing—impossible to avoid it—scandalous episodes between these ladies-in-waiting and sailors who should have known better. It became a matter of picking his way among lovers. As to Pomare herself, Charles hints rather darkly. She shared in the presents, anyhow.

Much of this animus may be due to the first violent reactions produced when Queen Pomare received the party, herself squatting on the floor of a palm-thatched hut. Her smile enchantingly toothy in her dusky face, the Queen was wearing dilapidated blue dungarees, a man's cotton shirt, wide open over prodigious breasts, and an astonishing plug hat of dingy felt, pulled down over her shining black hair. Her remaining beauties, sparkling teeth, lustrous treacle-dark eyes, were not set off to perfection by this costume. But to crown all, when the Baroness modestly offered Her Majesty a gift of beautiful shawls bought in Panama, the Queen unhesitatingly pulled off her shirt and donned the brightest.

However, the auspices under which the party were introduecd to Tahitian life seemed favourable, if not formal. Three days after, Pomare visited the de Thierrys, coming followed by two canoes, laden with breadfruits, yams, and taro roots. The de Thierry boys, less prone to standing on ceremony than their father the King, quite took to Her Majesty, and thus found themselves delightfully initiated into the ways of her outlandish world.

Old Pritchard, the missionary, was the man to whom one must turn for everything . . . information about the royal mind, about the best aspect for a house, about which sea captain was an honest fellow and which a villain. The missionary escorted Charles around the leafy houses which looked over Papeete Bay, grumbling all the time about the demoralizing effect of religion on the energies of the natives.

"Teaches them respect, Baron, right enough. But when it comes to work, and I have to choose between a Church boy and a Tahitian 'devil', give me the devil every time."

This Tahitian passion for repose was the occasion for the Affair of the Roast Pig. It was Charles who wrecked the Tahitian Sabbath, which has never been the same again. Those unacquainted with the islanders can have no idea how seriously, upon conversion, they will insist on taking *some* of the Commandments. Especially "Thou shalt do no manner of work". When Pomare joined the ranks of Mr. Pritchard's converts, it became a fantastic impossibility to persuade a native to do any work on Sundays. After some thought, the Queen passed an edict forbidding hot Sabbath meals.

This affronted the King of Nukahiva. He was still enough of an Englishman to enjoy his solid Sunday dinner. The roast pork of Tahiti was delicious ; to waste it seemed a crime. He consulted the Rev. Mr. Pritchard, who, physically at least, gave no sign of despising the pleasures of the table. Mr. Pritchard shook his head. He couldn't very well, having converted the Queen and half the islanders, go back on his own commandments.

From the two palm-thatched cottages where the de Thierrys and Major Fergus had installed themselves, curls of smoke, next Sunday, defied all strictures. Nothing was said. Charles was amazed to see that the Sunday after, the Queen's own residence brandished a smoke-plume. One week more, and the Pritchard mansion fell into line.

Major Fergus, now right-hand man and sole remaining support of the King, wins his heart's desire. Major Fergus is placed in command of an army. Run up the blue-and-crimson flag!

Halte, la! It is perhaps a very small army, only eighteen soldiers, all natives; seven of them New Zealanders, the rest Tahitian boys. At first sight it may seem one can't do much with so tiny a force, but that is the unimaginative point of view. For example, one can dress the good fellows. The army donned white cotton jackets and trousers, palm-leaf hats with the de Thierry colours in silk cockades, silver-studded belts. The sun was hot, the army sweated as Major Fergus roared, "Right *wheel*!" But no native was going to sacrifice a kit like that, not if he melted in it. They were armed with muskets, and every evening at eight o'clock a gigantic Maori, hewn like a statue, fired off his musket to warn the anchored ships of the hour. The sunset gun became the signal for each ship to strike eight bells. Behind the furled sails, gleaming white or stained and sea-worn russet, would flare and sink the copper ball of the sun, so fierce that one would expect the sea to hiss as that molten rim drove into it.

They bought two horses, a raw-boned brown for Fergus, for Charles a white-stockinged chestnut, with a white star on his noble brow. Black Aladdin was waxing fat. And the three—little dark-haired maiden, Frenchman, and bony Scot—would ride far into the long Tahitian grass. They saw Fiamali, the sweet-scented marriage of the flowers. The vanilla plant would remain sterile, but that brown fingers yearly wed pollen to blossom, in evenings of scent so intoxicating that life is no longer a concrete affair of problems and necessities, but only this drowning sweetness, ebbing over the world, sweeping men away more surely than did the Deluge; but not into death, only into that long, reasonless enchantment which is perfect happiness.

Ride on, ride on, into the long Tahitian grasses. The moon is slumbering somewhere at the heart of it, at lair like a golden beast of fairy-tale. Ride through the swishing shadows . . . you may startle the moon into rising up and taking pterodactylic flight above that blue crag of trees. You cannot fail now, there is no failure while the magic strength of this night's love-philtre stings in your senses. See, the little vanilla flowers are wedded and happy; it is to be a fertile and prospering world. Your dreams must surely be fertile too, since you have brought their petals here, to spread out and accept their destiny in this long grass.

They saw one night a Tahitian ghost. There was a strange oppression over the plains of long grass. Fergus prophesied a thunderstorm. Isabel's black curls, tied with a cherry ribbon, bobbed behind a face too pointed and phantasmal for a child's. Charles felt his horse's coat thick with sweat under his hand. They reined in. Then they heard a scream of horror from a native boy who was riding some distance ahead. The grasses, half a mile away, seemed suddenly to catch alight, yet they were not consumed. Afar there, under the knotted palms, something round and blazing whirled, moving rapidly towards them. It had no shape, yet it was more unearthly than any shadow of the human form could have been. Charles felt his horse plunge, saw Fergus catch Isabel's bridle and swing her across to his saddle, leaving her mount to follow as best it pleased. The rest was a wild chase through the jungle of grass. The native's account next day was a mere terrified babble, with the word "spirit" repeated again and again. They never found any explanation of this apparition, and the boy remained sick for many days.

The ends of the New Zealand settlement were far from being forgotten during these Tahitian months when M. Vigneti and the *Active* were expected to heave in sight again at any moment. Charles made public his proposals wherever he could think of a possible audience. Where the project of the little Independent State was concerned, he acted with considerable stateliness. Wrote to His Majesty the King of England, through the Duke of Wellington, Secretary for Foreign Affairs; to the King of France; to the President of the United States of America. He discovered from the sea captains that a British Resident, Mr. James Busby, had crossed from Sydney to the Bay of Islands in New Zealand, endeavouring to keep some check upon the activities of British subjects in that wild No Man's Land. With old-fashioned courtesy, Our Charles instantly places his plans in full before Mr. Busby too; thereby, as events proved, creating more sensation than anything that had happened since Abel Tasman found the place.

Were I going on a piratical expedition, I would not be so anxious to keep the British Government apprised of my plans. I have made known to His Majesty . . . that I am on my way to establish an independent government, having for object the diffusion of commerce and agriculture, and the civilization of the aboriginals. . . . I respectfully assured His Majesty's Ministers that I would withdraw from all political arrangements at once, if New Zealand were in any way considered a possession of the British Crown. But unless such is the case, and if New Zealand is really unfettered, I must, either as an Englishman or a French citizen, be allowed to bring my arrangements to maturity, and, calling myself a Sovereign Chief, will exert my best energies to check the growth of Republicanism.

(Extract from a letter written to the Governor of New South Wales, Sir Richard Bourke, of whom, together with the little matters of Republicanism, Mr. Busby, the eating of hats by various gentlemen, and what the New Zealand Aboriginals said about it all, considerably more must be said anon.)

The sea captains who made Pomare's Papeete their home away from home were mostly friendly souls. Many a summer's evening, after the sunset gun, charts of New Zealand and Australia were spread out, and the wealth, dangers, and possibilities of his Hokianga lands were explained by men who knew the country. Captain Crozier, of the *Victor*, struck up a friendship, and warned Charles of the white settlers who had made their homes on his 40,000 acres.

"Thirteen years, Baron . . . it's a long while, you know, and there's many a *kauri*-tree you might once have called your own sailing the seas as pretty as you like, stuck in some ship's masthold. I'm afraid you'll find dirty weather ahead in New Zealand. But in Sydney I can give you introductions which may smooth the way."

The outstanding exception to this rule of genial Jack Tars was supplied by Captain Fitzroy, of the ship *Beagle* (at a later day to become Governor of New Zealand). Captain Fitzroy had transported Charles Darwin around New Zealand coasts. "We were all glad to leave New Zealand," wrote the man of science, ungratefully. "It is not a pleasant place."

Fitzroy arrives from Point Venus at the de Thierry house,

in company with another of the *Beagle's* officers. Charles welcomes him in, offers him lemonade. But the conversation that ensues ! . . . Complexions go slowly through half a spectrum, rosy pinks, brilliant scarlets, fine, mottled purples. In ten minutes Charles is on his feet, expostulating, losing his breath through indignation, popping off again. A pirate and a smuggler ! . . . To be accused of these machinations would be enough at a sitting, one would think. But the Captain has another fowl to pluck. The Baron de Thierry, according to this sailor, is impersonating the Baron de Thierry. The proper Baron de Thierry lies tucked away in his grave, the whole time.

"That one's dead, poor fool, as many of us are aware. As for you, sir, it has come to my knowledge that you're no better than a pirate and an impostor, and have robbed this unfortunate gentleman both of name and credit."

"Captain Fitzroy, it seems that you are not intoxicated. Are you insane, then ?" A duel between them is only averted by shrieks from the Baroness. Charles spends the night writing enormous, wrathful letters . . . one to Captain Fitzroy, providing a list of references long enough to have stunned the Pope, the other to Sir Richard Bourke.

Otaheiti,
November 21st, 1835.

Sir,
I am truly sorry that my first letter to Your Excellency should be dictated by a sense of injuries done me and premeditated by an officer in His Majesty's service. . . . The enclosed copy of a letter addressed by me to Captain Fitzroy of H.M.S. Beagle will make known the subject of my complaint. Trusting in Almighty God and my own integrity, I have brought my project thus far. The cutting of the Isthmus of Darien, which is destined to have such an immense effect on the commercial importance of His Majesty's colonies in these seas, is but part of our designs. . . .

In his house at Sydney, that exceptionally fair-minded man, Sir Richard Bourke, was to become all too familiar with the great scooped G's and T's of his noble correspondent. Sir Richard was a patient man. From the hour when he received his first immense letter from Charles, he behaved with a calmness which did him credit. . . .

Yet how often he must have longed for just one thing: that the Baron de Thierry should cease to moralize to the tune of ten pages a time.

Vigneti's ship never comes, nor any word from Panama. The lustrous orb of the Baron's sun is dimmed a little ; but quite suddenly the cloud lifts. There arrives a copy of the *Sydney Morning Herald*, dated August 25th, 1835. Months after he should have heard the news direct from Panama, Charles learns that by acclamation the Congress of Bogota have granted to the Baron de Thierry, for fifty years, all rights in the cutting of the Panama Canal. His plans for the Canal direction have been accepted with not a hair out of place.

Provided that M. Salomon and the allied mercantile houses at Panama, London, and Havre will only keep faith as they promised, here sits the King and Sovereign Chief, just forty, and with one of the world's most important concessions safe in his hands.

Everyone becomes polite.

About this time, Tahiti was plunged into a religious disturbance which ended its run as an independent kingdom. In 1835 England had no Consulate in the island, and the natives badly needed protection in trade, also representation when their grievances boiled over the domestic pot. Mr. Pritchard was the most influential white man in Tahiti. With his consent, then, and at the request of Queen Pomare and a large body of Tahitians, Charles drew up the most beautiful petition, praying that the Rev. Mr. Pritchard be appointed His Britannic Majesty's Consul.

In due course, the British colours flew proudly over Mr. Pritchard's house. America had also appointed a Consul, a kindly individual named Moerenhaut. Mr. Pritchard, though gruff and forthright, was a shrewd old philosopher, but he presented one drawback. His Christianity was too muscular. Of the Church of England himself, he could not abide horses of any other colour. Especially not Roman Catholics.

On November 24th, all Tahiti was set astir by a strange sight. From a tiny schooner, sailed by Captain Henry from Gambier Island, landed the two first French priests to visit Tahiti. Two miles they trudged to Papeete, speaking nothing but the French language, and having with them no interpreter. Word flew from one house to another, as the strangers walked slowly between them : two men in soutanes of a heavy white woollen stuff, not unlike camlet, the trains of their gowns tucked up into their girdles. One was a giant, whose great strides seemed to be hurrying him over the edge of the world into some visionary abyss. The slighter of the priests appeared not much more than a boy.

The pair walked hatless, carrying flat black hats under one arm. Each bore a massive Bible, its black covers sealed and crossed with gold. As they advanced, they bowed and smiled to every man who passed them, white or native.

There was more fuss than if the phoenix had not only landed in Tahiti, but had at once sat down and laid an egg.

George de Thierry came in, red-faced from a morning gallop. The island sun had done well by the boys. They wore the minimum of clothing and spent their lives out of doors. Will, now a golden-brown urchin highly polished with coconut-oil, mixed native words with his first attempts on the English language.

"There's trouble ahead for the two French priests, sir. What possessed them to land without the Queen's permission, and with no interpreter ?"

Charles mutters a reference to the improbability of early Christians taking out permits before entering the dens of lions and offering themselves as a meal for the famished creatures.

"But surely . . . Mr. Pritchard ?"

The two priests had at once turned their steps to the English missionary's house. Mr. Pritchard, warned, had taken to his heels, and was discovered later aboard a whaler and drinking grog. He would have nothing to do, he said, with the Scarlet Woman. The unfortunate Mrs. Pritchard, unable to take refuge on a whaler, unwilling to be free with any Scarlet Woman, was obliged with her family to adjourn to the waterfront, and remain there in the trying heat of the day. Before nightfall, the island kingdom was split violently into two factions. One wanted the French priests either knocked on the head or thrown off the island. The others desired to see fair play. In the latter camp, the prime movers were the American Consul and Charles de Thierry.

Mr. Moerenhaut unhesitatingly put a thatched house on his own grounds at the disposal of the Frenchmen. Charles, plunging quill into ink, sat busily translating into English a protest which the priests were submitting to Pomare against the forbidding attitude of the islanders. The one and only available interpreter of French, Charles is indispensable now ; nor can he resist appending his own notes to the plea, mentioning that while his father-in-law is a dignitary of the English Church, the priests, being Frenchmen, would doubtless command French protection ; that it was high-handed of Her Majesty to prevent peaceable folk from landing at Tahiti ; and, finally, a pious hope that all would be smoothly arranged.

Meanwhile, stories of the Scarlet Woman were inflaming the natives. Moerenhaut influenced in the Frenchmen's favour two very powerful chieftains, Etote and Paofai, of whom Pomare herself was reputed to be nervous. Etote and Paofai gave orders that the priests' luggage was to be brought ashore from the little ship, which still lay anchored. This was done, their belongings being installed in the house on Moerenhaut's land. The landing was made on a Sunday.

Next day the priests won ground in a royal audience, and persuaded Pomare to accept some golden doubloons and a chest of shawls. But outside, the island was in confusion. Mr. Pritchard roamed everywhere, explaining that his God was no relation to that of the Scarlet Woman, and giving highly coloured descriptions of the Beast on which the latter sat.

So much for the supernatural. But throughout the Pacific, wherever the French approached the native races, there was another weapon to turn against them. "Children of Marion . . . Children of Marion. . . ."

That began after poor Marion du Fresne's shocking butchery, on New Zealand shores, and in the latter part of the eighteenth century. The terrible vengeance taken by survivors of the French expedition on the natives, innocent and guilty alike, would be remembered for centuries. When the "Children of Marion", as the terrified natives christened them, had finished their bloody work, villages smouldered in ruins ; men, women, and children lay slaughtered. It was in the doctrine of that day ; but it did not make for French popularity among the natives. "Children of Marion. . . ." True, when the French priests landed at Tahiti, they had come on a tiny ship, unarmed, unaccompanied. What did that matter ?

Where they stayed, surely the grim ships of the "Children of Marion" would follow?

Tahiti murmured like the forest before the hurricane. But where Etote and Paofai stood by the priests, Pomare, her wavering mind at last decided, gave orders that the Frenchmen should be thrust off her soil.

The priests spent the night in Mr. Moerenhaut's hut. Here in early morning came a shouting, yelling crowd of natives. There was some parody of law in the proceedings. Moré, the Chief Justice of the island, took charge. The native constabulary levelled their guns at the victims. The roof was torn bodily off the hut, and they were dragged out, offering no resistance.

The younger man was weeping, the blind, helpless tears of humiliation. His companion lifted a great voice over the storm, thundering out Latin with such a defiant solemnity that for a moment all was still. Then the crowd broke. The luggage which the two had brought with them was pitched pell-mell from hand to hand. The natives set off for Pritchard's wharf, followed by Mr. Moerenhaut, actually in tears with indignation, and shouting to the de Thierry boys to remember what they saw that day.

The priests were hoisted on the shoulders of the natives, then carried dangling, head downwards, like the carcases of slaughtered sheep. The great bronzed children, cruel now as only children can be, bore them along to the strip of sand. A canoe was drawn up on shore. Half a mile out tossed the little ship which had brought them from Gambier Island.

Their luggage, such of it as remained, was tossed into the canoe. Then, with as little compunction as if they had been the dead bodies of animals, the priests were heaved on board. The canoe heeled over and sank, pitching them into breast-deep water. Moerenhaut pushed through the crowd, his hand outthrust to assist the taller priest, who, with his soutane girt up dripping around his chest, had his arms around the shoulders of the younger companion. The young man's eyes were closed, as if he were in a stupor. On the face of the other was a strange composure. The anger which had corded the veins in his high forehead was gone. He was still steadily repeating the words of some Latin prayer.

The little craft was righted. Luggage lost, work undone, the occupants set out for their ship, the taller priest plying the paddle. On the ship they were received with brutal insolence, and white residents of Tahiti learned that the vessel was so ill-provisioned her passengers would probably suffer both hunger and thirst before she made port again.

In the afternoon Charles met Mr. Pritchard, who had not yet recovered from the towering passion into which the Scarlet Woman had thrown him.

"Had they refused to go, wouldn't the Queen have been justified in shooting them ?" he demanded.

According to Charles, his reply was that had Her Majesty done so, the first French ship that called at Tahiti would have been justified in hanging the murderers and turning the Queen off the throne. Whether this is staircase indignation or not it is impossible now to discover. Charles became progressively more French as, through the later years of his life, the English were more and more rude to him.

A sample of this occurs now. Why should the Baron de Thierry, in Tahiti, begin to suffer slights and mistrust ?

The person who could best have explained was not, in himself, of much importance, being a Mr. Smith, supercargo on the brig *Charles Doggatt*, which some months before had put into Papeete from the Bay of Islands, New Zealand.

Shortly after his arrival, papers were passed round among the residents, provoking equal parts of gossip and guffaw. They were, as a matter of fact, the very severe letters written by Mr. James Busby, British Resident at the Bay of Islands, in response to Charles's all too candid confession of his intentions. The papers, coming into Mr. Smith's hands, seemed too good a joke for him to keep to himself. So he stole them, and earned many an extra drink in Tahiti.

Thus, although Mr. Busby had taken up his pen on October 30th, 1835 to demolish the Sovereign Chief and all his works, it was not until August 30th of the following year that the brig *Criterion*, arriving at Papeete, brought copies of the communications, which this time fell into the right hands.

In the months between, all Tahiti, with the forlorn exception of the de Thierry party, had known of Mr. Busby's intentions. Charles, however, had gone blissfully about his business, waiting gilded news from half a dozen quarters at once, and quite unaware that most of the population considered him a ruined man.

CHAPTER TEN

DUEL WITH QUILL PENS

[MAY be omitted by those with a constitutional dislike of historical detail: proves mainly how two Gentlemen can waste everybody's time writing Impassioned Letters.]

.   .   .   .   .

I can imagine few things that the British Resident at the Bay of Islands would have hated more; but the fact remains that in certain lights Mr. Busby bore a marked resemblance to Charles, Baron de Thierry.

Mr. Busby adored writing letters. Mr. Busby waxed eloquent—though at times a thought unconvincing—in argument. Mr. Busby was apt to take steps which staider men regarded as fantastic, and which won him small thanks from authority.

Show me where this departs from the faithful image of Our Charles.

At a distance of thousands of miles, then—one lodged at his Residency, one poised for flight at Tahiti—these two porcupines commenced firing off quills at each other. On the whole, Charles may be said to have won. Time meant nothing to him, once left with his ink-pot.

Busby and his family landed in New Zealand in 1831. Someone acting in official capacity there had long been craved by the distracted Government of New South Wales, whose convicts kept escaping to New Zealand, and there—since no law existed—cocking long noses at them. The first British Resident, however, was one of Downing Street's own little touches; neither soldier nor sailor, not even so much as a broken-down politician. This put him out of favour with New South Wales, which had wanted red jackets and brass buttons to subdue its wild neighbour.

The idea was that, by the throwing of a British lamb, a Resident, to these wolves, law might be encouraged, at least among British subjects in New Zealand, while the escape of convicts to that country might be seriously checked.

James Busby was the son of a John Busby, who had served the British Government well, but without much reward. His son gave the Government very useful information on waste lands, pounded away at the subject of viticulture, which might help establish the wine trade in Australia, wrote in 1831 a brochure on the subject of Residencies: *A Brief Memoir, Relative to the Islands of New Zealand.* Authority sniffed, and was satisfied. Mr. Busby was packed off to New Zealand, with a salary of £500 a year, and £200 extra to be used as palm-oil among native potentates.

He was an upright, rather pompous man, standing too much on his dignity for the liking of the raffish whites. The fact that British law in New Zealand could touch only British subjects, and that these could only be legally tried by the expensive method of sending them over to the New South Wales Courts, did much to cramp his style. He was in constant trouble with his escaped convicts. Australia was still much attached to rough and ready punishments for crime. A little time before, a former Governor of an Australian state had officially recommended that convicts found guilty of offences warranting the death penalty should, in lieu of mere execution, be cast adrift on New Zealand shores, where the natives would eat them. "The fear of this," wrote Captain Phillip, "will operate much stronger than the dread of death." Of the first six New South Wales convicts sentenced to death, only one cost the Government the price of a rope. The remaining five were driven out to be massacred among the Australian blacks.

Incidents bearing on the lawlessness of the country were not without their quaint humour. A homicidal maniac had escaped by ship to the Bay of Islands. Mr. Busby hurriedly shipped him back again. But, as it happened, the gentleman was not a British subject.

"What is this?" howled Authority. "What power entitled you to drive a man, not a British subject, from a country which is not a British possession?"

DUEL WITH QUILL PENS

Friend Maniac was shipped, grinning, back to New Zealand, where his subsequent history remains wrapped in darkness.

Two New Zealand natives, as late as 1838, were tried by the Resident for murdering one Henry Buddle. Mr. Busby had the chief offender shot, as he deserved. The Attorney-General in New South Wales was not only most annoyed, but also refused to pay the expenses.

Whatever Mr. Busby did, he could be certain that Sydney would reprimand and discourage him. He had been pointedly insulted by the appointment of an "Additional British Resident", Lieutenant Thomas McDonnell, a man with a genius for getting on with nobody and, by the way, one of the white men who had settled on Charles's 40,000 acres in the Hokianga district.

The Baron de Thierry's letter from Tahiti, informing Mr. Busby of his intention to found an Independent State on his lands at Hokianga, gave the latter, at last, an opportunity for the legal and technical manœuvres which he loved.

This marauding Baron might wax eloquent. But there was ink and blood in old England yet. Mr. Busby bit the end of his pen and settled to it.

British Residency at New Zealand,
Bay of Islands,
30th October, 1835.

Sir,

In adopting the measures I have thought necessary to defeat the enterprise which you have announced to me in your letter dated from Papeete Bay, Otaheiti, on the 14th ultimo, I have acted on the discretion which as an accredited representative of the British Government I have considered it my duty to exercise, under circumstances of so extraordinary a character. But even had I been entrusted with no powers at all in this respect, I should have thought it my duty upon the broad principles of common justice and humanity to have used whatever influence I possessed to prevent the occurrence of so much mischief as would be the inevitable result of an attempt upon the liberties of a free people....

The British Government has extended to the natives of this country, as well as to His Britannic Majesty's subjects, the protection of British laws, so far as regards the conduct of British subjects. But with the present independence of the natives, or with their personal or territorial rights, it has not interfered, nor permitted its subjects to interfere. . . .

Mr. Busby goes on to discuss at length the de Thierry land claims, and the price paid thereon, described by him as "two dozen of axes".

Even if the chiefs mentioned in the deed would have considered this the price, instead of the earnest thereof (as the axes were considered by them to be) you would have had to satisfy the claims of probably five hundred other individuals before you would have been permitted to take possession of your property, for the meanest of the New Zealanders is not a person to submit quietly to the most trivial inroad upon his rights. This disposes of your claim to any property in the soil of this country. But however well-founded a claim might have been, the chiefs are well aware that it would have been forfeited by your pretensions to Sovereign Rights : and they request me to warn you against approaching their lands, in whatever capacity you may choose to present yourself, or however accompanied, on pain of being treated as Independent States have a right to treat persons who attempt the usurpation of their sovereign rights within their territories.

(Mr. Busby's dismissal of the purchase price paid for the 40,000 acres hardly takes into account the fact that the Church Missionary Society also purchased New Zealand land with axes ; while the New Zealand Company later, for property valued at £50 in trade, acquired nearly a million acres.)

Being persuaded that the utter hopelessness of success will present itself to your mind in so strong a light as to prove to you the madness of persisting in your enterprise, and the criminality of engaging persons less qualified to judge to embark upon it, it seems almost supererogatory to add that should you present yourself, with whatever face, you may be sure of meeting with the most spirited resistance from the whole population . . . a population with whom warfare in its fiercest form has been a sport, and who are far from being ill-provided with arms and ammunition.

If the steps I have taken should, under Providence, be the means of preventing the sacrifice of even one life in a bad cause, I

know I shall be held excused by His Majesty's Government for giving an appearance of importance to your enterprise, to which, apart from such a consideration, it has not the remotest title.
I am, Sir,
Your most obedient servant,
James Busby,
British Resident.

Nor had the Baron's most obedient servant contented himself with a letter. Enclosed were other documents, the first a circular composed by Mr. Busby for distribution among "His Britannic Majesty's Subjects, who are residing or trading in New Zealand".

Extracts from this quaint document—a very early printing effort in New Zealand—emphasize the warm welcome being prepared for the Baron de Thierry, who is rather off-handedly referred to as "a person styling himself Charles, Baron de Thierry, Sovereign Chief of New Zealand, and King of Nukahiva, an Island of the Marquesas". The little pamphlet goes into horror-stricken capitals every now and again. It is mentioned that Charles proceeds on an alleged invitation from Shunghie, and "an alleged purchase made for him in 1822 by Mr. Kendall of three districts on the Hokianga, from three chiefs who had only a partial right in these districts, *parts of which are now settled by British subjects*, by right of purchase from the rightful proprietors."

Charles is further accused of sending Mr. Busby "an elaborate exposition of his views" (this has the ring of truth), and of sending letters to the missionaries of the Church Missionary Society, "in which he makes the most ample promises to all persons, whether white or native, who will accept his invitation to live under his Government : and in which he offers a stipulated salary to each individual missionary, in order to induce them to act as his magistrates."

(Mr. Busby refers feelingly here to his faith in the loyalty and good sense of the missionaries.)

"If such a person were once allowed to obtain a footing in this country, he might acquire such an influence over the Simple-minded Natives as would produce effects which cannot be too Anxiously Deprecated. My Duty is to request all British settlers of all classes to use all the Influence they possess with the Natives, of every rank, in order to counteract the effect of any Emissaries who have arrived or may arrive among them. And to inspire both Chiefs and People with a spirit of the most Determined Resistance to the landing of a Person on their Shores, who comes with the Avowed Intention of Usurping a Sovereignty over them."

Once again the signature of James Busby, British Resident. The date of October 10th, 1835.

The printing of the pamphlet was achieved at the press of the Church Missionary Society, set up in Paihia, in the Bay of Islands, where missionaries were most earnestly engaged in preaching goodwill to all men among the Simple-minded Natives.

The right hand of the missionaries, the Rev. Mr. Henry Williams (established at Paihia by old Samuel Marsden), sacrificed time and energy distributing the circular among the settlers.

But was this the limit of Mr. Busby's activities? Unfortunately, no. A third document was in the packet. No less than the Declaration of the Independence of New Zealand.

Patience. I am not about to quote it in full.

It suffices to say that at Waitangi in the Bay of Islands, October 28th, 1835, the hereditary chiefs and heads of the tribes of the North Part of New Zealand, assembled by Mr. Busby, formally declared the independence of their country, which they thereby constituted an Independent State, under the designation of "The United Tribes of New Zealand".

All sovereign power and authority were to be vested in the chiefs within their territory, in their collective capacity. No legislative authority or function of Government separate from themselves was to be permitted, save by their own permission, legally given by themselves in congress assembled. They were pledged to meet thus in congress, in the autumn of each year, for the enactment of laws. And a copy of the declaration was to be sent to King George IV, with a request that he might act "as the parent of their Infant State".

In 1838, giving evidence before the Select Committee in the House of Lords, one New Zealand witness explained that the Rev. Henry Williams had distributed the circular, whilst the residents had also been informed that the Baron de Thierry was really a French general, taking part in planned French aggression.

Allowing for the profitable footing which British subjects had obtained on that 40,000 acres of debatable country, it is still possible that Charles might have found tolerance had he come without pomp and circumstance. But the fine ring of the Sovereign Chieftaincy . . . the glitter of that baby Nukahivan Crown . . . the guns exploding at Panama . . . it was too much for Englishmen to digest.

They were happily combined against a Foreign Usurper.

A cloud upon Mr. Busby's horizon : Sydney disapproved. Sydney was never done disapproving. Sir George Gipps contemptuously referred to the Declaration of Independence as "a paper pellet, fired off against the Baron de Thierry".

But Mr. Busby lay back at Waitangi, blissfully exhausted. He had done his duty ; and he had thoroughly written himself out.

On the other hand, Mr. Busby knew very little about Charles. One might perhaps abolish him by firing a sufficiency of well-directed cannon-balls. But with pen and ink ? Never.

Note the characteristic beginning of his address in reply :

Having but a few hours to write, *I must refrain from entering as minutely as I could wish on the contents on your letter, which seems to have been written with intent to intimidate a man of weak nerve, who would feebly renounce his rights and forgo the objects which have brought him to these remote regions.*

(Have at you, Mr. British Resident !)

But in this, Sir, you mistake me, for I am neither very ignorant of worldly affairs, nor very easily frightened out of my plans. The which, with the blessing of God, I will bring ere long to desired maturity.

(You will note that either side claims a complete monopoly of the right side of Providence.)

Acting on the broad principle that New Zealand is not a possession of the British Crown, I come forward as the humble champion of present and future New Zealand liberties. That my timber has been cut and is daily cutting, is sold and is daily selling, to my great loss, the loss of many thousands of pounds, all this I well know. But what I never expected to know is that an agent of the Crown of England would warn me not to approach my own property. Were we living under a Dey of Algiers, such things might be believed, but they are monstrous in British annals. . . . Such a thing is impossible, for were the King to deprive me of my lands, I would be an oppressed man ; and if warned off my property by the King, a persecuted man ; and thirty millions of voices would be raised in my defence, for there is not a person in Great Britain, from the peer to the peasant, but will side with the oppressed.

I must ask in what I have aimed a blow at the liberties of the people of New Zealand? Is it by coming thousands of miles to arrest their too rapid demoralization and degradation, and by wishing to raise them to the level of civilization ? Is it by devoting all my earthly substance to them ? Is it by bringing a young family to dwell among them ? By encountering dangers and privations, and by my willingness to live and die in their cause, that I show myself to be the dangerous man you are pleased to picture me ?

Look at the United States, the Canadas, the West Indies, South America, the Cape of Good Hope, New Holland and Van Diemen's Land : and you may point an instructive moral to the New Zealanders. When the New Zealand chiefs who received a flag (for the benefit of a few white people who wanted registers for New Zealand-built ships), assisted at this extraordinary ceremony, how were they treated? As equals, or as inferiors ? Did they dine at the same table with the whites ; or is it true, as newspapers report, that they "were supplied with a plentiful mess of flour sweetened with sugar, on which they feasted" ?

Is this the manner in which hereditary chiefs are to be treated? It is thus, sir, that the proud spirit of the native race is broken and degraded. They are spoken of as sovereigns, and treated as slaves. But there is yet a voice which shall be heard by these devoted people ; they shall learn the truth, they shall see how hereditary chiefs ought to be treated. And then, if they think it to their interest to treat me as you have so humanely advised, they may kill and eat me, *and history shall tell her own version, which will never redound very greatly to the credit of those who represented me other than one of the earliest and best friends of the New Zealand people.*

      I am, Sir,
        Yours very obediently,
         Charles, Baron de Thierry.

Forwarded by the brig Criterion, *August 3cth, 1836.*

Ink . . . the man was a cuttlefish for it. His track across the globe is marked with swamps of ink. But amid all the words, you will notice one small, honest, and painstaking star.

He has a sincere regard for the native peoples : a desire to treat them as equals.

Thousands of white men read that account of the distribution of a flour-sweetened mess among the chieftains. (*"Ko rodirodi"*, or *"wai ma"*.)

Charles was the only one who burst into flames at the idea. Years after he had assured Mr. Busby that this was no way to handle the proud spirit of the native people, a catch-cry went round among the North Island Maoris.

"Have you eaten the White Queen's stir-about ?"

The eyes of warriors smouldered as they heard that gibe. They had eaten, with childlike enthusiasm. Their pride had not quite digested the stir-about, and the circumstance, among others, helped in preparing them for war.

It is about this time that Major Edward Fergus disappears, perhaps a little sadly, from the picture. The army in their white trousers and striking cockades were now less vital than renewed support from Panama. Thither Fergus bent his sails, with many promises of return. The Princess Isabel wept bitterly over her lost cavalier. Major Fergus, equestrian statue of the kingdom, fades into the dull security of private life.

It is now or never. If one doesn't get to New Zealand, one may, from the vehemence of this Busby, find the whole place entrenched by brigades of ravenous cannibals. *"Frère, il faut partir !"* Who was it had made that suggestion ? Sister Caroline, of course, that time when he had endeavoured to raise funds in Paris. Money is there, if you demonstrate to the capitalists that you actually possess the nuts to insert in their large pouches. They will never be optimistic in advance.

To get out of Tahiti is easier said than done. Skippers develop an invincible prejudice against transporting the de Thierrys to any British shore at all. For months, attempts to obtain a passage to Sydney are a mere beating the wind. The ships will have none of Charles. He devotes his time to correspondence with Sir Richard Bourke, laying before him his plans, with a fullness of detail which must have made the Governor's brain reel. As for the Australian newspapers, they cannot have been so amiable, for in one letter to Sir Richard, Charles complains bitterly of "the low scurrility of the Sydney press".

Suddenly he discovers for himself the way of escape from Tahiti. He makes himself a nuisance, such a nuisance. . . .

It was a blow that could not have been expected. The man has bought up the coconut-oil in Tahiti, effected a corner in supplies. He will not sell until his passage to Sydney is arranged.

That against which all the elements, thunder especially, have warred, has come to pass. On May 3rd, 1837, Captain Lincoln gives the de Thierry party passage to Sydney in the Yankee brig *Draco*.

Thus, with a flourish of trumpets, however small and forlorn it may sound in that vast ocean, things begin to move again. The Sovereign Chief is really on his way to New Zealand.

CHAPTER ELEVEN

CONTEMPLATION AND LOQUATS

THE loquat-tree in the yard was covered with pointed golden fruits about the size of bantams' eggs. These, though dusty and rather disappointing to bite into—the big loquat-stones taking up nearly all the room—were fun in a way, because their tart flavour, though queer, was not *too* queer. With the Island fruits, you simply couldn't tell. Some tasted like whipped cream, others oily and horrible. You ate grenadilla, which was lovely, with a spoon, and Margaret stood over you grimly, saying, "Don't you swallow them nasty little pips, Miss Isabel." When there are millions of pips in one grenadilla, how can you help swallowing some ? You can't keep spitting them out: it isn't ladylike ; and to extract them under cover of your hanky makes you feel self-conscious. People who laugh too loud are horrible . . . like Hateful Captain Jones, who made you bite the gorgeous scarlet capsicum pod, and then shouted while your eyes streamed tears and you coughed and spluttered.

Papa knew how to handle Hateful Captain Jones. He didn't say much, but they played nap that evening; and when they had been at it for an hour, Hateful Captain Jones was as red as a beet, and Papa kept saying gently, "Dear me, how unfortunate !" Later, he jingled pieces of gold in his pocket. They had formerly belonged to Hateful Captain Jones. "I am *not* a gambler," said Papa, with his Divine Right of Kings look. "Let me see, I wonder if we can buy a doll anywhere on this wild island ?"

Now it wasn't the wild island any more, but Sydney, with dusty loquats in the back yard, and the wind lifting more dust, fierce and reddish, from raw clay roads. The heat was a great sticky blanket over everything. At night you wriggled out of your night-gown and lay quite bare between the sheets, trying to extract their cool linen feel. You had to be careful to wake up earlier than Margaret, however, for if she caught you bare, she would be in a state.

Mamma's room smelt lovely of toilet-vinegar and sixpenny bunches of the wild, cheeky little native roses. Why they were called roses, goodness knows. They were pale pink and curly, but otherwise there was no resemblance. However, most of the people in New South Wales were English-born, and Mamma said that they must feel homesick for roses. She smiled when she said this, but her eyes grew wide and a little queer. She wore her lovely fair hair down over the strawberry-coloured *peignoir*; and when you came in to kiss her good night, she would squirt toilet-vinegar at you from the little gold-topped bottle—toilet-vinegar smelling heavenly cool.

Mamma had a *friendly* smile, Isabel decided, though Papa was more exciting. Once, on a reckless impulse, she had confided in Mamma that she had been sleeping bare between the sheets. Then she hung her head, overcome with sudden shame. Already she could hear Margaret's voice. "Fie, Miss Isabel! . . . A great girl of nine years old! Whatever will your papa say?" She caught her lip between her teeth, so that she wouldn't cry out, "Please don't tell Papa!"

But Mamma only smiled that funny smile. "Look," she said, and whisked one leg out from the strawberry-coloured *peignoir*. It was a cream-coloured leg, with slim ankle and pretty foot, but the amazing thing about Mamma's leg was that it, too, was perfectly bare. Before Isabel could remark on this the leg whisked out of sight again. It was the first time, really, that she had thought about Mamma as having legs at all. With Papa you couldn't help noticing, because gentlemen wear pantaloons.

Isabel sighed a little, stretching her own sunburnt toes. Ladies became such queer shapes as soon as they grew up. Sydney was quite a fashionable place, and on several occasions they had gone driving through Pitt Street and George Street, the main roads of the town. There you saw ladies shaped like vases and hour-glasses, with bonnets like coal-scuttles or flower-pots. The gayest things about them were their darling parasols, which opened up in big frothy petals of silk and lace. Even Margaret admitted that Sydney was "ceevilized", though, of course, there were black fellows on the outskirts. You never saw them in town. They lived outside somewhere, probably where the little native roses grew curly and wild.

There were queer enough people hanging about in Sydney itself . . . a terrible man with stony blue eyes who wore a snake-skin waistcoat, and let great coiled snakes, black and mottled, fix their fangs in his savage bare arms and hang on. Then he shouted in a hoarse voice about his infallible remedy for snake-bite. Once they saw a gang of men with immobile, square-cut faces who were all chained together at the ankles. . . . Once an old woman, who said, "Listen to the mocking-bird, my pretty dearie." The mocking-bird, which had a sharp-pointed bill and was about as big as a kingfisher, but buff-coloured instead of shining blue, suddenly opened its beak and gave screech after screech of laughter. Isabel didn't like it.

"Are we going to live here, Papa?" That was what Baby Will asked wherever they went, because he was too little to know better. But Isabel knew the answer off by heart. "We're going to live in New Zealand, we're only tarrying here."

Odd to think of the different places where they had tarried. . . . She built up a picture of the place where they would live for ever. It was not large. It had rooms with flowered curtains, and a piano with a really fine tone, so that Papa could play without making a face. He was always bothered because the piano in this Sydney house had one bad tooth, and you had to keep pressing on the pedal if you wanted any expression. There would have to be fowls outside, red-brown, speckly, and white, because they make such funny sleepy noises in their chests, and when you slide your hand under them, feeling for the new-laid eggs, it is lovely and warm. Isabel would have one special fowl, who would lay a brown egg regularly every day. They could have a golden setter dog, named Rover, and inside the house would be a bedroom smelling always of toilet-vinegar and native roses, with pale blue curtains and a blue silken brush-and-comb bag on one wall.

Isabel paused. "Why, that's just like our house here," she thought. But then an improvement occurred to her.

In their own house, there would never be any need to wriggle under ghostly white tents of mosquito-netting at night—because, if you didn't, in the morning you had to keep scratching at horrible little red mounds, which came up all over you in the most awkward places. And then Margaret made you show your legs, dabbing at you with cotton-wool and citronella, and saying, "Well, them skeeters certainly had a fine dinner off you last night, Miss Isabel. What did I tell you, now?"

Still, even without the skeeters, it would not be practicable to draw this house for Papa. When they played together in the evenings, "Little house, big house, pig-sty, barn?" Papa would wrinkle up his nose and smile, saying, "Pig-sty?" Then you must look offended and haughty, and cry, "Palace!"

.   .   .   .   .

In September of '37, Sir Richard Bourke mentioned Charles in an official dispatch to Lord Glenelg.

"I have declined interfering in any way. Nor have I considered it my duty to interpose any obstacle to his proceeding to New Zealand, of which country he claims to be a Sovereign Chief by right of his purchases. He denies all intention of interfering with the interests of Great Britain, and professes a reliance on moral influence alone for the authority he expects to acquire among the natives."

This is the result of a private interview granted by the amiable Governor. "I found him what I had expected," writes Charles. "A courtly and polished English gentleman." Encouraged by this reception, he unbosomed himself at once concerning the threats of the former Assistant British Resident, Lieutenant Thomas McDonnell, who, on vacating his office, had become one of the British subjects to dig their toes in on the disputable 40,000 acres. With many oaths, the Lieutenant now declared that if the Baron de Thierry sailed up the Hokianga river, he would be received by the battery of guns in front of the Lieutenant's house, Te Horeke.

"Has he Your Excellency's authority to do this?"

Sir Richard smiled.

"Certainly not. I have only to tell you, Baron, if he annoys you, that the battery at Te Horeke is commanded by a high hill at the rear. You should know what to do."

His Excellency goes even further in fatherly advice and warning.

"I shouldn't like to see you in trouble with the British Crown. If any crime which requires capital punishment should be committed on your territories, don't under any circumstances take matters into your own hands. That would mean trouble. Leave it to the natives."

Both by letter and in this audience, Charles offered to resign his cherished Sovereign Rights if he could be assured of British protection for his settlers. Sir Richard maintained that he had no authority to extend this protection; Our Charles therefore stood firm on the necessity of "a paternal Independence, and the power to make laws". His demeanour in Sydney seems to have been rational. Learning of the many British subjects settled on his Hokianga claims, he wrote to Sir Richard, offering to permit the lot to remain, on receipt of a very nominal rent, and "the overlordship of the soil" ; to allow those who had contracted to supply timber from trees cut on his estates to confirm their contracts, on paying him a royalty of ten shillings a ton of 40 cubic feet ; and in the case of native residents, not only to leave them undisturbed, but for every acre they had under cultivation to allow them freehold of three further acres. Another suggestion, which would doubtless have struck a frightful blow at the dignity of the whites, was his calm proposal that every white man on his demesne should devote one day per month to the construction of public roads.

"As a further proof of my goodwill towards the natives, I offer to distribute among them two hundred red flannel shirts (or one hundred to be distributed half-yearly), for a period of ten years from the day I am confirmed in possession of my lands. I go not among the natives to obtain cargoes of produce for muskets, gunpowder, and ardent liquors. . . ." (This high-mindedness is terribly tactless, by the way. So many white men do go among the natives for precisely the reasons cited.) He further proposes to Sir Richard that every white man caught trafficking in arms or liquor with the natives shall forfeit a bond of £100 on first conviction. Imagine the embarrassment of numbers of the Hokianga population !

Old, blind, worn down with the years, Samuel Marsden,

who started mission work in his wild New Zealand, lingered on in Sydney, longing in vain for the strength to revisit the country where he had left his heart.

"I have this day seen a Frenchman, his name is the Baron de Teirny. . . . He expects to do great things there. Whether he will give the missionaries any trouble or no, I know not. I shall write to put them on their guard. I have had an interview with the Baron. I shall see him again before he sails. He tells me he purchased for the purpose of improving the natives of New Zealand. . . . I fear he will be greatly disappointed in the end. . . . I fear you will not be able to make out my writing. I am so blind. . . ."*

Samuel Marsden warned Charles against the dangers of raising his settlers in Sydney, but the advice came after a considerable number of recruits had been gathered together by newspaper advertisement. In all, ninety-three white settlers, men and women, collected for the expedition. One authority primly describes them as "persons of a very infamous description", but this is exaggeration. They were rag, tag, and bobtail, but Charles took the precaution of securing with every prospective settler a written official guarantee that no criminal conviction stood against his or her name. He appointed a Keeper of the Stores, Hargreaves, whose pretty daughter, Jane, was to marry his young surgeon, Dr. Cooke, before the expedition sailed. There was a tutor also, a gentleman, Charles says, of High Classical Attainments.

Old friends and new turned up in Sydney. Charles shook hands with Captain Hobson of H.M.S. *Racehorse*, who dropped a hint that the present lawlessness of New Zealand was likely to have a short run for its backers' money. Richard Jones and Stewart Donaldson, both well acquainted with the Hokianga, drank Margaret Neilsen's lemonade, and warned Charles against all manner of serpentine scoundrels, especially the ex-Assistant British Resident, Lieutenant McDonnell, who, it would seem, on retiring from his official capacity, had devoted himself unswervingly to unneighbourly practices, and was the chief lopper-off of *kauri* timber on the de Thierry estate.

"Honest missionaries, honest merchants, honest Lieutenants

---

*Historical Records of New Zealand.

of the Navy," writes Charles, referring to the timber-wolves. The British frigate *Buffalo* passes through Sydney waters, refitted with spars at Hokianga ; the timber, every stick of it, had come from those acres which Charles still believed to be as surely his own as parchment, ink, and law could make them.

The quaintest protégé fished up from the vasty deeps was nothing less than an authentic Maori chieftain. As the adventurous Maoris so often did, Chief Tiro had slipped aboard a sailing-ship at the Hokianga, and was now wandering happily through New South Wales. Charles received him like a brother. The large chief sat at table with the family, and slept under their roof. Tiro was not unappreciative. The original of the quaint and eloquent document in which he breaks the news of Our Charles to his Hokianga friends still survives.

The words of Tiro to his friends, tribes and visitors at Hokianga.

Listen attentively to my words, O Rewa, Kaweaka, Pura, Tau, Nue and Nene.

I am on my return to my country in the Nimrod, *one month will scarcely elapse before I arrive at Hokianga.*

O my friends, let your hearts rejoice for the coming of the great Chief, of the Baron de Thierry, who will teach our children and people, who will make our country reputable, and protect it.

Hearken not, I beseech you, to the words of the English, who state that the Baron de Thierry intends the enslavement of the country. On the contrary, his intention is to leglislate for, protect, and enrich us. The Baron has explained his intentions to me. I am satisfied. I have been an inmate of his house and have eaten at his table ever since my arrival, my heart cleaves to him.

Fathers! Sons! Prepare a great feast for the reception of our illustrious guest. Evince the greatest respect for the Person who comes to rule and enrich you.

These are my words, and they are true. I have seen the Baron de Thierry, he is the original owner of Te Papa, Mata Kura, Wai Hou, Te Te One, paid for by Mr. Kendall in axes a long time since. He holds documents from Mudi Wai, Patu One, and Nene. Friends, do justice to your high chief, listen to his commands! Friends, farewell! In a short time I shall be with you, and my tongue shall relate the words of our Chief, which, when you have heard, your hearts will cleave to him, as mine does at this moment.

Farewell!

Tiro, Chief of Munga-Muka.

The truth is, one couldn't help liking Our Charles. He had, of course, no sense of proportion. This made him, in a way, immoral. He would have thought nothing of putting Greenland's icy mountains in the pocket of his pantaloons, or the Crown of Arabia, in an absent-minded moment, on his head; all for the good of the natives. His commercial morality was terrible. If he hit on a scheme with profits in it, he was certain to twine it round and round with idealism, until a business man, touching the thing, would feel like a kitten tied up in pink wool. But, in nine instances out of ten, he meant well; and in the tenth, he could argue so reasonably, so exhaustively. . . . People from a distance denounced him with true passion. They met him and conversed with him, or, to be more exact, they were conversed at by him. The glare of suspicion faded from their eyes, to be replaced by that slightly dazed look. One finds it throughout his history. If he could have got them into one bunch together, and kept them there, they could never have held out against him. Imagine what Charles could have done, equipped with radio and television! It won't bear thinking about, when we see the dimensions of the mess we are in today. Charles would have stood the world on its head. What a good thing!

Do you know that in Sydney he persuaded His Majesty's Customs Office to accept both the flag and seals of his Independent State?

"Colonel Gibbs, the Collector of Customs at Sydney, was very civil to me, and it was arranged that vessels from New Zealand carrying my flag should be treated as ships belonging to the Colony. I was furnished with all the different printed customs-house forms which are used in Sydney, from register of vessels to clearances. More could not be asked, unless it were official recognition in the Gazette, and that would have been for the Sydney authorities to concede much more than was prudent."

See, then, the west, clear and tranquilly green in dusk, and clouds like ships passing through those strange lakes, where instantly their wake is obliterated. There is the creak of Emily's American rocking-chair, from which she will not be parted by any deceit or stratagem. Each shadow wavering in the dusty garden seems to have a human face. . . . Francis de Thierry, Salomon, Feraud in his brown brick house, Captain d'Orsay waving a scarf from the *Momus*. The dead men, the dead women, in Dominica. Vigneti, pale-faced, ardent, serious. Fergus, his long legs sprawling, and his terrible tobacco-smoke wreathing into the fragrance of the vanilla-scented Tahitian evening. . . .

Emily is privileged to hear all the most important documents, exhortations, Addresses-in-Reply. "The Address of the Baron de Thierry to the White Residents of Hokianga." Its ink is still wet from the press of the *Sydney Morning Herald*, whose office stands in Lower George Street. The *Herald* staff are not the scurrilous crowd, the more than yellow, the absolutely bright orange rag who have dared to christen Charles "the Baron de Theory".

Little stitches slip in and out of snowy cambric as Emily listens.

"I interfere with no part, save my own territories. As yet, no nation can enter into treaty with you. Your possessions and property are exposed to every vicissitude, you are bound by no common sympathies, you have no certain protection against danger, because your very pursuits divide your interests. You have no strength to oppose foreign and domestic invasion, no power to prevent and punish crime. You are oppressed by monopolies, little better than outcasts, where you have the power to be happy, secure and prosperous. . . . I take with me a Surgeon, whose duty it will be to give gratuitous attention to the poor of either colour. I bring experienced agriculturists, who will foster the planting of cotton and tobacco. A gentleman of high classical attainments has been engaged as tutor to my sons, and will be given permission to take the sons of respectable settlers under his care. The lady who will instruct my daughter may make similar arrangements as regards the daughters of New Zealand families. My Keeper of the Stores will purchase goods from all traders at a fair colonial price, deducting profit, freight and assurance. . . ."

The first suggestion of assurance on cargoes shipped from New Zealand. Surely an appealing point. Charles wrinkles his nose anxiously, looking at Emily to see what impression his Address has made.

He is forty now. The mould has set; the last mould but one. Nature, you know, experiments on our features with a number of moulds. First there is that button-nosed, hairless, toothless effect, not much to brag about. Then suddenly there is individuality; a face has taken shape. The child may be quite ridiculously like its father or mother, and yet, in its own right, the little face is so clear, so unspoiled by wrinkles and sly disguises, so clean, with its soft, downy skin, that it exists in a world apart. We understand, looking at it, why poor Ponce de Leon dragged himself about looking for a Fountain of Youth.

Then that perfection is marred. The legs are too long, there are hairs on the boyish chin ; or the little girl's flat chest—to her tearful embarrassment—produces overnight the elements of a bosom. What a pity! We avert our eyes. Behold, when we look back, the shining new mould, perfect again, so bright that it hurts our tired eyes. Youth stands before us, swaggering a little, kicking up the winged sandals. "Oh, God . . . Oh, God," cries that unreasoning, thwarted voice in our heart, "I was like that, too. . . . It isn't fair."

A peal of thunder, and the beautiful silver-gilt mould, which looked as though it would last for ever, has fallen in pieces to the ground. Now the face emerges as it is going to look for a long time . . . for Nature, growing impatient, has constructed the mask to last. It still retains a little of youth, even a little of childhood. But, with deft, sardonic touch, the fine details have been added, wrinkle, spot, and scar.

Portrait of a gentleman in broadcloth. His face is long, shield-shaped, his fringes of chestnut whiskers are turning iron-grey. Otherwise, he is clean-shaven, revealing the fact that his mouth is long, sensitive, obstinate as a mule's. He has a long nose with a bump at the end. His eyebrows are bushy, and beneath them the hazel eyes look out with a glance at once fierce and appealing. He is not—for which one may be grateful—in the least bald. His hands are beautiful . . . long-fingered, slender, determined.

Yes, it is a scarred face. That twitch of the mouth, that rather too arrogant stare of the eyes, followed by the humble, appealing glance. The face of a sensitive man who has quarrelled frequently with his inferiors, and thought too much, in the subsequent hours, of what he has said, and what an immortal, ineffaceable fool he was to say anything at all.

He will stay like this for a long while, until there is that strange little chiming stroke of the gong, not hard at all, this time, merely as if the gilt clock had sounded the hour. Then the mould will split in halves, and out of it will emerge the incredibly fragile figure of old age.

"I'll be glad when this waiting is over. Ah, listen!" From the hot little room across the passage, children's voices lifted in singing . . . a boy's treble, a girl's sweet, clear soprano, the last a voice which could sometimes bring tears to the eyes. He crosses the passage, stands behind them, listening.

The Princess, lifting her face, quite misunderstands.

"I'm sorry, Papa. The old keys are all muffled; I *have* to loud-pedal."

"What are you singing, children?"

"It's 'Over the Hills and Far Away', Papa. The words are so pretty. Willy and I made a tune for them ourselves."

"Isabel did," says round-faced Will, stoutly surrendering all the glory.

"Sing it again, children. 'Over the Hills and Far Away'."

CHAPTER TWELVE

GOD OMITS TO SAVE THE KING

VISIONARY as the movement of the Baron de Thierry may seem to some, and insidious as it is considered by others, we cannot help entertaining an opinion that he might be the means of effecting a moral and political good for New Zealand.

(Thus handsomely declared the *Sydney Colonist*, October 5th, 1837.)

Animated, as he appears to be, by an ardent desire to benefit the country, and indifferent to all the difficulties and obstacles he must inevitably encounter, he will, if his intentions be carried into effect, contribute to exalt the character of the natives, and extend the interests of commerce. But let him recollect that going, as he proposes to do, independent of all assistance from Government, and relying solely on his individual energies to satisfy the wants and defend the lives of those persons accompanying him, he has no ordinary task to accomplish.

"I had well considered all that," writes Charles, in one of his unavoidable footnotes.

On the evening of October 21st, the New Zealand missionary, Mr. Henry Williams (by then Archdeacon Williams), supped with the de Thierrys; in the morning he arrived at the *Nimrod* with a package of eleven letters of introduction to other missionaries and residents on the Hokianga and Bay of Islands shores.

"What !" cry in scandalized tones those who know anything of the inner workings of New Zealand history. "Our Henry forgathering with your Charles ? Writing him letters of introduction ? Incredible !"

But wait a moment. It was not for some months that Charles, having delivered his letters, discovered their nature. Far from being the complimentary epistles he had supposed, they warned the fold to beware of him.

GOD OMITS TO SAVE THE KING

It was a little astute, even for a missionary.

Mr. Henry Williams, his wife, and his two young children had settled in the wild country in 1823, when he founded the Church of England mission station at Paihia, in the Bay of Islands. Somewhat later he was joined by his brother, the scholarly and gentle Mr. William Williams.

Centred around the Bay of Islands—a day's journey from the Hokianga—was the stir of a slowly developing civilization, for most of which the early missionaries were responsible. A plough turned soil there in 1820. "Behold, I bring glad tidings," old Samuel Marsden declared to the natives, from an improvised pulpit draped with black-dyed flax.

Shunghie swept down on the Whangaroa Mission Station and destroyed it in 1827, to perish a few years later from wounds received on the battlefield. Foreign colours dipped through the shining waters. The Republican explorer, Dumont d'Urville, had taken the *Astrolabe* through the whirlpools of French Pass, in the south, and his ship had lain anchored in the northern harbours. These picturesque gentry came and went. The missionaries dug their toes in, reigning over folds of ever-increasing size. Archdeacon Williams, acknowledged leader with the Church of England group, worked hand in hand with Mr. James Busby against the "French aggression" of the much-discussed Baron de Thierry. The *rencontre* in Sydney was seemingly of diplomatic nature only. Perhaps it was morally justifiable. There are numerous sticky patches in the Bible.

The *Nimrod* sailed with her King, her royal family, and her consignment of settlers on October 22nd, 1837, and, under the captaincy of a first-rate seaman, made an excellent crossing of the Tasman Sea in ten days.

The lower decks were gay as a village fair, with squeaking Jew's-harps and concertinas. In his cabin, the Sovereign Chief had begun to build up the etiquette of his little Court. There are still tremendous yarns about all that. Some say that Charles made all who entered the Presence retreat tail foremost, for all the world as if he were a Hapsburg, a Hohenzollern, a Bourbon itself. Others insist that he wished, on landing, to create his Captain an Admiral. In this there may be truth. He would certainly have coveted an Admiral.

That he sailed with an Archbishop is little less than a miracle, and can only be explained by the notorious conservatism of Archbishops.

Was the voyage without calamity? Alas, no. On the fifth day out, he was called to preside over a burial at sea.

Poor Strawberry. And he had been so proud of her. She lives for ever in his records. . . . "A fine cow, which I bought myself for New Zealand, and which died by *gross neglect*."

There was a sadder loss—though one should not underestimate Strawberry, for cows, at this time, were scarcer in New Zealand than virtuous matrons, and the scarcity of virtuous matrons had to be personally investigated to be believed. You remember the "gentleman of high classical attainments", the tutor? Charles lost him, too. He did not die—not at all. Worse than death. The day before the *Nimrod* sailed, he revealed still another attainment, also classical.

"He was seized with a violent fit of delirium tremens," says Charles. "And I was forced to leave him in Sydney, convinced that he was no fit associate for the sons of gentlemen."

On Charles de Thierry's own *jour de fête*, St. Charles's Day, November 4th, 1837, the *Nimrod*, flying bunting stem and stern, and at her mast-head the great crimson-and-azure flag of the de Thierrys, entered the river-mouth of the Hokianga.

"Where was the hostile array of natives which was to warn me from New Zealand? The *Nimrod* carried my flag at the main, the ships in the anchorage were gaily dressed in their colours, and my arrival was hailed with warm congratulations, except by two or three persons whose sullen look portended that they had much rather I had not interfered with their operations."

Already, when the *Nimrod* anchored, twilight had dimmed the glitter of the waters. Settlers chattered, gaped, shouted, argued, sang. A splendid moon arose. Landing was for the morrow.

Close to one hundred years ago. What was it they saw?

Yes, it is beautiful, the Hokianga. At that time it must have been much more animated, less forsaken, than today. As an anchorage for traders, whalers, frigates, stormy petrels of the Seven Seas, it was only less than the Bay of Islands in importance. It appeared to have a future. Those ships, dressed in gay colours . . . one might now lie for a whole year in the warm sands and see never one of them. There still exists the crazy old wall of stone blocks, quarried in the convict hell of Botany Bay, and brought over as ballast in the sailing-ships. Mounted on this wall, slowly rusting into decrepitude, still scowl the ancient pieces of ordnance that the native gunners used to pop off so merrily when given the chance.

Beautiful ; neither with that overblown, *cocotte* beauty of the Pacific isles, nor with the farouche beauty of the South Island, its white mountains mirrored in the staggering turquoise of the cold lakes. The tidal river of the Hokianga extends a warm blue arm between yellow sand-faces. On one side, as you advance up-stream, the hills are piled up with patterned drifts of gold. The lupins, whose yellow matches the sand so well, and whose honey-scent so intoxicates the bees, cannot have been growing there when Charles saw the place, for the plant is not indigenous. Otherwise, I should imagine it much the same. On the side where he landed, the sands lie disposed in a smooth stretch, warm and fine, below little foothills which precede the darker and wilder slopes, given over to native forest. In November, when the *Nimrod* arrived, the *pohutukawa*, whose unreasonable name is usually avoided by calling it "the New Zealand Christmas-tree", would have been in first flower, whole leagues of it. The tree cannot live away from the sea-shores. Its grey, twisted boughs burst suddenly into a perfect bonfire of blossom, shading from pale coral to richest crimson. These impressive flowers, when inspected, prove to be nothing but millions and millions of inch-long stamens, protruding from pale little honey-cups. The massed effect, however, is very spectacular, like Brunhilde's curtain of flame. When the brief flowering-time is done, the stamens fall to make a deep crimson carpet.

Possibly, if one thinks in terms of the picturesque, Captain Hobson, who was to be first British Governor of the Colony, did the Hokianga a service when, by sacrificing all the far north to build up a city at Auckland, he drained this inlet, like the Bay of Islands, of population and commercial importance.

The Bay of Islands took its depletion hard. The first capital, Russell, was builded there, and then forgotten, forsaken, washed out. But there's more to it than that. The Bay had advanced, through hectic intercourse with the world's ships, so far along the road to importance—it was everywhere called "The Hell of the Pacific"—that it couldn't go under tamely. Even now, under its tourist gloze (my God, those fishermen, sitting about under stuffed sword-fishes, and talking like tadpoles!), all that part of the country is sick and sullen, like a caged beast. One is always expecting it to break loose, and yet aware that it lacks the force. It is haunted, and not by genteel presences.

The Hokianga was neither so wicked nor so vigorous. It held the promise of a future for so short a time, and now it remains the sort of place where one wants to sleep in the sands and the sun ... to sleep for a long, long time, in sands that, unlike the others, are really golden. One might easily see, through half-shut eyes, moving up the glittering blue waters of the river-mouth, that preposterous and delightful ship.

Ships.... New Zealand gets them now by the thousand. Old Te Rauparaha, one of the most skittish among that bunch of wild horses the English found so difficult to break in, put the matter in a nutshell. "*E rara!* This land is destined to be the nest of ships." But of all the squadrons, I like the *Nimrod* best. To begin with, Charles meant so well. The others, when you look into them, do not. Their intentions are both terrifying and depressing, especially when they believe themselves to be virtuous. And then they are so self-assertive. The earthquakes growl a little when they come and they go; but only a little, in slumber.

He must have heard the more-pork owl from the decks of the *Nimrod* that first night. A little banshee of a thing, fluffy, but with an enormous voice, which wails incessantly, "More-pork ... more-porrrk," like a starving orphan.

We return to the first official *communiqué*, delivered per dinghy as the *Nimrod* lay at anchor. This *billet-doux* was from a person of importance—nobody less than Lieutenant Thomas McDonnell, "the ex-Assistant British Resident"

My Dear Baron,
         Captains Robson and Cabell will wait on the Baroness in the morning, to escort her to Te Horeke. They will take care that your lady shall leave the Nimrod with due honours, and I will take especial care to receive you with the battery of Te Horeke.
    With my kind regards to the Baroness, believe me,
                         Yours sincerely,
                                Thomas McDonnell.

"Had he been sincere," writes Charles, sadly, "the day would have been among the brightest of my life."

It was, at all events, a sensational day, all blue sky and little flags twinkling in the wind. In the brilliant morning sunshine the de Thierry settlers were landed—the largest expedition till then brought to New Zealand shores. They were pressed at the deck-rails, shouting, chattering, all in their finest feathers ; the men wearing fustian, corduroy, white moleskin trousers, and caps of skin ; the women with bonnets strangely plumed or beflowered, jackets pulled rigidly upon waists not yet escaped from the leather corset. There were hands outstretched as the Sovereign Chief, the Baroness, and the young family mounted the gangway, and many a voice cried, "God bless you!", at which Charles, for once in his life too overcome to make a speech, could only smile and wave a hand.

Then, breaking the mirror of the morning and making the women almost jump out of their petticoats, the battery before Te Horeke spoke. The hills shook, the guns roared and roared ; the ships lying at anchor, their flags brilliant tatters against the white sheet of the sky, took up the chorus. Twenty-one guns . . . the royal salute, thundered in unison by Lieutenant McDonnell's battery and by ships in the Hokianga.

It was thus that the King of Nukahiva and Sovereign Chief came into his own, thus that he was welcomed. We have had a duke or so since, one or two heirs apparent. Never another king.

How did he feel about it ? Devilish, I should imagine, until his feet were set upon earth again. There is something very reassuring about soil. It's a talisman, destroying the sense of unreality. You crumble it between your fingers, tread it lightly, knowing that it remains the same the world over. Everything goes into it, everything comes out of it. Once you have soil, you have the lot. It is the principle of the kingdom.

When one is getting on for ten years old, when one wears a white cashmere pelisse, white stockings, and a snood of white velvet beneath an almost grown-up bonnet, the fairy-tale is very real. The proud, burnished colours cannot be flicked away with a touch, a rough word. There are dragons, but merely for the convenience of the stripling princes who get their exercise and enjoyment disposing of them.

Thus Isabel, her hand tucked decorously into her papa's arm, landed like what she was. The lost Princess. One to do credit to the Brothers Grimm.

Lieutenant McDonnell, obliging as his word, pressed upon Charles the use of his upper house at Te Horeke, with storehouses as a temporary residence for the settlers. As an afterthought, he spent the afternoon trying to sell for £2000 these desirable abodes. "Not worth a quarter of the money," writes Charles, "and besides, I told Lieutenant McDonnell frankly that I had not at this time the means."

There is a good deal of awful truth in the last hint. Just what means *had* the expedition? It had faith . . . and Charles had made the most beautiful plans for disposing of the produce of his settlement to reputable merchant-houses, though it is true that he had yet to catch his settlement and grow his produce.

It may be imagined that a shipload of nearly a hundred emigrants, under the leadership of the notorious Baron, would not be taken lying down by the Hokianga settlers, especially not by those who were living on Charles's claim of 40,000 acres. Immediate attempts were made to perturb the newcomers, who were separately and collectively harangued, being assured that the Baron de Thierry had no lands at all, and had but brought them to New Zealand as sacrificial victims for the orgies of perfectly insatiable cannibals. That reminds me. I had almost forgotten Tarea. Tarea was the chieftain who, before Charles ever left Tahiti, sent word that if the Baron de Thierry ever landed in New Zealand he would both kill and eat him. They had their methods, too. One was the swallowing of eyes, supposed to give additional strength in battle. Another involved the significantly named "brain-pots". However, history gives no record of Tarea's actual performance after the landing. He was evidently in no position to make himself a pest.

Numbers of people wished to meet Charles at once. But what they all wanted, especially the missionaries, was to convince him that he would never do any good for himself, and had better go away without delay. On the day after his arrival, he was summoned to a meeting under the leadership of the Rev. Nathaniel Turner. "To persuade me that I possessed no land," Charles puts it. The fine-looking chief Nene (one of the three signatories to that famous deed) turned up. Horrors! Nene has been converted, they have baptized him by the name of Thomas Walker, and he is now known throughout the land as Tamati Waaka Nene. This in itself would not matter, but from the first it becomes plain that Nene means to please the missionaries, and that the missionaries intend to render Charles, Baron de Thierry, completely powerless to form an Independent or any other variety of State.

Charles, of course, is furious about this. Refers to Nene as "the crafty chieftain", and to the missionaries in terms as forbidding. However, Nene is actually a man of scruple, and, admitting having received a share in the purchase price of the land, he offers one of those "without prejudice" settlements to the Baron's claim.

"The distance was rather more than three miles from where we first landed, which was to be the first boundary. The farther boundary was a great *totara*-tree, on which Nene now cut the letter T. The depth of my lands was to be bounded by the horse-road, and was rather more than four miles. Under existing circumstances, I was willing to accept this, and concluded that as this point was conceded, and the sale to Mr. Kendall at least so far acknowledged, time might do more for me."

Time might, perhaps. . . . It would have been a very minute kingdom, set upon twelve square miles, grimly wooded, deep of ravine, and with no knowing what might befall the

settlers should they poach beyond the giant *totara* marked
"T". But, for a few days, the Sovereign Chief rode or
strode about his Utopia with the air of a Napoleon. He
picked up an interpreter, little Ted Davis, and continually
made speeches to the Maoris, exalting his own aims, and
the unsuspected possibilities of the Maori character.

This concentration on virtue . . . one can have too much
of it in the long run. It is not comfortable. One might have
known that sooner or later it would get him into bad odour
with the multitude, and it did.

Lieutenant Thomas McDonnell commenced to bribe the
emigrants. His bribe came out of bottles.

"The ex-Assistant British Resident," Charles writes,
"told my emigrants that they should get a pint of wine a day . . .
and that he would bestow this on them if they would desert
me."

Lieutenant McDonnell, of course, had two motives—
self-interest and patriotism. He himself was established on
part of the land-claims. Again, while Charles could produce
ninety-three settlers at his back, and no end of talk concerning
the excellent business prospects for their produce overseas,
he remained the nucleus of a power in the land. Other
white men, not all of them satisfied with the Hokianga's condition, might have been attracted. Most serious of all, he
might have obtained considerable influence over some strong
native tribe, as Thomas Kendall had once possessed with
Shunghie.

Mr. Hargreaves, Keeper of the Stores, turns out to be the
leader of the rebellious faction among the emigrants. It is
represented to them that Nene's land-grant is precarious,
and that, in all probability, once committed to that isolated
region, they will find their throats slit, their wives and daughters
ravished or devoured—or both—by the natives. Offers of
secure employment at the highest rates are made by Lieutenant
McDonnell, who, incidentally, forgot all that with bland
disregard, once the damage to the expedition was done.

Meanwhile, the Sovereign Chief is out riding in the Long
Bush, and falling in love with his first *tui* . . . that very same
bird whose morning song and seemly little bib and tucker
of white feathers, spotless against glossy black chest, did not

prevent Captain Cook from putting him in a pie. Permitted to give his concert uninterrupted, the *tui* can speak as one musician to another. His instrument is a peal of silvery bells, compassing the best part of an octave, then starting again from the other end. He is also a famous mimic, and can imitate a running stream, or a benighted native woman scolding her husband. Charles is infatuated. He comes back to Te Horeke, covered with grime and leaf-mould, but talking about his enchanted kingdom. Until . . .

In the dusk, a moon like a gipsy's fire, smouldering over the edge of Te Horeke's hill, as they rein in at the bridle-track. The boughs of the ragged, lean *manuka*-trees, edged with that light, crackle in a crisp fire. Only one window of the upper house remains lighted ; there is a barricade placed against the inside of the front door.

What is all this ? An attack by cannibals ? Charles, green about the gills, rattles the door and shouts. It is opened. The company are discovered weeping in the kitchen, with the exception of Margaret Neilsen, who, armed with a poker, snorts terribly, and between snorts ejaculates, "Fine goings-on !"

The emigrants have finally decided to desert. This, however, is not the limit of human baseness. With a very few exceptions, the emigrants are mad drunk. (Who supplied them with the liquor ? Ask the ex-Assistant British Resident.) Already shouting insults, they have swarmed around the house half the afternoon, led by Mr. Hargreaves, Keeper of the Stores. Those stores present the problem of the moment. The emigrants' idea is to broach and plunder them. Lieutenant McDonnell has filled them with a sense that they are wronged men. Charles shouldn't have brought them here, to be eaten by the cannibals. Or, if they have not yet been eaten, it is only because the cannibals have lacked time and space. Again, have they been given a pint of wine a day ? These and other notions, which will instantly be recognized as the very ones that from time immemorial have placed kings and generals in a fix, have been so firmly implanted in their heads that it is doubtful whether they will ever again be eradicated . . . certainly not until the emigrants have sobered up. The question remains : are they to be allowed to broach the stores and leave the remnants of the expedition absolutely without resources ? Or shall we resist them ?

Everyone, from Margaret with her poker to the sons of the family, cried, "Resist them !" Little Ted Davis remained loyal, and offered himself as intermediary between the besieged and the rebels. Charles was positive that among the ninety-three must remain at least a few uncorrupted.

The situation became picturesque. Subduing the Boadicea tendencies of the Faithful Nurse, and quieting the fears of the Baroness, Charles commanded the whole family to retreat to a back bedroom, the door of which he barricaded with a couple of tables. Then, in majestic loneliness, he took out a pair of pistols that had travelled with him since his Paris days. There were two double-barrelled fowling-pieces in his luggage. He loaded each barrel with two balls, laid them on the table beside the pistols, and sat facing the door. Faintly he could hear the shouts and songs of the revolutionary party. However, nobody came ; something of an anti-climax. His head started to nod as he sat with eyes fixed on the bright barrels of the guns. . . .

Faces and pictures flickered through the shadows. Fowling-pieces . . . he remembered giving Shunghie and Waikato a gun apiece, the barrels engraved with their names and his own, on plates of silver, just before the chieftains left Cambridge. Guns, that is what the native thanks you for . . . or axes ; they will give anything for axes. But were thirty-six axes paid, or only twenty-four, and could it be true that these were of an inferior make, turned out by a Hokianga blacksmith ? He must speak to Thomas Kendall about this. . . '. But Kendall came swimming heavily now into sight, his body a whitish mass, revolving slowly in the purple and green caverns of shadow. As it turned face upwards (ah, that destroyed face, where the brown eyes had shone so brightly !), the lips moved stiffly, and said, "Yes, but in Sydney Shunghie sold it all for muskets and powder. . . . He should have remembered to wear the King's armour, poor fool. Once a native acquires a superstition, he lives by it, my dear Baron. And I spent my share on an estate ; but it is greener here under the sea. You are wrong, I paid thirty-six axes. If I remembered, I could tell you the names of the men who received them. . . ."

"Children of Marion, Children of Marion. . . . You are a pirate and a thief, sir, and have stolen this unfortunate gentleman's name together with his papers. But Sir Richard Bourke won't allow that, Captain Fitzroy; I am told he is most gentlemanlike and polite. At the Congress of Vienna, where the Marquis of Marialva was as a father to me . . . My God, Moerenhaut, did you see the face of that tall priest . . . ? 'I have only to tell you, Baron, that the guns of Te Horeke are commanded by a high eminence at the rear, and you will know what to do. . . . You will know what to do. . . .'"

A yellow spear of light thrust under the door-sill. Reality hardened in outline. The morning was young, the shouting still far away. Margaret Neilsen brought him coffee, and he noticed, with momentary absorption, that a large portion of her brown bun of hair had consisted of a switch, which she had forgotten to restore to its position. However, there was no time for speculation. Quite suddenly the shouts increased, thick and large, like bodies in a crowd.

"Pull him out! Pull him out!" Little Ted Davis went down the hill under a flag of truce and announced the Sovereign Chief's decisions. He would receive a deputation if the deputation promised to behave. Otherwise, he would defend family, honour, dignity, the whole concern with his fowling-pieces and pistols. He reminded them that he was an excellent shot. By this time he was feeling more in the vein, a flash of excitement which would pass as soon as the cold truth of the expedition's failure leaked into his heart. Nothing, he says, could have given him greater pleasure than to pepper the retreating behinds of the blackguards. But that was the question; would they retreat? He had the women to consider. . . .

The mob, incensed by the idea of sending a deputation, or in any way handling things on a basis of respectability, approached until right beneath his balcony, and then howled continuously. Unable either as musician or as gentleman to stand another moment of it, the Sovereign Chief emerged, and stood on the balcony, arms folded.

Unwilling men, he said, were useless; pretended loyalty worse. He endeavoured to make a speech restoring their faith and courage. It was hopeless. Most of them were still full of bad liquor and worse morality.

If they wished to go, he said, then let them break their articles of agreement and be free.

At the end he found that he was not quite alone. Of the settlers, Ted Davis and his family, William Southerland, Richard Dwyer, Robert Mowbray, Matthew McCrea, William and Charles Lee, William McCready and his wife, and, after much hesitation, a tall, red-headed fellow named Thomas Kearney, stepped forward to join him. ("Amid the howls and execrations of the rest," says Charles.) Dr. Cooke stood at his side one moment, but a determined hand grasped the young surgeon's coat-tails. Charles looked down into the far from visionary countenance of Mr. Hargreaves, his surgeon's father-in-law.

"I bring a surgeon, whose duty it will be to afford gratuitous attention to the poor of either colour. . . . I bring with me also a gentleman of high classical attainments," thought Charles.

Dr. Cooke said, "I'm sorry, Baron"; and so, with that large brown paw drawing him back to respectability, disappeared for ever from the chronicles of Utopia.

The stores, at all events, were safe for the moment. After debate as to whether they should attack or not, the deserters decided to make off over the hills to Kororareka, the main settlement of the Bay of Islands, where they were promised employment. Thus, straggling through the *manuka*, passing frankly anti-Royalist comments and singing bawdy ballads, fades away the largest organized white colony which had up to that date arrived in New Zealand.

The next thing was to get out of the fateful clutches of McDonnell, which Charles did without delay. "Leaving," he says, "the baser materials of the expedition to the contempt of posterity."

While half the party stayed behind to care for the women, the rest of the settlers, with Charles and his two eldest sons in command, went up the river that same day by canoe to his farther boundary, the *totara* marked with Nene's "T". Here he supervised the building of a fair-sized wattle-and-daub house . . . refuge, palace, whichever you please. The natives appeared most friendly. Brown lads slipped in from the trees to lend a hand. Negro-head tobacco and thick, milkless tea was doled out in the heat of the day, and magnificent teeth flashed in thanks. Charles discovered, however, that the natives had already a name for him. "Pokeno", they called him, "Te Pokeno". He requested a translation from Ted Davis, who squirmed and looked embarrassed. Charles insisted.

It meant "The Pretender". Nene started it. . . .

Well, after all, they did the same thing in England to Charles Edward Stuart. If every pretender had his rights today . . . Nevertheless, coming on top of the rest, it smarts a trifle. But something suddenly happens which does quite a lot for Te Pokeno's failing popularity. There is an attempted assassination.

Just in time, somebody shouted a warning. Charles leapt like a buck, and Thomas Kearney's axe crashed down on the spot where his head had been a moment before.

To acquire the prestige of a martyr without the resultant inconvenience . . . it couldn't have happened at a more opportune time. The loyalists, roused to fury, kick the rebel out of camp. The natives, with no small enthusiasm, offer to pursue him and knife him as he goes down the trail. Charles refuses . . . you can imagine with what a benevolent air. The whole atmosphere is cleared. Several native houses, flax-thatched, nothing much wrong with them barring appalling ventilation and a preponderance of active-bodied fleas, are purchased for the temporary use of the settlers.

The goods from the *Nimrod* were stowed next day—the seventh after her arrival—in boats and canoes. They left the house at Te Horeke, with no sign either of Lieutenant McDonnell or the runaway settlers, as they filed past the battery which had volunteered the royal salute. "And that night, we slept in our wild habitation."

All the night was disturbed by the quaint, flurried voices of animals . . . bawling goats, pigs, and poultry, landed from the *Nimrod* and driven overland by excited Maoris. The morning of November 12th commenced with *élan*, the sky transparent as a vast bubble, the wattle-and-daub house sprawling like a child's castle, pieced together for some earnest little game.

Below lay deeply wooded valleys, misty with the rising blue smoke of many streams.

Over the breakfast-table ("Thanking Providence, the hens lay here as elsewhere," was Margaret's greeting) the family were very mysterious. The coffee, ground fresh in the little steel mill which was the boon companion of their travels, comforted his nose with an Arabian redolence. But they weren't willing that he should linger over breakfast that day.

"Come outside, Papa. There's something to show you."

They had chosen a sapling, slim as the mast of some baby Argo. Against the blue sky shone out the rising colours. The silken de Thierry flag, brought from the *Nimrod*, curled slowly to the top of the flagstaff, then took the wind and flapped free. The settlers, discreetly arranged in a half-circle, threw up their caps and cheered.

What could a Sovereign Chief do? Felt his eyes tingle, of course; congratulated everybody, male or female, on loyalty, and passed within his heart the most splendid resolutions. He christened the new habitation Mount Isabel, which might have been expected from the first.

The world said, in this little game of consequences, that the flag wouldn't last a week. Actually, its crimson and azure continued to disport themselves in the breeze for years. And, much later, the flag again played a dramatic part, though an obscure one, in history.

As for the maiden now married to a mountain, she, with dark eyes solemn, watched the morning paint great ruffled flowers of shade on the valleys of her remarkable kingdom, which was not at all what she had expected. It was perhaps a drawback that there were no other children to play with, since she had acquired in Sydney a rose-patterned tea-set, and dearly liked pouring out tea for the dolls of the other young ladies. However, perhaps there would be brown playfellows, like the almost naked little boy who had presented her with a *paua* shell at Mr. McDonnell's house. For the rest, there were the compensations of the family circle, presided over by Papa.

CHAPTER THIRTEEN

FIAT JUSTITIA

ON the whole, I think that, with the exception of the little Nukahivan epic, this next step shows more real flair than anything else he had done. To be sure, the Court-room wasn't much—a good-sized barn, haunted in summer weather by that strong stench of dried shark and eel which is the poignant result of gathering too many natives together into an enclosed space.

There, in December 1837, himself seated on the Bench with a violet gown draped over his shoulders, Charles presided at the first trial by jury ever held in New Zealand. His jurymen consisted of four white settlers and four leading lights among the natives, all as respectable as he could possibly get, and all pledged to meet fortnightly for the trial of minor crimes ; once monthly, in Supreme Court, for consideration of major errors. All the natives from miles around, sweating under their best blankets, came to look on. So did the white settlers, most of them with a forbidding look in their eye. What did that matter ? Justice, my girl, off with those bandages and mufflers !

You will remember that in New Zealand there was no such thing as law. Mr. Busby pursued the tail-lights of vanishing British criminals and homicidal maniacs, club-law kings bullied and swaggered. Where many another marooned monarch would have been down in the taverns, weeping himself maudlin on the bosom of any low fellow agreeable to listen to him, Charles preferred to act as bear-leader to Justice herself.

You may be a little disappointed in the criminal. A native, caught stealing twenty bars of soap . . . one can't make much of an impression with that. But it was better to begin with small offences. The Maoris were very impulsive. Charles didn't want to get them into the way of hanging one another for every little thing. On the other hand, if his Court took their fancy, it was hard to see how his worst enemies could deny him a step in the proper direction. The first man to introduce trial by jury, and with whites and natives on a footing of equality . . . surely that was a feather in a king's cap ?

Gravely His Honour—the prisoner at the bar having been found guilty—sentences him to the punishment of working three weeks without payment on the construction of public roads ; and further declares that he shall be known hereafter as "Soap-Stealer". Little Ted Davis interprets with religious zeal. The mahogany faces of the jurors break into toothy grins. After the trial His Honour whisks his violet gown from the Bench, and shakes hands with his jurymen, tall and imposing in their blankets. The inevitable fig of negro-head is doled out among the natives. Maori *rangatira*, quite impressed, promise that in future jury trial shall be observed at stated intervals for all manner of transgressions : grand and petty larceny, breaking and entering, sabotage, arson, rapine, seduction, disregard for property, intemperance and riot, murder, armed revolution, high treason, fracture of by-laws—when the King has made them. . . .

A track runs from the Court-room, uphill to the house, down to the waterfront, through that part of the de Thierry estates which is known as the Long Bush. It is still a shiny little track, with no depth of wear to its raw surface. On either side hang the yellow grasses, brown fern, and scrubby bushes. One can see how it could be as easily wiped out as an old promise, leaving no trace.

It is hard, all the same (watching the Sovereign Chief remove the judicial gown from his shoulders) to believe that a man could do so much and leave standing so little.

· · · · ·

Manuka, its slender stakes and pungent little leaves thick-massed for fencing, had been cut into great piles, bound together with flax lashings for stockades, enclosing the main residence and the settlers' huts. The slim naked slips of thousands of fruit-trees, as disconsolate as small girls caught out of their petticoats, showed on the slope behind the house. The men had put plough to the soil, and already several acres were broken up and dressed, ready to take wheat and potatoes in season. The womenfolk were busy over a flower-patch, where dozens of seed-packets, optimistically labelled with the high names and titles of pansies, double balsam, wax-lilies, and gillyflowers, had been introduced to their new soil.

The house was built in straggling formation, with a central blockhouse, where valuables and the comfortable furniture brought over from Sydney were installed—His Majesty's State Apartments—and on either side a boarded wing ; one for stores, kitchen, and dairy purposes ; one where the boys had their sleeping-quarters. For the present Charles shared these rougher quarters with his sons, leaving the centre block for the women. The east wing faced the path most readily accessible from the valleys, and, after nightfall, was not a restful place. Moths, attracted by tales of those stores brought over from Sydney, continued to flutter around its window-panes. A number of the deserters, finding Lieutenant McDonnell's promises of employment more comprehensive before than after their exit, had taken to the bush as outlaws, and were perpetually requiring, after dusk, to be scared off with charges of buckshot.

The central house, however, was comfortable. Cases of books ; the writing-desk, of beautifully grained teak ; Emily's American rocking-chair, like a portly throne on the verandah, where, as she hoped, rambling roses would make a pretty canopy in a year's time. On the little round table, close at hand, always waited the long frosted glasses, filled with Margaret's inevitable lemonade. That lemonade ! . . . The grimaces with which it was received by some of the stout villains used to burning their gizzards out with rum and arrack ! As soon as Charles could manage it, there was to be a piano again. Meanwhile, they contented themselves with the gilt Irish harp, whose music was soft and cool enough . . . water-nymph music, in these hot evenings, when the arguments of the day seemed suddenly as overwhelming as a landslide, everything booming together in slippery confusion. . . .

> Music . . . that gentlier on the spirit lies
> Than tired eyelids upon tired eyes.

The young man Shelley had written that. He had known what it is to be weary, though he was beloved of the gods, and died very young.

As regards the white settlers, the King of Mount Isabel's castle made small progress. One suspects that he argued too much. Here and there he won a friend by sheer persistence. A tough old fire-eater of the name of Jellico lived just beyond his boundaries, and had gone about breathing threatenings and slaughter, swearing that if this Baron, begad, trespassed upon his properties, then he, begad, would let him have a charge of shot in the pantaloons. This was too much for the dignity of the Sovereign Chief. Over the boundaries he strode, head in the air. He discovered Mr. Jellico, fortunately unarmed at the time. They conversed together. In the end, they shook hands like long-lost brothers, and Mr. Jellico came home to supper.

In Sydney, the newspapers continued to take an interest in the movements of the Baron de Thierry . . . some, of course, declared they were not movements, but machinations. These Charles ignored, but with the friendly he was delighted to unbosom himself. The teak writing-desk comes into play. On December 17th, for milords of the *Sydney Gazette*, was concluded the first letter to the outer world from Mount Isabel.

The Wesleyan missionaries had purchased a portion of my lands over me, and Mr. Russell and Mr. White had also purchased, in full knowledge of my previous claims. . . . Nene (now called Thomas Walker) at length agreed to give me possession of a district, part of which had been repurchased by Captain Young, who acceded to the arrangement on condition of receiving £100 to withdraw his pretensions.

(This, by the way, Charles, not having the cash in his pockets at the time, paid off in negro-head tobacco, a fact out of which the historians have had some fun. But no doubt Captain Young turned his profit.)

In my absence from Mr. McDonnell's place, he began the most diabolical tissue of false representations, and seduced the greater part of my emigrants from me. He offered to find them in provisions for twelve months, to build them good residences, to give them lands and furnish them with oxen to plough them. . . . Each individual was to have repaid me his passage money and that of his wife and children if he left my employ before the expiration of twelve months, but McDonnell told them that they might snap their fingers at me, for there was no law in New Zealand. He employed my boat-builder to repair his boats, my painter in repainting his long-boats, my tailor in making clothes, and without permission or compunction appropriated to his service all those I had brought at such heavy cost for my own. . . . Thanks to this plausible man, I have been left without carpenters to build my houses, without blacksmiths to work the iron I had brought with me, and am reduced to the necessity of employing my farming men as carpenters. McDonnell's aim was the frustration of my expedition, but he has failed. I have a few men remaining who are faithful, and have already gained the confidence and affection of the natives, whom I treat in all respects as white men. I have a sufficiency of labourers. My white farming men have already broken up and dressed several acres, ready now to receive corn and potatoes. I have cleared a road upwards of a mile long, and have made other smaller roads. We have a house and outbuildings. I have sunk a deep well, and given to this previously wild place an appearance of civilization. . . .

Good as my opinion has always been of the New Zealanders, it is greatly improved by a closer connection with them. They are mere children, it is true, but they are gifted with kind and friendly feelings and I find them both intelligent and trustworthy, and that they are willing to work cannot be better illustrated than by the great portion of labour which in a few weeks has been done on this place.

The greatest bar to their improvement is the blanket, which they prefer to other garments because they are poor and unprotected, and it serves them for clothing by day and covering by night. If properly paid and receiving a fair remuneration for their labours, they would soon be supplied with coverings for the night, and proper clothing for their persons. It is their incessant aim, and I find that those who possess a few articles of dress wear them until they no longer hold together. . . .

The country abounds with natural resources. The timber is magnificent, and I am surrounded by thousands of acres ready for the plough. On my own lands, I have shell for lime, abundance of fine timber, stone enough to erect houses for centuries to come, fine gravel for roads, river sand for mortar, clay for bricks and earthenware, potters' clay, abundance of clear and delicious water. . . .

Crusoe signed his long letter *Charles, Baron de Thierry, Sovereign Chief.* The "King of Nukahiva" could keep for the moment.

Gloaming drew on, a veil of gossamer over the valleys. Below, like the lances of an army, rose trees strangely turbaned and tufted with great bushes of parasites, some burning-flowered, some lolling out green tongues.

All Canaan there ; queer, dark Canaan, difficult of understanding to any white man. Some of the Maoris delighted in pointing out the exact districts that should, under the original deed, have been his own. But now, as dusk spread softly into the crevices of that deep-cut world, vapour thickened until it streamed densely as an aquamarine fluid, he had a picture of encampments in other virgin forests.

Here were camps springing mushroom-like, and strange men in leather and steel rested among them. He knew that the words shouted by one and another were in the Latin tongue, and that the inky darkness spreading north was the woodland of Gaul . . . forests to subdue and colonize. Where they passed, a presence stayed behind them ; Rome, the unconquerable.

There were rough log-cabins, their interiors glowing with the sappy fires of green spruce, maple, and hickory. The skins of deer and black bear sprawled on the floors. Long-legged, taciturn men smoked their great corncob pipes here, stretching their limbs in firelight. He saw the settlers of the Canadian and North American wilds, the pioneers, whose valour had touched his imagination often enough in childhood.

Now a last green cloud swam in the blackness. That was a lake in the desert, a mirage lake, and the bewildered caravans would never find it. Those men had set out to find a legendary city. (Many names, many names has she borne since the beginning of time.) There was a story of old and half-forgotten beauty somewhere beyond the dunes, of loveliness struggling, pitiful and deserted, against the inroads of the tiny sands. But to that city would the seekers never come, and the green lake would shimmer and die away, and an unfriendly sun shine in fierce pride and anger over their bones, distinguishing not between seeker and injurious conqueror, between dreamer and blind braggart. Useless,

useless. . . . Yet God knows whether it is ever useless to seek and to be lost.

"From Mount Isabel I could view almost the whole of the lands that should have been my own. I could not behold these broad, wild-looking acres without a deep and heartfelt regret that I could not bring to them the air of comfort and civilization which I had planned for wherever my authority should extend. . . . The chiefs from distant parts came to me for advice, and made me offers of vast tracts of land, which I might have secured but for my unfortunate paucity of means. The six months which first elapsed after my arrival had placed me in so favourable a position as to make it certain that if money should arrive, as I still expected it would, I might in little time have become possessed of a power which very little effort would have consolidated."

Poor Charles ! . . . Put your trust in princes, if you must ; they are at least capricious, and therefore subject to a decent whim like the rest of us. But to have reposed your faith in financiers !

The Maori passion for tobacco proved a terrible nuisance to the de Thierrys. (At that time, for a fig of negro-head, sixty figs going to the pound, unscrupulous whites were rooking the natives for eighty-pound kits of *kumaras*, the Maori sweet potato.) A wretch from a passing schooner got hold of a chief in the district, persuaded him to pay heavily for three sacks of "tobacco seed". Three valleys were assiduously planted by the natives, and, as the infernal luck would have it, one bordered on Mount Isabel. Springtime, up came the plant, leagues of it . . . not tobacco, but rank dock. To get rid of it meant burning acres of timber. What would you say to a fellow like that sea-captain ? And the trouble is that sort don't even know that they are dogs. If you asked them they would admit that they found themselves very amusing.

In Kororareka, Benjamin Spar, old sailor, ship-owner, and proud possessor also of a celebrated grog-shop and native brothel, sat down and with many oaths and misspellings wrote a letter threatening to make war over the Baron de Thierry's bones. Charles says he most likely wrote it in a fit of the horrors. At home, what with deserters and the satellites of the opposition, things remain in a state to make one jump. Margaret Neilsen develops a periodic *crise de nerfs*, when, unless she is propped in an arm-chair and comforted, she goes about all day long with a vinegar poultice over the jumping tic in her cheek. Our Charles sleeps—so he says—with an open keg of gunpowder under his bed, and a pistol beneath the pillow. How lucky that he was a non-smoker! Nevertheless, one wonders whether the Baroness would not have preferred the risk of marauders to that of being blown up. There's an open-air shooting-gallery behind the house, and Charles writes, in his naïve way, "As none of the natives could equal what I could do with a pistol, it was easy to make an impression."

The brown sheep of the fold are not only the most interesting, but the most affable. Mount Isabel becomes a Maori meeting-place. In summer evenings, with the cleared ring of hill-top smouldering under moonlight crisp as a fern-fire, one goes out to find a circle of squatting natives around the flagstaff. (A flag in its own right has enormous *mana** among the Maori people.) Charles, as a conversationalist and *raconteur*, is not bad, but he can't equal the gesticulations and fire of the Maori orator. The chiefs have so prodigious a vehemence, so fine an impartiality. One grey-haired man, tears in his eyes, describes Charles as his father, protector, and king. Up leaps another, flourishing his feather-tufted spear, and with extraordinary force denounces Charles as an invader. Both accept the inevitable negro-head tobacco afterwards without the faintest show of ill-feeling.

What does one know, in actual fact, about the dark races of the world? A number of generalizations; about the Maori (though there are excellent books on the subject, few of them read), little or nothing. It is said that the race is picturesque. Anyone with a conscience must sooner or later develop a dread of that word.

Thus, when a distinguished visitor to New Zealand today asks for particulars about the Maori race, the odds are ten to one that he will get an oration. The Maoris will be superlative in valour, poesy, beauty, loyalty, wit, and insensate adoration for the *pakeha's* ways and works. Nobody offers a hint

---

*Prestige.

of criticism. The distinguished visitor may later be surprised that he sees so little of the race, or that those whom he does meet often live in habitations both wretched and slovenly.

Always these encomiums ; they are a surface of glass, firm, slippery and chill, distorting everything. But apart from the habit of intemperate praise, the white man contributes very little to the Maori race of today. There are a few authors and old-timers, a few surveyors and station-owners, who have a genuine knowledge of and regard for the people they are talking about. But in the seats of the mighty there are few who can call themselves the Maoris' devoted and practical-minded friends.

What were they really like ? What were the essentials in their little manual ?

For the most part, in youth, everyone agrees that they were good to look upon ; at their best, kingly. A tall race, the hair ranging in colour from the red of some districts to the shining black of the north ; sometimes with thin, chiselled features, sometimes much thicker of lip and nostril. In the north, the most feared and warlike tribe were the Ngapuhis, living up beyond the great forests of *kauri*-trees, and led once by Shunghie in battle. The remnants of them live on like ghosts.

The blue tattooing covering the lips and chin of women, the full face of the male, was used only on the features of persons of high rank. It was not a disfigurement, but an added distinction. And these tall people, especially the men, were capable of growing old with a dignity which still looks darkly out from the paint of a few ancient portraits. They wore pieces of *mako* tooth in the lobe of the ear, or greenstone carved into queer little amulets, some of which, the *hei-tikis*, were in the shape of the human embryo, and a potent charm against the spirits of stillborn children.

They were superstitious, cunning, terrible in revenge, holding it just to wipe out a whole tribe as payment for a single death ; patience itself, in waiting their opportunity for this revenge, or *utu* ; impressionable to the point of being fickle ; capable not only of great fortitude, but of acts of chivalry which no white race could better.

They respected their word when it was given to an honest

man. But they had a shrewd instinct for the cheat ; once having detected him, they stung him like a swarm of mosquitoes. Early New Zealand history resounds with the bellowings of white biters bit.

For a long time they did not seem to take the *pakeha* overlordship of the land very seriously. They liked the rum and arrack, the white man's weapons, the rough fellowship of the sailing-ships. But one feels that many of them had a strong idea that all this would vanish away as suddenly as it began. They traded their lands, parting with them, as it were, only for the moment.

In these land-bargains, whites found them most unscrupulous. Great was the roaring of gentlemen who bought enormous holdings for nothing, receiving, duly, the deed adorned with the vendor's *"moko"*, the tattooing upon his buttock. Unluckily, scores and scores of exactly similar deeds, adorned with exactly similar *mokos*, might be furnished by the owner of the same brown and brazen buttock. Discovering their plight, the white buyers would comb the length and breadth of the land for their beguilers, but Buttock had gone a-hunting.

Sometimes it was worse than that. Land might be sold to the one person, the deed sweetly water-tight. Immediately then, up would pop the heads of scores of others who claimed to possess a share in the land, and wanted a purchase-price themselves. If the chief vendor went about a bargain with a white buyer properly, he could conciliate the tribe and see to it that the ground was clear for its new tenants. This, however, he frequently omitted to do. My own theory is that he got a good deal of innocent pleasure watching them fight it out. The classic example is that quoted by F. E. Maning, when everything on a land-transfer was held up because an important Maori claimed that the land belonged to his ancestor. But, as it turned out, the ancestor was a large green lizard, said to have lived in a cave on the property.

In business, then, 'ware land-sales . . . as Charles had already discovered to his sorrow. In the Arts, about the time when John Keats was dying like a rat, the Maoris were maintaining tribal poets and poetesses of distinction as something between fetishes and pets. Far from there being any snobbish prejudice against authorship, great chieftains themselves—

Te Rauparaha, for instance—composed famous and bloody-minded epics.

There was no written language, but an amazing and priest-taught skill in memorizing history, legend, and poesy. There were musical instruments, some carved from the thigh-bones of gentlemen who had previously been disposed of by way of the cannibal oven. There was double value in this idea ; firstly, the practical Maoris were getting the use of the bone article, and secondly, they were dealing a terrible insult to the relatives and friends of the person eaten. They made a business of insulting one another, like the Scottish clansmen, who are, indeed, their nearest white analogy.

Cannibalism, when the de Thierrys arrived, was at a much less forbidding strength than during Shunghie's wars a few years before. It was still practised in isolated cases, and on various warlike pretexts rose to popularity now and again. Nevertheless, that impressionable and sensitive regard of the Maoris for the white man's custom was forcing the cannibal feast into disgrace and desuetude. Less than ten years after Charles landed in New Zealand, a young chief named Hone Heke had a little war on in the north. The Maoris were successful in one encounter with the whites, and after the affray the body of an English captain was found to have disappeared completely. Instantly the papers—the colony then sported two regular papers—raised a terrific howl of cannibalism. A few days later the captain's body was found where the Maoris had buried it, with all honour and dignity. The newspapers observed a journalistic maxim of today: "Never apologize. Never explain."

The influence of white man over brown has always been boundless. Those tall savages at Mount Isabel, curling up in their red blankets and pining for waistcoats and breeches *à la mode* . . . they have, today, a parallel in the little island of Puka-Puka. It is very touching. You won't believe a word of it, but that makes it none the less true.

Puka-Puka achieved two things: pants and cricket. When the depression came, the tiny export trade, which, after all, was nothing but bananas and coconuts, dwindled away. The natives wore their European clothes until, piece by piece, the rags fell from their backs. . . .

That was the end of the cricketing fixtures. The Puka-Puka islanders were not merely naked, but ashamed. They mourned their condition more sonorously than did Adam, led by the ear out of Paradise.

Happily, the island mind soon forgets. The sunshine continued to glow, beneficent, unperturbed, in that little isle whose bananas the great world would not buy. Arriving at Puka-Puka a year ago, a white voyager who knows the locale found them merrily pitching the leather up the crease again, their old straw mats back in place, bronze nudity disporting itself everywhere. The scene, he says, was one of an idyllic charm. Puka-Puka had gone back to Nature. What a good thing nobody would buy those wretched bananas!

Among the Maoris, unfortunately, such a consummation was impossible. Their beautiful mats, flax, feather, and dog-skin, went to the moth and the museum. They had blankets; and they coveted breeches, which in the end brought them nothing but trouble.

Shunghie had left behind him a mighty tradition. One day to Mount Isabel came two young chieftains, his sons. Learning that Charles possessed their father's famous battle-mere, they begged for a sight of it. Charles brought out the exquisitely polished weapon, its stone smooth as jade, but of darker green. He had an immediate instance of the reverence in which such relics were held. Shunghie's sons dissolved into tears and prolonged lamentations. An old man, near-blind, near-naked, a *tohunga* of their tribe, fingered the greenstone softly, and raised his shrivelled hands as if in blessing, repeating the weapon's sacred names. That night great flax-kits of *kumaras* and fresh fish were left outside the door. Ten years later, Shunghie's sons approached Charles and begged to be allowed to purchase the mere. "Of course I gave it to them," writes Charles, who at that time was in a state of bewilderment as to where his next week's rent could be coming from.

In the house at night, an oil-lamp, a mere tin pannikin, its contents bubbling and sizzling like a witch's cauldron, shared the honours with that oddest of their possessions, the little Sèvres nymph. Her tiny porcelain breasts rose from their fichu of pale chiffon. The light of the candles held in her raised hands had flickered in the New York room where Isabel was born. Now they lighted a besieged peace in the wilderness. The damsel, nevertheless, maintained her porcelain air of remoteness. She was born to it.

A native who drifted in one day for tobacco brought with him a great flaxen kit of provisions. (The Maori way of cooking is fascinating. Earth-ovens are scooped out and lined with red-hot stones, over which green fern is layered. Your wild pigeon (*kuku*), pork, or sweet *kumara*, beds itself on the fern ; flax matting is drawn over the whole, and dinner steams slowly and deliciously.)

Richard and George de Thierry—Richard now seventeen, his brother two years younger—went exploring in the kit. Later, their father discovered them lying green-faced among the *manuka*, overwhelmed by violent fits of retching.

Inside the kit were the hacked and bloody arms and breasts of a native woman. The Maori, when Charles remonstrated with him, seemed to have no understanding of the rebuke. Charles stared at the phlegmatic brown face. It did not look particularly repulsive, brutal, or bloodthirsty. Customs of a country. . . . "What a farce it is," he thought, "to teach psalms and texts to these men ! Civilization . . . what they need first is civilization."

The boys hung together like a brace of young gun-dogs. Cannibalism is not a topic to be discussed at table, with white women living under the dubious protection of under twenty settlers, and savages on every hand. But there was a little crusade established between them.

On a day when they had been out shooting pigeons in the Long Bush, they came on a shouting mob of natives down at Herd's Point. (Named after that same old Captain Herd of the ship *Providence*, mentioned in Charles's famous deed.) The man tied at the stake, whilst native women prepared green fern and stones, they recognized as a Maori who had visited Mount Isabel.

There are fairy-tales, many of them so obviously for children that you laugh at them, and don't turn a hair going down the dark corridor afterwards. The guzzling witch in the cake and candy house was of that breed. There was a beautiful queen ogress, with deep red hair . . . she could be rather petrifying, because it was so easy to understand how one might be taken in by her. She was not merely like a normal person, but like a lovely and fascinating person.

The women and children, running about picking up stones and pieces of fern, were precisely the same as those who sat round the flagstaff in the evenings, and sang as though there were nothing but music inside them.

The bound man, then? There must be something extraordinary about him. Richard called to him in Maori. He was quite conscious, and muttered a few words in reply.

Richard unslung his new musket, and stepped forward, over the borderland into one of those violent, highly coloured fairy-tales. He didn't in the least know his way about, and his eyes filled with nervous tears. A tall, finely tattooed native lounged some way apart. Richard, with a desperate gesture, shoved his musket into the chief's hand, and pointed at the bound man. Everything went spinning round before his eyes. He wanted to laugh, and cry out, "Oh, stop it, Margaret, we're not babies!" But when he looked up, the face wasn't that of Margaret, who looked rather like a solemn and faithful old horse, but the face of the ogre. He couldn't understand what its lips were saying. The ogre squinted down the barrel of his gun, said tersely, "Good," and then pointed imperiously to George, who, his musket held between shaking hands, stood on the outskirts of the circle.

George said, "You're a fool," between stiff lips, as he unslung his musket and passed it over. The ogre handed Richard a sheath-knife. He stepped forward, his knees shaking, and a black mist surging before his eyes. He knelt down by the bound man, who lay still as if he were already dead. The knife took a frightful time to cut through the stiff thongs, and at any moment Richard expected the crash of axe or mere on his head. The man on the ground had little bright beads of blood pointing the ends of his fingers where the tightness of the bonds had forced the blood down and burst his skin. It was the ogre-place, and Richard, sawing with the knife, couldn't wake up.

The man stared at him with cloudy eyes. Then, as if something had looked out from behind a mist, a glance came, brightened, and passed. Richard thought, "Those were a man's eyes," and then became confused over his thought. The knots gave. He tripped over a stone in rising, and went sprawling to the ground again, spraining his ankle. He wanted badly to crook his arm over his face and cry, but dared not. George walked behind him stolidly, as they forced their way out of the circle. The women and children started to scream and chatter, in the most horrible high voices. Ogreland . . . when they had seemed to be getting on so well, when they had joined in games with the enormous Maori tops, which fly up higher than the roofs of houses. He wondered if George were terribly annoyed at losing his new musket ; and his foot throbbed.

He looked back, after a hundred yards' limping progress, along the steep way, red-carpeted with the myriad fallen stamens of the *pohutukawa*. The crowd at Herd's Point were out of sight, but the man bought with two muskets was following them, limping as sorely as Richard. Those bonds must have hurt.

Suddenly Richard's heart sang. He didn't look back again, but for the moment he felt that nobody in the world, white or native, would ever have the power to laugh at the de Thierrys again.

CHAPTER FOURTEEN

TWO AND A HALF FRENCHMEN

Now there, at least, he might have kept his coat-tails clear of the barbed wire of ambiguity. After all, his papa-in-law was the Archdeacon Thomas Rudge of Gloucester, a dignitary of the Church of England. One might really think he did it out of spite. The next thing we find is that the Sovereign Chief has embroiled himself in the first serious civil war of religion to affect New Zealand.

The occasion of the strife is Monseigneur Jean Baptiste François Pompallier, Bishop of Maronée, Vicar Apostolic of Western Oceania. (In effect, the long title means that the young Bishop is expected to make his headquarters in New Zealand, and in some unexplained manner, though not assisted by any great financial resources, to keep a fatherly eye on the unsophisticated heathen prancing on a thousand islands here and there in the Pacific.) Bishop Pompallier is provided with two junior colleagues, a priest, and a religious brother, when he arrives in New Zealand, disembarking at the Hokianga from the little schooner *Raiatea*, on January 10th, 1838. The *Raiatea* sailed again for Tahiti next day.

Since M. the Bishop and M. the Baron have never met before, there must be some reason, if one can only get at it, for the actions of the Sovereign Chief in ranging himself on a side which would not naturally be considered his own. Here are the only reasonable conclusions :

M. the Baron arranged himself beside M. the Bishop (1) because the missionaries of his own fold, the Church of England, not to mention the Dissenters, had been rude to him, snubbed him, and opposed his land-claims. (2) Much more important, because the Bishop not only belonged to France, a nation of which Charles grew ever fonder as the English became more impolite, but because he brought with him personal letters of introduction which cannot but have been flattering to a man in the Baron de Thierry's position. The English were taking no notice of him at all, unless of such a disparaging sort that he would rather they had left his name out altogether.

One must not forget reason (3). Charles was essentially chivalrous. The lonely and dangerous situation of Bishop Pompallier at this time appealed at once to his generosity. He would scarcely have left a Long-Haired Israelite or a Mormon isolated under the same conditions. In the Bishop, he met a gentleman whom he could greatly admire, and whose purposes towards the native seemed to him exemplary.

Few others in the Hokianga agreed with him. There was a mere handful of Roman Catholics. One of them, Mr. Thomas Poynton, immediately placed a ship-shape boarded house at the Bishop's service, and when the natives of tribes converted to other sects became warlike and marched on to the premises, threatening to hurl the Bishop into the river, Mr. Poynton collected his own natives and scared the first lot back again. It was like the legend of the Grand Old Duke of York, but on a miniature scale.

From the letters which Bishop Pompallier brought to Charles, one can only assume that in France there was a complete misapprehension as to the extent and powers of the Sovereign Chieftaincy. Can it be that Charles lied to them a little? I cannot see why not; after all, he needed their money.

The first letter, a friendly note, was from Bishop Polding in Sydney. France was represented in the epistle of M. de St. Hilaire, Councillor of State, Director of Colonies, who, from the French Ministry of the Navy and the Colonies, addressed himself thus:

Monsieur the Baron de Thierry,
 Sir, I deliver this letter to Monseigneur F. Pompallier, Bishop of Maronée, Vicar Apostolic for Western Oceania. Being informed that his mission will take him to New Zealand, I apprised him that he would find you in that country in a position to second his evangelical labours, and I pray you please to render to the honourable Bishop all the good offices which may depend

on you. Serving religion and a Frenchman will, I am persuaded, Sir, be a great satisfaction to you.

I can give you news of your brother, who is attached here to the Department of Foreign Affairs, at present in Paris, but on the point of departing for St. Petersburg.

I would be very happy to receive from you, Sir, some token of your remembrance. And if I could be useful to you, I would very willingly place myself at your service.

I have the honour to be, Sir,
Your most obedient servant,
de St. Hilaire,
Councillor of State,
Director of Colonies.

Fair enough; but in Mr. Thomas Poynton's house—where he called on Bishop Pompallier three days after the latter's arrival—Charles must have rubbed his chin a little, perusing the letter. That the Bishop stood in need of protection could not be questioned. But how was the Sovereign Chief to afford it? (Did I mention it? The envelope of St. Hilaire's letter bears the address "Sovereign Chief of New Zealand.")

But paramount over all disturbances, there is the delight of talking once again to a man of intellect and feeling, a gentleman and a Frenchman.

"Notwithstanding differences in religion, we have never, as yet, ceased to be friends, and when he comes to enliven my solitude, as he often does, I feel increasing admiration for the excellence of the man, whilst I must ever admire the mild, courteous, and amiable deportment, as well as the noble and truly catholic virtues of the Bishop. I have known him intimately for nineteen years, and I have not yet come to the end of his good qualities."

From this little testimonial (written in 1856), one might have supposed the Bishop would be welcomed in New Zealand with open arms. But the rivalry between religious sects was at that time perhaps more bitter in the Pacific and the Tasman Sea than anywhere else in the world. Sometimes the consequences were distinctly funny. There was the chieftain, William Repa. He was converted, in the first place, to

Wesleyanism, but Bishop Pompallier weaned him to the Roman Catholic fold. However, when Bishop Selwyn came along, he made Repa an Anglican over the heads of his former conversions. After this, Repa turned "devil", took three wives to illustrate his independence, and marched with the war-parties against the white men. Who can blame him?

The last years of the 'thirties were a most trying confusion of religion and politics in the Pacific; inevitably so, for whilst most orthodox and dissenting missionaries were English, most priests were French, with a sprinkling of Italians and Spaniards. For a time, especially in New Zealand, the missionaries tried hard to maintain native independence, less because they adored the native and wished to see him for ever free than because their autocratic leaders had entrenched themselves in a power, sometimes in a very material prosperity, which could not be maintained were the country to pass under a European sovereignty. They were the gods of the independent native principalities. But a civilized and dependent country has no gods, and even its God is confined within a limited space.

This wish for native independence could not survive the beginnings of the struggle for power in the Pacific between two great maritime powers, England and France. In the islands, priest-baiting had furnished an excuse for the arrival of French war-sloops. At the time of Pompallier's entrance, the French admiral du Petit-Thouars paid a social call on Queen Pomare of Tahiti, and fined her 2000 dollars for her treatment of the French priests driven back to Bambier Island. Rumours of similiar French *coups de foudre* were everywhere. Naturally, the English missionary became Englishman first; to his already profound dislike of Roman Catholicism was added his resistance against possible French domination. His entrenchments had better pass civilly into English possession before France grabbed them.

Nobody could say that Charles hadn't extended an open hand to the Hokianga missionaries at first. Did he not implore them to become the magistrates of his Independent State? That they, very naturally, refused to do any such thing he might have forgiven; but not their opposition to his land-claims. Doubtless he was overjoyed when Bishop

Pompallier's arrival gave him the chance to furnish them with a poke in the eye. Passing in his canoe from Mount Isabel, on that first visit to the Bishop, he was called into the little Wesleyan Mission Station at Munga-Muka. Here the Wesleyan leader, the fire-eating Rev. Mr. White, was presiding over a meeting of protest. For the first time, Charles was greeted by missionaries and settlers as a man and a brother. His voice was as good as another's, if he would but join them in protesting.

When the Baron de Thierry revealed that, despite the Archdeacon in his family, he was actually on his way to visit the Bishop, a storm broke out.

"Would I go near the Scarlet Woman ? Near the agent of the Beast of Rome ? ... I was really pained by their deep groans, and vexed by their personalities," he writes, with that exasperating superiority which did so much to get him generally disliked.

St. Hilaire, from the tone of his letter, concluded that the Sovereign Chief could put a brigantine, at the least, to watch over the Bishop. This was not to be, but Charles did what he could. A fast canoe, manned by one white settler and four Maoris, sped daily from Mount Isabel to the Bishop's residence, inquiring after his welfare. The entire garrison at Mount Isabel stood ready to render assistance if necessary.

It was not a navy or an army. But it was something.

On the third day after his visit, Charles heard that the natives were gathering, their warlike inclinations roused by pointed reminders about the Scarlet Woman and the "Children of Marion". They meant, said the runner, to throw the Bishop and his two priests into the Hokianga.

There is only one way in which the Baron can meet this sort of crisis: mounted upon his witch's broomstick, his quill pen. This time the entire household is pressed into service, copying out duplicates of the circular, which he then distributed—whether they wanted it or not—to the white residents of the district.

CIRCULAR

Being informed that an attempt is to be made by residents of the Bay of Islands and by others of this River to drive away from this Island Monseigneur F. Pompallier, Vicar Apostolic of Western Oceania, Bishop of Maronée, the Baron de Thierry appeals to their sense of justice and humanity, as well as to their best feelings as Christians, that they may pause before they commit an act which must inevitably occasion much loss of blood, and which would bring the severest punishment on the native race, who can never be suspected of such measures but at the instigation of the whites. The Baron de Thierry makes this appeal under the persuasion that all men, of all nations, have a right to worship God in their own manner. New Zealand is not a British land, and no British subject has the right to persecute the subjects of another nation whilst they live after the usages of civilized society. The Baron's right to interfere in the matter would be sufficiently founded upon principles of humanity, if a more immediate reason had not been offered in the shape of an official letter from France. . . .

And more in the same vein. Whether his circular, signed with that flourishing "Sovereign Chief of New Zealand", and sealed in black with the dear little prancing lion accepted by H.M. Customs Offices in Sydney, had any effect but to decided the settlers more finally that the Baron de Thierry was the damnedest of all damned souls, is to be doubted. Meanwhile, owing to a combination of events, the expected attack on the Bishop did not prevail, though twice the natives were heated to boiling-point.

In the first instance, Thomas Poynton's boarded house—where Bishop Pompallier had dedicated a room as chapel, and was baptizing at a steady rate every convert he could get hold of—was threatened by a hostile party, Methodists by persuasion. These natives were disarmed by the courteous refusal of the Bishop and his priests to take any notice of their threats. Then, on the banks of the Munga-Muka, the Rev. Mr. White and his natives had a brush with Thomas Poynton and his, confined to verbiage on both sides. Mr. Poynton's party being of superior strength, the battle went to him by default, as already related.

Then the Bishop himself took a hand. He was reported to be picking up Maori at record speed. At first, the results of this were disconcerting to himself, for he discovered that the long name with which he was everywhere addressed by the natives meant "Anti-Christ". The little mission press at Paihia, learning of his impending arrival, produced a printed pamphlet about him under this title. Since he himself possessed no press, he remained "Anti-Christ" for a considerable time, but did his best to wean the innocents on to "Episcopo" instead. "Pikopo" was the best their tongues could make of it.

Then he was diplomatic with the downright hostile. Those who came to execute war-dances remained to fall in love . . . perhaps not so much with the Bishop as with the Bishop's blankets. They were superb. More brilliant by far than any rainbow. Striped rosy, purple, vivid green, orange. Something to intoxicate the average Maori even more surely than the thrill of battle.

In Pompalleranian blankets, the tribes stalked through their *pas*, as vain as peacocks, and twice as harmless.

Failing in any success in their scheme to duck the Bishop, the white settlers had to find some other outlet for their annoyance. This, naturally, proved to be Charles.

From that time onwards, his position grew steadily worse. Regarding the land ceded by Nene, one Maori claimant after another popped up an insatiable head, explaining that he had a right to be consulted. Acres here, acres there, were whittled off. Of course, the settlers were putting the natives up to this game.

Then there were the depredations on his remaining estates. He would hear an axe ring among the blue-grey *kauri* trunks in the Long Bush, and know that in the heart of the forest whites and natives were felling timber which would be rafted down-stream under his very nose. His flock of goats had settled down cheerfully as Crusoe's, and the boys were chaperons to the rabble of turkey chicks, fowls, and ducklings. But there was never a night when some two-legged fox did not invade the hen-houses. White men of the baser sort helped themselves as they pleased. "And they set on the native dogs," mourns Charles, "to worry my poor goats." The Maoris had a sly humour in their sins. Many a time he would strive to see the faintest trace of remorse in some stolid brown face, as the possessor, having lugged in a stolen pig from the Long Bush, tried to sell this to Charles at his own back door. The animals themselves turned rebel. Charles had brought some fine breeding-sows from Sydney, which did their duty by their Chieftaincy, and littered; however, when kept in pens, these aristocrats raged and devoured their piglets, and when Charles released them they roamed into the Long Bush, there to be ravished and devoured.

Always in the mornings the blockhouse door would open, and, as early sunlight crept silverly across the lintel, there would appear a slight figure, dark curls loose over its dressing-gown. A sober command: "Drink this, Papa." It was admitted that Isabel's coffee was a masterpiece. The child was not domesticated . . . too much of a dreamer, though she had such a coaxing way with plants that Charles swore they put their green heads out of the ground to look at her. But his morning coffee was a solemn rite. Always, as she stood beside his sofa-bed, he would watch for her quick, anxious glance, which said, "I understand. But perhaps today will be a lucky one."

A campaign of petty persecution, of offences so small that taken individually every one of them is a joke, and the man who complains against it a mean fellow, devoid of any sense of humour; this type of stratagem is about the last suited to improve the nerves, common sense, or stability of the sensitive. The more they prodded, with their little pieces of stick, the more entertainingly he behaved, proving by his lashings of the tail, his pawings of the earth, that they had been right in treating him as a dangerous madman.

Charles began to lose his head. With him, that could mean only one thing. He talked too much . . . this time, about the handsome things the French would do for him, the moment they got wind of his treatment.

Perhaps he believed it. (How often does the persecuted child threaten his tormentors with a policeman?) At all events, he made speeches about it, lots of speeches . . . to his native friends, squatting around the flagstaff; to the white settlers when he could manage to buttonhole them. The French ships would sail up the Hokianga, their theme-song a combination of "God Save the King" and "Pop Go the British". Above all, they would restore his prestige by giving him the royal salute.

Naturally, this interested both settlers and natives. From the first, it had been their idea that the Baron was a secret emissary of France. Now, with French warships prowling at large about the coasts, the natives declared freely that the French were going to land, and force the chiefs who had withheld the debatable land-claims to hand them over.

At the time when things were at their worst on Mount Isabel, another Frenchman, just as lonely, and perhaps in greater personal danger than Charles, was placed by the intervention of a third in a position of safety.

Word came that the French corvette *L'Héroine*, captained by Cécille, stood off the northern coast, heading for the Bay of Islands.

In Sydney, Cécille had heard rumours of the Catholic Bishop's situation. It was reported that the threatened attack on the mission had been successful, obliging the Bishop to spread his sails for New South Wales. Cécille wasted no time. Leaving word in Sydney that, should the Bishop take refuge there, it would be safe for him to re-embark immediately for New Zealand, where *L'Héroine* would have cleared up his difficulties, the French captain headed for Kororareka, chief settlement of the Bay of Islands.

The approach of the corvette plunged both the de Thierry household and the Hokianga settlers into a whirlpool of speculations, doubts, and hopes.

"They're making it a test case . . . more French generals riding on dragons, or this time it might be on a sea-serpent. But, oh, Emily, if Cécille will only come!"

"Yes," she said quietly, looking from Mount Isabel's windows to the far shine of the sea below. "If only. . . ."

She went out, and the door closed almost noiselessly. Yet the sound re-echoed somewhere in his heart. Sunset was a great pavilion of royal colours, the sea below an empty blue carpet, unrolled to the feet of the glowing hills. His fancy painted it with the ship, moving under full sail.

"Why shouldn't she come?" he asked himself childishly. "Why shouldn't she come? I am a good Frenchman." France was everything now. Lieutenant McDonnell had quite cleared up his position in regard to England. Before the "ex-Assistant British Resident" had stolen away his emigrants, his papers very frequently referred to himself as an Englishman; never afterwards, though he was still inclined to flourish his long-extinct commission in the 23rd Light Dragoons under one's nose.

Meanwhile, at Cécille's invitation, Bishop Pompallier made his way overland to Kororareka, sleeping the night at Benjamin Turner's grog-shop. . . . "A wild place, frequented by savages," he wrote, years later. The Hokianga, for all its heathen ways, was milk and water compared with the activities of the Bay of Islands.

Where the waters deepened into milky jade, fortified islands thrust up their topknots, tufted bush parting over the earthworks of old Maori trenches. A few miles up the Bay, within spearshot of the mission station at Keri-Keri ("the Place of the Rumbling Waters"), stood the carved war *pa* of Hone Heke, Shunghie's nephew. The *pa* in old days was a living blood-stain, soaking into the clear waters. Under the eyes of the missionaries, whose stone blockhouse was built like a fortress, in Shunghie's time had shot in the red-ochred war-canoes, laden with bound and living captives. These were butchered for the cannibal feasts within full sight of the mission station. Girl-children grew up in houses where the blinds were always drawn, for fear of what they might see across the riband of water.

There was more than brown man's custom to reckon with in the Bay. Here captains from whalers and trading-schooners put in, drinking rum and arrack at the peak-gabled taverns, and frequenting the native brothels. Runaway 'prentice boys, bold after six weeks' clearance of the ships they had deserted, poked their noses out of their rat-holes and rubbed shoulders with unkempt, bearded men, escaped convicts from Botany Bay and Van Diemen's Land. White grog-shops at Kororareka ran in competition with the native brothels. Handsome Maori women of middle age, their breasts swelling against the gaudy cotton bodices of striped scarlet and orange print, herded the deer-eyed, slender wilderness girls into the upper rooms pent beneath the high gables. Kororareka was a sleepless, restless town, life burning with a hot scarlet flame behind its shuttered windows.

Captain Cécille himself came ashore in the ship's long-boat to breakfast with Bishop Pompallier in the tavern parlour. The French flag flew gaily over the Bishop's head, as he left

L'Héroine after his first visit ; and as the long-boat neared shore again, the corvette's guns rattled in a military salute. Cécille, aware that the eyes of white settlers and native chiefs were watching his reception of the Catholic Bishop, was doing the thing in style.

With the fresh breeze swelling the cloud-sails on that vast blue, Bishop Pompallier relaxed for a moment the iron discipline under which he had locked away hesitation and fear. For long months, since in the Vatican the Pope had placed the episcopal ring on the finger of a young priest from Lyons, he had put childish things away.

He must be no longer a Frenchman, no longer even a human being. He, the pilgrim in a strange and pagan country, must be only the symbol of his spiritual authority. He had forced himself to seem immune from ordinary weakness. In the Wallis Islands, hostile natives had boarded the little ship on which he journeyed. He had stood side by side with a giant native determined on his murder. He had never once turned his eyes to the tomahawk brandished in that man's hands, his lips had never uttered the plea for mercy. He compelled himself to think, "This is nothing." As a man, he was helpless, unarmed, to be smashed to pieces and cast aside like a toy by these savage children. But if the tomahawk in that moment had swung, splitting his skull, spattering the deck with the human body and brain, that which dominated body and brain must still have endured. . . .

For a moment he was in France again, and could remember the voices of his mother and sisters, calling his name. A long-bearded sailor from *L'Héroine* came to him, and asked for his first Communion. Forty-eight years old, and a sailor since childhood, the man could neither read nor write. The Bishop's heart stirred at finding this simplicity after the desert of quarrelsome days.

Eighteen of the sailors on the corvette desired to make their first Communion ; others among the crew, sun-tanned fellows who had spent years afloat, came with them to the Holy Table. Bishop Pompallier gave them instruction twice a day, either aboard the ship or on shore. The few who could read painstakingly guided the others. It was a strange sight, that little knot of jerseyed men sitting on Kororareka's pale, wind-sifted sands, whilst before them shone the broken opal of the sea, and behind slanted the peaked gables of the unclean houses.

When the Bishop finally celebrated Mass aboard *L'Héroine*, there were over three hundred people present, many of them Protestants. Cécille and his officers, in full uniform, stood erect and motionless. At the Elevation of the Host, a squad of gunners knelt bare-headed, and the sound of the corvette's drum echoed along the wild shore. The sailors who had been prepared for Communion now came forward and knelt in a half-circle about the altar. The glance of their eyes, the roughness of the tanned and bearded faces, brought tears to the eyes of the man who served them.

The visit of *L'Héroine* meant a considerable improvement, in security and in prestige, for Bishop Pompallier. He busied himself with finding a place in the Bay of Islands where he might establish a central mission. For long years, an old two-storeyed house in Kororareka was to harbour him and his priests. In the meantime, the Hokianga mission moved out of Thomas Poynton's boarded house to a new refuge, a house built at Papakauwa. He took possession of this in June, his approach heralded by a salvo of musketry. The heart of the house was its little *kauri*-wood chapel, where were unfolded, for the first time since his arrival, beautiful old tapestries from the Flemish looms.

The worst days were over. In some part, they would return again . . . shortage of funds, political crises, enmity, misunderstanding. But he had his feet on the soil. Later comer than the missionaries of other creeds, he had, despite his disadvantage, planted a tree that would grow.

The last months of King Pokeno's little chieftaincy. There he sat, waiting for the help which obstinately refused to come. Every day he watched the narrowing bright blue of the Hokianga, hoping against hope that he might see *L'Héroine's* sails moving there, and knowing perfectly well that he himself was to blame for his isolation. Cécille's letters were more than courteous. They one and all addressed him with the "Sovereign Chief" in a conspicuous position. Only, as it happened, Charles had quite fatally committed himself, both with white men and natives, over that infernal royal salute.

The first French ship to arrive in New Zealand would give him the royal salute. . . . Ah, for his own part, they might take away their royal salute and bake it in a pie, if he could only sit down again at table with civilized men, after this existence ! On the other hand, was it possible to back down ?

There he sat on Mount Isabel, and the rising tide of British power swirled higher about his footstool.

"King Pokeno doesn't abdicate," said Charles, and sat on.

"The desire which you express, my dear Baron, to make known to the officers of the French Navy the beautiful river and fine country over which your sovereignty extends, that they may give an account of them to their Government, comes from a good Frenchman, and no other sentiment could have been expected from you. But I do not share with you, M. le Baron, the fear of ever seeing England take possession of this country, either by force or by stratagem. A few adventurers might ardently wish it for their own private ends, but I do not believe that the loyalty of the British Government would give way to such an enterprise against an inoffensive people. The English have already too many colonies, which enervate the Motherland, and increasing their number would not be to increase their strength. It is evident to everyone that that great power, the forces of which are scattered all over the globe, rests but on a naval engagement. The example of Spain is there to prove that. Two great maritime nations are, moreover, interested in New Zealand's remaining an independent country, and if they so will it, so it will be."

Charles writes again offering to take as settlers any sailors who do not wish to return to France. Cécille, making up from his own crew the deserters from his sister-ship, the *Ganges*, and short-handed by the loss of more men lent to a French vessel in distress on the high seas, refuses the offer.

"I am sorry, M. le Baron, that the etiquette to which your position compels you should have deprived me of the pleasure of seeing you on board *L'Héroine*, but you are too well informed of the nature of things not to know that it does not belong to one who is simply a Captain in the Navy to take the lead in what does not come within his instructions. . . . It is then with much regret, my dear Baron, that I find myself deprived of the pleasure of seeing you. However, I am returning to the Bay of Islands at the end of the season, that is to say, in August ; so I do not altogether lose the hope."

One Frenchman assists another. The example of Bishop Pompallier is there to prove it.

On the other hand, is Charles de Thierry a Frenchman ? Born in London, after all.

But, say the English, the perfect type of French agent and aggressor.

But, say the French, not our responsibility.

About half and half, then ; and furnished with no assistance from either side. One cannot blame them. Leaving the wishes of great maritime nations out of the question, Charles belonged in his heart to a remarkable little nation of one.

June is the bitterly cold month of the year, midwinter, when all the evanescent gorgeousness of *pohutukawa* and *rata* abandons the grey boughs, shivering miserably in a shroud of driving sleet. Sea, sky, and earth are all overcome by the profound discomfort of remaining alive. Never come to New Zealand in June. Neither the animals nor the people have learned how to hibernate. For another thing, the buildings are all draughty, and the inhabitants cannot be taught to build proper fire-places.

Isabel's garden showed the first pale and frantic streaks of despairing daffodils, brought from half across the world. Her moss rose, wet as a suicide from London Bridge, had just managed to survive. (Charles once wrote a poem to "Her mossy rose" ; but his poetry is so bad that one dares not quote it.)

There was little shipping in the Hokianga that month, and no more need to keep an eye on it. He had let a friend go past. No sunrise nor sunset would ever produce the white sails whose eyrie was France.

CHAPTER FIFTEEN

THERE WAS A GLORY

THE scene-shifters complain that the stage is too full, the whole thing cumbersome. "Take it from me, an empty house tomorrow night," grumbles one old gaffer, striking a match on his corduroy pants. "Yes, all those hams and heroines on together, and all talking at once. . . . What do they suppose the audience will make of that clack? We'll all be lying to our landladies the day after tomorrow, and on the roads the day after that."

"Here," says one enterprising old curmudgeon, "why can't we have a revolving stage? Sort of thing they use in the modern shows, so that you can see a million legs at once, each more ravishing than the last?"

"But," protests the author wearily, "you can't have a revolving stage, for revolving stages weren't invented in your day. Use sense, I implore. . . ."

But upon that, they all blur together, like the blue smoke-rings from a long churchwarden pipe. "Who distinguishes us, one from another? We are the years."

"Very well. For peace and pity's sake, you shall have your revolving stage. Listen, now. We are in England. This is the House of Lords."

"Hadn't you better give some idea of the cast?"

"Oh, later, later. First let us rehearse this House of Lords, and the Nanto-Bordelaise scene. It weighs on my mind, I can bear no more. Don't knock out your pipe-ashes where the audience can see them. Ring up the curtain. . . ."

"Resolved in Select Committee of the House of Lords: that it appears to this Committee that the extension of the Colonial Possessions of the Crown is a matter of public policy which belongs to Her Majesty's Government: but that it appears to this Committee that support, in whichever way it may be deemed most expedient to afford it, of the exertions which have already beneficially affected the rapid advancement of the religious and social conditions of the aborigines of New Zealand, affords the best present hope of their future in civilization."

The Earl of Devon is in the Chair. Men appear for a moment in London limelight, called in to report on New Zealand conditions. Mr. John Liddiard, expert by reason of a ten weeks' stay in the country, makes his bow.

"You have stated that the New Zealanders appeared anxious to have Europeans among them. Do you suppose this was solely for the purpose of instructing them in religion and the Arts, or for giving them laws and acting with authority?"

"For the purpose of bettering their condition in giving them greater comforts of life, and introducing the arts of civilization."

Another witness, the Hon. F. Baring, Member of Parliament, is questioned.

"Lord Durham's New Zealand Company did not give for their million of acres more than about forty or fifty pounds?"

"Probably not. They would give a certain number of muskets or blankets."

To the uninitiated, this deal might seem no more respectable than that made by the Baron de Thierry; and then there was the land purchase made for the missionaries in 1815, and paid for with twelve axes. . . .

Captain Fitzroy, of the old *Beagle*, gives evidence before the Lords, and makes an excellent impression in this awakening England. The Earl of This, the Marquis of That, the Duke of The Other, are known to be strongly in favour of the settlement of New Zealand. No one can too powerfully emphasize the fact that Mr. Edward Gibbon Wakefield (the power in the New Zealand Company's steam-engine) has absolutely no official status in connection with the project. "Oh no, we never mention him, his name is never heard," writes Mr. Wakefield, and clears his decks for action. Poor Mr. Wakefield. . . . He supplied most of the energy and action, and what did he get for it? Begrudged fame, precious little fortune. But then, Mr. Wakefield sometimes looked like a buccaneer, which was what the others, also buccaneers at heart, but so overgrown with whiskers and respectability, could not tolerate.

Two kings on the English throne since that poor old man under whom the elder and now deceased Baron de Thierry had come from the French shambles. Now a woman, with Victory for her name. England wakes out of the introspective, *poseur*-ridden phase into which she had passed after the Napoleonic wars, shakes out lion's mane on the wind.

Yet there are strange happenings also in France. (Swing over that revolving stage. Ah, how it creaks!) Almost you'd think life moved again, life better than shadow, among the gilt and the ghosts of Versailles. Even the lack-lustre Court, with Louis Philippe's curled hair, fleshy face, and twinkling eyes stamped on its gold bits, is astir over the subject of Nanto-Bordelaise. It's rumoured that His Majesty stoops to pat the shoulder of a French whaling-master, Jean Victor Langlois, who sailed his ship, the *Cachalot*, all round New Zealand, and from an old South Island chieftain has bought the whole of Banks' Peninsula for a French settlement.

Before Cécille turned *L'Héroine* back towards France, at the request of this Jean Victor Langlois he took possession of the South Island, with salvo of heavy guns and the tricolour flying. This is not official annexation, but it's a step on the road. France is very tired of M. Guizot, the autocrat of the Chamber of Deputies, who leans back in his chair, sighs that he is a man of peace, and watches England snatch one prize after another. The Paris quill-drivers tickle that rhinoceros hide of his, and if they don't wake much more in him than a lazy enmity, they attract the attention of the crowd. If Charles de Thierry were in France today, they wouldn't talk to him about Brazilian coffee-beans. Quite suddenly, Charles is a penny-a-liners' hero in Paris.

Captain Langlois advertises for settlers, and they come pelting. Journalists mirror the fertile lands of Banks' Peninsula as a little Arcady. The big fellows of the moneyed world take a hand in mixing the pie. Captain Cécille, arriving in France early in 1839, endorses the project of a French colony in the south of New Zealand. His word settles the matter. The Nanto-Bordelaise Company, with a capital running into many million francs, is successfully floated at Bordeaux, with Captain Langlois of the *Cachalot* a fifth partner for his pains.

On December 11th, 1839, the French Government have positively made up their mind. Nanto-Bordelaise is to be supported to the limit of discretion. The naval transport vessel, the *Mahé*, is to sail with arms and provisions, under orders to remain with the settlers for eighteen months in New Zealand, wet-nursing the infant colony. The insurance on the pioneers' vessel runs into 300,000 francs. Louis Philippe remains good-humoured with his whaling-master. At a royal hint, the *Mahé* is renamed the *Comte de Paris*, after the baby heir to the French throne.

In Paris, the Chamber of Deputies now argue whether to send a French Consul to the Confederacy of Chiefs under Parore (Mr. Busby's "United Tribes of New Zealand") or to the Court of the Baron de Thierry. Francis de Thierry puts in an appearance, working day and night for his brother's interests. Charles's name is hoisted up, a queer little flag bobbing about in journals whose editors know nothing very valid about his circumstances. Their pictures of the "Court" are of a grandiloquence to make the bells of Utopia burst into peals of mirth. There was a little girl in a French *conte de fées* who went out one morning and found strawberries under the snow ; but that's nothing. Charles, when he had found the strawberries, looked once again, and behold, the snow wasn't snow at all, it was ice-cream !

Fantastic letters, all addressed to the "Sovereign Chief of New Zealand", begin to pour in at Mount Isabel. There are protests of loyalty and promises of support from men whose names had faded into limbo years ago.

The great balance sways. The King at Mount Isabel cannot help wishing that both sides would suddenly become involved in some crisis . . . a war, a new revue, a fashion, anything to take their minds away from New Zealand. In the sovereignty of a great power, whether England or France, commerce stands to gain much, political strategy still more. But the native ? Men of the greenstone age, tall, chivalrous, barbarous, childish, friendly. . . . Facing them, in a truce more dangerous than open warfare, the powers of Europe.

Meantime, King Pokeno continues the offices of his alleged Court.

"I, Charles, Baron de Thierry, do hereby decree . . ." This time it was a document relating to the sale of native lands, one of the last issued for circulation by the Sovereign Chief. Re-affirmation of his benign wish to encourage all Maoris settled on what he religiously describes as "my lands". (Did I mention it ? He had commenced what he hoped would be a twelve-mile carriage-drive through the Long Bush. This was probably the most optimistic enterprise in the world.) A suggestion follows that, to guard against unscrupulous land-sharks, a minimum money price of five shillings per acre should be paid on all sales ; and, to safeguard native interests, let all such lands coming into the market be disposed of at three-monthly auctions, held in Sydney. Let 25 per cent of the proceeds be set aside for roading and public improvements ; 25 per cent for native hospitals and schools ; 12½ per cent for a native trust fund, banked in Sydney ; 12½ per cent for native needs in clothing and tools. All, of course, perfectly illegal. The native vendors would sooner have cut his throat, any day, than have seen their hard-earned gains stuck in a bank, or expended on hospitals and schools. Also the white settlers, clinching their bargains with raw spirits, must have found the circular diverting.

It was put forward, presumably in all seriousness, in March 1839, and carries as its final clause a suggested limitation of all land-holdings to a maximum of 100,000 acres "free for ever of land-tax".

He was to write of 1839 as "the last year of my political existence".

Slow burning of those massive Christmas candles, alight on the *pohutukawa* trees. The Wakefield brothers' ship, the brig *Tory*, lies anchored in the Hokianga that Christmas, and twice Colonel Wakefield—Mr. Edward Gibbon Wakefield's adventurous brother—tramps to the canoe which takes one up-stream to Mount Isabel. The English voyager writes down Charles as "a most interesting conversationalist". He does more. On Christmas Day arrives a letter from Colonel Wakefield, promising the Baron a much-needed supply of caps and gunpowder, and begging "Miss de Thierry" to honour him with the acceptance of a toy from her friend. That was civil. The Hokianga bushes don't sprout wax dolls, or green and yellow dancing wooden mannikins, either.

We can no longer delay it. Here they come, the cast, the cast . . . all drawn up in order at Waitangi, in the Bay of Islands ; which is, of course, the home of Mr. James Busby, British Resident. Mr. Busby has an important role to play in the drama, that of superman among the clerks. I often reflect that it is really the clerks who made the British Empire, but they never got any thanks for it.

Cast Assembled at Waitangi

Captain Hobson (formerly, you may remember, of H.M.S. *Racehorse*). A British officer. A gentleman. A man of unimpeachable integrity, who might have served as model for that cliché, "An Englishman's word is his bond." Later, first Lieutenant-Governor of New Zealand. Later again, an untimely corpse.

Captain Nias, of H.M.S. *Herald*, Captain Hobson's convoy from Sydney. An officer. No gentleman. With a cold in the head.

Archdeacon Henry Williams. Driving force among the missionaries. Official interpreter of the Treaty of Waitangi to the natives, and of the native orations to Captain Hobson and the other whites.

Other Missionaries : Any number of them.

Bishop Pompallier : Regarded by the above as representing the Scarlet Woman. Wears purple. Not popular. Not expected. Attended by his two assistants.

Hone Heke : Fighting spirit among the younger Maoria chiefs. Likes to be always first. A temperamental young man, regarded by some as a Maori Paladin, by others as the makings of a brigand. Something in both views. Hone Heke has acquired much *mana* by marrying the daughter of the late Shunghie, Hariata the Beautiful. He makes good speeches.

Tamati Waaka Nene : The greatest of the chiefs. From the independents' point of view, a defeatist. Actually, the spirit of the Maori race.

Other Chiefs : All have speaking parts. All make excellent speeches. All are more than half prepared to fall on the white men and devour them. All secretly await a lead.

Our Charles : Present only in the spirit. To the English, an exploded cracker, a mare's nest. To the French, a good agent ruined by temperament and a fad for native independence. To the natives, King Pokeno. To himself, King of Nukahiva, Sovereign Chief of New Zealand, Defender of the Maori faith.

.   .   .   .

It would be idle to deny that the first scenes passed off without their little hitches. When Captain Hobson and Captain Nias landed from the *Herald*, Hobson was almost distracted, Nias in a vile temper. He refused to recognize Captain Hobson as Lieutenant-Governor, or to give him a salute from the *Herald's* guns, until this Treaty was signed and done with. Hobson's landing was contrived with the maximum of discomfort and the minimum of respect. A few settlers arrived, just in time to prevent the future Lieutenant-Governor from delivering his first speech to the walls of a wooden shed. Later—when the treaty was signed—Hobson from his bunk on the *Herald* offered to fight Captain Nias "across a pocket handkerchief". The settlers were wroth with Nias. "He fell off his horse, he got wet, he caught a cold in the head", joyously relates a scribe of the period.

Mr. Busby and his two clerks had the next scene to themselves. All night they sat, putting the finishing touches to the beautiful Treaty, under which the chiefs were to cede their sovereignty to Queen Victoria, but must not be forced to part with any of their land unless they wished to sell. The British Crown was to acquire pre-emptive right of land purchase. All the blessings, all the curse of white man's rule and civilization, are the chiefs' hereafter, for a mere scratch of pen on parchment.

But the real show begins in that great beflagged marquee at Waitangi, in which the Treaty is to be read out to the natives, and the perorations of the latter will be heard. Very impressive settings; flags—though all the bunting in the Hokianga must have been scraped up to supplement that of the Bay of Islands —clean outshone by the spectacular garments of the Maoris: white plumes nodding in dark hair, inky blue of the *huia* feather, red of the *kaka*, greenstone earrings, clubs, amulets. Numerous gold-laced coats, representing the pomp of Great Britain. Bishop Pompallier, a dramatic figure, purple from head to foot—even purple stockings—with a gold cross on his breast, and the great episcopal ruby on his finger. How the black-frocked missionaries suck in their breath! . . . Especially when the Bishop somehow manœuvres his person between themselves and Captain Hobson, and appears on the dais in a seat of honour. All eyes, however, are distracted by the entrance of a dandy robed in glistening white dog-skin. The splendour of the old pagan world rises up tall and implacable in this tent, for a moment its full sunlight streams in the Lieutenant-Governor's eyes. He does not see, seated on his dais, that the sun passes its meridian on that day.

There was a glory. Let us admit that, and salute it, before we turn the page.

Rangatira, tohunga . . . let the spirits of your old meanings creep like lizards out of that cavern where you have taken refuge, the Silence of the Ancestors.

See, the white man has collected a handful of your ancient words, as a child gathers the bright worn pebbles from the glassy rub of the sea-waves; knowing nothing of their meanings, knowing only, as their smooth kiss lies in the palm of his hand, "This is significant and beautiful."

He was set like a rock above the tribesmen. The shadow of his hand was like the swaying of the mighty *totara*-tree.

Where he moved in anger, the enemies were afraid before him: as sweeps the wave back, under the thrust of the great storm.

When he came in friendship, there was raised to him in obedience and love the heart of things: as the tide is lifted unto the moon.

He was the touch of greenstone, clear, hard and cold. He was the wind that challenges dawn alone from the horn of a mountain. He was the forest that flared in that fire kindled by the white man, the *pakeha*; and in his going, majesty was stolen from the earth, and her natural garment was withdrawn. *Haere mai*, thou who comest from the caves of the spirit. *Haere mai, O rangatira.*

And thou, *tohunga*, what was it, elder brother of the Maori race, that was too subtle for thee? Was it the fiery metal of the white stars, or the clay of the human heart?

Nay, for both were written on the doors of thine understanding: in that speech which is older than all speech. And something of this thou taught'st to the sons of chieftains. But all thou didst not teach.

Tell me, then, wise one, old one, that could conquer so much: were they so easily defeated, your kinsmen, the *atua* of the Maori race?

Nay, but the lizard runs from one cavern into another; and who shall say which is the larger, when the second cavern lieth unseen?

Since thou hast withdrawn into the darkness, old one, and come now only to the threshold, with the dryness of Time on thy tongue, and its scorn in thy glittering eyes, I think it is a vast cavern, that Unseen which we have not conquered. Slip back then into your darkness, Lizard; begone like the cold trail of a thought. Yet, because thou wert wise and secret, never yet surprised, never yet defeated, *haere mai* to thee also, O *tohunga*.

.   .   .   .   .

The stateliness, the gesticulations, the play of passion in the mannered speeches of the dark orators, drift slowly together in that hot whirlpool of memory. Here and there a splendid face stands out; the reproachful dignity in an old man's eyes makes the Lieutenant-Governor wish that he could understand what is said, without the services of an interpreter. There is dispute over the settlers' and missionaries' land. Hobson gathers that Mr. Busby, Archdeacon Williams, a score of others, are accused by the natives of over-shrewdness. The accused men are quick in their own defence. One by one, they explain how their young families are growing up in this wilderness, with no secure inheritance but in their fathers' estates. True enough. . . . If the white children are to be secured, the native children must be . . . what is the word? Dispossessed? No, no, a friendly mingling together. For how many? Room for how many? Mr. Williams is once again requested to speak up.

Hone Heke makes an oration, of which Captain Hobson understands nothing except that the young man expresses fire in every line of his clean-run body. There is trouble over the interpretation. Mr. Williams says that Heke is favourable to the Treaty; a score of voices shout that Heke is for no surrender.

The afternoon has wearied the white men; eyes have grown vacant and tough bodies listless. Not only the stuffiness of the marquee, but the invisible conflict in the air is telling on them. Captain Hobson, his strength sapped by a sickness of months' standing, thinks grimly that he is like a ventriloquist's doll. At the right moment, his voice will say the correct words. But the lips that utter them might as well be a dead man's, for all the sense of physical reality that remains to him.

Something in the presence of Nene stirs him to life again. He leans forward from the dais, studying the finely tattooed face, the look of deep-set eyes under a noble forehead.

Nene, baptized in the name of the Father, the Son, and

the Holy Ghost as Thomas Walker, says, "Too late." If you had kept your country from the white men, he tells the natives, we could stand together now. If you had never invited the ships and the traders, the country would still be your own, and we should rule it. But you have brought the white men to New Zealand; your whole strength will never suffice to drive them away where once they have settled. To master the bad among the white men, you must have the white man's law.

The level voice spoke on. Nene was a friend to the *pakeha*, a zealous convert to Christianity. Yet, far more than those moved quickly to anger and loud talk, he remained a prince of the Maori race. On this afternoon, when he offered himself valiantly as ally to the white men, the spirit of his race spoke through his lips, and its sad cry was, "Too late."

It would never speak so clearly and bitterly again, until besieged and thirsting in sun-baked Maori trenches, Maori men and women, the forces of the chieftain Rewi Maniapoto, huddled together, and death watched them with empty eyes from a little distance. The officers sent them an offer of surrender and safeguard. The blackened lips returned a message of one sentence.

"Friends, we will fight against you for ever . . . for ever."

. . . . .

A few months of bearing the Treaty here and there, among the more distant tribes of the North Island. (The South has not yet been taken into consideration. Do not forget the Comte de Paris, Captain Jean Victor Langlois, the French settlers for Banks' Peninsula, now on the high seas.) Occasionally, a chieftain sticks out his tongue at the Treaty. One in particular declares he will never accept the petticoat government of "the woman, Victoria". But that's a bagatelle. New Zealand has an English Queen. There is officially a British Lieutenant-Governor.

It might seem that Captain Nias of the *Herald* could no longer refuse to be polite . . . but that's because one does not know Captain Nias. After that desperate quarrel in the cabin of the *Herald* (Hobson, already a sick man, propping himself up on one elbow in his bunk), quite suddenly the Governor's head swims, the world becomes very dark. The managing spirit, for the moment, loses control of the ventriloquist's doll.

"The Governor has had a stroke," whisper dismayed settlers, one to another. He was ominous, that very aged chieftain who came to Waitangi especially to see the White Queen's first representative ; who teetered forward across the green lawns, stared in the Governor's face, pointed a finger as shrivelled as a crow's claw, and cried : "Alas, an old man ! . . . He will soon be dead !"

. . . . .

"An aboriginal people saved . . . a marvellous consummation. A native race protected and perpetuated, brought forward instead of being driven back into the wilderness, and a people taught to love the God that permitted these things, instead of trembling at the denunciations of the missionaries. It might have been. Poor doomed, poor devoted people. But England is mistress here, and Fate has sounded their funeral-knell. Where they might have been taught to command, they must be content now to obey : and where in ages to come they would have shone and reflected glory and light upon their country, they must hang their heads in servile despondency, and grope their way in darkness."

Yes, yes, at Mount Isabel. The Sovereign Chief discovered at his teak writing-desk. Where else could it possibly be ?

That epitaph of his upon Waitangi is rather good. But it wouldn't be Charles if he didn't ruin the effect by adding, farther down the page, "If in the years to come the natives ever set eyes on what I have written here, how they will weep !"

Apart from the possible weeping of the natives, there's the vastly important matter of the first letter from the Sovereign Chief to the Lieutenant-Governor.

Charles congratulates Captain Hobson on his landing and successful achievements, and begs information as to what attitude Her Majesty's Government would take up regarding "French possessions in New Zealand". (This is a bit mystifying. But the Nation of One being obviously unsuited to defend itself, the French wing may have seemed the one remaining refuge.)

I have very few comforts to offer the traveller, but, should you come this way, I need not say that I shall feel proud of an opportunity to welcome you.
   Sir,
         Yours very sincerely,
            Charles, Baron de Thierry,
               Sovereign Chief of New Zealand.

("Was I to hide away like a guilty man? Was I to pull down my flag, and hide it in some obscure corner?")
   There is in Captain Hobson's exquisitely neat letter—the Lieutenant-Governor was a genuine penman—a courtesy which takes the sting out of its tail.
   "When you do me the honour to address me again, pray avoid the title you assume of Sovereign Chief." Hobson points out that the French neither held nor could hold any possessions in Her Majesty's dominions, "though individual French settlers have large holdings, and these shall receive exactly the same treatment as the other white settlers".
   There was half a promise to visit Mount Isabel. Indeed, a few days later a young Maori arrived, mud-splashed and panting, with a pencilled note from the Governor, explaining that the visit which the Baron had expected from him that day had gone awry, owing to the sudden illness of Captain Nias, and a mishap with a guide who had lost the way, delaying until it was too late to make the difficult journey to Mount Isabel. So the supper for which one of the turkeys had died the death was consumed *en famille*.
   "My flag remained. I desired one of my children to lower the ill-omened colours, and fold them and put them away, in memory of the lost liberties of the natives of New Zealand."
   The Princess Isabel secreted herself, alone for once, in that quaint thatched temple where they counted the stars together, she and her papa. It was next to the grotesquely deformed *kauri* which, owing to its proboscis, was known far and near as the "Elephant Tree". A green lizard, perhaps half an inch in length, ran out from under a strip of grey bark, with an air of great importance, and at sight of her finger suddenly froze, as if his mere existence were a piece of bad manners, which she would perhaps be good enough to overlook.

The lizards of New Zealand are extraordinarily old and wise. One of them, the *tuatara*, is said to be the Oldest Member in his entire society, and lives in a burrow, proving that nothing can ruffle his philosophic calm by allowing white seagulls to bunk with him. Could any but a reptilian Diogenes live placidly with such a shrew?

The little green lizards are not so wise as all that, but they have good sense also, and a certain degree of magic. The dry slithering sound they make is as if the hot restless leaves had come unstuck and gone travelling on a summer's day.

"O Lizard, advise me!... We are all plunged into sorrow, for my papa, the King—whom the English insist is a pirate, or else a French general—has been obliged to strike his colours. What shall we do?"

Wisdom in its solid form is incommunicable. Dissolve it, then, into streams, sieve it into the yeast of almost invisible air-bubbles, dancing between earth and sky. The prickle of tiny straw-coloured grass stems, the warmth of the sun, were grateful to her bare knees. Perhaps they were wisdom of a sort. Friendliness, at all events.

Part Three
SOUND THE RETREAT

CHAPTER SIXTEEN

THE KING GOES BACK TO NATURE

THOUGH it may seem unbalanced, I would like here to present a few notions concerning another monarch, who also, owing to pressure of circumstance, went back to Nature.

>Nebuchadnezzar grew sick of King's dishes,
>Weary of peacock, flamingo and venison.
>Said he to Unperturbed, "Yield me a benison,
>Grant Thine old reprobate three ploughboy wishes.
>Lord, let it come to pass
>Hot flesh be cooled with grass,
>Gross paunch anticipate
>Appetite's fate.
>Give me the cud of the slow-browsing kine
>Grazing on dreams in the silken blue shadow,
>Out of Thy mercy, let healing be mine
>That the sick, snarling cur tears from the meadow.
>Yield me a bellyful
>Of that blest cool
>Meat on which earth of Thine
>Nurtures the swine."
>
>God said to reprobate, "Taste then of earth.
>Learn ere thy grave-clothes the smack of the soil.
>Blunt tooth and nail in a scavenger's toil,
>Lair with my wild things : be butt of men's mirth.
>Spittle on beard and cheek,
>Thou shalt grow meek,
>Vacant eyes peer afar
>For my white-mantled star.
>Woo my wild almond, with snow for her wimple,
>Run to the palace gates, babbling of wonder—
>Knotted hands, bleeding feet, stumble and blunder—
>*There are yet splendours I save for the simple.*
>Schooled of my living grass
>Thou shalt surpass
>Kings whose worm-hearts are fed
>On a pride void and dead."

Everyone, you see, takes it for granted that Nebuchadnezzar was induced to crawl on all fours, eating grass, because God, wishing to punish him, could think of nothing better than to make him ridiculous. On the other hand, isn't it possible that God and Nebuchadnezzar came to an agreement about the desirability of grass . . . roots tangled in sunny soil, stains and sweetness of berries, queer little flavours pent up in nuts ? It sounds Shavian, and it would be too much to represent God as Shavian. However, under some circumstances, the reversion to Nature can be cure, not chastisement.

Not that Charles went so far back to Nature as all this. He did not crawl on all fours, unless when looking for tintacks, as a tiresome detail of his job-carpentering about the place. He did not quite eat grass, though he grew and ground his own grain, and Margaret helped Emily to bake the long loaves.

But in all his monumental papers, there are two periods concerning which he writes, not like an optimist, but like a thoroughly happy man. One was that moment in the orange-groves of Nukahiva. The other was the few months after he had hauled down his colours, and before he had had time to get into any fresh trouble.

It was not all bliss. He couldn't go near the empty flagstaff. The Maoris had grown used to it as a *rencontre* when they wished to deliver themselves of great ideas, and thought very poorly of Charles for letting the White Queen deprive him of his flag. Yells of "Have you eaten the White Queen's stirabout ?" greeted him whenever he approached the old meeting-place. The tribal elders buttonholed him and made reproachful speeches. You can imagine how galling this must have been to Charles, who was accustomed to a monopoly of that sort of thing for himself.

"They'll forget," he decided. As it happened, they never did, and the flag was to make a dramatic little reappearance later in history. In the meantime, however . . .

There was a crackle of resiny wood in the fire-place, whose smoke wreathed solemnly up the vast clay chimney affected by the pioneers. One still sees them sometimes, built outside the house, their hand-baked bricks sprawling over a whole wall. Their fires were tremendous. Nearly all the cooking was done in three-legged iron camp-ovens, like witches' cauldrons. As for lighting, isolated settlers—picking up the trick from the Maoris—attended to that in an odd way. Liver of a shark, no less. The fish was split open, his liver suspended between two sticks until a sufficiency of oil had appeared. This was burnt in little bowls of clay, with wicks of white calico twisted round long sticks. Charles, however, must have more dignity in his surroundings than that . . . candles, and wax ones, if it breaks him. The little Sèvres nymph supported her candlesticks so that their banners of gold fluttered directly over the pride of Mount Isabel—a piano, a genuine piano, shipped from Sydney to the Hokianga, and packed by horse through bush to "our mountain home". Probably it was the only piano in the district, but wasn't it worth the trouble ? Now Charles could play "When the King shall have his own again."

The wild autumn, with its tattered leaves, its tattered regrets, blew itself out of breath. Down in the bay, a hurricane tore the sails of H.M.S. *Herald* to shreds, and beached scores of smaller craft on the ribs of the rocks. Winter mists rose up, and shut Mount Isabel away from the world. The Long Bush, with its unmetalled if ambitious road, its beautiful beginning of a twelve-mile carriage-drive, was almost impassable. The smaller tracks were a mire of heavy yellow clay, nightmare stuff clinging in great dollops to a man's boots, and suddenly oozing into quivering bog where the tracks were lipped by the urgent, restive green of the high-growing *raupo*.

"I was glazier, tinsmith, carpenter, joiner, carriage-builder, well-digger. I drove my team of six bullocks, and so did my sons, as to the manner born. There were no drones in our hive."

They were worth talking about, those bullocks ; great, burly, bony, buffalo bullocks, with immense brandishing horns and surprisingly meek eyes. To feel the tug of their great shoulders straining, as the cart pitches out of the mud . . . to crack the rawhide in a figure S, using language unbecoming a baron and a gentleman . . . to smell the resin bleeding in sticky red drops from white timber . . . that's not such a bad variety of conquest for a beaten man. And then the de

Thierrys were perpetually on the track of timber-thieves, white and native. The impudence of the scoundrels was almost unnerving. No less than ten thousand feet of timber, cut, squared, and dressed, hauled down by his own bullocks to river's edge, were stacked overnight. What happens? Every stick is stolen, shipped down the Hokianga, loaded on board the piratical schooners whose skippers will thumb their noses at the law, provided they've got their spars at a cut rate.

There's enough trade, however, to keep the pot boiling. Timber is the principal export, finding a ready market in Sydney. Then there are always stray boats in the Hokianga, ready to pay well for quick provisioning. Not so bad, when one considers that, a few years before, the only considerable trade from New Zealand was in native birds—stuffed, for women's bonnets—and dried Maori heads, for curios. The latter industry was a bad business. When the native found he could get a price for the dried and tattooed head of his brother-man, what did he do? Sit about under a tree, waiting for someone to be good enough to die? Not likely. . . . He devised ambushes, knocked his enemy on the head, doctored the head in the steam, according to specification, and was down at the trading-vessels bright and early, demanding a cash price. The purchasers, no doubt, went to church on Sundays, and were models of respectability in their own home towns.

Charles Frederick, the eldest de Thierry boy, is twenty-one now; the rest follow him in steps and stairs. The daughter of the house is half past eleven. The natives, who love Isabel, can't make anything of her little name but "Irapera", which greeting salutes her whenever she goes abroad. Charles uses "my Isabel", or, alternately, "my angel girl". No companions for any of them, barring their papa's handful of faithful and so persecuted settlers, and the Maoris. That has its results. Charles Frederick, who kept on the title of Baron de Thierry after his father's death, married three times, leaving successors in plenty. The second wedding certificate, which began a line of Maori de Thierrys, gives his name, but the bride is registered simply as "a native woman". That comes strangely from his father's son. But it was a road as rough as the track through the Long Bush that ended in such bitterness.

They made their own bread, grinding wheat and maize

in the little steel mill from Sydney, and devising loaves and rolls of eccentric shape, twisted like pig-tails or sticks of barley-sugar. Two water-mills turned across the clear stream which furnished their main household supply. A solemn old Chinaman, wandering down from the Bay of Islands, his yellow turnip-lantern face and white tufty beard regarded as a terrible apparition by the innocent Maoris, showed the boys where tree-stumps in burnt-off patches of land provided delicious edible fungi. Richard and George would tramp home, their flaxen kits heavy with the sleek-plumed bodies of the wood-pigeon. Charles hired an old Maori fisherman, who for three figs of tobacco a day did precisely nothing except decorate the landscape with the most beautiful and lavish curls of blue that ever came out of a stumpy clay pipe.

They learned the how and where of spearing fish by torchlight. The torches, thonged with flax and soaked in resin, burned with a pumpkin-yellow flame, spitting across the dark like prowling salamanders. There were flounders and green-boned butterfish, and the forest pools supplied eels, mud-coloured creatures repulsive to look upon, but edible when dried golden in the smoke of the chimneyless native *whares*.

Leaving out the Maoris, most of the strangers who entered Mount Isabel that year were sailors spending a few weeks ashore—deserters, in some cases—and willing, both for money and curiosity, to join forces with King Pokeno as casual labourers. Any guests Charles could get hold of, he treated like brothers. He must have been dying for an audience.

It is rather amusing; perhaps a little sad as well. Among his casual labourers, he now extols the French, and can't find a good word to say for the English. The French wear red caps, they are versatile, they botanize, they sing love-songs, they do not require more than beer or light wine. But the English, with their faces ruddy as harvest moons, demand whisky. He stigmatizes their brawling very ponderously, but can't help admitting that, of all men in the world, the so-drunken English are the best sawyers, while the long-legged Americans —also, for the most part, intoxicated and riotous—win by a short head from the English as axe-men.

It is too chilly, however, to stand on ceremony or grievance. All human creatures, in awe of the storms outside, a little imbued with that languor which sends the northern animals into the sleep of hibernation, crowd into the kitchen at Mount Isabel. Red and lusty as wine, the flames pour up the throttle of the clay chimney, casting their spirited reflections on walls whitewashed over a foundation of wattle-boughs and mud. The red-capped men sing in French, the red-faced ones in that English tongue which didn't sound so bad when it was the season of cider-making in Bathampton, County Somerset.

It is curious to look back at a place which the wilderness has taken again, these many years, and see flaunted against the bush the little defiances of firelight and candlelight; to press one's face, in fancy, against a window-pane that has fallen starred into the long grass, and see behind it, in a kitchen big as Cheiron's cavern, the fire leaping up. A man with his back to the window sits at the piano. One has only a glimpse of a swart profile, but his hands move swiftly over the keyboard. The red-capped men chant their Breton ditty. Then they make a circle, and she comes among them, her frills rampant with snowy starch, all airs and graces, as was the custom when a young lady was about to render a Musical Item. But the little voice is so artless, so sweet, and it strikes so truly on the chord of memory.

> "*Sur le pont d'Avignon*
> *L'on y danse, tout en ronde*. . . ."

Rightwards and leftwards, bows of a depth that no Messieur, however beau, could manage without splitting the buttons off his waistcoat and pantaloons. But what would a young lady know of that?

Then it is whirled away, and the bitter leaves fly there from an old alien tree, helplessly, angrily stranded among its perennial neighbours, whose leaves, with their air of self-command, are always that same glossy dark green. There is nothing more, the place is empty.

Only once that winter Charles stirred from Mount Isabel: when he went to Paihia, in the Bay of Islands, to pay his respects to Captain Hobson. The Governor, recovering from the paralytic stroke brought on by his over-exertions and Captain Nias's impertinence, was staying at the Church of

England Mission Station, sheltered beneath the wing of the Rev. Mr. William Williams, the scholar of his family, and much less of an autocrat than his brother, Archdeacon Henry Williams.

Land, land, land ! They were all at it; some nibbling, some openly showing their greed, widening their jaws to gulp down great tracts of it. They called it commerce, the insolent and patent injustice of their dealings with the native. They expected him to submit, to be tame and purchasable. They had paid for their many thousands of acres, they claimed. A fool and his money . . . But Captain Hobson and his honour . . . not so soon parted, as they would find.

Still, the darkness of his bedroom was for ever invaded by them. He could get no peace. The bedclothes writhed into heaps, at one minute clammy with cold, at the next drenched with sweat. He fought out wars, knowing, at the back of his mind, that his own health and stamina were ruined, or he could calmly have ruled this disorder, which, after all, was not provoked by people of so considerable a character that Her Majesty's representative need take great note of them.

Edward Gibbon Wakefield and his clan, down in Wellington, biting off a million acres for the company, refusing to disgorge ; and strong men stood behind that deal at home. In the north, every second person who addressed him had an axe to grind. No civility you could trust, until you found what petition was embedded in the butter. He forced on himself the cold and repellent personality which was not naturally his own. "The matter will be settled in due course by the forthcoming Land Commissions, which at Her Majesty's wish will be set up . . ." He said that perhaps a hundred times in the day ; becoming ever more aware of hatred, resentment, and greed, huge and active spirits in the air, having quite as much personality as the human beings through whom they whined and blustered. Personality. . . . Sometimes it seemed to the Lieutenant-Governor that these land-sharks had literally sacrificed their own spiritual integrity, that out of their eyes looked nothing more human than a monstrous greed. He thought of the devil-possessed in the Scriptures. But the casting out of devils was out of date . . . though one cannot conceive of anything more lacking in dignity than that a man should allow himself to be governed by such instincts.

"Oh, Liz! Liz, my dear," thought the sick man, remembering how, in her vital gaiety, his wife had always seemed able to barricade the world against meanness. It was the Bermudas she had liked best, where they had been stationed in a place like a floating dream, all colours. And she could be childish, too. The delight she took in modelling those wax fruits after the Bermudan oddities. "Couldn't you almost bite them, Will?" with a pomegranate of wax in the palm of one hand, and in the other a contrivance which might have been a grenadilla.

He was subject now, he knew, to sudden fits of exasperation and fury. That forced calm of his was the steel door on the cage; and behind it, the beasts of Ephesus. But when one met him half-way in civility, he could still smile and converse, over Mr. William Williams's long-nosed silver coffee-pot, upon any topic at all except land. . . .

Unfortunately, of course, land was the burden of old Crusoe de Thierry's song, as with all the others. Captain Hobson was a little sorry for old Crusoe. "The forthcoming Land Commissions will soon be held."

Charles went home disconsolate. But, be it counted unto him for virtue, he was sorry himself for the Lieutenant-Governor. "Much as I like the Lieutenant-Governor as a man," he invariably begins his preambles concerning the injustice with which he was treated.

It seems impossible. But, nevertheless, at this time Charles has contrived to get himself into another tangle, quite a new one, and there are two chiefs threatening to cut his liver out; and Ohlsen, the club-law King of the Hokianga, advising Tau Nui, the fiercest, to march upon him and seize house and possessions in return for that promissory note.

Thus: Tau Nui, an important Hokianga chief, approached Charles with an offer of an enormous acreage, stretching up the Whangaroa Peninsula. The area would be more than 100,000 acres. Tau Nui wanted £400 for it.

Charles accepts, signs a promissory note for £400, gives it to Tau Nui with an earnest of the bargain, and writes to Sydney, where he has a lawyer, to raise the cash.

THE KING GOES BACK TO NATURE 197

But Tamati Waaka Nene then appears, says Tau Nui is a thief and a liar, that the land belongs to him, and that he wants to sell it to Captain Hobson for the Government.

Tau Nui learns of this, says Nene is thief and liar himself, and the land fairly his, as he earned it by right of conquest.

Patuone, Nene's brother, comes hurrying to Mount Isabel, warning Charles that if he takes the land, the Maoris will attack him.

Charles refuses, in the meantime, to pay the promissory note or to accept delivery of the land, and refers the matter to Captain Hobson.

Tau Nui first offers to see Charles safely installed in the land, then to fight Nene, then to fight Charles himself, if he won't pay up. In this he is seconded by club-law Mr. Ohlsen, who says Tau Nui has a claim on all de Thierry properties until he gets his £400, and should take them by force.

Charles tears his hair, and starts sleeping over gunpowder-barrels once again, talking about what a good shot he is, and writing indignant letters.

Both Tau Nui and Nene go off to the Bay of Islands, to pester the life out of Governor Hobson.

Governor Hobson wishes he were back at the Bermudas, and had never heard the word "land-sale".

It is discovered that Tau Nui wasn't lying, after all. He did conquer the land, and has right of vending. Nene was wrong.

But by this time, either Charles has discovered he can't raise the £400, or he has spent it on something else. Anyhow, he hasn't got it.

Ultima thule: The status quo is maintained, but under passionate protest all round. Maoris steal more and more timber and pigs, and feel more and more sanctimoniously in the right about it. Charles still can't see where he was wrong. He hopes to heaven the Land Commission will sit, and quick about it, for, what with Maori depredations and argument, he has only about 300 safe acres left at Mount Isabel. Yet he's afraid. . . . One can do with friends at Courts and Commissions, and where will the Baron de Thierry find them? How he wishes the French ships would darken New Zealand's door, as was promised all those months ago. . . .

Time, time, how slowly you creep! Why aren't you like

the fox in the fairy-tale ? The Prince sat on his back, and away they went, so fast that the wind whistled through their hair. But here . . . one has time to hear the grasses grow.

Thunderclouds split over Mount Isabel, for a spectacular fall of raindrops fat and round as marbles. Up from the Long Bush, one sopping June night, tears a Maori runner, explaining that Lieutenant Smart, riding over to Mount Isabel at Hobson's request, has bogged himself in the forests, and, if not drowned by this time, will at least be perishing of the cold.

One can imagine the excitement. Charles and the boys lugging on great gum-boots, Charles forgetting his principles and slipping a flask of best brandy into his pocket, the lanthorns winding like a procession of large scarlet ladybirds down the hills. The hero, Lieutenant Smart, is discovered a mile down the track, sitting quite unconcerned by the body of a fine black horse, which had its neck broken by a falling tree, throwing its rider clear. Exclamations of horror and concern are all wasted.

"I've lost my little black pipe, Baron. I'd not have broken that pipe for twenty horses. Do you smoke, Baron ? A man can't feel the same if he hasn't got his pipe."

A man can't feel the same, either, if in enemy territory he is at once rubbed dry before a roaring fire, and then sits down to a bowl of macaroni soup, draped in a spare pair of his host's pantaloons, which are luckily not too bad a fit. Still, the whole effect might have been ruined if Lieutenant Smart hadn't been able to borrow from one of the farm-hands a terrible black little stub of clay, at which Charles nearly fainted with horror, resisting a primitive instinct which urged him to cross himself. Deep puffs at this instrument : beautiful blue rings curling into the air.

"Ah ! . . ." (Puff.) "That's good, Baron." (Puff.) "A man can't feel the same without his pipe." (Puff, puff, puff.)

Add to that a reasonably sound claret. . . . Affairs march. Lieutenant Smart sits cross-legged, telling about the rumoured majesty of the portable house to be shipped out from England, for service as Government House.

"Like that we provided on St. Helena for old Boney . . . oh, saving your presence, Baron."

"Boney him all you please"—contentedly from Charles, who loves claret and damns the Bonapartists.

"Just as you say, Baron. But the Governor's house will be a fine one ; it's to cost £4000, which is more than the Crown paid for Boney's housing, and quite right too. It will be part marble, with forty-two french windows, and cedar-wood doors, and iron arches outside, where English roses may climb, if God gives 'em grace to bloom here. The settlement has a tavern that's supposed to be respectable now, though I can't say I ever tried it for myself. And there's a savings bank open twice weekly, and down at Port Nicholson, where the Wakefields' chicken settlement crows so loud, what do you think they've got for entertainment ? Nothing less than a Pickwick Club. Have you read the old rascal, Baron ? Next time you come to Russell, I'll lend you my copy. Next only to my pipe, I do love Sammy Pickwick."

Lieutenant Smart stayed the week-end. Officially, he was there to look into land-claims. Actually, he was a good, kind, lazy soul, who would marshal chessmen with the best, applaud loudly when Isabel was bidden to stand by the piano and give another musical item, and praise Margaret's pigeon stew until her snorts changed to some such doleful agreement as, "Best we can do, in this land of heathen blacks and cannibals." In the evenings they brought out the sheeted procession of the de Thierry ghost-stories, only to be told when the twigs were spitting like fairy cats in the fire-place.

There were the candles at the King of Norway's banquet, Great-uncle de Laville was consul there, and when the Revolution broke out, he didn't go home to be guillotined, but stayed on at the Norwegian Court, joining in state ceremonials, but thinking all the time of his mother, who was in Paris. One night, when Great-uncle de Laville sat at a royal banquet, candles leaning from porcelain sticks on either side of each guest, tall candles with flames silver like little haloes, his two candles went out. The servant in green quickly relighted them ; but, with not a breath of wind in the hall, they guttered and sank again.

Then the diners fell to watching, and the candles were lit and lit, but always their flames seemed cowed into darkness. At last Great-uncle de Laville's face was very white, and the guests looked at him as they would at a man under some heavy misfortune. So he excused himself and left the hall, and that night started on his journey to Paris. But he was too late, for the Revolutionists had found his mother, who was once a very wealthy old lady, and still very proud. Her serving-girl helped her to escape from the empty house, where shadows scuttled about like rats on the sinking ship. But the streets terrified her, and she turned aside into the lofty sad darkness of a church, where white altar candles burned low. There the Revolutionists found her, and killed her with pikes at the high altar, the faces of stained-glass saints looking down, still-lipped as though they saw but did not understand.

Great-uncle de Laville's coach never rattled back to Norway, for in Paris the Terror caught him too.

And there was Caroline's doll and the stranger on the stairs. Caroline, the children's aunt and Papa's own sister, had been only seven, with long, thin legs and a satin hair-ribbon, when they lived in the London house where the attic was always locked up, because the landlord said he had stored rare drugs there—after turning the little apothecary-shop which was once the front of the house into a parlour with a bay window.

Caroline had a beautiful doll, with long, shining hair. She would sit out on the staircase in the evenings, teaching it lullabies. One night they heard her say, "No, no, you shan't have my doll. Go away, pray do." But when they went out into the shadow, only Caroline and her doll were there. Often, after that, they heard the little girl talking to someone on the stairs, and decided that perhaps somebody in the next house, whose peaked gable joined their own, was making his way through the empty attic. But no; when they looked, the door above the stair squeezed in behind the cisterns was securely nailed up, with great bent rusty nails. When at last they forced the door, and looked in at the room whose spirit was all sheathed in cobwebs, there was no stranger, but only on the floor wide-spreading stains, rusty in colour as the nails, groping their way to the door. Then the landlord confessed that the last tenant, Dr. Parmentier, had killed himself there, when he could no longer make a living from dispensing behind the counter in the apothecary-shop, whose jars of dragon's blood, mouse-ear, vervein, wild ginger, old man root, were too far away from the press of London for customers to be attracted by its wavering green and blue bottles of light.

So the de Thierrys went away from the house, and at the last moment Caroline ran back and left her beautiful doll sitting on the stairs, its white-stockinged legs dangling neat and prim, its face pouting beneath its sunbonnet, waiting for Dr. Parmentier to come down and play with it.

And when the shadows drew back into the black-throated chimney, where a thousand minute soot-demons danced wildly in the smoky flames, Charles would make them laugh again by telling about sixteen-year-old Aunt Caroline, who was so brave and chased a burglar away from their house in Somerset, with nothing but a candlestick for her weapon. The children, however, were undecided whether to admire Aunt Caroline or the burglar, who was nothing but a chimney-sweep's little black boy, and who marched into the house in broad daylight, as bold as brass, with his soot-bag on his shoulder, and would have cleared the sideboard of silver if Aunt Caroline hadn't come running down and caught him at it.

But the story not often told was of Grandfather de Thierry's dream in Grave, after the Revolutionists drove him into exile. In the morning, he couldn't, even when cool sunshine dazzled on the round white pebbles of the paths where he walked with two French nobles and their beautiful greyhounds, forget the tall, sad man in the brown camlet coat, with a flat hat pulled over his eyes, and very high boots. As they turned a corner in the park, whose oaks and dreaming sunlight seemed to know no sorrows at all, Grandfather de Thierry caught his breath, and plucked at his companion's sleeve. For the man in brown camlet was walking straight towards them. As he would have passed, Grandfather de Thierry stepped forward and touched his arm, saying, "You are from Paris?"

"Since yesterday," said the tall man indifferently. "And I do not go back."

"Not after what you have seen," said Grandfather de Thierry.

The man's face whitened suddenly, and his eyes peered out under his flat hat.

"How do you know what I have seen?" he asked hardly.

"You were with those who saw the King led to the scaffold. You came out of the gates of a tall house built like a triangle, with carved and gilded gryphons on the cornice. It was you who saw His Majesty drop his kerchief, and stepped forward to pick it up. But you remembered that he was captive, and it would be most dangerous to show him any kindness. So you watched."

And the tall man said curtly, "Keep your dreams," and was gone. Like the black-eyed gipsy who came to the London lodging-house and told the Baroness, his mother, so many queer things about the squirming little boy who stamped his foot, and declared that gipsies were friends of the Devil and he wouldn't listen to them. But she smiled at him out of her old eyes, red-black as rubies, and said, "It's all true, my little dear, so sure as you've got three teeny moles over your heart." And when he slipped inside and pulled up his high white shirt, with its starched frill, there were the three teeny moles plain in the looking-glass. And long and long he thought of the many queer things the gipsy woman had told, and again afterwards, when one or another of them seemed to come true.

Winter outside, a great, high-ribbed cave, its roof pierced with the white, freezing, stalactites of starlight. The winds came roaring in, like those demonic spirits of whom the Maoris were so fond : Hau-Tuia, who is Piercing Wind, Hau Ngangana, who is Blustering Wind, and their mother, Te Mangu, who is Darkness. The Haumaringiringi, who are the Mist Gods ; Hauauru, Mauru, Tamauru, and Tauru, the four spirits of the West Wind ; Haumia-Tikitiki, Lord of Fern Root and all Wild Foods. Not the Haumarotoroto, the Fine-Weather Gods, those had been blown away by the cold and evil ones. But Rangiwhenua was there, the Lord over Thunder, and his servants the Kahui-Tipua, the Ogre-band.

Ghostly voices around the house. But within, Lieutenant Smart beats His Majesty over the chessboard, two nights out of three. Both gentlemen are eased with claret, after being blistered with Margaret's unforgettable parsnip wine. They discuss the Wakefield plans, the gentlemanlike conduct of Governor Hobson, the prospective personnel of the Land Commission. The windy house is stranded like the Ark on Ararat, there is nothing to see outside the windows but a tossing and rebellious darkness of high-stomached trees. Within the charmed circle, firelight and candlelight fall gently as the lustre known in a dream.

CHAPTER SEVENTEEN

SISTER ANNE, SISTER ANNE . . .

LIEUTENANT SMART is gone through the Long Bush. At Russell, Governor Hobson is holding out against the land filibusters, at the cost of popularity, patience, and life itself. The Land Commission is the only subject discussed among the settlers, though men of discernment might find something to interest them in the temper of the Maoris. Chiefs from northern and coastal districts drift through the Hokianga. They have never set eyes on the Treaty of Waitangi, they treat Queen Victoria's sovereignty as a false rumour. "Stir-about, stir-about, have you too eaten the White Queen's stir-about?"

The *tohungas* of the north are speaking in prophecy. To come upon them at their rites is death. The *tohunga* teaches in the way praised by Plato, that of direct discipleship. His disciple sits at his feet in the smoke of the wood-fire, hearing by word of mouth what a nation with no written language has kept intact for centuries. He sees the old man with foam on his lips, in the time of the darkened moon, when the dead cry through him with their reedy voices, or call in jest from the thatched roof of the *whare*. He handles the genealogical trees, scored pieces of whalebone. He watches the bathing of the dead, whose flesh has rotted from their bones before they are taken from the *tapu* place, washed carefully thrice with oils, and then decked for the last time in the splendour of plumes, greenstone ornaments, and feathered cloak. Over the *pa* the dead man looks down, and the women cut their flesh with sharp *paua* shell until blood streams, and wail with voices like dark birds flocking over the moon. When the lament is ended and the tribe feasted, the dead man is taken to the burying-place.

In the south, the island named Te Wahe Pounamou, the Greenstone Place, where Poutini the Fish-God guards the greenstone ornaments and weapons quarried there, the dead lie in cave-tombs of secret access. In the north, the chief rests in kindlier earth, but where he lies the ground becomes *tapu*, forbidden.

The dead, who do not lose power in their dying, are angry. Their messages are not sent in peace. Those whose spirits have plunged from Te Reinga, the cliffs of ghosts, down into waters churned to whirlpools of milky thunder, have crept to earth's surface once again, back through the hollow stems of flax and *toi-toi*. The spirit tribes are abroad in the land, and seek for their inheritance.

At Mount Isabel, nothing is sure except that the sons of the house have grown broad-shouldered and tall, and a child with dark hair walks in the forest. Winter stars stand over the house, angry stars, the Sword and Belt glittering as if heaven bent to a crusade, the Cross lifted up in a stream of chilly fire.

"But not my star." Charles wonders if he will ever again see that star. It was caught low in the branches of Somerset's apple-orchards, when a dim golden green melted day into twilight, and the west grew slowly transparent, a drowned wood under veils of sea. Hesperus rose there, the star of far-off islands that men seek for ever, moving in sudden freedom over the restless sea of their dreams.

. . . . .

May 2nd, of 1840. A native runner hastens to Mount Isabel with news of two French warships anchored at the Bay of Islands. The Maori bears the invitation of Captain Dumont d'Urville, Commander of the *Zélée* and the *Astrolabe*, cordially bidding the Baron de Thierry to call on him at his earliest pleasure.

In his wardrobe, Charles hunts desperately through suits respectable enough when Captain d'Orsay clinked glasses with him in the cabin of the *Momus*. Ah, thunder of God! . . . what a position for a Baron! To have nothing; no shirts that have not become distasteful to fashionable men years ago, no hat but one whose beaver brim flaps lamentably over his eyes, no pantaloons that do not bag—hardly a stitch to his back. At the last moment, Margaret Neilsen produces a suit which has certainly retained an air of respectability, but which smells horribly of the camphor-balls in which she has smothered it. Charles fixes her with the glassy eye of despair.

"Would ye rather go to company in holes, then?" She stalks away, looking as vulnerable as an iceberg, and Charles flings up his hands. What a race! He cannot understand how even the English contrived to conquer the Scots, and what, in any case, they expected to get out of it.

I have always had a weakness for Dumont d'Urville, on account of the spot to which he attached his name. The average explorer and his admirers become, one can't help noticing, very ostentatious. Nothing short of the largest snow-peaks and lengthiest lakes will do them, if they don't decide to afflict whole continents and seas with their often unreasonable names. However, d'Urville, one of the first navigators to nose about the New Zealand coast-line, and first of all to take his ship through the whirlpools of French Pass, contented himself with an island measuring perhaps twenty-five miles from tip to toe.

D'Urville Island, even today, is the oddest place. From a small town named Picton, which is noted only for a regatta, a special kind of bloater, and the fact that its harbour is allegedly so fine and deep it could accommodate the whole British Navy (but what the devil would the British Navy be doing there?), one sails between the wooded edges of the Marlborough Sounds over a sea of incredible transparency. Fishes designed in *outré* shape, fishes sapphire, scarlet, silver, lie palpitating on the ocean floor. There is a ridiculous isle where a million starlings live and striped yellow lilies grow; just there, nowhere else on earth. Everywhere the vegetation bordering or island-studding this crystal sea is indigenous, except for a few peach-trees, whose flaky pink scallops blow across their background as if sent scudding by the brush of a Japanese fan-painter.

Here, at the head of Tory Channel, Charles has recorded the scandalous existence—just before he himself sailed from Sydney—of an old shark who issued his own currency among the whalers and traders; a royal prerogative on which Charles had doubtless fixed his own eye. What happened to this first New Zealand note-issue I do not know. Farther along, there is Endeavour Inlet, with a stone anchor marking where Captain Cook's ship put in.

Then French Pass. The purple-headed mountains, as in the hymn, all scissored out of cardboard. Whirlpools, and funny little baked islands which are ancient Maori burying-grounds. Their rocky soil is so shallow and the confraternity of the dead so large that the corpses, for years, have been buried one on top of the other. What white people live here inhabit ramshackle houses half buried in jasmine and the beautiful clematis, which produces starlike blossoms, white and indigo. The population is so small, everyone has thirteen children to make up for it. Then it doesn't matter when their boats overturn in the whirlpools and they are drowned. I have a recollection of the squealing of innumerable children and pink piglets around these parts. Also there were ruddy strings of onions, very handsome ; and the wharfinger, when at 3 a.m. the vessel touched at French Pass, removed from the jetty its only illumination, a tin lanthorn, and employed this for guiding guests to the only hotel, where the bedrooms each possessed half a tallow candle, and there was no supper whatsoever. Again, there was a monstrous spider, which unravelled its legs and leapt from a watercock over the bath, where one had to pump one's bath-water. Great God . . . is it possible ?

Whirlpools, whirlpools . . . the sun glittering, and d'Urville Island ineffably secure behind its nobody-wants-to-see-me barricade. There are no roads on the island. One has to swarm over huge rocks, like a cat. The wild birds are small, and delicious minstrels. For some reason there are no mice or rats on the island, and this pleases the inhabitants. But the ferrets got there, perhaps by swimming. "Ah, there's those ferrets," they say, solemnly looking up from behind their periodicals, which are read over driftwood fires, and which are exclusively farming journals, containing pictures of immense rams, bullocks, and castrators.

Why did Captain d'Urville give his name to a little island like this ? It was exceptional. He was a good fellow, anyhow, and particularly kind and sympathetic towards Charles.

Remember the bombast of the Paris journals, their portraits of "the Court of the Baron de Thierry", all sprinkled with flunkeys and fleurs-de-lis ?

There in the door of Bishop Pompallier's dining-room

at Russell—where the gentlemen of the *Zélée* and the *Astrolabe* were entertaining themselves as the Bishop's guests at dinner— they beheld the King ; hands broadened and roughened from odd jobs about the farm ; hair grey at the temples ; hazel eyes, with that look of nervous anxiety, of mental quarrel, advance and retreat ; and, what was worse, reeking of mothballs.

To the eternal credit of these young officers, seeing him dilapidated, they put their generous hearts into lionizing him. Charles warms to it. Half an hour, and he is better than a hero. He is a martyr, with an uncommon gift of the gab.

("I dare say I have long been forgotten by them. But I shall ever remember.")

Captain d'Urville, with his great leonine head, his flowing brown hair, his shaggy brows, is an impressive figure. It was not only that he bequeathed his name to irrational islands containing neither roads nor rats. There was something about him . . . a slightly heavy-handed but definite air of command, amounting to stateliness. He was a staunch Republican. In fact, it was d'Urville who had the pleasure of escorting the fallen Charles X to England in the ship *Great Britain*, after the French had kicked him off the throne.

You may remember this Charles X as the Comte d'Artois, godfather—so Charles never wearied of claiming—to himself, the King of Nukahiva and Sovereign Chief? One might have expected some awkwardness between the godson of the fallen monarch and the Republican skipper. And there was another difficulty. After his earlier New Zealand voyages, in 1827, Captain d'Urville published *The Voyage of the Astrolabe*, in which scathing references were made to the Baron de Thierry, the authority being the early missionaries.

Charles doubtless brings these little matters up, and disposes of them in mind, before accepting d'Urville's invitation. After all, they lie in the past. Now, he is warmed by a cordial reception, by the smile in Bishop Pompallier's quiet eyes, by wine, by firelight, by the impressiveness of the Republican Commander's tawny head. Something more than a man to be played with, this one. The scoundrels will see for themselves. . . .

I mentioned how, when Charles feels on terms of amity

with another man, he cannot bear that the poor fellow should be anything less than right out of the top drawer. So, on the next morning—according again to Charles—we have the Republican Commander expressing himself in these remarkable terms :

"I also, M. le Baron, am a Baron, but I allow nobody on these ships to call me so. When in 1830 I conducted your godfather from the shores of France, I treated that priest-ridden monarch as he deserved to be treated by a Republican. He was called Charles Capet on my ship. But you I address as M. le Baron, because you have been a persecuted man, and the English have done their best to put you down."

About that you must decide for yourself. Even if Captain ("I also am a Baron") d'Urville did not actually make these remarks, they would have been tactful in him ; and Charles loved tact.

The sails were flapping when next day a long-boat put out, taking the Baron de Thierry to visit Captain d'Urville on his flagship, the *Astrolabe*. The cabin was panelled in polished wood, its only ornaments a great globe, and d'Urville's own beautiful pictorial charts of New Zealand and the South Seas. On these the Captain indicated where the French settlement in the South Island—its transport vessel and convoy now due in New Zealand waters—would be located. This nearness of a French settlement might make considerable difference to the de Thierrys. At worst, if driven from Mount Isabel, Akaroa would not be far to go, and there they could settle in honour under the French flag. However, better than this was hoped for. In Captain d'Urville's opinion, French influence would be consolidated in the South Island, and such an interest would serve to secure the Baron in his tenure at Mount Isabel, as an act of friendship between two nations sharing in New Zealand.

D'Urville himself left letters strongly supporting the Baron's land-claims, and mentioning that in 1824 he himself had met Thomas Kendall and learned from the missionary's own lips of the purchase made on Charles de Thierry's behalf. More he could not do. But "soon" was the word on the lips of both men.

Suddenly, as they talked, the port-hole dipped, a blue rim

of sea swung across their view. The vessel quivered as if her heart had begun to beat. Captain d'Urville smiled, and drew back the curtains from the port-hole. The *Astrolabe* was moving towards open sea. She stood a full mile out from Russell, her narrow helm turning northwards. The *Zélée*, too, was moving out from shore. Beyond the ships lay the long journey whose end was France.

"If you had your family with you, I'd take you with me now to France. You could not seek justice in vain, M. le Baron."

A handshake, before Charles put his foot on the swaying rope ladder. He looked up, saw the stern face watching him, forced himself to smile and wave as he took his place in the long-boat. The sailors of the *Astrolabe* and *Zélée* flourished their red caps and raised a cheer for him. Spray stung sharp and bitter on his face, for a stiff breeze was bellying the sails of the moving ships. The long-boat had to fight an hour against a heavy swell before it made the beach.

Help would certainly come, declared Dumont d'Urville.

Sister Anne, Sister Anne . . . do you see horsemen?

. . . . .

On the sixth day he was back at Mount Isabel, to find that three of the eight white labourers now left to him had deserted. One couldn't blame them. The place was cut off from the world. Governor Hobson was arranging postal services, but his line of communication stopped short twenty miles down-river, and with winter churning the roads into bog, they might as well have been at the Pole.

From the Long Bush, £180 worth of squared timber arose and walked one dark night.

There's comedy in it. Margaret Neilsen, for the first time, received an immoral proposal. It's that riff-raff who deserted the expedition, hung about at Lieutenant McDonnell's heels until that engaging gentleman kicked them off, then settled down for themselves, surly and penniless, hangers-on at the Maori villages. By and by, times are hard, or their ways too rough. The Maoris also expel them, and they are forced to earning their own living. This they accomplish best as brigands, but are pining for the softening influence of a woman's association . . . more than one woman, if possible, but one would do to go on with.

Therefore, an unkempt gentleman, whose ragged moleskins might have moved Margaret to pity if his breath hadn't smelt of mightily bad whisky, barred her path one day, and invited her to share the couch of an outlaw . . . of half a dozen outlaws.

"The loon's daft!" she snorted, drawing up her petticoats as though from the nimbleness of a singularly vile beetle. But the bush-dwellers were not so easily discouraged.

Margaret Neilsen, a grim little figure with spinsterly mittens hiding her mottled crimson hands, made her way home from the nearest approach to a store, a crazy hillside shanty, its tinned goods piled beneath its dirty thatch. The store kept treacle, tea, weevily flour, and split peas, but the inebriated store-keeper, with his very wet lower lip and his chuckle, went against the core of her being. She picked her way disdainfully among the *manuka*, thinking, "Men . . . they're all alike—fair disgusting." At this moment came a shout from the *manuka*. "At her, lads!"

The first thing she saw about her aggressors was that they were the lowest of the low. They were ragged and drunken, their chins were blue, their language was coarse. Nothing about them could impress or daunt a Scot who for fifteen years had seen service with a noble, albeit a slightly erratic, family. She lifted her chin, and as the first outlaw staggered towards her, her hand went up to a majestic black steeple of a hat. The gentleman dropped howling, three inches of steel hatpin in his belly.

"There, ye randy!" said Margaret, pale but undaunted, and took to her heels, thanking heaven that men who live on liquor are mostly short in the wind.

Richard was working in the garden, and rubbed his eyes at the sight of his mother's pocket Napoleon approaching on the run, her hat flapping dissolutely over one eye. Then he observed the pursuit, seized his potato-shovel, and with a roar of delight sprang down the track.

Margaret, straightening her hat, suddenly and anxiously burrowed in the bowels of her string bag, and sank down among the newly dug potatoes, crying as if her heart would break.

"The tea!" she sobbed. "The tea! Those randies have lost the tea on me, and it's seven shillings the pound!"

Nothing comforted her that night—not even Charles, shaking his head over the vileness of his own sex, and goin outside to refill the double barrels of his best shot-gun.

Tea at seven shillings the pound isn't the worst of it. The valleys are flooded this winter, the Maoris suffering a cruel loss of their crops, *kumaras*, and maize. Casual traders in the Hokianga are taking advantage of what looks like a famine. The little steel mill, which has ground the de Thierry wheat and maize since their arrival, is silent for want of feeding. To keep alive until the Land Commissioners sit becomes a problem. The three hundred acres left seem about as profitable as the Sahara.

Nene offers for £300 cash to drive natives and white men from the whole of the original 40,000 acres. Everyone, drenched, sodden, and disheartened, needs money and food. Charles shakes his head. He hasn't got £300. Moreover, how would Captain Hobson like a war on white settlers and natives? The French . . . that's the trump left in his pack.

Out of winter darkness came a message from Bishop Pompallier, warning the Baron de Thierry of Captain Lavaud's arrival with the French warship, *L'Aube*, in New Zealand waters.

CHAPTER EIGHTEEN

THE ROSY SOFA

THE storms, sweeping away the few poor roads, had rendered part of the journey to the Bay of Islands, where Captain Lavaud's ship lay anchored, impassable by land. But Lavaud had been warned of Crusoe's marooned condition, and his letter gave instructions for a signal-fire to be kindled on the high bluff overlooking the Bay as soon as he arrived there. Under these wet auspices comes Charles out of the wilderness, cursing when flint and steel can't start a spark in the sodden heap of brushwood, blessing the Maoris when they drag their dry fern bedding from a near-by hut and use it to start the fire. The tongue of flame thrusts up ; a long-boat detaches itself from *L'Aube*.

"France, I come !" cries Charles, and precipitates himself into the long-boat, manned by twelve hefty fellows from Brittany.

"I was received on board *L'Aube* with unexpected distinction, and Captain Lavaud immediately intimated that he expected to retain me as his guest during my stay. A boat was to be placed at my disposal whenever I wished to go on shore, and I began to think that my long trials were at last brought to a close, and I should once again see my family in circumstances of happiness and comfort. In the morning, Captain Lavaud showed me the orders he had received concerning me from the King of France, given under the sign manual. . . ."

This attention, comprising an order for "*protection toute espéciale*" to be afforded the Baron, had a shade less than its face value in the New Zealand market. Captain Lavaud had immediate problems to face ; Charles, he discovered, was simpler in every respect if treated as an elementary sum in subtraction. This is perhaps why, after his first optimism,

Charles adds ruefully: "I can never forget the civilities with which Captain Lavaud received me, but I cannot forget either . . ."

It is no use. Captain Lavaud had a most difficult role to enact, the role of the good loser. He did it perfectly, with a gallantry which still calls forth admiration from historians of all nationalities.

I cannot like the man. Because he was such a good loser. Because he lost with an air; while the others, surly old Jean Victor Langlois, Charles de Thierry, the French settlers for Akaroa, merely looked fools.

That insensate passion for losing magnificently . . . consider a pair of fingers snapped under the nose of the man who invented it.

If ever my own dream-army were beaten—which is, however, impossible—it would receive no instructions to form in a square, give a performance with the cavalry, and die with band playing, colours flying. On the contrary, it would be instructed to run like blazes, taking cover in the rough country. Then, when the oncoming forces assembled to repose themselves, they would be tactfully received by a specially selected corps of beautiful virgins—indigenous to the country. To *"fraterniser et les corrompier"*, as did the citizens with the Guard of Paris during the French Revolution, would be the duty of these young women, for whom the *élan* of martyrdom would be added to the natural human satisfaction attached to any new experience. After a few weeks, re-assembling my army on a dozen sides at once, I would strike with any weapons available. If the virgins also were killed, no matter. They would have lived.

Captain Lavaud's position was this. He had arrived in command of *L'Aube*, ostensibly, at least, to see established upon French soil in Southern New Zealand a French colony.

But by the time he arrived, there was no French soil in New Zealand. From June to September of '39, the French Chamber of Deputies had argued as to what steps should be taken in the matter of this colonization. On November 4th, they got as far as their diplomatic recognition of the independence of New Zealand. Meanwhile, Captain Hobson was on his way from England to Sydney, and they were still talking when he arrived.

Four years later, M. Guizot, who placidly ruled the Chamber of Deputies, *"dormant fort bien sans gloire"*, and describing all more energetic souls as "the war-party", explained that Lavaud was but crossing the Line when English sovereignty was proclaimed in New Zealand.

After Waitangi, the sovereignty of the North Island was never in dispute. But much less clearly understood was the process by which British power became established in the South and Stewart Islands, and many people never understood at the time that such power had been assumed at all. (It was in the South Island, of course, that Captain Langlois had made his land-purchases, and that the French proposed to settle.)

At a later date, Guizot took the Deputies into his confidence, alleging that he had received formal notification that on May 31st, 1840, the Queen's sovereignty was declared over both South and Stewart Islands, by proclamation of Lieutenant-Governor Hobson, and again on June 17th, when, at a native *pa* in Cloudy Bay, Major Bunbury, of the 58th Regiment, who had gone south to collect signatures for the Treaty of Waitangi, hoisted the Union Jack, and received from Captain Nias and a party of marines landed from H.M.S. *Herald* the royal salute of twenty-one guns.

That the original business was a ceding of New Zealand by the chiefs under treaty, and that the signatures of the southern chiefs were far from complete at this time, occasioned much bristling of moustaches in the Chamber of Deputies. What use? New Zealand, after all, was a small island group; the matter was ended.

On the soil thus narrowly lost to France, a very different view prevailed. For a time the fact of English sovereignty in the South Island was kept secret from the French emigrants. None of this debate, as far as men knew, was apparent to Captain Lavaud while *L'Aube* lay anchored at Russell. Whatever he had learned before arrival, whatever Captain Hobson had told him the moment he came ashore, he was there ostensibly to see French settlers established-on French soil. The game must be played out. Why? Because there were the Nanto-Bordelaise chestnuts to be pulled out of the fire. Once establish the settlers—whoever really owned the soil—and there was a much better chance that England would pay compensation to the company. This reasoning proved correct. Some years later, the Nanto-Bordelaise Company was bought out, or, rather, recompensed by a very considerable sum from the English Government.

The French settlers themselves lost nothing by the arrangement except their right to live under their national flag, which you may rate according to your views. They made a charming settlement, at all events, retaining their French characteristics, and bestowing on the little settlement of Akaroa—still extant—a touch of individuality.

Meanwhile, the things Captain Lavaud must avoid were these: He must not run his nose into serious trouble with the English. Guizot wouldn't like it.

He must not create a panic among the French settlers on the *Comte de Paris*, or the sailors on his own vessel.

He must not unnecessarily complicate the issue with minor details. Of these, Charles was one.

All this necessitated an elaborate little comedy-drama, perfectly staged, with the green Russell hills as back-drop, the trolling voices of sailors as chorus, and that ramshackle old gabled residence, Government House—until the famous portable house should arrive and be set up at the new settlement of Auckland—as its setting.

L'Aube carried two French priests for Bishop Pompallier's mission. The weather sparkled into a false springtime, sun danced on the wavelets, powdery foam glistened white as the seagulls' wings. The tiny town stood out in morning light. English colours floated bravely there. A little north lay anchored Her Majesty's ship of war, the *Britomart*.

Captain Lavaud saluted the *Britomart's* colours as his ship drew near shore, but not the Union Jack over Russell. No formal acknowledgment, then, of British domination. The sailors chant, the gulls bob about like scraps of white paper . . . how tempting to a literary man! Charles, glorious in a new broadcloth, expands his chest four inches. What a fine place the world is! He is going to pay a visit to the Lieutenant-Governor. ("For Hobson the man I had every possible regard, though I often wished the Lieutenant-Governor at No. 10 Downing Street, and No. 10 Downing Street at Timbuctoo.")

Winter roses had been planted at the arches and pilasters of the old house, their soft flurry of petals dropped against the dark green of wrought iron. The house smelt agreeably of the resinous wood which had built its high doors. At mid-morning, for the first time, Charles made his bow to the Lieutenant-Governor's lady, Mrs. Hobson, who was wearing a crinoline of lavender-flowered soubrise, opened in front to show the waterfalls of lace with which this year's fashion had deluged London and Paris. Her throat showed creamy and rounded above the stiff-shouldered gown which descended into leg-of-mutton sleeves, jutting out above tight bodice and tiny waist. Canova had ridded women of their Iron Maiden, the steel corset; but the whalebone and leather receptacles in which the little creatures must move, breathe, and even smile, still kept them vase-shaped. Women are wonderful. . . .

You are about to meet an enchantress. It doesn't happen every day with the wives of Lieutenant-Governors, Governors, Residents. Most of them smile and smile and refuse to be villains, however one wishes they would. They are all silver photograph-frames—corralling signed pictures of Royalty—inferior orchestras, fat red lines of women waiting to be presented, and nothing to drink. But not Mrs. Hobson. She makes Captain Lavaud forget the hard knot in his thoughts, and muse, "After all, there's nobody in the world who can lose as well as a Frenchman." Her husband thinks, "Dear Liz! How she carries it off. If anyone in this world can turn a swarm of buzz-flies into Red Admirals!" And as for the Baron de Thierry . . .

"She was surrounded by so many of the elegancies of civilized life that I felt a pang at having brought my family to a country where they were still unknown, and which, even now, they had no chance of enjoying. I would have forgotten past troubles if I could have carried my family to comforts like those with which I was now, for a moment, surrounded."

Enchanted Liz! Life is so transitory for the male, so

lasting under the touch of a woman. A deer trots by in an English park, a rose flowers, its petals swish softly to the turf, and you think, "Over and done with." Oh, but not at all. Circe threads her needle. Come back in a week's time, and you will see the fine antlers branching on tapestry, the rose-petal redder than ever Nature meant it, efflorescent on her plump cushions. You find it tiresome ? I don't know. Nearly all the genuine ghostliness in the world is created by women. Powder-closets, mirrors, just those unnecessary, fitful things which are so inescapably intimate. A woman, you see, is the one who knows how to desire the past, because her life is all one smiling regret for that particular bough or dingle of youth which she never had. Men make the past their servants; that achieves tradition. But women are slaves to the past, and that achieves ghostliness.

Everywhere in the Governor's surroundings, Circe had been at work. The drawing-room where they chattered was ornamented with rosy sofas and chairs, all hung in tapestries upon which English countryside scenes were depicted with a good deal of vigour, stiffness, and beautifully tucked-in corners. The whole of it was the work of Mrs. Hobson's fingers. Cherubs looked impudently through their frozen storm of buds. There were gentlemen in hunting-pink, raising sleek hats to young English misses. This little strife-less world. . . . How exquisite, really, were women, who could fancy a world without strife, and then seat themselves in their high, apple-scented chambers, and like devout little girls stitch it into being.

Nor were the rosy sofas all Mrs. Hobson had contrived. Hadn't that sick, weary man, her husband, been once a bronzed sailor, stationed at the Bermudas ? Now Fate had taken the ripe juices of those days away from their lips. But see Liz, with her finger at her mouth : "There's my beloved Bermudas," she whispers to Charles, and indicates a pile of the most ravishing tropical fruits, sultry as a harem's jewels.

Charles feels his mouth water. Wax, every man of them. "Impossible to have detected them from the works of Nature," he writes fervently.

Mrs. Hobson plays the harp, and there is a grand piano, its keys honey-coloured from the touch of the years that so loved it. Harp's music ripples soft and dim, an obscure creek, carrying the sad thoughts far away. "The Baron de Thierry played a harp solo at the masquerade, and an Imperial lady fell in love with him." He looks at his own hands, which can control the machinations of six bullocks. By and by, he plucks up courage. The company is quite silent; for once in his New Zealand life Charles has an audience that don't argue. Governor Hobson sits with his eyes shut, his face waxen pale. The chords speak on, declaring out of the cavern of dreams their oracular message. Mrs. Hobson doesn't fall in love with him like the Imperial lady, but she smiles and is very amiable.

"I left with an invitation to spend the night at Government House whenever I pleased, with a bed on one of those delicious rosy sofas."

I wonder if Crusoe came into her mind that night, when Captain Hobson officiated with the back hooks on the lavender frock? No other gentleman present has put on record his admiration of her wax Bermudan fruits. But no. . . . In the lamplight, she must have wished only that the sharp face seen over her shoulder were less the colour of untinted wax itself.

At one o'clock next day the Hobsons lunched at Bishop Pompallier's house. There was a party of fifteen at table, among them Captain Lavaud, Charles de Thierry, and Captain Stanley, of the brig *Britomart*. Mrs. Hobson's presence seems to have gone to these gentlemen's heads. She was a sprite, setting wit and laughter loose among them. See how Captain Lavaud smiles and raises his glass. . . .

"There was one at table whose intelligent countenance bespoke a man ready for any daring enterprise. That one was Captain Stanley. Towards the end of the dinner, he asked Captain Lavaud if he had any letters for Sydney, as the *Britomart* was sailing there at the close of the day. Lavaud seemed taken aback, and murmured something about the shortness of the notice. I did not quite collect what he said. I was struck with an air of mischief which brightened Captain Stanley's eyes. Dinner was a very cheerful meal, with Captain Hobson in high good humour, and everyone in better spirits than I was, but I kept up appearances as well as I could."

At the end of the meal he had opportunity for a word with Lavaud, and asked when *L'Aube* left for Akaroa.

"In a day or two, Baron, in a day or two."

"Captain Lavaud, they are tricking you. You'll find the British flag flying when you get there. Captain Stanley is bound south in the *Britomart*."

Lavaud's handsome face reddened angrily.

"What do you mean, Baron? He has asked me for letters for Sydney, where the *Britomart* sails this evening."

"He may send your letters, but he will never deliver them. He means to get the start of you."

"You are deceived, Baron." Lavaud turned on his heel. But his anger was a thing of the moment. Next morning, he was the same light-hearted host, taking part like any schoolboy in fishing for crayfish off the stern; and, when a prodigious rusty-brown monster had been hauled up protesting from the deeps, sending it off, beautifully garnished, as a gift for Mrs. Hobson. Each morning of *L'Aube's* stay, Government House was regaled with fresh French bread; the ship's boat, in charge of a young "aspirant", making the three-mile journey to Russell. One night there was a brilliant ball for the officers at Government House; the following day Captain and Mrs. Hobson lunched aboard *L'Aube*. Rivals for territory . . . who could credit it?

Charles contrives to extract a word or two about his own affairs. Once the Captain, in high good humour, buttonholed him and told him to ask for 20,000 acres. "Hobson's all but promised me you shall have 10,000, Baron, and he's a man of his word." But two days after the *Britomart* sailed there was a change in Lavaud's attitude. Charles was summoned to the Captain's cabin.

"Baron, persuade your family to join us here. I'll take you all down to Akaroa, and thence you can sail for France in the transport vessel. Come, you'll travel as guests of the French Government, and you'll create a sensation in Paris. I give you my word of honour you shall have employment in France. I could wait here three or four days to enable your household to be taken on board."

That prospect of creating a sensation in Paris, with his little travelling-circus, the wheels all polished . . . it should have appealed. What then? Roots put down at last in a hard soil, when he had drifted over three-quarters of the globe, and never yet called a country "home"?

"I told Captain Lavaud it was too important a matter for me to decide without consulting my family, and, asking him to put me on shore on the Waitangi side of the Bay, left at once for Mount Isabel."

One has next to consider these de Thierrys, in their kitchen with the wattle-and-daub walls, the boys stretched out before the fire like young animals, changed into homely, shapeless clothing after their day's wrestle with the mud ; Emily in her rocking-chair ; Isabel helping Margaret Neilsen to put away the supper-things, the blue-and-white earthenware, the silver tea-pot said to be an heirloom, and, anyhow, with a fine Jewish nose.

Do you remember the celluloid mannikins, with the most serious faces and inch-high bodies, whom you could tip about to fantastic angles, never over-balancing them? Concealed under their pantaloons or petticoats was a secret weight of lead.

Emily de Thierry must have resembled one of those sensible mannikins. The world tipped her this way and that. She was never overbalanced. She must have been secretly weighted with something . . . common sense, dignity, humour.

Perhaps the taste for fantasy grew upon her, until finally a curate's face looked just as odd, or, rather, as normal-odd, as a cannibal chieftain's ; while neither looked as sane as the face of a cow. One will never be able to tell. She stuck to Charles. She went on cutting bread-and-butter. She was a great woman, a heroine, a martyr, too, and in appearance she strongly resembled Queen Victoria.

Then the children themselves ; they were born all over the world ; in London, Cambridge, Paris, New York, Baltimore. They had inhabited three separate kingdoms, counting in Queen Pomare's, and leaving out the extra two provided by their father ; also America, the West Indies, Colonial possessions in the crudest phase, and a native republic. (I suppose that is what one must call New Zealand, before the British Crown took it over.)

By the time one has ended such a career, one is more than

an *émigré*, one is a Wandering Jew—a fugitive, trying to escape from the habit of insecurity.

They had been two years on Mount Isabel, in a life wild, rough, risky, and very lonely. The eldest was twenty-one, the youngest not quite seven. Whether they were tired of being at one moment sprung from royal loins, at the next merely a spinnet-tuner's brats ; whether the royal salutes and dog-fights were a confusion in their ears, nobody can say. They are not here to present their case. Unlike their father, they were all very uncommunicative, proud, peculiar, secretive. They never destroyed any of their father's papers or souvenirs. They merely locked them up, hid them, and refused to elucidate. That they ever wrote a line or made a speech themselves is more than I have been able to discover.

Does not this proud silence indicate that perhaps, even at an early stage of the game, Mount Isabel was to them more a home than a hated shore of castaways ? They made a good deal of their own fun. They had the piano. They loved one another dearly. Of Isabel, Charles says she never in her whole life did anything wrong ; but I am sure that is one of the pardonable exaggerations with which people make the dead sound so dull. A friend of her Uncle Francis saw her in young maidenhood at Mount Isabel, and wrote to Paris giving Francis a *précis*. "Everyone coming from there is amazed at her beauty," wrote Uncle Francis to Uncle Frederick.

Charles told his family of Captain Lavaud's suggestions. 10,000 acres—perhaps—from Governor Hobson, or the journey to France as guests of the nation, with employment promised at the end of it. Then he informed them that they must make up their minds and let him know. But if he stayed on and everything went wrong, he added cautiously, they mustn't blame him. After this, he went out and sat in the parlour, its windows all a-weep with rain. The impossibility of getting his geese and turkeys back to civilization occurred to him. Here they must stay, running wild like Crusoe's flocks.

The door opened; he was standing again at his fireside. All the flushed faces smiled, all were decided. "Mount Isabel . . . Mount Isabel . . . Mount Isabel." Only one said another thing, and that so low that the others did not hear it. She said "*Irapera,*" and smiled at him, as she gave the little name the natives used.

The young voices ring around him like swords. The de Thierrys have no nation. What of it? They are a nation in themselves.

Almostly immediately Charles is back on *L'Aube*, getting scolded by Captain Lavaud, who is really vexed at the minor problem which insists on remaining problematic. Lavaud assures Charles that he is distrusted among the white settlers.

"Do you think, Baron, that France will risk a war with England in order to determine your rights?"

"I spoke to him very seriously," writes Charles, who, of course, would think a war with England none too strong a means for France to express her annoyance at his treatment. He recalls, with considerable dignity, that he is a Frenchman, and that one who has rendered his country service should not with impunity be molested.

Captain Lavaud takes down from a shelf the *Code Napoleon*. It has tricoloured edges.

"To my mind, Baron, there is only one test whether a man is French or not. It is here in the *Code Napoleon*. Has a man been drawn for conscription in the French army? If so, he is French. If he cannot produce his ticket, then he may belong to what nation he pleases, but he is not a Frenchman."

Captain Lavaud bows and turns away. Charles stares after him.

"I might have said, 'What, then, are a Duc de Guiche, a Duc d'Harcourt, a Viscount de Chateaubriand, a thousand more, doing in France?' "

Staircase wit. For once, argument sticks in his throat.

He left *L'Aube* with Captain Lavaud's handclap on his shoulder, and in his pocket a letter of recommendation to the captains of French warships and merchant vessels which might need provisioning at the Hokianga.

"I also ask the Captains of French merchant vessels to have the goodness to comply with this invitation," wrote Captain Lavaud, "being perfectly convinced that they will take pleasure in assisting a countryman who for so many reasons deserves, as you do, that everything should be done in his favour. . . ." Lavaud refers further to the provisioning as "the means of repairing the ills which have been inflicted upon you by robbing you foot by foot of what you had so rightfully bought and paid for".

Some months later, we have Lavaud's letter endorsed by one Varien Leveque, commander of *L'Héroine*, who, having fully provisioned his brig at Mount Isabel, is satisfied with the prices and quality of the goods supplied.

A Monsieur de Belligny, arriving a few weeks later with letters from Captain Lavaud, whom he had met at Akaroa, told them the end of the mock battle between *L'Aube* and Captain Stanley, of H.M.S. *Britomart*.

The three days' start that the *Britomart* had of *L'Aube* was lost in a heavy gale, which caught the English brig before she won to Cook Straits, tearing her sails, and carrying away so much of her sparring that she limped along wounded over a sea still very rough, and was sighted by *L'Aube*, coming along undamaged by the wind, but farther out from the south coast than the *Britomart*.

The race ended in something like earnest. *L'Aube* cracked on every stitch of canvas, and her white sails moved like a tower towards shore. But Stanley ran up every rag of sail on the *Britomart*, and his inshore position won him the race to Akaroa.

The Jack flew gaily, and not without Lavaud's good graces, for the French ship's carpenter was lent to put up a flagstaff and help in building a house for the first English magistrate at Akaroa. Tragically enough, two graves were the first French imprints on shore ; for the first solemn occasion, when the transport ship, *Comte de Paris*, put in, was the burying of two infant colonists, dead on the voyage. The vessel arrived at Akaroa three days after *L'Aube*.

"Captain Lavaud pushes his attentions to the English to heroism . . . poor old Langlois grumbles like a bear with a sore head, but nobody cares to take any notice of him. The settlers will live on, unmolested and peaceful. Akaroa is won, the French have lost, and I am again for France, my dear Baron."

M. de Belligny's prophecy was perfectly correct. Langlois's emigrants were landed on August 19th, 1840, and in '45 Lord Stanley directed the payment of a grant of £30,000 to the

Nanto-Bordelaise Company, for their somewhat problematical "rights" in New Zealand. It is scarcely necessary to add that Jean Victor Langlois quickly fell out of favour, in France as in New Zealand; sulked, argued, apologized, argued again, became a discredited man.

Extract from a letter written in 1840 by the Baron de Thierry to Governor Hobson.

> *All my people, with the exception of three Frenchmen who are also going, have left me in consequence of the persecution to which we are exposed. . . . I do more for the satisfaction of an English administration than a Frenchman should, but I have already mentioned in former letters that I have strong English sympathies, and cannot help listening to them. It is now for Your Excellency to decide whether I must apply for redress to the Government of France, for the justice you are so well able to do. For your own sake, this must be my last appeal.*
>
>   *I have the honour to be,*
>   *My dear Sir,*
>   *Very faithfully yours,*
>   *Charles, Baron de Thierry.*

Extract from the letter in reply:

> *If the French Government should feel disposed to support the claims of a subject of France, I can contemplate no other course of proceeding by that nation, or any other nation in amity with Great Britain, than by friendly negotiation through their respective Governments. . . .*

The *Code Napoleon* has tricoloured edges, and says one cannot be a Frenchman.

A letter comes from the Bay of Islands, informing Charles he must take the Oath of Allegiance to Queen Victoria before his land-claims can be considered at all by the Commissioners.

He writes all night, pointing out that he has been educated at English universities, held a commission in the 23rd Light Dragoons. "The father of my wife is a dignitary of the Church of England. . . ."

From the hinterlands of memory comes the picture of an

old man ; indeed, he seems amazingly old, seen through these wise shadows. He sits at a table in a horribly clean little cell, writing, writing, justifying existence with a quill pen. "The candle a little closer, Charles. Ah . . . so. Your Royal Highness will then remember. . . . Always, they cry, I push myself to the fore."

The old man looks up, though the thin-legged boy at his side keeps his eyes studiously averted. The face of the old man, weary, querulous, bitter, is Charles de Thierry's own.

CHAPTER NINETEEN

THE SMITHY IN THE WOODS

THERE is one thing never likely to be forgotten by the man who has witnessed it. That is the spectacle of the earth, just before some natural calamity, an earthquake, a hurricane, or a great drought, comes upon it.

The structuralists of language have their own term for the poetic conceit which figures the earth in sympathy with the moods and passions of men. But what of that other mood, in which no man seems more than a straw? That atmosphere of dreadful impatience, pouring out of ground and sky, as disturbing as the difficult breath of a man dying of fever? Men, beasts, bending trees, become infected with a shadowy fear. Familiar landscapes are suddenly weird and harsh, with the mocking lineaments of a dream, whose sign-posts seem to have a significance that always escapes the dreamer. Among human quarrels and attachments there is a dividing sense of awe. The puppets almost realize that their voices are too squeaky for the immense stage.

Incidentally, a land overthrown by this sudden unfair mastery by Nature is frequently an excellent theatre for war. The survivors among the pigmies must forget their insignificance, so they rush into heroism. It was so in the Hokianga, and farther north, which first suffered flood, then famine and war.

1841 . . . 1842. Black years for many, drifting by in confusion of argument and disappointment. Mr. Willoughby Shortland writes from the Colonial Secretary's office, advising the Baron de Thierry that in due course his land-claims will be investigated. The Commissioners, Mr. Richmond and Mr. Godfrey, are selected; the date of the sittings fixed. To Mr. Richmond goes a fee of £6 for the service of investigating the de Thierry claims, to Commissioner Godfrey, £3 10s. 0d.

Tamati Waaka Nene opposes the claims, which are cut down by the Commissioners to 1500 acres, of which, according to their overlord, only ten acres are any good for cultivation, without the expenditure of far more money than he possesses.

In retort discourteous, the Baron de Thierry formally opposes the claims of white settlers to lands originally part of the 40,000 acres. Of these settlers, Mr. William Young, of Terawera, shows remarkable forbearance, declaring that if the others give back the lands purchased through Mr. Kendall, he considers it will be his duty as a Christian to follow suit. Unfortunately, his duty as a Christian does not impel him to take the lead, and there the matter rests.

"A little thing in swaddling-clothes got its 2560 acres," writes Charles of the land-grants acquired by certain missionaries for their children. "One old missionary, King, a contemporary of Mr. Kendall, got 25,000 acres for his family of nine." To be fair, by no means all the missionaries were as acquisitive as the so-prolific Mr. King. Numbers made no attempt to claim any land at all, and the really rapacious were, if anything, more frequently catechists and lay assistants than the actual clergy. None the less, for generations the catch-phrase among the Maoris has been, "The missionary told us to turn our eyes to heaven. When our eyes were turned to heaven, he took our land."

Government Houses in New Zealand seem to have been burned down almost as a habit in early days. The old house in Russell flared up first. Governor Hobson, in September 1840, removed his capital and seat of residence to the settlement of Auckland, on the Waitemata Harbour—a town named after his friend and patron, Lord Auckland. Here, seven years later, the portable house shipped from England also went up in smoke, but Hobson was not there to see it. By that time he was safely in his grave; and the country, which ran through its governors as quickly as through its Government Houses, had also wrecked the career of his successor, Captain Fitzroy, formerly of the *Beagle*. The wild mare of the Tasman Sea had an unpleasant knack of bucking all comers off her rump. Hobson died at Auckland in September 1842, worn out, lonely, misunderstood, with little to leave behind him but the tradition of his infuriating fairness over land-deals. Mr. Willoughby Shortland, as stop-gap, stepped into the shoes of Acting-Governor.

Troubles began to be dreaded through the north, in consequence of the barbarous murder of Mrs. Robertson and her family by the natives, near Paihia. This was no chance outrage, but the first omen of stormy weather. In the Hokianga, where civilization and trade had ebbed deplorably as Auckland moved towards closer settlement and prosperity, there was as much consternation among the natives as in the isolated houses of the whites. The Hokianga tribes dreaded the attack of stronger northern war-parties. War-*pas* were being built and fortified everywhere in the district, and a desultory trade in muskets strengthened and extended inland. The poorer of the settlers, cut off from the world, and with two days' heavy going before them if they wanted to dispatch or pick up a letter, lost heart over their stubborn little farms. Many of them actually took refuge with the Maoris, huddling into the war-*pas*. There was the strangest mingling of white men and brown, a refuge of forest creatures uneasy in the far-off crackle of the fire drifting slowly towards them.

Mr. Shortland, our fine new Acting-Governor, purses his lips and shakes his head over a rather engaging letter from the Baron de Thierry, who wants to raise in Her Majesty's service a combined militia of Hokianga's white settlers and friendly natives. He points out that hundreds of the Maoris harbour brotherly sentiments, and that these browner brethren should be caught young. Himself, he has held a commission in His Majesty's 23rd Light Dragoons, and will very willingly act as drill-master over such a militia, not for reward, but for the pleasure of serving his country. "I can offer three grown sons, two European labourers and myself, and am very willing to take charge of forming such a militia." He is dying for brass buttons and gold braid again. Who knows? Perhaps some of the sky-blue and scarlet cloth, the plumage and swords bought at St. Thomas, are here eating their heads off at Mount Isabel, where moth and rust do corrupt. Incidentally, also, the idea of the militia was not such a bad one.

Alas! Mr. Shortland is like the rest, unimpressionable. He does not even answer the letter.

Across the stage walk the new and terrible actors, beasts of a nightmare, the seven lean kine.

Crops fail, prices soar. From the few ships putting in at the river-mouth they buy vile flour at £100 a ton. Potatoes, which were bought for a fig of tobacco a few years before, now cost 10s. a kit, and as the stilt-legged native store-houses become empty, to obtain them at all is almost impossible.

"Fern-root," chant the tribes. "We have fern-root." This is by no means a grace before or after meals. Fern-root is the most despised food, eaten only when the store-houses are empty. Native logicians wax eloquent. The white man is here, you have given him the land. "Fern-root, we have fern-root."

The plight of the Hokianga Maoris becomes desperate, and their manner threatening. They capture and drag in the few remaining pigs, offering them for tremendous prices at the back door. Charles dares not retort aggressively, though it wrings his heart to pay fifteen golden sovereigns for three of his own hogs—and in such an apologetic condition, too. The family are driven to kill off their poultry and some of the unhappy goats, which, having furnished them with milk and cheese all these years, have a genuine place in their affection. The labourers subsist on a scrawny fowl per day. Green-stuffs and potatoes are beautiful dreams. The steel flour-mill is always silent now. Four acres of wheat promised well, but torrential rains came in the autumn. "And where one day there was a field of ripened gold, on the next it was a sea of bright green. The wheat had begun to germinate."

For three days the household lived on a pottage made from dock-leaves—not so far removed from Nebuchadnezzar's grass, that—but the vile stuff made them deathly sick. Isabel and Will came in with a fantastic tale of seeing the side of a hill disintegrate into silent, brown, moving forms, like loping forest beasts. They had been playing at carriages on the stranded old gig which had lost one wheel in the mire of the Long Bush. They were mud to the tops of their high boots, boots so often soled and repaired at home that they scarcely looked like footwear at all. The little boy ran about in tattered woollen jersey and home-made breeches. He was brown as a native, and spoke more frequently in Maori than in English.

Often, commencing reasonably enough with a sentence, he got excited, and out tumbled the native words, helter-skelter. Then he would be annoyed, and stamp his foot.

The little girl—she was fourteen now—wore a long shabby frock of strawberry-coloured print. Her black hair fell in ringlets over this garment. She was beautiful, Charles told himself, but if you deprive a plant of sunlight, of course it looks white and strange ; of course, its beauty is seen under an opaque glass. Her pointed face, with its odd, knowledgeable smile, pricked at his heart.

He was responsible for these children ; he took their docility for granted. But they were not quite the same as himself, as the older children, who were reared in civilization. What were they ? He did not know. At present, they must certainly be hungry and physically wretched, but they gave no sign of it. They merely went on playing carriages in the Long Bush, and spinning yarns about a hillside which was all brown and moving.

On the third day of their semi-starvation, a native came from the Long Bush, bringing with him a fine double-barrelled Menton gun. The weapon was out of repair, no spark flew from the flint. The native offered potatoes in payment if "Te Parena"—"The Baron" in Maori, and the name Charles tried assiduously to substitute for their "Te Pokeno"—would mend the gun.

He was Jack-of-all-trades here, but the gun was a delicate job for which he had no proper equipment. Potatoes, however, were potatoes. He sent the boys out to cut firewood in the bush.

"My Isabel helped me to collect some old shoes and bones. Margaret brought out a fry-pan and an iron pot. I took off the hammers, filed smooth faces on them, wrapped them in leather, and carefully placed them in the iron pot, which I filled with old shoes and bones. I took blacksmith's tongs, and turned a hook at the end of a round bar of iron half an inch thick. Here we placed the pot on the brushwood pile that the boys had made ready, and set the whole blazing. In two hours, I called to my sons to bring a bucket and a tub of water. The whole contents of the iron pot were emptied into the tub, and I drew out the hammers and wiped them clean. Then the gun-flint, with the aid of my hooked iron bar . . ."

A second's waiting, while the fire smouldered down among the *manuka*-sticks. Then the smithy's first triumph is complete.

"Lo, the sparks flew! I kissed my Isabel. "Cheer up, my darling. There, thank God, we are safe again."

Somebody once said that the most significant moment in time occurred when Robinson Crusoe found the print of a human foot on his island sands.

Perhaps, in early New Zealand history, the most significant moment arrived when Charles, probably with a smut on his nose, and stinking of burning leather and cremated bones, drew forth the gun-flint. "Lo, the sparks flew!"

The owner of the gun had eight kits of *kumaras* brought up before light had faded that day. This was the beginning of a period which seemed, after the menace of sheer starvation, more blossomy than anything in the past.

Was it moral that Charles de Thierry should turn gunsmith for the natives? Probably not. Everyone knew perfectly well that there was a scrap coming, though it took longer to eventuate than was expected.

On the other hand, which really *was* his side? The French were out of it, the English wouldn't let him form a militia, and otherwise sat on him. This left him again the Nation of One; its customers, a conglomeration of tribes, some of which had every intention of marching with the war-parties, whilst others preferred to remain friendly with the white man who was supported by the powerful forces of Tamati Waaka Nene. Most likely Charles was as impartial as the armament manufacturers of every civilized nation today.

In six weeks he had earned eight hundred kits of potatoes and maize, several of his stolen hogs, smoked shark and eel. "The little steel mill worked merrily on, and our household had an abundance of Johnny-cakes and corn bread once more."

The Johnny-cakes were all very well for the de Thierrys, but the Maoris were still tightening their belts. Their foodstores were so low that they had not enough both for themselves and for their normal trade, which was all in return for produce. If they sold, they had to go hungry. If they remained unarmed, they were at the mercy of possible war-parties from the north;

or would be prevented from marching out to glory when Hone Heke, the leader of the rebels, showed the white man his hand.

The Maoris chose tight belts. They sold their produce, got their muskets repaired, then, half-starved, begged at the doors of Mount Isabel for food. That they were never turned away, or unkindly treated by the de Thierrys, is illustrated by what came next.

Summer, and the natives were setting out from the whole Hokianga district for a great meeting at the Bay of Islands. The northern tribes would be represented there more fully than at Waitangi, and the fate of hundreds of white settlers might depend on what the native leaders had to say. But for a night and a day there was no time at Mount Isabel to speculate over the issue of the meeting. On the Utoia side of the house, columns of smoke moved tall and threatening as great genii, sprung from the brass bottles of the valleys. Night brought a magnificent and unforgettable scene. The fire was marching upon Mount Isabel from the far side of the river, the whole sky an immense crater of molten gold. The wind was up, blowing straight towards the house. In frantic haste, the supplies of gunpowder were dragged out and dampened.

From the Long Bush, where a brushwood pile had seen the beginning of the smithy in the woods, came a sound that made Charles catch his breath. Before the natives were in sight, he heard them shouting and singing, as they tramped up the red-lit road. He wondered for a moment if the native humour was come to enjoy the fall of King Pokeno's castle. But the party of five hundred natives, men and women, running together, settled his doubts. Naked to the waist, the Maoris tied their old mats about their loins, and dipped their blankets, their most valued possessions, in the stream that ran through Mount Isabel's holding. The women snatched boughs from the Long Bush. In a moment, they were swarming over house and outbuildings, blanketing the thatch with the dripping felt. The air was bright and dangerous with rosy sparks, and the great pantomime of the fire moved splendidly a few yards away, across the sluggish water. One wing caught, and a room was charred out, but they were able to keep the blaze from spreading. There was something breath-taking in the coppery limbs, naked in that beautiful and terrible light. Animals, panting for breath and conscious that humanity was their friend for the night, had run from the bush and crouched close to the house.

"This vast illumination, which seemed laid out by the hand of Art to celebrate some great event, was magnificent beyond words. And I watched them there on the roofs of my house and outbuildings."

Dawn rose coppery over a world where the columns of flame had whirled past on their solemn way. The natives, their hands blistered, their precious blankets stained and spoiled, would accept no payment but a fig of negro-head apiece for what they had done. They filed past, chattering and laughing. The western house was badly charred; a case of books and documents was burned. For the rest, Mount Isabel's wattle-and-daub integrity remained—for what it was worth. And, although the fire had devastated hundreds of acres, flood and famine had so despoiled the land beforehand, and Hokianga trade had dwindled so pitiably, that nobody had much to lose.

But that dawn was the happiest Charles had known since Nukahiva. Dangerous happiness—he might have guessed it. The flagstaff stood, lean and bare, its colours hidden inside the house. Once again there was a great circle of squatting Maoris about its base. He was stiff, exhausted, weary, moving among them. Somehow everyone was carried away; bosoms, brown and white, suffered an expansive moment. They made speeches. So did Charles. They gave him the impassioned and yet childish greetings he had so much wanted.

In the Long Bush, the great *kauri*-tree, known on account of its proboscis as the Elephant Tree, had been burned to cinders. This was a pity, as it was the landmark and cornerstone of the thatched temple where he explained the movements of the stars to Isabel. But the air in bushland where *kauri* has been burned off holds a wonderful fragrance. It smelt as though a thousand censers had been swung, making the cathedral ready for that long-delayed coronation service.

CHAPTER TWENTY

THE KING DECLINES AN OFFER

MODERN science has done us the service of making all war vile and intolerable. A war today is no place for any honest man, horse, dog, ship, *vivandière*, or artist ; and these should draw in their horns, leaving the others, who will not be missed, to fight it out.

But a hundred years ago there were still some good touches. One could find something to recommend, here and there. I shall always approve of Hone Heke's herald, who appeared among the startled whites to inform them that Heke would not think of disturbing the Sabbath, but would begin his war punctually on Tuesday morning. What a lot that young chieftain could have taught some of the rough-necks let loose in Europe today ! . . .

And there was the time—in '48—when a regiment lay encamped in the newly fortified settlements of Wanganui. The fact was, the Maoris outside so outnumbered the red-coats, and the latter knew so little of the lie of the land, that they were not enthusiastic about a sortie, and played cards instead. For weeks and weeks, large brown men kept appearing out of the horizon, to sit on their haunches and loll out their tongues like patient dogs waiting to be taken rabbit-hunting. Steadfastly, the red-coats declined to come forth. The chiefs at last conferred, and sent a message under flag of truce. They must now withdraw, as they had to go fishing—a seasonal occupation ; but they would gladly return and fight the regiment, any time, any place, given one week's notice.

Heke's war, compared with the later Waikato wars, was a mere flash in the pan, almost a one-man show. The young chief was handsome, showy, chivalrous, domineering. In the north he reigned like a bronze Robin Hood, permitting no traders to do business near his territories without milking them. His activities annoyed H.M. Customs Office. They had as much control over the wind as over Hone Heke, who now declared he had never liked the Treaty of Waitangi, and intended to do as he pleased. He had many admirers among the smaller northern fry ; a redoubtable enemy in Nene, whose great prestige Heke both hated and feared ; and a grand, fire-eating, beaky-nosed, leather-hided old general in Kawhiti, who backed him up, not because he was a prey to any high-falutin notions or cared much who won, but because Kawhiti would go anywhere for a fight.

In time to keep Christmas of '43 on New Zealand soil, Captain Fitzroy arrived to take up the duties of Governor. It might be written on the grave of this sailor, "He aimed to please." Hobson had wrecked both health and popularity by his habit of saying "No". Governor Fitzroy simply reversed the process. Land-sharks swarmed, growing fatter and fatter. Whole forests passed overnight into a single and inelegant pair of hands, and were at once hacked down or burned off, leaving the land deteriorated for the next hundred years.

From Auckland's main streets blew an appalling reek of horse-dung, beer, and carcases, the latter dumped by the stockships, which unloaded right at the gates of the town and thought nothing of leaving dead beasts in the roadway. These roads were nothing but tunnels of mud, triumphantly bridged by one tavern-keeper with empty barrels, sawn in two and placed end to end, like a series of fantastic Japanese bridges. Yet there were livery stables, carriages, flutter of fine ladies . . . a bloom of quickly grown beauty, an orchid thriving on a dung-heap.

Other ladies, quite as fine in their own way, with their lavish bosoms and long feathers, leaned bawling from the red-and-white brothels in Fort Street and Chancery Lane. Should the passer-by seem curt, they emptied their chambers on his stove-pipe hat, and thus had the better of him either way. The taverns had beautiful, lusty names : the "Fortune of War", the "Naked Indian", the "Spread Eagle", the "Black Joke".

Miser Annersley's son came into the fortune which his father could not take with him to the grave, though the old man groaned enough at parting with all those golden jimmies.

The lad hired a four-wheeler, and drove past the red-and-white houses, flinging handfuls of gold from his silk hat, his young face bright-flushed and excited. The girls from Black Julia's ran out in their shifts, to scramble in the mud for his bounty. He made a denunciatory speech to them, came sprawling down, to be picked up by Black Julia in person. Against that immense bosom, he wept that everybody misjudged him; he was no miser. "Yas, dear . . . yas, Honey," soothed Black Julia, rocking him like a doll, while her girls went through his pockets.

"*When did our troubles begin? It was when we were told that the White Queen was to be our mother.*"

But Auckland was a white town, divorced from the wilderness, as Russell with its leaning hills, Hokianga with its wooded valleys, could never be. The Maori was a legend here, an ornament. Nobody was afraid of him. Native canoes came from the Bay of Islands, offering loads of huge golden honey-peaches at a penny a kit. Town-Maoris, their clothing grotesquely Europeanized, squatted under little calico tents, selling anything and everything from flax kits. Delicious rock oysters were sixpence a kit of three hundred.

Governor Fitzroy and his friends did not make any comprehensive study of the secret societies forming among northern tribes—societies whose flax-paper messages were replacing the old and conspicuous means of the *korero** as a call to arms.

Population flowed steadily to Auckland, its movement facilitated by Fitzroy's system of land exchange. Auckland was to be a town, a safe and flourishing settlement, though to effect this might drain the outlying districts of their sparse holdings.

A value of £1 an acre was put on all lands held by country settlers. This was paid for, not in cash, but in Government scrip, and the scrip then auctioned in Auckland, where the buyers were mostly investors who could afford to hold remote land purchases until the day came when they were safe territory, and their value worth mention. Meanwhile, with the proceeds of the scrip-auctions in their pockets, smaller settlers from Hokianga and Bay of Islands farms drifted down to the seat of Government.

---

* Native gathering.

Driven for money—not precisely a new situation for him—Charles put his lands in the auctioneer's hands, only to find that, owing to the fear of native disturbances, Government scrip in the Hokianga district was fetching a miserable price. So the plans of migration were abandoned, and the family stayed on at Mount Isabel, with a bundle of more or less worthless scrip—which was, none the less, what Charles used for money when he could persuade people to accept it—and a mortgage over the farm to cover the auction proceeds. The wattle-and-daub house was falling to pieces, into the bargain, and its large three-block structure had outlived its usefulness, now that not a single courtier, labourer, or admirer —except "my faithful Margaret Neilsen"—remained at the Court of the Baron de Thierry.

At this opportune moment, when the rest flee the land as if the Devil were in it, Charles determines on a new castle.

"In September 1844, I purchased from Mr. Russell 23,000 feet of board, for £50. For this he took £333 in scrip."

The carpenter, having demanded that he should be paid in advance for building the new house (because the natives are raising such a dust that the Hokianga is no place for honest workmen), puts the scrip in his pocket, turns tail, and disappears, heading for Auckland, pursued by the laments of the family.

Do you remember Chief Tiro? ("O my friends, rejoice with me.... He is coming to civilize our country and make it reputable.") Out of the past comes Tiro now, eloquent as ever, and bursting with information for the authorities in Auckland, which he demands that Charles shall at once communicate to Governor Fitzroy. Tiro then sits down on the doorstep, and awaits an official reply with beautiful red lions in sealing-wax. Alas! Governor Fitzroy is lacking in any sense of the picturesque. He never summons Tiro to a private audience in Auckland, nor even condescends to take notice of his information about the war-parties. Tiro, in a huff, turns north, and joins the rebels, taking with him his family and all his adherents.

The Long Bush is closing softly, with the little crumpled hands of bracken and long tendrils of creeper, over the clay roads leading from Mount Isabel. This invasion is harder to resist than all the others. The house, unable to execute a strategic retreat, stands on, with a perpetually surprised look on its staring window-panes. They are such small shields to bear up against such immense and overpowering sunsets.

In this year of its isolation, many chiefs, and natives of lower caste also, drift around Mount Isabel. A nervous man might compare them to the troops of Midian, but Charles thinks they have come to ask his advice. He asks them indoors, and makes Margaret give them lemonade, which is, in its way, a superb insult.

Hone Heke, the paramount war-chief, once puts in an appearance. About this Charles narrated an incident which might have come more appropriately from the Baron Munchausen than from the Baron de Thierry. Heke, he says, came unannounced, and made himself a little fresh in the kitchen, where nobody knew his name. There was a fine musket over the door, the pride of Charles's heart and the admiration of the Maoris. Heke, after examining it, indicated that he wanted the gun for himself. Charles said "No". Heke retained his hold of the musket, while sitting on a three-legged stool. Charles grasped the butt, and pulled with such vigour that the stool gave way, precipitating the war-lord to the floor.

Charles, regaining possession of his weapon, was a little disconcerted—but not too much—to learn when one of his sons came home that it was Heke whom he had thus bowled over. Heke, however, took it all in excellent part, suddenly bursting into a shout of laughter. "He sprang to his feet and shook my hands," says Charles.

No other white family remains in the neighbourhood. He must have engendered immense curiosity—he and his empty flagstaff, his open hand, his homilies—among the restive tribes, padding about on their flax-paper errands. Perhaps they grew fond of him in the end . . . "wild things out of the wet, wild woods". Perhaps, also, he talked too freely of his sympathies with the brown man's losing fight for national identity. That got him into a pickle.

There were shouting and singing of a tribe on the march, one misty day, with the little nectarines and apricots just sufficiently green-ripe for the wax-eyes from the bush to be interested. Charles got home in time to open his door to heavy knockings. The women, used to alarms, stayed in the background. Papa did the arguing for everybody.

William Repa, who came that day to Mount Isabel at the head of his tribe, has already been mentioned for his religious vagaries—Wesleyan one moment, then Roman Catholic, good High Church of England next, and, at the time of this social call, plain, polygamous "devil".

William Repa was the only chief who had ever pestered Charles for strong liquors, though all the natives liked light wines. Repa was a drunkard; yet he was not unimpressive, and not a revolting figure. A strange, bitter-mouthed, lonely man, feared for his outbursts of temper, avoided by the white men, Repa had been one of those who helped to install the de Thierrys at Mount Isabel.

He was by no means the species of penny ogre who lives by terrorizing the weak. Something smouldered in him . . . a distortion of Nene's deep love for the race, Hone Heke's love of a fight, without that young warrior's clean-run chivalry. An old scar slashed his cheek, marring the blue tattoo-pattern. Repa eschewed European dress, but the bloodshot eyes showed how *pakeha* vices had caught him far more securely than any open surrender to *pakeha* authority. There was something pitiable about him—pitiable and frightening together. He spoke in a blurred voice. It was some time before Charles could make out what he wanted. Behind him, the murmured approval from the listening Maoris was like a wind rising among the trees.

William Repa wanted the flag of the de Thierrys, the flag that had flown from the empty flagstaff. A flag is something sacred to the native. Because the White Queen's flag had flown at Russell, her power was mighty there. Because the English flag was set in Maori soil, the land belonged no more to its people. The hoarse voice rose in bitter eloquence as Repa reminded Charles of his coming.

"You promised that you would be our father. You said you would lead us, and do good for us. You said that all would be the same together, Maori and white man. Then the White Queen sent her ships; your flag was taken down. Have you, too, eaten the White Queen's stir-about? No, no, it is not so. I, Repa, say now that you are a good man, you are Repa's father. We are going to drive the White Queen's people into the sea; the land will be ours again. Give us the flag, to take with us into battle."

The hills seemed locked in silence, though the oration went on and on. There was nothing in Charles de Thierry's mind but an empty flagstaff, a kingdom non-existent outside of a dream. Trial by jury of whites and natives . . . roads, hospitals, schools . . . teach English, all English, nothing but English; would they be so easily cheated, then? . . . If any white settler marries a native woman, he must in every respect treat her as his wife . . . for every acre you have now under cultivation, I will give you freehold of three more. . . . It seemed very clear, in the waning light, the kingdom unbuilded.

He began to speak, hardly knowing what he said, about the flag which they wanted. . . .

"Then the Queen's flag was hoisted in New Zealand, the sovereignty of the land belonged to her, and only to her. It was the word of the Maori people. When I flew my flag, here on Mount Isabel, none of you would listen to me. You would not take part in the things I had planned, you let the lands I had bought be taken away. When you gave over the country to the White Queen, all my power to help you was gone, and I was forced to take down my flag. I am a white man, my flag can never be raised in battle against other white men. If you fight against the white man, you will be lost. The White Queen's ships will come from Sydney."

All the while the words on his lips meant precisely nothing. Deep and formless, that love of the native races which had been the keynote of his spirit since youth struggled for some means of expression. Greenstone against guns, bravery against organization. . . . I am a white man; to betray that could not help. . . . Too late now for a militia of friendly forces; even Tiro, poor, vain old Tiro, they never troubled to take any notice of him, and his loyalty's dead and gone. A man can't make speeches with his heart torn in two.

He looked up and saw Isabel on the other side of the door. For the moment the girl looked at him like a shadow, like a ghost, her hair was so black, her eyes so wide and dark in the peaked face. She was silent and obedient. Somehow he had contrived to fail her, like the others, but she understood him now, and without words. That look between them, and she slipped away into the house. For five minutes more, Charles strove to hold the natives with the lamest speech he had ever made in his life. Then Isabel came out of the house, white as death, and smiling. She nodded to him.

Charles said : "You cannot have the flag, William Repa. There is no flag in my house any more. While we were talking, my daughter went to the place where it was kept and cut it to pieces."

"It is true," said Isabel, watching Repa. "I have cut my father's flag into tiny bits."

The chieftain talked rapidly to the men behind him. There was that hideous shout, and their line surged forward. Repa's face was distorted with anger.

"We will kill her now," he said ; and Charles saw Repa's two hands close on the white line where Isabel's print dress was drawn over her shoulders.

She was terrified at his touch, and cried out, "Kill me yourself, kill me yourself ! Don't let them touch me !" Then she burst into bitter sobbing. He knew that she was alienated from the normal world, so much so that it seemed strange to see Isabel frightened at last. It was only the other day that Colonel Wakefield had sent her the green-and-yellow mannikin from the *Tory*. Now she was grown up, almost seventeen, and the Maoris were going to kill her.

"Why, Repa, you knew her as a child," he said, feeling very old.

Then, quite suddenly, it was over. As once Richard de Thierry, leaning over a native whose bonds he had just cut, had thought, "Those were a man's eyes," Charles now saw something in Repa's look which, for all his continual idealizing of the native race, he had never seen in any Maori face before. Repa took his hands, enormous brown hands, away from Isabel's shoulders. There was a look between them, as of people who have met suddenly and strangely in a wilderness, and greet one another quietly, knowing that in a moment they must part again. And no greater jungle could have surged around them than that tangle of errors and misapprehension in which they stood. White man, brown man. The hostility of race to race ; two quick prides drawn like swords against each other ; disease, warfare, and death—a tangle in which the human being stands utterly bewildered. It is only for an instant that men can meet one another so. But that instant is never forgotten, and no matter how obscure its circumstances, it is cast in immortality.

Some few words, and then Repa, with his tribe at his heels, went off into the Long Bush. Charles lifted Isabel, and carried her to the couch in the room whose wide windows looked over the wooded valleys. All that afternoon, as he moved about the house, he could hear her sobbing. She was too utterly a part of his dream. He had dedicated her to it, shut her up in it, under the streaming colours at Panama, in the sweet groves of Nukahiva, here at Mount Isabel in the secret flax-roofed temple where none but the two of them had ever come. As the dream, from its original fair lineaments, had become puzzling, violent, and distorted, Isabel suffered as even he could never suffer. For it was he who made the dream, but Isabel was its fabric.

Tiro came on the next day, to turn the knife in his heart. He begged for the flag, even in pieces, even a shred of it, to bring luck in the wars. He was the same light-hearted, friendly creature as of old, and went off after dinner, full of the heroic deeds he was about to perform.

A day later, Nene himself came to Mount Isabel, with the news that meant "War Declared". Hone Heke had cut down the British flagstaff on the hill at Kororareka.

Unless they took refuge with the Maoris, the family could remain no longer at Mount Isabel. A struggling war-party, a torch dropped in the Long Bush, that would be the end ; and not a single neighbour left to befriend them. Russell was the nearest refuge. Charles set off on horse, a day later, for Paihia, near which the chief Mokatu had first fired the grass in this war by the murder of the Robertson family.

In the orchard apricots were in season, little flushed drippy fruits which the children gathered by the bushel from the long grass. There were dusky grapes coming on, soon to be purplish under the vine-leaves. The house, with its shabby, unpainted walls, stood out from the screen of the Long Bush as Charles looked back. He wondered why he had ever left the empty flagstaff standing there, a useless provocation to the natives; or if, had he been without wife and family, he would have abandoned the white races, for better, for worse. He never saw Mount Isabel again.

On March 3rd, Charles sent for his family, William Repa coming from his fortified *pa* to see the family through to Kororareka. The Maoris brought three horses. Old Black Aladdin had departed with Charles, and the native ponies carried Emily and Isabel, with Margaret balanced precariously on the third saddle, clutching Will, who, in his twelfth year, was finding the exodus a high peak of adventure.

The furniture was abandoned, though thirty natives trotted alongside, bearing personal belongings, bedding, and what lighter goods they could manage. Behind them bees murmured in the green-and-golden orchard. The goats and turkeys suffered the Crusoe fate so often prophesied, and remained to run wild in the bush. Little by little, the trees took back the breathing-space they had given, and the road where King Pokeno had demanded a carriage-drive complete with prancing greys was forgotten. Only, perhaps, in the springtime, snow and rose, drift the petals of foreign fruit trees, strangling among the lustier native inhabitants. Or there is a night-fountain of sweetness, where Isabel's "mossy rose" shows its pink cap through the straggle of weeds, and the double balsam opens its healing leaves secretly, to cure the hurt dream that seeks it out while the dreamer lies sleeping and far away. And where the Hokianga glitters through its yellow dunes, sickle leaves dance on the eucalyptus-tree planted on the day of his landing by Charles, Baron de Thierry, King of Nukahiva, Sovereign Chief of New Zealand.

The journey from Mount Isabel was more picturesque than perilous. War in those days was conducted along pleasantly unconventional lines. When they were sitting at breakfast with Repa, in the stone *pa* just beyond the Long Bush, who should appear but Hone Heke, the war-lord himself. Did he, aroused against the white man, promptly massacre these innocents? On the contrary, he had breakfast too, made himself quite charming, and pressed on them the offer of any help they needed in transport. He had been visiting friends at the little Waimate Mission Station. Right up to the outbreak of fighting, Heke was the kindest of district visitors to the young son of a missionary family, who had fallen desperately ill. Earnestly he impressed on the parents of this dying boy the necessity of resigning themselves to the will of God ; and then went away, lithe as a forest animal, to put the fear of death into the entire white population of the Bay of Islands. It had no logic, but there was a queer kind of beauty about it. That is why I say, curse your machine-fighting. The blood of Nene, of Heke, of the illogical and gallant, must never be offered in a machine war, since they share none of the blood-guilt attached to the machines of destruction. Do what you feel is most becoming to you in Europe. But a ram must be found for Isaac.

Keri-Keri was white and jade in morning sun. The missionaries had settled here since early days, and among them the name of the de Thierrys was as popular as *tutu* poison—as Emily discovered when she knocked at the door of Mrs. Colman's* house and asked for shelter overnight.

Emily de Thierry, a lady in middle life, somewhat past forty-five, and attired in muddy riding-boots and a habit whose pristine beauty has long departed. All the light gold of her hair, no longer cleverly arranged, has become indeterminate and streaky. Her small waist, which doubtless gave her some innocent pride when in Gloucester she poured tea for her papa's curates, has disappeared owing to the efforts involved in producing five children, wandering round a world, working hard on an isolated farm, eating what she could get, and being quite unable to procure new corsets. The Archdeacon Thomas Rudge, if then alive, would have passed her in the street, never dreaming that so weather-beaten a piece of flesh could have sprung from his own dignified loins.

She did not know, when she rang the bell-pull, whether she most wanted to take off her boots, which were mountainous with clay, or to sit down and burst into tears. It was one of the two. Emily badly needed a bosom to cry on. Mrs. Colman gave her black bombasine.

They sat in the parlour, where everything was stuffed with

---

*"Mrs. Colman" is an alias. There are many living descendants of the family mentioned by Charles, and probably, even if the lady were unkind to the notorious de Thierrys, she was otherwise a Christian.

horsehair. Mrs. Colman had taken tea, but a servant brought the travellers cups, one each, on a tray, and a plate on which reposed four virginal-looking slices of bread. Mrs. Colman did not drink with the refugees. Her replies were monosyllabic, and in between she offered no comments. One leapt from precipice to precipice, across great chasms of silence, chasms that had never known the sun. The black china dogs on the mantelshelf looked also as if they were prepared to bark, but could not release their tiny, infuriated voices from prison.

None of the family was invited to stay the night. Emily, Isabel, and Margaret were given an attic between them in an old building on the other side of the road. The de Thierry boys Mrs. Colman refused to harbour at all, and they remained out of doors, in Repa's charge. The three women slept on shake-downs, their first New Zealand night in civilized surroundings since Lieutenant McDonnell had sent his two Captains to escort the Baroness de Thierry to Te Horeke.

"No place," thought Emily, lying with pale moonlight tossed through the shutters, like great blond pear-petals. Little details of the journey became painfully clear in her mind. A curve of the Long Bush road, between great banks of the ragged-barked, slender *manuka*. A sick child at the stone *pa*, lying on a heap of smelly mats, its black hair tangled over its beaky face, which was just like the face of a starved fledgeling bird. Isabel sitting still as a wax doll in Mrs. Colman's parlour, a doll holding up the sleeves and high shoulders of her shabby cherry-coloured dress. "Her clothes are in rags," fretted Emily, and then saw a worn patch on Mrs. Colman's green sofa, and wondered if this made Mrs. Colman human. Mrs. Colman's heaven would be filled with angels all in starched and laundered white. If any of them developed a worn patch, the sky would be filled with the slender, stabbing light of their darning-needles, as they stitched and stitched, endlessly, viciously . . . covering things up, and gossiping as they worked.

Her mind, like the worn-out, ungainly machine of her body, was aching with tiredness, but the stream of thought refused to break. She thought of the boys, and wondered what mischief they were up to with Repa. "The Bay of Islands is full of native brothels," coldly prompted the enemy. She saw her sons, for a moment, as the strange white women of the Bay of Islands, used to neighbourhood if not to full civilization, must see them. Big, uncouth, walking alternately, when unwatched, with the queer grace of animals, or, when eyes were on them, with a sullen, self-conscious slouch of hips and shoulders. Their hands were the broad, coarse hands of farm labourers. Though they could talk enough among themselves —dropping far too readily into Maori—with outsiders they were dumb, or sat staring. All creatures on the defensive.

"But they are beautiful boys," said Emily to the world. "Look at them as I have seen them." She stripped away their clumsy rags, and, to an audience of admiring mothers, showed them as they had been at the successive ages of two, four, seven —little golden-brown bodies, with deep chests, slender hips and loins, more beautiful, more beautiful than the body of a girl. Yes; Isabel belonged to her father. "He loves her so," Emily defended herself. But her sons were her own. They were encamped in a hateful, hostile place, full of suspicion. She was their camp-follower—a ridiculous role for a woman of her age, and one for which the boys wouldn't thank her.

Something closed tight, like a small door shutting in her mind. From that night, she was other than the woman who had so often lain awake, wondering where next Charles would contrive to lead them all. That Emily was finished with, in the attic room. For the rest of her life, her reserve with the outside world was implacable. In her last years, she bore the oddest resemblance to the woman who, of all women, would have been least likely to tolerate Their Majesties of Utopia— Queen Victoria. Wearing ruffled black silks and bonnets firmly seated on her faded hair, she moved with dignity and resolution through the medley. But she was never Emily of the moonlight again.

Outside, the boys were having the time of their lives with the native caravanserai, digesting a huge Maori supper of mussels and *kumaras* while their mother and sister famished. But Repa was in a peevish frame of mind. The missionary-woman, he considered, had insulted his personal dignity by refusing his charges hospitality. He debated whether to cut her throat. The boys dissuaded him. Suddenly Repa's face relaxed in its nearest approach to a grin. He revenged himself by turning the whole tribe loose in the Colman orchard, where they stripped the trees and pelted one another with apples.

The Colmans had already dealt with Charles. The infamous Baron de Thierry arrived there with a hurricane of a cold upon him, beseeching Mr. Colman to tell the one and only lodging-house keeper in the vicinity that he was a safe tenant for the night. Mr. Colman refused, remarking that there was a native *pa* about four miles away. Rain came howling down as Charles and his guide—later discovered to have been a notorious cannibal—tramped the hills, only to lose themselves in a swamp where they must abide till morning.

"The native curled up under his blanket. I sat on my trunk—it contained about £250 in scrip, all I possessed in the world—with my umbrella up." Was even the dignity of the Baron de Thierry proof against the quaintness of this occasion? If only there had been a cartoonist at hand! . . .

Potatoes and delicious little rock oysters were the family fare next morning. From Keri-Keri Repa launched the long, red-ochred canoes, and waves tossed bright around them for a very rough journey to Kororareka. The natives sang as they paddled, a plaintive chant with a steady rhythm.

They saw ships black-sparred against the watered grey silk of the Bay, and Kororareka growing clearer in detail of gabled houses and foreshore road. It was their first glimpse of a town since their arrival in New Zealand. At a little distance lay the old Government settlement of Russell. The sun shone brilliantly over that rounded green hill on which stood the flagstaff that Hone Heke had thrice cut down.

A mile out from shore, there was a sound like a dull start of thunder, and the water clipped up in a white column, not a hundred yards ahead. H.M.S. *Hazard*, seeing war-canoes making for the beach, and ready for anything on the part of an enemy whose quaint rules of fighting had already demoralized the opposition, had put a shot across the bows of Repa's canoe.

On shore Charles, white-faced, cursed all officers, military and naval, in terms deserving of prompt arrest. But they were landing now, with the quite unnecessary admonition from the *Hazard* that Repa must at once take his canoe and tribe out of the Bay.

Cherry frock crumpled, black curls loose and shining where the spray had touched them . . . she was too exhausted then for the officers to notice how pretty she was ; but they discovered it later.

A word from Charles to Repa. The chief shook his head.

"We will take no pay from our father. Good-bye."

The canoes are launched on the sleek, pigeon-plume waves. Repa sits immobile as a carved figure-head ; the red prows pierce northwards once again. Good-bye, then . . . with a dazzle of sun on the waters, blurring the vision of him who stares after you. The man who commands those canoes is good and bad, as are most men. And he knows the meaning of friendship. And now he is gone. A week later, Repa was fighting with the war-parties.

In the sack of Kororareka, the attacking natives kept a red shirt flying . . . all the flag they could secure.

In the piecemeal records preserved by Charles, there is one entry scratched out, all but illegible. A few words can be distinguished.

"And if I could ask for any . . . would ask for certain pieces of crimson and azure . . . would be respected everywhere. . . ."

I wish he had done it. Traitor or not, he belonged with them, and with nobody else. He would have been in the way, in the hurrying lights and hurrying shadows of the native *pa*. However, the Maoris needed a flag, and in between rush-hours they would have enjoyed talking with him. They also are discursive, with an eloquence so luscious that it makes one almost embarrassed at first, like the too-much-juice of tropical fruits. But Charles, who understood this language to a marked degree, was their man. And over the whole of the world today, it is hard to think of a single place where the white man's game may fairly be said to be worth the candle.

CHAPTER TWENTY-ONE

KORORAREKA

AT noon on March 9th, 1845, a cloud of dust was seen moving, brown, thick, and slow along the clay road from Paroa Bay into Kororareka. Glasses were turned on it from the decks of the British war-sloop, H.M.S. *Hazard*, and the whisper, "Heke's on the move," went the rounds. Then a young officer clicked his heels, made his report to Acting-Commander David Robertson. The jest was tossed down to the waiting men like an orange; a roar of laughter went up. The Maoris were coming, all right . . . stragglers from a nearby *pa*, driving a great number of sheep past the danger zone. Apparently the shore defences were annoyed that natives, however peaceable, should be trapesing around the countryside, for the hill gun grumbled. Two shots went over the dusty river of men and beasts, but no damage was done, and the Maori drovers showed no alarm.

Diverting attention by this manœuvre, Heke brought his forces more securely into position around the hills above Kororareka.

Russell, a few miles from Kororareka, became a ghost town when Hobson shifted the seat of government to Auckland. The two Bay of Islands settlements drifted together, their identities became slowly merged. At the time of Heke's attack, most of the settlers had established themselves in Kororareka. Later, the little settlement dropped the long-winded native name, and became Russell, *tout court*. This is where the tourist goes today when he wishes to haul tons of mako and marlin out of the obligingly vasty deeps. Of the original Russell, nothing remains. It has turned its back on history.

When Heke's behaviour was at its most spectacular, then, the defences of the Bay were pretty well concentrated in Kororareka. And the trouble with the campaign was that nobody knew from one day to the next whether it was a war or a game of tiddlywinks.

Governor Fitzroy, as has been mentioned, liked to make himself pleasant. Convinced that a war with Hone Heke was not the best means to this, he gave a fatal impression of weakness, now offering concessions, now making difficulties. The fact was, Captain Fitzroy was a good sailor, but no administrator. An attempt to change his vocation cost him his career.

Heke, assured by enemy agencies (the Americans were suspected) that British power stood or fell with the Union Jack, centred his dislike on the flagstaff. It stood, he said, on ground never ceded under the Treaty of Waitangi, and consequently not the property of the Crown. Troops were brought from Sydney to change this attitude of mind. Then a parcel of chieftains made their submission to the Governor, handing in their muskets—which, by the way, proved to be ancient weapons, badly out of repair. Governor Fitzroy's friendliness got the better of him. He sent the troops back to Sydney, and gave back the muskets as well. A second and a third time Heke, his warriors at once re-arming throughout the north, cut down the flagstaff. Fitzroy passed the hopeful stage, and the *Hazard* took up her station in the Bay of Islands, lying off Kororareka.

The sight of a British ship, it was expected, would change the plans of the natives. That might have been all right. Unfortunately, the Bay of Islands was so accustomed to dealing in its own manner with ships of all nations. Something in the garish, noisy streets, whose red gables made a narrow flange under the leaning hills, got into discipline like the weevil into ship's biscuit. And this was such a comic-opera campaign.

There can be no denying it. By a combination of bad luck, bad management, and protracted optimism, the defenders contrived rather to encourage than to impress the natives, who, in any case, utterly outnumbered the whites, and were by no means badly off for arms. They might have been afraid of the *Hazard's* roundshot, but the sloop removed this difficulty by giving several preliminary displays of outrageous marksmanship, and by permitting several of her crew, in Mary Lockhart's brothel, to talk too much about the low state of her ammunition.

The situation, too late, was understood as serious. Fitzroy

made frantic attempts to procure more warships from Sydney. Auckland itself was suffering a nervous crisis, expecting Heke to arrive and butcher the population at any moment. (He intended to do this. But Nene and Te Whero Whero, another great chieftain, between them spoiled the plan.) Meanwhile, the warships did not come, and did not come. . . .

The first exchange of hostilities was quaint. A week before, the *Hazard's* pinnace had fired on Heke's own canoe, as the chief passed blandly by to Keri-Keri, and by damned bad marksmanship contrived to miss. Governor Fitzroy put a price on Heke's head. Heke retorted by offering exactly the same figure for the Governor's topknot . . . and for that, alone, the young man deserves immortality. Acting-Commander Robertson's deputy in the shore defences, a hot-headed Lieutenant named Philpots, had galloped in the wrong direction a few mornings ago, with the midshipmite he was pleased to call his "aide-de-camp", and both were taken by the Maoris. To their relief and humiliation, they were turned loose with only the loss of a pistol.

On shore, Mr. Beckham, a magistrate, had joined forces with Lieutenant Philpots in effecting martial law. This had the result of making everyone tense, excited, and uncomfortable, but it is not known to have achieved any positive good. Mr. Hector, a choleric Russell attorney, was the Left Wing, and fought Mr. Beckham's ideas every inch of the way.

Charles states that Mr. Hector's roar was much more dreaded in Kororareka than the native tomahawks, but this may be mere libel.

Then there was Mary Lockhart's, representing the fair deserved, and inexpensively achieved, by the brave. A two-storeyed, russet-painted house at the corner of the main street, it had been rented by white men, and the lowest of Maori prostitutes moved in, gaudy in their European clothing and mock jewellery. Intercourse between sailors and native women was the custom of the Bay of Islands, and the sudden sparkle of brown eyes, the unexpected point of Maori wit, put a polish on the crudity of such affairs.

Three nights before the attack, Mary Lockhart, a handsome, middle-aged native woman, had slipped out of the house, a black shawl over her head, feet bare like any poor girl from the country, and hurried to the conference of chiefs at Pomare's *pa*. Heke was there, tall and confident . . . listening. From that hour, the war-party knew more than it should have done concerning the quantity of the defenders' ammunition.

Meanwhile, Charles de Thierry was making himself a little more unpopular. It sounds grotesque. But it is so much easier to start this practice than to stop it.

Sleeping in the guard-room at nights, while his sons patrolled the hills on sentry-duty, he learned what it is to be an insignificant unit attached to a world in a hurry. Everyone at the settlement was on edge, secretly or openly flustered, striving to summon up an air of command by barking and growling. It is not pleasant to go to sleep at night expecting to be wakened by the glare of flames and the uncouth yells of savages. Moreover, the settlers had their women and children on their hands. For so long they had taken the timely arrival of the warships from Sydney for granted, that now a safe evacuation of Kororareka seemed less feasible than staying to brave things out. A thousand times in a day they visioned the sails of the war-sloops spreading over the Bay, saw themselves, grouped on the foreshore, cheering and shaking hands. They lived on illusions, and in great discomfort. Little Kororareka was on the outer edge of panic.

Charles began to feel that they were rude to him. He felt that they were treading him underfoot. He had grown so used to that state of being in which every man's hand was against him that he could not believe all the singing hostility and excitement in the air was not directed against his own grey head. The tepid coffee, doled out in dirty tin pannikins, the need of sleeping in his greatcoat, the snappy manners of passers-by . . . it gave him the impression of another conspiracy against him. More, he was the stranger. These people, under their curtness and nervousness, knew one another very well, and could understand abbreviations. But who had time to listen to the high-flown de Thierry periods ? If they spoke of him at all, it was not in complimentary terms.

He became a lightning-conductor for insults. In the end, of course, he exasperated them into behaving as crudely as anyone could have wished.

There is the other side. He had left his heart at Mount

Isabel and with the natives ; Mrs. Colman offered the Baroness four miserable slices of bread-and-butter ; the women of his household were immured in an attic bedroom.

Despite all this, he was longing to shine. Immediately he did all the wrong things. He offered advice, pointing out to the defenders that their methods were wrong from first to last, and their position untenable. He mentioned that he had held a commission in His Majesty's 23rd Light Dragoons, and was very experienced with the natives.

Kororareka looked savage.

A score of times he told himself he'd not be dictated to by that little upstart Philpots. Defence organization . . . a civil request, and he'd show the jackanapes what defence was, and teach them a thing or two about the Maori that had seemingly escaped their intelligence.

Lieutenant Philpots sent a terse command that the Baron de Thierry was to join the Civic Guard. It was not an invitation, and he said nothing about a commission . . . gold lace, not an inch of it.

The Baron de Thierry sent his compliments, and refused.

The Baron de Thierry was informed that if he did not immediately do as he was told, his family would be denied all British protection.

"Then, sir," retorted the Baron, purple in the face, "I shall place my wife, children, and household under the protection of the American flag."

If he had merely announced his intention of proceeding into Buckingham Palace with a bomb and lighted match, they might have thought it improper. But when he mentioned American protection, they could cheerfully have torn him limb from limb.

A few miles across the Bay, at Paihia, lay anchored the United States frigate, *St. Louis*, much better armed than H.M.S. *Hazard*. Her assistance against the natives, in the settlers' opinion, would put Kororareka out of danger. But the Captain of the *St. Louis*, quite properly, from his own point of view, determined to remain neutral. After the sack of the town, he gave considerable assistance in taking off refugees, under heavy fire. Before hostilities commenced, he refused to make himself useful. Sparks were flying between the

Captain of the *St. Louis* and Lieutenant Philpots, who had the safety of women and children on his mind.

Twenty minutes after Charles had stalked out of the defence committee's office, meaning to arrange a passage for himself and his family on the *Sir John Franklin*, a schooner which undertook to sail for Auckland as soon as the disturbances were over, he was greeted in the main street by a ragged shout which ran from mouth to mouth.

"French bastard ! . . . French bastard ! . . . French bastard ! . . ."

It was a narrow street, all taverns and straggling houses. Out of these poured the citizens and sailors, the native girls, until the world was nothing but a shout. Kororareka was in that frame of mind when people burn a witch because the cows have gone dry and too many children are breaking out in spots. Afterwards they feel happier and more efficient, until they notice that the cows are drier and the children spottier than ever. Their world was no longer safe nor coherent. Some blamed the natives, some Governor Fitzroy, Mr. Hector, Mr. Beckham, the *St. Louis*. Now they had the satisfaction of saying the same thing in chorus. Those at the far end of the street had no idea what it was all about. They simply saw a man walking, and heard their friends and acquaintances roaring, "Bastard !" "French bastard !" shrieked the seagulls. Charles stalked along, red in the face, and thinking obscurely of Lavaud's *Code Napoleon*, with the tricoloured edges.

Since the noise, like a vulgar neighbour, marched up the garden path and intruded itself into the house where the de Thierry women had taken refuge, Isabel, sitting in the window-seat of a parlour with shabby pink wallpaper, for an instant thrust her fingers into her ears. Then she let her hands fall into her lap again, and sat listening, a peculiarly intent look on her face.

A blockhouse, supposedly invincible, stood on Flagstaff Hill ; another behind Mr. Polack's house, with a palisade of sharpened *ti*-tree stakes. Mr. Polack's house also was crudely fortified, and acted as a third blockhouse. Charles had a glimpse of his old acquaintance, Archdeacon Williams, hurrying from Paihia to dispose of the mission goods in Mr. Polack's house, where already £10,000 worth of the settlers' valuables had been deposited. Archdeacon Williams, even at that date, did his best to assure the frightened women that the attack would come to nothing. In Polack's cellars the ammunition for the shore defences was stored away, making the place, as events proved, a dangerous refuge for the women and children, who were ordered there on the Monday after Heke's challenge arrived.

A hasty breakfast next morning, and the de Thierrys—Emily, Isabel, and Margaret Neilsen had refused the shelter of the blockhouse—boarded the *Sir John Franklin*, leaving old Black Aladdin tethered in a grass plot behind Bishop Pompallier's house. The schooner, which had lent her only gun to the settlers, lay right inshore. Bishop Pompallier, who had first offered the de Thierrys the shelter of his mission, decided himself to board the schooner, and await the turn of events. The clergy of other denominations were well represented. Out of the west arrived the tall young Anglican Bishop Selwyn, on his little schooner. In the Bay lay the Colonial brig, *Victoria*, Benjamin Turner's schooners, *Flying Fish* and *Dolphin*, H.M.S. *Hazard* ; the *St. Louis* at a distance of some miles, lying near Paihia, and coming up from the north, her sails rusty over her cumbersome black bulk ; the squat old whaler, *Matilda*. The smaller ships were anchored so close inshore that their decks were within musket-range, and every word of command shouted from the *Hazard's* decks could be heard aboard the *Sir John Franklin*.

The storm broke on Tuesday, March 10th, in still early morning, with the guns of the lower blockhouse, under Mr. Hector's direction, firing the first shot at a native party. Not a man fell, but a shout from the *Hazard* greeted the Maori rush down the hillsides. A seaman dropped with a musket-ball through his chest, as the gun behind Polack's fell to the enemy, without a single native casualty.

The barricaded doors of the upper blockhouse were seen to open, and the defenders, headed by Lieutenant Philpots, poured out in a sortie as brave as it was indiscreet. In five minutes the party was cut off from the blockhouse, and both blockhouse and flagstaff fell to the natives. The flagstaff was sheathed in a heavy iron casing, but not even this could withstand the battering of tomahawks. There was a wild yell as the Union Jack was torn down, to be pulled instantly into fragments, while the red shirt of the war-party ran up in sight of the watching ships.

Had the Maoris now turned the guns of the captured blockhouse on the whites cut off from shelter, they must have inflicted terrible losses. But, throughout the battle, Heke kept the pledge he had made to his friend, Bishop Pompallier. His warriors had come to break British dominance and haul down the colours, not to massacre the whites. He had sworn that people who kept their shutters fastened would not be attacked, and his party dared not disobey. This forbearance, however, put the defenders in a difficult position. Realizing that the Maoris were holding their fire from the exposed whites, they dared not fire directly into the mass of natives, and infuriate them towards a general slaughter. The settlers and their defenders were hopelessly outnumbered.

Lieutenant Philpots wrung his hands, as the *St. Louis*, coming nearer shore, refused to land an attacking-party. From H.M.S. *Hazard* was shouted bad news. Acting-Commander Robertson, leading a shore party, was down and desperately wounded. The sloop's gunners were firing blind, her ammunition at a low ebb. From the *Sir John Franklin*, every detail of the disaster was visible. A man would drop suddenly, huddled and limp against the blockhouse wall, another give a queer little leap and fall with arms outstretched, a puppet jerked and dropped by hidden wires.

A wild, continuous yell told the climax of the native attack. From old Maori trenches, tufted with long grass on the slopes behind Kororareka, a withering fire poured down. The *Hazard's* shore party, caught in the open, paid for their daring with a heavy casualty list.

Another shout, as the red shirt is pulled down and a white flag of truce flutters up. Nobody can guess what the victorious savages want.

Then exhausted men, some propped wounded against bullet-scarred walls, others with sweat pouring down powder-blackened faces, raised a straggling cheer. The Maoris were seen leading down from their trenches Signalman Tapper's wife and children, believed to have been massacred some days before. But the eldest girl, her blue eyes distraught, the bodice of her torn dress stiff with blood, collapsed, fainting at the sailors' feet. The Maoris would spare the whites . . . but Captain Wing's half-caste child, three years old, had clung in her arms and hidden its little dark face against her breast. They butchered the child with tomahawks in the white girl's arms.

Hurriedly, under cover of the flag of truce, the white women and children were evacuated to the ships, some families boarding the *Hazard*, the rest coming at a stumbling run to the gang-planks of the schooners and the *St. Louis*, which had anchored under heavy fire to take on refugees. The last women were not clear of the blockhouse when there was a terrific roar, and the roof of Polack's house lifted sheer off, under a fountain of flame. The gunpowder had caught. Mr. Polack was blown up, and crashed down among his ruined cellars, but by some amazing chance was unhurt except for a few bruises. A seaman wriggled clear like a snake with a broken back, his face hideously disfigured. From the shore came the dreadful intermittent sobbing of a girl who lay with a broken thigh. The firing started again. Peppery little Mr. Hector stuck gamely to his post, and his three guns continued to hold off the Maoris from the second blockhouse.

"My Isabel stood beside me on the deck. A musket-ball struck the cathead beside her, and another passed between us. She laughed, and said, 'That one was close, wasn't it, Papa? How cold the wind blew.' I begged her to come below, but she shook her head. 'If we go below, they will say you are afraid. We must stay where we are.'"

Mr. Hector's gun ceased firing. In late afternoon, the Maoris began the sack of Kororareka. Some of the whites, half dazed, remained on shore, and took part unmolested in the plundering of their own property. Comic opera, like the rest.

"Seeing others go ashore, I left the *Sir John Franklin* myself, to try to effect the rescue of my poor affrighted horse, which had rolled over and over in his rope, and looked like a great cocoon. I untied him, and came back to the ship to see if he could be brought on board. But when I looked back, it was to see a party of natives leading him away. I believe that many other horses suffered the same fate."

So Black Aladdin, with a brown hand at his halter, trots

R

into a world far removed from sugar-loaves and striped winter apples.

Twilight made the Bay a place of ghosts. One after another, like great grey moths, the ships spread sail. There was a sobbing of exhausted women on each of those ships. The *Hazard* had taken as many refugees as she could carry, the *St. Louis* one hundred and nineteen. The *Matilda's* big hulk carried two hundred and twelve, with thirteen wounded soldiers in an improvised sick bay. The rest huddled on the schooners. No food had been provided in the blockhouses, and the ships' provisions were quite inadequate. Famished, weary, and facing destitution, the refugees left their dead at Kororareka. With the houses destroyed there, the losses in property amounted to about £50,000.

Auckland waited with desperate eagerness for the ships from Sydney, and cheered when three ships came into harbour. Then the *St. Louis*, the *Hazard*, and the *Matilda* drew alongside, and the town went into mourning.

The little *Sir John Franklin*, well ahead of heavier craft, berthed in Auckland on the same day that Hone Heke gave Kororareka to the flames, sparing only a few mission buildings. Heke's campaign saw its last big triumph with this assault. The warships arrived at last from Sydney, bringing with them Captain Grey, who first, with the able assistance of Nene and other leading chiefs, proceeded in the most business-like way to clean up the war-parties, and then replaced Captain Fitzroy as Governor of the Colony. Heke's fire smouldered in northern grass for a long time, but it was only at Kororareka that really large letters of flame told the world of his intentions.

"In Auckland, I found the value of Government scrip down to 1s. 9d. in the £. My first call was to my land agent.... When I had paid him the £40 required for his services, I had almost nothing left. I was nearly broken-hearted, wondering what I could contrive now for my family. But one of the Hokianga's respectable white settlers, to whom I had lent money in times past, now assisted me. ... I called on Governor Fitzroy, and was given an extremely friendly interview. When the men from H.M.S. *Hazard* came to Auckland, I was exposed again to insult and assault, and threatened on all sides as the Frenchman who said he would take refuge under

American colours. It was stated that I was a spy of France, and only waiting for a native rising to usurp power for her. . . . I was knocked down in the streets, kicked and insulted. . . . A few days after my arrival, a native came up to my son Richard in the street, and spoke to him in a confused manner, asking if the white man would fight again against the Maoris. My son replied that he had better ask someone else, and walked on. That night, my three eldest sons were arrested and taken to the police-station, where an attempt was made to implicate them on a treasonable charge. But the whole was exposed as a plot, in which a Mr. Hancock had endeavoured to induce the native to set a trap for my sons. Fortunately, he was overheard. . . . If ever I am an enemy, which God forbid, I shall be an open one.

"As far greater men have done, I decided now to make existence possible for my family by the employment of what talents I had. . . ."

Then began the music-stool, dangling schoolboy legs, a nailed boot pressed down in grim determination on the loud pedal. The Baron de Thierry gives a concert to display the talent of his pupils, and mothers are requested not to bring infants in arms.

Far away on Mount Isabel, apricots drop, flushed and downy-cheeked, into the grass; there are still sleek grapes under the unkempt vines. "Fruit," wrote Charles, in 1856, "of which I never see a particle."

The Sèvres nymph watches him through her misty halo of candlelight. She has seen more kings fall than one.

CHAPTER TWENTY-TWO

WIND OF THE SEA

THE door of her room was open, the song floated through.

> Wind of the sea, come fill my sail;
> Lend me the breath of a favouring gale
> And bear my port-worn ship away.
> For it's oh, the greed of the tedious town,
> The shutters up, and the shutters down,
> Wind of the sea, sweep over the bay,
> And bear me away, away.
>
> Whither you bear me, wind of the sea,
> Matters never the least to me;
> Give me your fogs, with the sails a-drip,
> Or the weltering path through the starless night.
> On, somewhere beacons the new daylight,
> And the cheery gleam of a sister-ship
> As its colours shine and dip.
>
> Wind of the sea, sweep over the bay. . . .

Isabel Matson, who since her marriage had almost forgotten that she had tried to escape from her father's domination, thought confusedly, "Not that song . . . I hate it." He didn't sing it badly, though his voice was apt to crack on the top notes now. He was singing it for her benefit; he knew she'd be awake.

Coherence slid out of her mind. The moonlight was hot and restive, window-bars cast shadows over the counterpane, like the steel bars of a cage. Any other song. . . . But Papa likes that one best; oh, of course, he sails tomorrow. Frederick and Will in California already. Will's far too young to be away from home. . . . Where have we gone to? It was safe by the fire, the room like a big cave with the winds roaring outside, and we used to tell ghost-stories. Papa had one about an old gipsy-woman who told his fortune. "You shall sleep in a strange bed, pretty gentleman, pretty little lady." This is a strange bed. Strange to be sleeping again under my father's roof, and only for the one night, because tomorrow he sails. I am not Isabel de Thierry, I am Mrs. Matson; there was a baby, and she died. The room smells of apples. Oh, if only somebody would cut open my side and take the pain out. . . .

The memories began in Baltimore, where Will was born. Isabel could see a high house, with a yard behind it, and trees very broad and leafy over a wooden swing. There was a boy who used to push the swing for her, and say, "Higher, higher," in a funny, sing-song voice, and points of light came glittering down through the leaves; not white, but deep blue, orange, and scarlet, all in tiny flecks.

But she was sad, of course, and they had to give her strawberries, because Papa and Mamma and all-the-little-brothers were living in another house, queer and sickly-smelling, with the blinds like shut eyes. She was told they were ill of the cholera, and she must say her prayers for them every night. This she did obediently, first brushing out her hair with the blue-enamelled hair-brush, as she had been taught, then kneeling with her hands like a church-steeple against the white counterpane. "Please-God-bless-Papa-and-Mamma-and-all-the-little-brothers-and-Margaret-Amen." But that wasn't the same as saying them with Papa there to listen, and to tell stories afterwards, sometimes with the lights out, and no Papa visible at all—just a voice talking reflectively in the darkness about old, curious things that happened to princesses, and a shaggy coat-sleeve if she put out a hand to feel where the voice came from.

Then she remembered candles lighted, a million of them, dancing and funny behind the enormous melons in Jamaica, and a black man sitting beside each melon, his teeth white and laughing. She had been wearing a brown velvet coat with pink scallops, and a poke-bonnet which came down over her eyes. . . . There were riding-lessons; he was lifting her on the back of an enormously tall black horse, somewhere in a town with blue and pink houses, and palm-trees pointing stiff, dark fingers at the sky. Sand scattered deliciously under her horse's hooves, and their sound was like a drum in a great hurry, and her hair went flying, flying.

The boys were opening a door in the attic of Mr. Feraud's store, and she was frightened because it might have been a pirate door. But when they were inside, there were only cobwebs and big chests of tea, which smelt clean and nice. Then the sea streamed green and white under the keel of a ship, streamed out V-shaped, and the clouds were a crimson V above, and between them shone the flag. Her father was excited, and pointed at it, talking of golden castles in the woods, and princesses. This was what made him so different from the fathers of other children. She couldn't have imagined other fathers asking her to help choose plumes and swords in a big store, with a little dark shopman, like a monkey, doubled up with bowing.

Sometimes she had wished he *would* look more like the others. She had wanted to cry out, "Oh, don't!" when he did things more and more like Papa. On this she had trodden as if on a serpent. And, anyhow, those moments came so rarely that she could afford to laugh at them.

She thought she could remember a white island, and her father saying very importantly, "This is the first marmoset that the natives have ever seen." There was a delicious smell in the air, a smell like Paradise. Oh, far away. . . . Yes, that came next. Willy and she had made up the tune for "Over the Hills and Far Away", and she had played it in Sydney, where the piano was so old that its keys stuck under her fingers. But Papa had liked the tune. She could remember his coming in from the hall, and making her sing it over and over ; and his eyes were bright—that was tears. Because the night was hot, because "Over the Hills and Far Away" is a sad song.

Then it was New Zealand, and she was three people rolled into one. She was Princess Isabel. She was Isabel de Thierry, whose father is always in trouble. And she was herself.

Princess Isabel had vanished now, years ago. The last time she had been taken out of the box was at Kororareka, when Isabel didn't want the English to think that the de Thierrys were afraid. Of course, the de Thierrys were really just as much afraid as anyone else, and she had been terrified of

Repa, his hands were so large and his eyes so queer. But it had been necessary to pretend.

Isabel who was herself belonged mostly to the thatched temple in the forest, where nobody else had ever come but her father. The boughs were closely plaited overhead, and the greedy wood-pigeons would plump down berries with soft, dull little thudding noises from the *karaka*-trees. They had an altar of piled stones, and used to leave gifts for Tane Mahuta, who was lord of the wildwoods—bright bits of cloth, flowers, notes on white paper, scraps of food stolen from the table. These were always gone next day, but that was the work of the *wekas*, incorrigible thieves, with their beady bright eyes and their long-billed heads cocked on one side.

It had been best here with the stars coming out on summer evenings, pointing down like long white swords with jewelled hilts. He would tell her their lovely names. In that thin, streaming darkness, taking its own soft colour from fern and smoke and star, Papa never seemed to be acting at all. She could feel the curve of the earth, enormous and placid, through the thin cotton of her frock. She loved to feel it against her, it was a sort of secret. It seemed to move and bear her along with it, ón a vast circle that rolled through the shadows into some peaceful place . . . the Garden of the Hesperides, perhaps, with the singing women white as starlight around the jewel-fruited trees. Her father's voice, talking of the Nature of God and of the way the planets were made, was quite different, a part of the steadfastness. "Once this fiery orb was but a breath of vapour. Once man was nothing more than a pinch of dust. And if God could perform these wondrous works, and if we trust in Him . . ."

Yet it seemed strange that the God to whom one prayed wouldn't take away anything so dreadful as the pain in her side. It wasn't as if she had done any harm. God couldn't blame her, because unhappiness had poisoned her, and the baby nursed at her breast had died.

"I am dying too," thought Isabel, and thrust the heavy wet hair back from her forehead.

Isabel de Thierry, whose father was always in trouble. Since they had come to Auckland, it had been that from year's end to year's end. Her mother had grown cold and silent, despising the world. Isabel couldn't. She had to keep herself lovely, to smile and pretend, because her father always turned to her.

First it was the horrible shanty-house, and in the tangled, fenceless garden which ran down under dusty-flowered laurestinus stood the other cottage, where the negro and the worthless little white man lived together. She remembered the quick shiver of evil, sensed without perception, which had caught her one night as she sat brushing her hair before her looking-glass. She was eighteen then. She had looked round, her dressing-gown loose over white shoulders and breasts, hair tumbled around her young face. She saw the two faces, negroid and white, pressed, grinning, against the panes. Somehow they seemed a mere symbol of this world to which they were all exposed. She had run to her father that evening . . . and even as she felt his hand on her hair, she knew there was little he could do to protect his own.

She was opening the door to the mothers of her father's pianoforte pupils . . . not one of them that she hadn't disliked on sight, for she knew how hopelessly sensitive to discords poor Papa had always been ; and music, like the temple in the Long Bush, was a place where she could always join him. But she had forced herself to smile and curtsy, like a prim little governess. "And this is your daughter, Baron ?" Voices like bits of stick poking into a cage. They might as well have called him Great Auk. It was curiosity, not respect. Isabel wore starched dresses, the fichus crossing high at her throat, and plaited her hair tightly. When she was alone, she let it fall loose, and knew that it was beautiful.

People were always promising support and assistance. There were Governor Fitzroy's rather funny and nice letters about journalism.

"A few letters on the native question might be well received by the public through the medium of both papers, if *not* complimentary to the Governor. And might, if carefully written, be very useful at this time of excitement. The good points of the New Zealand character might be shown, his improvement described, and his faults stated with truth. The propriety of adapting law to his transitional state, the hope of raising and amalgamating the native race with the white, might with good effect be stated."

Papa had laughed, saying, "Well, at least he doesn't want bouquets from the French spy." But in Auckland, even the boys were suspected everywhere. Frederick was appointed to the Customs Office when Captain Grey became Governor; George was in charge of a Maori road-gang; Richard and Will both sent as interpreters where Maoris were used in constructional work. It never lasted. There was too much understanding between the boys and the natives, who came to them over the heads of older men. Then the white workmen treated the de Thierry name as a joke, which made the boys show at their worst. Even in these days of poverty, Maoris were always drifting in at Papa's gates, and making themselves at home. Frederick was at the Customs Office still, but they paid him five shillings a day, and labourers fresh from the emigrant ships wouldn't take less than eight.

General Dean Pitt, who came to take charge of the military, was an old friend of her father's, and tried hard to get him the post of Postmaster-General. Then the French ship, *Dido*, offered them all free passage to France, and Papa decided, happy and excited, to accept. But Governor Grey at once communicated through General Dean Pitt an offer to give the Baron de Thierry a resident magistracy and charge of a pensioners' settlement, at a place called Ruapekapeka. They promised him £650 a year . . . and the *Dido* sailed without him. A few days of silence, and after that, letters again. The family didn't need to be told what had come of it. It had happened again, that was all.

And two more years, like a strange dream, impossible to unravel. Long, hot nights before the baby was born, two terrible days of sheer agony, Margaret Neilsen actually in tears, the doctor bending over her, and the hall door opening for a moment, so that, through it all, she heard two voices lifted in quarrelling . . . her father's voice, her husband's voice. She wanted to shriek to them both, "Don't be ridiculous!" But the pain caught her, a great claw, and she lost herself in a different sort of cry, which carried her senses away. And baby Isabel hadn't lived three months; and she was only a guest for the night at the little Parnell house, which bore the unimaginative name, "Rosebank". Tomorrow, her father sailed for California, where men were making fortunes in the gold-fields. "Wind of the sea, sweep over the bay. . . ." He was making the most extravagant promises about the success he would have. The new golden dream glittered all about his nakedness. He was very nearly old, worn-out, ill ; and, worse than all, he hated leaving her so much that it was almost killing them both. Isabel hadn't the strength left to tell him that the golden dream was preposterous, and he, though he knew it, would not admit it. He was going in order to impress her. "Let him go, the damned old fool," said her husband.

"But I am dying, and I shall never see him again." Past pain, she turned into the short blackness of sleep, into the empty place where they had taken her child and her youth.

Lieutenant-Colonel Wynyard, later Acting-Governor of the Colony, wrote a sentimental little poem about Isabel. It began "I saw her as a bride", and told how she walked up the aisle in white satin and myrtle-sprays, to be married to Major Matson of the 58th Regiment. That was early in May 1848, when she was twenty. Her daughter, Isabel, was born on July 10th, 1849, and on the third day of October they buried the child in the Grafton Cemetery, a deep gully thick-matted with native trees. Of little Isabel Matson, Charles says, "She was the loveliest little thing imaginable, but she would not thrive." Isabel, her mother, dying, said she was glad the baby had not lived.

That Major Matson should have married Isabel de Thierry was a rather remarkable circumstance. The de Thierry stocks were low in Auckland, when the Major arrived there in 1848, to be given a paragraph in both newspapers, the *New Zealander* and the *Southern Cross*. They expressed the hope that "this distinguished officer will see his way to making his home permanently in our midst" ; and Major Matson strode further into popularity by becoming President of the Colony's first Horticultural Society. Then to marry the little de Thierry, when so many charming girls must have been setting their caps for him !

It can only have been her peculiar and haunting loveliness, of which all who saw her spoke ; the goose-girl effect, which presents a princess so much at her best, until one gets tired of fairy-tales and feels sheepish at having succumbed to them. And then, her very sense of unreality, the way in which she made a world for herself, as she and her papa proceeded on their fantastic course, must have puzzled and attracted Major Matson. But one must never let a materialist finger those bubble worlds.

Auckland at the time had a nickname. It was called "The English Garrison". The title sums up its society . . . red-coats, crinolines, camaraderie borrowing a glow from the dangers outside its window-panes. There was no place for Isabel Matson in that world, especially with her papa, like the superabundant tail of some small kite, for ever in the offing.

Soon there was open estrangement between the young couple. Her husband and her papa quarrelled bitterly. Major Matson somewhat neglected her; the baby pined and died. In the fifty black-bordered pages which he calls "Mysteries Surrounding the Death of my Daughter Isabel", Charles almost accuses Major Matson of murdering the girl. This was nonsense. But, in the realm of the spirit, they certainly harried her between them. Her death broke Charles de Thierry's life, and perhaps unhinged his mind. Those black-bordered pages were not written by a perfectly sane man.

Charles sailed in the *Noble*, in 1850. The house where he said good-bye looked across the harbour, and from its balcony the canvas and lifting spars of the brig could be plainly seen. He has left record of that parting . . . too long a record; dazed, confused, unwilling to believe that he could have sailed, never knowing that she was dying. What is life but a tall candle-flame blown out ? "Be buried quick with her, and so will I." He must have it so; carefully reconstruct the scene of her death, every word said, every look. Hundreds of flat little poems, all about "My poor Isabel", crowd themselves into his pages. Then he writes to a friend, "I have sworn that I will write no more poems."

All the words cannot obscure the fact that he loved her.

Margaret Neilsen sat in her rocking-chair, at the foot of Isabel's bed in Major Matson's house. The doctor had called, the last of three, and the one who discovered the hopeless condition of her lungs, after the others had declared her sound. She was in agony, and begged him to take the pain away.

"I wish I could, my dear child," he said, and hurried from the room. But then, unexpectedly, all pain left her. It was evening, and she persuaded her mother to go into the next room where her piano stood, and play over the music of her father's favourite songs. She seemed gay and animated all night, though sleepless, and for a few hours they believed she was getting better. But in early morning she asked them to carry her into the room where her baby had died. They called Major Matson, who lifted her and placed her on the great sofa where the child had lain. She said good-bye, then, and gave them various trinkets . . . a gold pin with a pearl for George, a prayer-book that her father had given her for Richard. All she asked of her husband was that he wouldn't quarrel with her father.

They closed her eyes and left her alone for a little while in the room. But there was something left for dead Isabel Matson to do.

The *Noble* was nearing Pitcairn Island. It had been a wretched voyage, on an ill-conditioned vessel. Charles had kept to himself. That night, he came on deck and stood watching the troubled green seas.

"Suddenly I saw my darling's face and form on the waters. Her eyes were closed, her arms outstretched as if in sleep, her long dark hair swept out around her. I called to her, but the vision was gone. Going back to my cabin, I wrote the whole in my diary, and sealed it and gave it to Mr. Barker. . . . While there is still an honest heart in my family, never let this page be destroyed. That vision was a link between heaven and earth, and I bless God who sent it to me."

At the French Hotel in Honolulu, months later, a sea-captain heard the Baron de Thierry talking about his daughter.

"Isabel Matson ? Why, she's dead," blurted out the sailor.

Twelve officers, one of them Lieutenant-Colonel Wynyard, were the pall-bearers when Isabel was buried in Grafton Cemetery, so soon after her baby's death that all the frocks in her wardrobe were the stifling black mourning of the day. Mrs. Mary Jane Brown, a friend of the family, wrote to the Baron that the girl of not quite twenty-three looked lovely in death, and that she herself had parted her hair and placed a scarlet rose against it. Her old friend, the Rev. Mr. Churton, who had been a second father to her in the absence of her own gold-seeking papa, was inconsolable, and locked himself in his room without victuals for a whole day after her death. Many shops were closed along the road as the funeral cortège, black plumes nodding from the heads of the horses and black crêpe weepers on the carriage doors, trailed past.

Isabel who was herself belonged to a flax-roofed temple on Mount Isabel, and had nothing to do with them. As far as they were concerned, she was simply Isabel whose father is always in trouble.

CHAPTER TWENTY-THREE

PARDONNE

"I SAILED in the *Noble*, February 10th, and was marooned on Pitcairn Island, where I remained with my kind friends, the descendants of the *Bounty* mutineers, for a whole month. The schooner *Velocity* took me to Honolulu, and thence to San Francisco, where I remained six months. . . . I later returned to Honolulu, where I remained in charge of the French Consulate until March 1853. I then returned to Auckland, in consequence of the news I received concerning the dangerous state of my wife's health. At Honolulu I left friends whom I shall love to the last day of my life, and if I came back with but scanty supplies of this world's goods, I was rich in the regard of many who won my warmest esteem and gratitude."

There again, that peculiar ability to magnetize the unexpected crops up. Almost any other man could have made the journey to the gold-fields without being marooned on Pitcairn Island and spending a month with his kind friends, the descendants of the *Bounty* mutineers. However, it is fair to add that the sailors of the *Noble* did not throw Charles de Thierry overside as a Jonah, and then speed away towards the horizon. Having been very seasick and miserable, he spent a day on Pitcairn sight-seeing, whilst the *Noble* took on fresh water. A sudden gale blew the brig out to sea, leaving five passengers stranded. The stiff wind held, and the *Noble's* captain, refusing to pile up his brig on the rocks for the sake of prospective gold-diggers, who were probably travelling steerage, departed for Honolulu, leaving his strays to Neptune and Chance.

Charles made the very best of his opportunities on Pitcairn Island, which is an idyllic spot. He could be very charming when he liked. Do you know the main passion of the inhabitants ? It is for organs. This sounds extravagant, but I have had it from the lips of Pitcairn Islanders themselves. The taste for organ music amounts to fanaticism, and one of the few things that will induce a Pitcairn man to leave home is in order that he may earn the money to buy himself a new organ. There is very little high finance on the island ; the women are all chaste—at a rough estimate—the men silent, efficient, and good-looking. They marry young and die centenarians. Only one man smokes a pipe on Pitcairn, and he is an American, who, for love of an island lady, settled himself there. For the rest, Pitcairn has some exports, but is off the track of ships.

In the beginning, John Adams, having no native Bible, taught the natives their religion and its language entirely in English, thus realizing Charles's long-lost dream of a native populace speaking "English, all English, and nothing but English". I forgot to mention that the entire island was converted to Seventh Day Adventism, which makes it a more respectable place than ever. Being sheltered from the greed of commerce, the viciousness of diplomacy, the brutality of war, and the weak though strident passions of society, the Pitcairn brand of respectability has charm. The natives had amalgamated peacefully and without deterioration with the whites ; there was no colour distinction. Probably at the time of Charles's unexpected visit they would be able to make only a rough guess at what a baron was. But Charles was a musician, too, and since he had the sense to parade this talent, he became very popular. A letter from Caroline Adams, one of the mutineers' descendants, illustrates this fact. It was written in 1850.

My Kind Friend,
Dull indeed have the days been since you left us. I am distressed to hear that you have received none of my letters. Your corner at table, the piano you used to play, the music-rule with which you taught us, all speak of you a hundred times in the day. John Noble read out your letter from the pulpit last Sunday, and asks me to tell you that your singing-classes have done as you bade them, and practise daily. . . . The children love the Bacon and Potatoes round, and the older girls do well in the Bread-making Song. But we shall be grateful to you if

you can possibly send us some music in the modern manner, from which we can learn part-singing in our church . . . unless you can come again yourself, for a few months or as long as you please, and teach us, which is what we would like best of all. I cannot say how grieved I was to hear of your loss. There is a little namesake here, for I have now a grand-daughter called after your Isabel. . . . The double balsam seeds you sent us have not come up, I am sorry to say, but the waxflowers and the paper-lilies are thriving splendidly, and should make a pretty show. . . . John is writing to you also today.

Caroline signs herself, *Ever your sincere friend.*
Other folded letters, their ink now faint, are written by Pitcairn Islanders to Charles, until within a few months of his death. The Adams family migrate to Norfolk Island, and send him cases of the island oranges, and boxes containing the seedlings of Norfolk Island's beautiful pines. If he wished, he might find a nook in the chimney-corner.

Come and spend your declining years with us. It is little we can offer, but there is a room looking over the sea, a garden, and a piano. . . .

But Charles has a fancy for dying on the soil of Utopia, though he stores the Adams letters carefully away.
"On Governor Grey's departure in 1853, my much valued and respected friend Colonel Wynyard became Acting-Governor. A more honourable, more kind-hearted, more gentlemanly and hospitable man than himself could not have been found. He and his truly amiable lady honoured me with their friendship since their arrival in the country. The natives hold Colonel Wynyard in great esteem. . . ."
Did Colonel Wynyard and his truly amiable lady also honour Emily de Thierry with their friendship, until in 1854 death took her into the quiet of his keeping? There is only the one portrait of her—a tiny, faded chromo-photograph, taken in old age. A stiff black gown, all ruffles and tucks, flows over a short little person from which the lines of youth have long departed. Her hair is drawn back, a bonnet perches above. The photograph is too sadly faded for one to see

whether there is still gentleness in her eyes, or about her mouth.

George de Thierry, who was drowned crossing a river, had himself photographed on glass, a modish device. He looks the beau ideal of a Victorian novel, all dashing sidewhiskers and wax moustache. But the eyes are very honest, ready to face the world. It is a good face.

Charles made his home in the suburb named after the gallant and unfortunate Parnell, and now known for its three P's: Pride, Poverty, and Pianos. His cottage had not much to its credit but that the piano was kept tuned. The pines took root firmly in the soil of a sloping garden, forget-me-nots made blue shores here and there among long grass which aided and abetted the strayings of his bantams, willing to lay anywhere on earth except in the nests which their lord provided for them. Music-pupils, loneliness, memories. . . .

"Shall I ever forget when crowds of smiling natives used to follow the footsteps of my lovely girl, the children calling "Irapera, Irapera", which was all they could make of her name? And she, poor thing, lies in New Zealand clay; and with her, her mother, who did so much for the natives. . . ."

"It is time now that I speak of the outlines I had planned for my Chieftaincy, before Waitangi ever took place."

He writes of the first days, and of how against the efforts of missionaries he fought two powers: the lawlessness of men embittered with civilization, and the covetousness of some of these missionaries themselves.

"During their fits of intemperance," he writes of the convicts escaped from the penal settlements, "these men became frantic. With the years of long and painful exile, the marks of their manacles deeply imprinted upon them, they represented to the native how guilty were the men who, under the cloak of religion, were betraying them into the hands of the nation that had robbed themselves of liberty. These men were not a little successful in neutralizing the efforts of the missionaries, as acid will neutralize an alkali. The refugee to these wild shores was as free as the air he breathed, and became a stranger to actual want, for the natives were generous and friendly, and supplied all his needs.

"Example has done its prodigies. The natives are keen observers. . . . They have to some extent progressed, by noting the usefulness of white men's appliances in commerce and labour. They have large flour mills, they grind their own wheat ; and dress, bag, and weigh their flour. They have fine horses, and now use ploughs, harrows, drays, powerful threshing machines. They have a great number of vessels, from brigantines down, and work these with skill. They have cattle, and are beginning to rear sheep. They gather vast quantities of wild honey, and bring into Auckland a considerable amount of fruit. But great as their strides have been in these matters, they remain absolutely stationary as civilized beings. Gunpowder is now manufactured secretly among the natives at three places, and there are men among them who have been abroad, working in factories where armaments are made. They delight in pointing out the ways in which Auckland could be attacked, and how the defences could be rendered useless. . . . At this moment, they are preparing for action. God only knows how it will end, and how it may retard the progress of a race which might have been happy and prosperous, had it been ruled with foresight.

"It is not a week from the writing of these lines that the natives declared that if the Governor attempted to seek restitution of the gunpowder stolen at Kawau by force of arms, they would do by Auckland what they did by Kororareka in 1845. In such a case, the outsettlers would be in deadly peril. The punishment of death by hanging has lowered us with the natives. They say we talk of being better than themselves, and then treat one another like dogs. This is because dogs are hung at the Auckland Police Office, if found wandering without collars. We were safe without soldiers, we are in danger now that we have two regiments to fight for us."

Writing in 1856, he does not prove a bad prophet. A few years later the Waikato wars were raging. Auckland was in a state of nerves. The old windmill, looking over the town like a quaint toy soldier, stopped grinding flour, for its space was used in melting and moulding bullets. But what even Charles never foresaw was the degree to which the clash between white and native would retard the development of the Maori race. Those promising industrial and commercial signs of the early years have for the most part melted like snow.

The museum-piece attitude used towards the native has, in the long run, an effect nothing less than a futility which proves it hypocritical. The race is now numerically on the increase. What that may mean, to the Maori or to anyone else, depends largely on the incidence of the next fifty years.

He speaks of the missionaries. "The Quakers in Pennsylvania did more good than the Puritans in Massachusetts, thereby proving by natural implication that the savages are more easily managed by gentle means than by despotic ones. When once the sort of mysterious halo which surrounded the New Zealand missionary began to be dispelled by the wider intercourse of the two races, their influence gradually lessened, and they are at this time little more regarded than any other men. . . . For this task" (the moral elevation of the native) "they were well qualified in every way, since most of them were mechanics, and could have assisted in every development of native life. But they must have remained content for some years with their fustian jackets, instead of indulging in fine linen and broadcloth."

Never once did he write, "All this was a fool's dream. The man who looks for advancement of the natives will be disappointed." He wrote, instead, of the obscure Sandwich Islands, civilized more by level and moral influence than by force of arms, trade, or mysticism. "In their homes I have seen fine furniture and splendid pianos . . . and these instruments were for use, not for ornament."

There were to have been villages in Utopia, starting off with a metalled road for each village, and settlements in which "respectable" whites and natives would live side by side. The schools were the pride of his heart. Respecting the Maori usage which divides the *rangatira* and his kin from lesser men, he planned separate schools, in which the sons of chiefs would be tutored with those of white gentlefolk, while the hoi-polloi should have free schooling in rival institutes. This, of course, was abominably snobbish ; but at least Charles insisted that schooling be free and compulsory. Parents keeping their offspring away were to be disqualified from holding "any State post or emolument" . . . and these, if he had only had his way, would have been many and gorgeous.

On the other hand, he was not opposed to a little discreet

bribery and corruption. Children were to be given clothing and attractive books as prizes, and he brought over much of these goods from Sydney, abandoning a whole trunk of picture-books at Mount Isabel. A new plan was attendance prizes for virtuous Maori parents, whose infants presented their "shining morning face" regularly at school. Punishments were to be strictly of a moral nature, but, lest one should think him soft, Charles explains that this was not because he minded beating boys, but because the chiefs wouldn't have their sons and daughters whacked. He was not a co-educationalist. "The sexes were to be kept apart," he writes primly. While the children were to be boarded when possible, they were to have separate beds. In their playtimes, the infant Utopians would speak only English.

From their juvenile schools his pupils were to graduate—by learning, not by pull—to District High Schools. (He is, I think, the first man to have suggested these institutions in New Zealand.) Every child, during its high-school education, was to be taught a trade of its choice. During the last year's schooling, all but two hours a day would be spent in apprenticeship to this trade, and the profits—if any—devoted to the "Public Fund", out of which everything from roading to native hospitals was expected to spring. As for this fund, its main resources would be the produce of the gigantic trading farm into which he hoped to turn his Chieftaincy. For the exports of this he had already arranged markets and insurance with established houses overseas. "I visioned the entire Chieftaincy as a hive, with no drones among it." Was it Communism? In any case, it was charming.

Temperance advocates might have found something to smile or scowl at, according to the rigidity of their natures, in his remarkable plan for a Temperate Utopia. How, puzzled Charles, was he to deal with the problem of the Low Dive? Eureka . . . he had it! There would be no sly grog-selling. Anyone, on paying a small licence fee, might sell the light wines and beers to be produced from the Chieftaincy's vineyards and hop-gardens. But nobody must get drunk.

"On a third offence of drunkenness, the offender is to be banished for a year from the Chieftaincy. If, after this absence, he has reformed, he will be received again, and offered employment in a position of moderate trust, as on probation. I do not desire to interfere with the pleasures of men, but I fear the effects of strong liquors sold by unscrupulous men among the natives. . . . Everything must be done by example, and by the love of good."

Was he in earnest, this aging gentleman who sat scribbling at his teak desk, when the last music-pupil had tucked flower-scrolled music-sheets into leathern satchel and stumped out of the room where the French dragon scolded so if one jumped on the loud pedal ? Before leaving Sydney for New Zealand, he had the *Sydney Herald* offices, in Lower George Street, print a form of agreement, to which each settler put signature or mark before boarding the ship. Here are the articles :

> Charles, Baron de Thierry, shall be Sovereign Chief over his own territories, and shall exercise all rights and prerogatives of an independent Chief within their limits.
> No neighbouring Chief or people of his tribe shall be molested in person or in property, nor compelled to lend, cede, give, barter, or sell anything in his possession.
> No New Zealander on the Baron de Thierry's properties shall be deprived of land or dwelling, but shall ever be protected in the same, unless guilty of some heinous crime or of open mutiny ; nor then shall be removed, without trial by a mixed jury.
> No New Zealander shall be compelled to work for a white man, unless in punishment for crime.
> No native tribe, Government, foreign State or power shall exercise jurisdiction within the Baron de Thierry's territory.
> No one shall be molested in the free exercise of any religion. But no nunneries or monasteries shall be permitted within the Baron de Thierry's lands.
> If any white man marry a native woman, he shall be bound to treat her in all respects as he would a white woman.
> No gambling is to be allowed.
> There shall be no distinction of colour within the Baron de Thierry's territories.

Incidentally, much as he admired friendship between white lambkins and brown, Charles did not approve of mixed marriages, and is quoted in Brett's *Early History of New Zealand*—one of the few histories mentioning him at all—as telling a tale against the Anglican Bishop Selwyn on this point.

"How would you like that fine young man for a husband?" asked the Bishop of a pretty girl, indicating a Maori.

"How would your lordship like him for a son-in-law?" was the damsel's demure retort.

I would not have you think, however, that the Chieftaincy was to be a tristful place, buried under mountainous morals, with never a ribbon on the maypole or a feather in the troubadour's bonnet. Right at the bottom of a pile of ancient, unsightly documents are some family letters written to Charles's sister, Caroline. There is an engaging frankness in one, dated March 1838.

I cannot live without female society. Louis and his wife; James and his; Frank, if he has one; and Frederick, if he has got tired of the single state, all joining my circle, and bring Georgiana and her kindred with her, with as many more amiable petticoats as you can add to the list. That indeed would make New Zealand a happy place for me.

And note the sunburst of optimism in which Caroline is asked to behold her brother's future, when in 1834 the Guadeloupe syndicate is playing about with crowns and thrones.

I am so completely harassed with preparations that I have with difficulty found time to scribble this horrid letter. The time is certainly come, for everything favours me; friends, followers, means, and good wishes. The blue and crimson flag will float in the Bay of Islands by the first week in February. The flag of whom? Of him, my ever dearest sister, who, humble or exalted, will ever be,

Your devoted Charles.

In 1856, the New Zealand Government made the Baron de Thierry a present. He was allowed one hundred and six acres of land, in recompense for a claim of 40,000 acres, an extravagant claim, over which, however, some said the old gentleman had been hardly done by. Various rumours associated with his name were recalled. Yet it was undeniable that the Baron de Thierry had never murdered, raped, pilfered, caroused, nor even led an armed rebellion against Her Majesty. Hence the gift.

But Isabel was dead, and there could be no second Mount Isabel. Emily was gone too; the family was scattered. And long ago a flag of crimson and azure had been cut into the tiniest pieces by fingers which no doubt trembled as they lifted it from the shelf where it had lain rolled up and hidden away. So he remained at Auckland.

One need not feel too sympathetic. There was a secret scandal. If the Government had known, they would never have given him a sniff of their hundred and six acres.

In his old age Charles was writing an epic poem on the invasion of England by the French. It concludes with a portrait of Queen Victoria kneeling in tears before a French General, who is stern but just, and who properly hauls Victoria over the coals. You will take this to be a lie. However, the whole poem is preserved in the Sir George Grey collection at the Auckland Library. It contains more cantos than those of Mr. Ezra Pound, and they are larger cantos, too; preferable in every way, those who don't like modern poetry might think. I cannot quote from the poem, it is too bad. But Charles is probably the only being who during his lifetime got the better of Queen Victoria in verse, even though she never knew it.

A clipping in a journal of 1864:

> There was much laughter in the New Plymouth Gentlemen's Club last night over an account of a Frenchman who thought he had bought vast lands in New Zealand by a payment of thirty-six axes, and came here meaning to set himself up as a King. But the natives drove him away, and the King was reduced to teach music for a living.

And a caustic enough little retort, written perhaps by an editor who had watched the old man making his way between the sailing-ships and the Parnell cottage.

> It is a pity that those *gentlemen* of the New Plymouth Club who laughed so heartily at a Frenchman's purchase of lands for thirty-six axes were not honest enough to admit how some of them paid for their own land, if they paid for it at all. If light were let in on their buyings, there would be more to wonder at than one Frenchman.

The last de Thierry documents I can trace are entirely in

the sanguine vein. One is a gold-prospector's licence for the new fields at Ballarat, Australia, taken out by Charles, Baron de Thierry, in 1863. It was never, so far as one can gather, put into use. The old gentleman was by then past sixty-five. Was that, however, to put him on the shelf? Here is his final (discoverable) letter, written, in May 1863, to that Captain Grey who had a second time been appointed Governor, and who now shone as Sir George Grey.

My Dear Sir,
I most sincerely congratulate you on your escape from the savage murderers whose deeds have filled the whole community with horror. Being in my sixty-eight year, I believe I am exempt from military service. But I once had the honour to hold a commission in His Majesty's 23rd Light Dragoons, and do not like the idea of skulking in the hour of danger. If Your Excellency should see fit to form a Company of elders for the city's defence, I beg to offer you my services. Most people have heard of plans for incendiarism among the Maoris, and a trusty Guard might be useful for the protection of life and property. Though so old, I have yet pluck enough to perform my duty. With best wishes for your health and service,
I am,
Charles, Baron de Thierry.

Ancient Pistol had not cooled off with the years. There is no record of decorations pinned on his veteran breast. Yet, after all, music . . . The young man Shelley had written:

> Music, when soft voices die,
> Vibrates in the memory. . . .

All the soft voices were long dead, long dead. Sitting in the dusk alone, his fingers on the keyboard, he let them wander as if they were no part of that discredited old man, the Baron de Thierry. They were changed, perhaps, with the years, swollen and knotted. Yet the beloved ivory keys still seemed familiar with them. They took him far away, and into other worlds.

"The Baron de Thierry played a harp solo at the Masquerade

and an Imperial lady fell in love with him." He wondered for a moment whom she had been. He couldn't remember. Soft voices die . . . soft voices die. . . .

"Over the Hills and Far Away." If he played it very quietly, like this, she came and stood beside him, and sang it again in that voice so clear and sweet that nobody else might hear it. It was the sacred thing, for him alone. There was a voice that would never die, a pure voice ringing in some eternal place . . . but not in the lofty, forgetting hymns, that go with the eyes turned away from earth and its poor people . . . not in these, but in the little song she had sung again and again, because it pleased him. The melody was her own, a silver master-key, and she was the child of his heart. The room filled with a tranquil light, clear and golden, light sweeter than any sunset. It wasn't a room any more, but a wider place, and he could see the waves rippling far below. "We are at Mount Isabel," he said. She laughed at him for thinking she might have forgotten.

The little nuns who had come to see him often of late, visited him together this evening. The Sèvres nymph held up her candlesticks, and looked down at him.

An old man, lying half out of his bed, his slippers off to reveal the fact that nobody has darned his worsted stockings, looks up at them, but cannot speak. They raise him between them. Although his thin body is tall enough to be still heavy, they have a singular impression that he has no more substance left than a dead leaf. The old man, however, feels terribly sick in the pit of his stomach. With a convulsive movement, he indicates that he wants them to give him the flowered chamber from under the bed. He leans over this for a moment, coughing, and then feels a little better. He says in a feeble whisper something that sounds like "Pardon", and they think he is apologizing for his plight. But then he raises his voice, and says with a questioning inflexion, *"Pardonne? Pardonne?"* as though requesting that some unseen person should speak up a little.

I think the Invisible Stranger repeated his demands: "You are Charles Philip Hippolytus, Baron de Thierry, King of Nukahiva, Sovereign Chief of New Zealand?"

A nod indicates that all this is true.

"Then," says the Invisible Stranger politely, "will you please explain why things happened in such and such a way? You must excuse me. . . . We have our records to keep, and it's no end of a job, with every unlicked cub of a cherub fancying himself a learned clerk. But we try to keep things tidy. Your case seems a little complicated at first sight. No doubt you will be able to put us right?" He smiles in the most affable way. A beam of golden light, which the nuns mistake for the last of sunset, pierces between the bed-curtains and all the dust-motes spring out from ambush and dance.

The old gentleman, for his part, smiled in return. And though he spoke no other word, and the little room was so quiet that they knew they could fold his hands on his breast, I am quite sure that the answer to it all was on his lips.

EPILOGUE

It is done, Charles. I only hope you will not be too much annoyed. When I first understood how this dunder-headed world had treated you, you know best what I wanted to do, and how that sentiment was aggravated by the sight of your own handwriting, setting forth your wrongs, until, like those terrible cannibals of yours at Cambridge, I could not part from you without a copious flow of tears. And then to discover, from an ancient sexton quite like a billy-goat, that he did not know where your grave was, among the slip-shod cream roses and wild onion-flowers of old Grafton Cemetery, because there was no sign, ancient or modern, to mark it! But, when patient investigation had at last uncovered the site, how much worse it was to find planted at the foot of your grave a rusty iron tin, once intended for bouquets, but at the time filled with drowned flies.

Time and thought, however, convinced me that we gain nothing by charging bull-headed at your old enemy, the brick wall of materialism. There are other means. And there are things within your gift which do not belong to other principalities; people will see that for themselves. It is not too late for you to be a very resplendent monarch. Many modern kings might be pleased and surprised to find their own boundaries march with those of so good a neighbour.

APPENDIX ONE

THE DEED OF PURCHASE

AGREEMENT between the Baron Charles Philip Hippolytus de Thierry, of Bathampton in the County of Somerset and of Queen's College, Cambridge, and Mudi Wai, Patu One and Nene, native residents on the banks of the river Yokianga, in the Islands of New Zealand. We the above-named chiefs and residents of New Zealand, for and in consideration of thirty-six axes to us now given, for us, our heirs and successors, by free will and common consent have sold and granted unto the said Baron Charles de Thierry, his heirs, executors, administrators and assignees for ever all the land, woods and waters situated in the following boundaries or limits, hereinafter specified : viz., the district called Te Troone, at the source or rise of the Yokianga River ; the district of Wai Hue, adjoining the aforesaid district ; also the district of Te Papa, adjoining the aforesaid district of Wai Hue ; also the district of Huta Kura, adjoining the aforesaid district called Te Papa ; all of which districts are situated at the source and on the eastern and western banks of the River Yokianga, and contain by estimation forty thousand acres, be the same more or less. And all lands, woods and waters, and whatever may be contained therein and situated within the aforesaid limits and boundaries, do from this day and shall for ever remain the property of the said Baron Charles de Thierry, his heirs, executors, administrators, and assigns, and no person or persons, whoever, shall on any pretence unlawfully seize, take, give, make over, distribute, molest, injure, or in any manner damage or injure the said lands, woods and waters and whatever may belong thereto or be contained therein and upon. And we, the aforementioned chiefs and natives do solemnly engage to defend the said property to the best of our power from any unlawful seizure or injury. We further declare having received full payment and satisfaction for the said lands, woods and waters, and everything belonging thereunto. In testimony of which, we do sign this our hand and deed in year of Christ, 1822, on board the ship *Providence* now in New Zealand.

> The mark of X Mudi Wai.
> The mark of X Patu One.
> The mark of X Nene.

Signed in the presence of James Herd, Master of the *Providence*,

APPENDIX ONE

Thomas Kendall, Missionary, and William Edward Green, First Officer of the *Providence*.

(Attested copies of the above are deposited at the Foreign Office, London, and at the Ministry of Foreign Affairs, Paris.)

APPENDIX TWO

I REGRET that full particulars cannot be given those who might be interested in the subsequent fate of the de Thierry family, which, even before the Baron's death, became widely scattered. One branch became extinct with the death of his daughter Isabel, who was pre-deceased by her baby daughter, Isabella Matson. These two, like the old Baron himself, are buried in an unmarked grave in Grafton Cemetery, Auckland.

After the Baron's death in 1865, his eldest son, Charles Frederick, assumed the title, and, strangely enough, there was still a Baroness de Thierry in the Auckland directory and telephone-book until a few years ago. Charles Frederick married three times, his eldest son by the first marriage, Mr. Frederick de Thierry, did not assume the title. The second marriage, of which there was plentiful issue, was with a Maori woman. The third wife, Mary Jane Brown, was a widow and a little Irish emigrant, and it was she who remained "the Baroness de Thierry" to all Auckland long after her husband's death. Mary Jane, who lived to be a hundred in a red-brick cottage in Symonds Street, Auckland, was a character. At ninety-odd, she had all her wits about her, did her own housework, and spun her own linen. But she was most punctilious about the title. Strictly speaking, she admitted, she was only the Baroness Dowager, but as the rightful heir, Mr. Frederick de Thierry, refused to make use of it, somebody must keep it up. However, she compromised in favour of the children of Mr. Frederick de Thierry, by invariably calling his daughters (who are still alive) Lady Emily and Lady Isabel.

Mr. Frederick de Thierry, who died only a few years ago, and whose widow is still alive, was a quiet and intensely reserved gentleman; the teak-wood writing-desk referred to in this book was in his possession, and it was only a few days before his death that he allowed anyone to explore its contents. Fortunately, nearly all his grandfather's records and papers had, on the latter's death, fallen into the hands of the late Sir George Grey, and were thus preserved intact.

Mr. Frederick de Thierry left a son, Lionel, who would thus be today's "Baron de Thierry" if the title were ever employed, but Mary Jane of the red-brick cottage was the last to insist on it. Incidentally, one of her younger relatives can remember seeing the Sèvres figure mentioned in this book on many visits to the old lady.

Mr. Richard de Thierry, another son of "Our Charles", made endeavours to recover from Chancery a very large fortune in France, to which his family lays claim. This sum, which amounts to nearly £7,000,000, has a romantic enough history in itself; the last member of the family who sought to lay hands on the phantom gold was a Lieutenant de Thierry in the French Navy, probably a descendant of one of Charles's younger brothers. Among the de Thierry papers is a letter from a Mr. Miller, of Dunedin, offering his services to Richard de Thierry in investigating the claim abroad.

Margaret Neilsen survived the old Baron, the Baroness, and her beloved Isabel, and was buried in Auckland.

Despite the reserve of the family—a quality of people whose parents were driven into cover by the hostility which surrounded their youth—they take a great deal of individual pride in the old Baron, and every now and again one sees a death notice with "Direct Descendant of the Baron de Thierry" attached as a footnote. Not many years ago there was an extraordinary affair in which a Mr. Terry—said to be really "de Thierry"—walked quietly out and murdered a Chinaman, because he did not believe that Chinese should be allowed to come into the country. Those who met him said that he was a most interesting personality. I cannot vouch for him as a member of the family, but certainly, though Our Charles had no colour prejudices, one feels that if he had ever murdered anyone, it would have been on a strong principle of this kind.

The youngest descendants today alive in Auckland are Della and Arnold Morrison, the children of a daughter of Mr. Frederick de Thierry. They take a great interest and pride in their great-great-grandfather, and warmly defend him when at school his memory arouses unfair comment from all those little Bolshevists and Heretics who do not Believe in Barons. (Still less Kings or Sovereign Chiefs.)